Bound by Fury

Jazmyne Ortiz

Contents

PROLOGUE

"Ms. Mars!"

I groan, moving my head and positioning it comfortably on my folded arms. I was tired. A lot more then tired. I couldn't believe it was already time for school, I just wanted to sleep for another eight hours. "Five more minutes," I mumble, reaching for my pillow to bury my head under it, only to find.. a pencil?

Why did I have a pencil in my bed? And why did my bed feel like wood? And why-

"Ms. Mars, wake up. This is a place for learning, not sleeping!"

I jump up abruptly from that. Only to be greeted by the face of Mr. Matthews staring down at me with his beady little eyes.

I hear numerous snickers from all around me. I look around the room slowly, seeing all my other class mates laughing. At me.

I glower at them, like they hadn't fallen asleep in class? Everyone has! Or well, I think so.

"Ms. Mars, if you fall asleep one more time in my class, I will be forced to give you a dentition." He warns, wagging a finger in my face like I was a naughty child who had just been caught with their hand in the cookie jar.

I sunk deeper into my seat and pulled my hoodie up closer to my face, as if I wanted to just bury myself away in it and hide. And I did. "It won't happen again." I say, although in the back of my head I knew it probably would.

He gave me one last glare before walking back to the front of the class, going on about something that didn't interest me one bit.

I glance to the clock. Five minutes. He had awaken me for five minutes to hear about his stupid lesson. Really?

I stuff all my books away in my bag, just wanting to get out of this damn school. Once the bell rung, I bolted from my seat like lightening, making my way out the door and to my locker.

Around me, students rushed and pushed their way out of the school, laughing and talking about what there plans were for the weekend. I, unfortunately, wasn't one of those teenagers who would make plans to hang out with friends.

Perhaps because it was because I didn't really have friends. More like I had a friend. Hence, the singular, not plural.

It's not that I was weird, or anti-social or anything, I just didn't.. well, get along with others greatly. I didn't even get along with my own pack.

But like that was no surprise. My dad wasn't in a high place like other kids parents. He was just.. A lap dog, I guess. What I mean by "lap dog" is that if the pack wanted, they could kick him--us-- out so easily. We were no importance of them. My dad just worked in the forest, cutting wood. Supplying them to other members of the pack and obeying any orders from the Alpha.

But he wasn't always like that. My dad use to be a soldier for the pack. Sure, that wasn't top rank, but he helped keep the pack safe. And that was far more honourable than being some lap dog. No one really knew what made him stop doing it. But I knew why.

My mom.

The moment she died, everything about him changed. He stopped taking risk. Stopped laughing. Stopped talking. Stopped everything. He just.. shut off. Although, who wouldn't? She was his mate. The other half of him. And he was doomed to this world to live without her. And everything I did, to my laugh, to my brown hair and blue eyes, reminded him so much of her. For a while, he couldn't look at me without bursting out into some kinda fit.

I didn't know how to deal with it for a while. I was only twelve, and I couldn't fully grasp what was happening. Why my mom wasn't coming home at night, why she wasn't tucking me in, or making us dinner. When my dad explained, I didn't cry. I wasn't really sure what to feel. Then again, I never could decide what to feel. I really wasn't one to cry. Maybe because crying was so foreign to me. I wasn't use to it. I was use to smiling. It all changed that night.

As I laid in bed, thinking back to what he said about my mom never coming home, I cried. I buried my head into a pillow and cried. I cried for her. I cried because I wanted her back so badly.

It never brought her back. The pleading, the crying. Nothing. That's when I discovered crying wasn't worth it.

Once my dad lost that position of fighting for the pack, my friends seemed to drop me. I guess because they all realized their parents were in much higher places. It didn't hurt till it came down to Adam. The Alpha's son.

We were child hood friends for as long as I could remember. And him suddenly just not wanting to be my friend anymore, just made me.. I don't know. Blame my father. Blame him for making me suffer more then I needed to. I'd lost not only my mom, but my friends.

And it just got much more worst when we got older. Of course I tried to make peace with them, but each time I even hung around them, they expected me to be like my father. To follow their commands. Which I certainly wasn't going to do.

Now I could see why people went rogue. Because they were tired of taking shit from the Alpha.

I shake my head as if to rid myself of the annoying thoughts.

"What's up with you?" I felt a hand touch my shoulder, it causes me to jump and swiftly turn, ready to punch whoever it is in the face when I realize it's just Anna. That one friend I was talking about earlier.

"Someone's jumpy," She says and eyes my raised fist.

I let out a breath I wasn't aware I was holding and close my locker. "Well, yeah. Who wouldn't be when people just come out of no where?"

"But I didn't come out of no where," She states as she begins to walk. "I was behind you for like, two minutes. What's got you lost in thought?"

I sigh and fall into step beside her and begin to tell her about how Mr. Matthews was all over my ass in six period, she just nods and agrees that he's horrible. Then Anna goes on to explain how she tried to talk to this cute boy from her Math class, and how when she asked him if he wanted to study for the up coming exam, In result, he told her he was gay.

I laugh at that, which causes Anna to smack me in my arm. "Ronnie! It's not funny! What if he really isn't gay? What if he just told me that because he thinks I'm ugly or something?"

I quickly shake my head at that. I know it's not true because Anna surely isn't ugly with her long blonde hair and her deep brown eyes. I didn't understand why she didn't have a boyfriend, or why she wasn't in the whole popular crowd.

I guess because the whole popular crowd consisted of werewolves. Anna wasn't one, so of course she couldn't be apart of it.

Yeah, that was the only difference between us. I was a werewolf while she was.. Normal. Something I had never experienced.

I practically told Anna everything. Well, close to everything. I couldn't tell her I was a werewolf, that'd be breaking a pack law.

But sometimes I wish I could. I think I even almost told her once. Thankfully, I bit my tongue before I could say anything more.

"Ronnie? Are you paying attention?" Anna asks, bringing me out of my trance.

"Um, yeah." I nod, pulling my bag closer to my body as I exit the school with her by my side. "Asked a guy out for studying. He told you he was gay. You think you're ugly. See? I'm listening."

She laughs slightly, and turns her head to look in the direction of my pack. She always seems to have a habit of doing that. Maybe because she yearns to hang out with them, instead of me.

I can see the frown etch at the curve of her lips as she stares. "Why do they have to be so perfect?" She mummers, probably thinking I don't catch it. If only she knew.

"They're not perfect," I object, stopping to get a better look at them. It's Adam, the Alpha's son, who catches me staring. Well, catches me and Anna. "They're probably stuck up snobs."

"Yeah," She nods. "But come on! Look at Adam Beckett. He's like.. a God."

I snort, "A God? Really?"

Sure, Adam's cute. But he's no God. In my eyes, at least. In others, I see where they're coming from. Adam wasn't like all the other boys in school. Maybe it's because he wasn't a boy, but a man with shaggy blonde hair, alluring hazel eyes, and a strong, lean, fit body. I know it's rather cliche to say this, but every girl really did want to be with him and every boy, wanted to be him.

I didn't know if it was his parents that he got his extremely good looks from, or his werewolf trait.

He seems to catch my gaze. For a while, we stare at each other. I'm trying to decipher what lays under those hazel of his. What is he thinking at this moment? I was never one good to read Adam. Even when we were the closets of friends. Maybe it's because when I look at him, I still see the little boy I use to play at the lake with. The clueless, kind, one.

Anna nudges me, causing me to pull my gaze away from him to her. "He's staring at you. You think he likes you? He has this dreamy look on his face, you know?"

No Anna, I don't know, I think warily. And shake my head. Like the Alpha's son would ever want something to do with me.

Chapter 1

It takes me an hour to get Anna off my case about Adam. And coming over for the weekend. It always takes this long to convince her she can't come over.

It's not that I don't want her to come over to my house, meet my dad and all that stuff, it's just that she can't. I lived with the pack. Bringing a human around wouldn't be smart with people in wolf form prancing around.

I bet Alpha Beckett would definitely have a fit then. I almost grin at the thought of him angry. I don't hate him, but I dislike him to a point where I only talk to him when necessary. I make no attempt to greet him whenever I see him. He doesn't either, just examines me with his blue eyes. The same eyes that Adam posses.

Something about that thought makes my skin crawl. I don't know what gives me the creeps about Alpha Beckett, but I can't seem to over come it.

I don't know why I even care for his existence, once I get old enough, I'm probably just gonna bail out on the pack. Maybe go off and do something I love in the human world.

Art? Maybe. I was no professional when it came down to it, though It seems to be a hobby of mine. People tell me I'm not bad. Who am I kidding, though? Being a artist in the real world must be hard, I can only imagine.

I gnaw on my nails as I think of this, walking into the clearing. My thoughts seem to drift away once I catch sight of Adam talking to his father. They both seem to be giving me occasional glances my way. It causes me to quicken my pace and direct my eyes towards my house, or well, shack. I hope they catch the drift I'm in no mood to stop and chat.

They don't.

"Ronnie!" It's Adam. I don't stop. I reach into my bag swiftly, grabbing my head phones and shoving it into my ears. At least if he catches up with me, I'll have the excuse that I was listening to music.

Still, he rushes over to me. "Ronnie!" He calls again. I ignore him the best I can and reach my house. Mentally, I'm cheering and thinking, yes! I made it!

The happiness I once felt dwindles as I feel Adam's hand make contact with my shoulder and twirls me around to face him. I stumble back, putting some distance between us when I notice just how close he's standing.

"Could you not hear me or-" He begins, but I shake my head rapidly and point to my ears, emphasizing the fact I have head phones on.

"What? Sorry, I can't hear you. I'm in a rush. I have.. my cat to feed. See you later!" I make a attempt to get away when he tugs on my head phones. They slip off my head and into his hands.

He dangles them between his fingers, staring down at the fact I have no iPod attached to them.

I cuss under my breath. How did the thought never occur to plug them in?

"So much for listening to music," He mutters. "And you have a cat?"

I fidget with my fingers, biting down on lip. "Um, yeah. Birthday present." It's a lie. And he can tell. I don't have a cat. Come to the think of it, I don't even like cats. Not that they aren't cute or anything, but I'm more of a dog person. How ironic is that?

"Well, that must be a bad birthday present since you don't like cats." He says and thrusts the headphones back into my reach. I nod numbly and take them from him.

"Yeah," I agree, "Totally. Nice chat we had. But I have to-" This time, it's not me who rushes to speak.

"Are you coming to the monthly bonfire tonight?" He asks. "Or do you have to feed your cat then, too?"

I flush, my face probably turning beet red before I glare at him. God, I'm so stupid for coming up with that excuse. "Uh, probably. It's mandatory, isn't it?"

"It is tonight," He answers with a nod. "We really need you there tonight. You've been ditching out on the last few. So that's why I came over to talk to you."

My eyebrows shoot up. For two reasons.

1. The, "We really need you there tonight" part.

And, 2. How he notices I've been missing from the other monthly bonfires. I never knew he realized I was gone from those. I guess I just figured my presence wasn't needed, nor cared for.

"Why do you need me there?" I manage to ask. He just stares at me, a ominous glint in his eyes that leads me to believe whatever they need me for is not gonna be something I like.

"We just do." He says nonchalantly and gives me a shrug. He turns on his heels, strutting away. "See you later, Ronnie."

I stare after him confused. Dumbstruck, even. Apparently, I'm not the only one who's watching him walk away. I notice other girls from the pack staring after. But all for the wrong reasons. They stare because they lust for him. I stare because I'm crossed between running after and demanding a answer for him, perhaps even punching the basterd who hasn't spoken to me in years.

I shake my head. He's not worth it. He never was.

I turn away from him and march into my house. Dropping my bag by the door. I know my father is aware I'm home since I hear the shuffle of his feet, his erratic breathing, and the sound of drawers closing.

I lean against the counter, shutting my eyes. I know what he's trying to do. Mask the fact he's been sitting on the couch, staring at the pictures of her. I wonder when he'll get over it and move on with his life. I have.

I came to accept the fact she isn't coming back. He hasn't. I pity him because he's pathetic. Not because I care. Though some part of me begs to differ.

I was so done trying to help him a long time ago. He refuses to even talk about it. Or her for the matter. So how can I help, when he doesn't clearly wanna help himself?

I can't even remember the last time we had a proper talk. I can't remember the last time he's told me he loves me.

But it's not like I need it. I'm fine on my own. With that thought, I abandon the support from the counter and place the dirty plates in the sink, then turn on the water and begin to scrub away from them.

"Ronnie?" He calls. "Is that you?"

"Who else would it be?" I call back with a edge to my voice and put my force into my washing, demanding that the chunks of food be removed from the plate. It doesn't. And I soon become frustrated. "Do you mind maybe occasionally washing your dishes, as well? Or are you so incompetent that you possibly can't?"

Most would be shocked at the way I speak to my Father. He deserves it. I practically had to raise myself, clean, cook, just to keep going. That was his job as a parent to do that for me. But he hasn't. He's never done anything.

I angrily toss the plate back into the sink and turn off the water. I'm in mood to be doing this. I dry my hands before I grab my bags and storm through the living room, catching sight of my Father. I frown at him at first.

He looks.. So weak. And well, miserable. I take in his hair black hair that now touches his ears, his dull gray eyes, and his pale, dry, skin. I almost can't believe this is him. He's changed so much. No longer does he wear a smile on his face, no longer does his skin glow a healthy golden tone. Now he's a ghost of what he use to be. A ghost of the father I wish he could be.

"I've been busy today," He counters. I scoff and gesture to the empty beer bottle and flickering tube that broadcasts the weather.

"Doing what? Wasting your life?" A sadistic laugh slips my lips, "You do realize how wrong this is, don't you? How wrong-"

"I don't need you to remind me, Ronnie. Just go to your room." He commands and stares at the TV.

I shake my head at him and grip at the strap of my bag, "Pathetic," I mutter before I go to my room and close the door behind me.

I remove my hoodie and toss it onto my small bed. I collapse in my office chair and convince myself to not go charging back into that room. To not scream till my voice gives out. No matter how much I scream, nothing will ever get through that thick skull of his.

Another reason I think I'm so angry with him is because I'm so much like him. I always was. We're both stubborn, thick headed, and just.. Shut off when it comes to emotions. We never talk about what's wrong with us. Or what's going on with us, really.

I do what I usually do when I no longer wish to think about something that bugs me. I occupy my mind, with painting. I take my mind off everything and just focus on the strokes of my brush and the picture that appears on the paper. It relaxes me for a while till night falls, reminding me of the fact I have to be at the bonfire. I contemplate ditching it. I think, what did Adam want to tell me?

It makes me stop what I'm doing and toss the dirty paint brushes into the glass of water. I wash off any paint on me and put on a clean white spaghetti strap with my black jeans and my combat boots. I style my long hair into a braid before I take a glance of myself in the mirror.

At least I look decent, I think as I chew on my lip. It's not like I really care what I look like. I don't really have much of a fashion sense. My wardrobe consist of jeans, T-shirts, and combat boots. I don't wear a lot of makeup. I don't even wear jewelry. Well, except for a leather bracelet but that shouldn't be considered jewelry. Isn't jewelry supposed to be feminine? Then again, who cares?

I don't marvel in my "beauty" for too long. I exit my room and find my Father in the same place that I left him. "Are you going to the bonfire?"

He shrugs, "Maybe. If I'm in the mood. I think the one they really need is you there."

The one they really need there? Is there something going on that I don't know about? Clearly. I sigh, "Is there something going on that I don't know about?" I ask, echoing my thoughts.

Again, he shrugs. "Go find out for yourself."

"Thanks," I drawl sarcastically. "For the help." I'm already out of the house before he can respond. Not that I expect him to.

I catch sight of everybody huddled around a glowing fire. The only source of light right now. I make my way over slowly, almost hesitantly.

Everybody's laughing and talking away. Even the Alpha who sports a unfamiliar smile on his face. He jokes, telling stories. Is this what pack meetings are like? Fun?

Some people are roasting marshmallows as well. Well, this isn't that bad. I think and I let my eyes roam over everybody's face, recognizing old friends and foes.

My eyes land and ulimately stop on Adam, who sits next to his father, oddly staring into the fire. I can see him playing with his fingers. He's nervous. But for what?

"Ron, is it?"

My head snaps to my side to see Adam's mom, Alpha Female Beckett. I haven't seen her since.. Well, since I was twelve years old. She rarely makes a appearance and insists on shopping almost constantly.

I remind myself to answer before she thinks I'm ignoring her. "Ronnie." I correct. "Ronnie Mars."

"Oh, of course! My bad!" She laughs, although I don't understand what's so funny. "How have you been, sweetie? You look so.. Different." Her eyes rake over my body. She frowns, obviously because of what I'm wearing.

"That's what growing up does to you." I rub at the back of my neck and focus my eyes on anything but her.

"Yeah. Those four years have done you good," She smiles and points a finger in Adam's direction. "So are you excited?"

"For what?"

"They haven't told you?" Her face scrunches in confusion and she mutters another, "Oh."

What the hell is everyone talking about? And what does it have to do with me? Before I can ask, she quickly darts away, handing off in the direction of her mate/husband.

People are getting weird-er by the day. I decide to not obsess over it and take a seat in front of the fire. Tossing pebbles around and aimlessly looking off into the dark woods.

Something about tonight just gives me a.. Well, off feeling. I imagine something just lurking in those woods. Weirdly, the thought excites me.

"Hey Ronnie," I don't need to turn to know it's Adam taking a seat by me.

"What's the big secret, huh?" I ask, cutting straight down to business.

He's silent for a minute before he murmurs, "You'll see." I'm about to reply when Adam's Father beats me to the chase.

"Attention everyone," He says. Everybody goes dead silent, staring at him. Including myself. "You all know what we discussed last time, yes?"

No, I mentally answer but everyone else seems to know. The girls are especially nodding and giggling. I don't understand why.

I feel Adam shift beside me, and glance to see him stand up and walk over to his Father. His dad clasps a hand on his back as he smiles at his son. "Well, Adam has made his choice. Would you like to announce who it is?"

I found myself more confused by the moment. But no on else is. I'm tempted to lean over and ask the person next to me what the hell they're talking about. I don't once I see the girl looks like she's about to burst with excitement.

"Ronnie Mars." I look in the direction of where they've called my name. I can't tell. Since everyone is staring at me with their mouth wide. I'm left to stare back at everyone in confusion. When I don't say anything, all the girls seem to go up into a uproar.

"She's not even happy!"

"Who the hell is that bitch?"

"I can't believe he choose her over me!"

Wait, what? Why am I being called a bitch and screamed at?

"Everybody, sit down!" Alpha Beckett commands. Again, they go silent and fall back into their seats. "Ronnie, how about you come up here?"

"But for what?" My eyebrows furrow as I stare them.

"Didn't you hear what we said?" Adam asks, and I shake my head. This just seems to piss people off more. Before they can break out into a angry fits again, Adam says, "I picked you to be my mate. You know, to be Alpha Female when I take my Dad's place in a few months."

My mouth falls a gape. The whole sentence just keeps running through my head. Why? Picking mates was.. rare. Most just waited to find their true mate. Though, finding your true mate is even more rare. And it takes quite long. He was supposed to be taking over in a few months, that's why he must have had to pick out of us girls in the pack. The thing I don't understand is why me? Why not some other girl?

"Did my Dad agree to this?" Is the first thing I say. Adam nods stiffly. So the basterd knew about this!

"Your father guaranteed that you'd willingly mate with Adam." His father answers. "He said he even spoke to you and agreed."

My fists clench at my sides and I glance back to my house. Ready to pound down that door and yell. How could he do that to me? Sell me off like I'm some piece of land?

I shake my head. I don't want this. Any of this. I stand abruptly, pressing a hand to my forehead. I feel suffocated. It's all too much to take in. That my fate was sealed by what my Father has said.

I find my feet carrying me away from the scene. Away from the pack. Away from Adam.

"Ronnie!" He yells after me and I break out in a run after that, running into the woods. I shift once I realize I'll never escape him like this in human form.

I land on my now four legs and run. Run till the only thing I think of is the wind blowing through my fur. I run till everything else fades away.

I dodge any plants or rocks. I run for what seems like hour. Finally, I come to a stop in front of the lake. The lake I use to come to when I was child. I fall helplessly to the ground and let my bones shift to where I become human again. Normal.

I bring my knees to my chest as I gaze hard into the black water.

Adam's words just keep replaying over and over again in my head. Like a broken record. I feel so betrayed. So.. Angry. I mean, it's my life. Shouldn't I pick who I want to be with? I could care less if Adam is the Alpha's son! I want to be with someone of my choice!

I stand, grabbing a rock and chucking it with a grunt. It flies before it hits the water with a thud. I keep chucking more. Letting out more angry cries as I throw them.

"What's got you so angry?"

It's that rough, masculine, melodic unfamiliar voice that makes me stop. Makes my shoulder bunch up and makes me in take a sharp breath.

It's not Adam. It's not the Alpha. It's someone else. Someone far worse.

I don't turn. I freeze, as if I'm afraid if I make any sudden movements, that they'll attack. I try my best to not make any noise, although I've already been spotted. The wind blows softly, rustling my loss strands.

It's when the intoxicating scent meets my nose. It smells like.. Pine trees and something else I can't detect. I can tell right away it's a male. A very, very big male.

I turn, slowly and come face to face with a chest. A very muscly one at that. My eyes travel up from his chest, the muscles he bares seems to go on forever. He's huge. In every single way and form. He towers over my 5'6 for so easily. He's 6'5 by what I can tell.

He could snap in freaking half if he wanted. But he doesn't. Something screams at me. My body? My mind? I'm not sure.

My eyes meet his straight away.

His eyes. Sea green eyes. Eyes of a killer.

Chapter 2

Mate - That's the word that screams at me just by gazing at him.

For a minute, I just stand. Watch him. I'm not even sure I breathe because I'm so shell shocked. My mind seems to be racing at a hundred miles a minute. The only thing that sticks out from the clutters of thoughts is the colour of his eyes. It's the only thing I can focus on.

My eyes trail further across his features. I find myself rapidly looking all over him, drinking in every part of him. I rush to examine every inch of exposed skin. His chiseled jaw, his five o'clock shadow, his perfect, slightly tanned skin. To his lips. His thin, but very kissable lips. Even his stance seems to have me fascinated. His muscles are constantly bunching, with every move he makes he flexes involuntarily. I can see him clenching his fist at his side. As if he's holding himself back. But from what? Killing me?

I step back once I realize what I'm dealing with. He looks familiar. So familiar. Not to mention deadly.

Who is he? I rake my brain for anything that leads me to revealing who he is. Nothing. But would you be able to focus with a guy this handsome in front of you?

"Well aren't you a small little thing," He smirks down at me, noticing how small I am compared to him. I literally have to bite my lip from letting out a dreamy sigh at the sound of his voice.

But I'm supposed to be feeling insulted, right? He had just called me small. And a thing.

I mange to direct a pointed look at - more like up - at him. "I'm not a 'thing' I'm a person. Also, don't small and little have the same definition? That's quite a range of vocabulary you have, giant big thing."

He chuckles, It's almost as sexy as his voice, if not, more. "And that's quite a attitude you have." He steps closer, getting right back in my personal space.

Oh god, how could I forgot how big he is? He could kill me! And here I am smart mouthing him. Talk about a death wish.

I cower back and glance back once I feel the sole of my shoe get wet. I notice that I'm standing in the lake by now.

I turn slowly back to the man before me and notice just how close he's standing. So close that I can feel the body heat that emanates off of him. I tilt my head upward at him, seeing him watching me the way I was doing to him minutes before.

The moonlight catches his face, allowing me better to get a look at him. It especially lights up a scar on his face. A scar directly above his eyebrow. How the hell did he get that scar? I think. I start to conjure up horrible scenarios of how it could have happened. I push it all away immediately.

He reaches out, almost hesitantly, before resting his hand on my face. His finger tips grazing my cheek bone. Just by that small touch, I can feel tingles run through all out of my body. It causes me to let out a shaky breath, but I don't move. "Do I make you nervous?" He asks, in a heated whisper, his hand traveling to my neck.

I swallow and shake my head, though my mind begs to differ. And so does my body. I tremble almost pleasurably under his touch and lean into him.

He chuckles, running his hand over my shoulder to the small of the back where he abruptly shoves me towards him. "Then you clearly don't know how I am."

"I know you look familiar. I just.. can't seem to think clearly enough to realize it." I mummer, glancing up at him. I watch the curve of his lips turn up into a smile.

"Can't seem to think clearly, eh? Am I distracting you?"

"No," I answer shakily.

He laughs at the obvious lie. "What's your name?"

"What's yours?" I counter.

"I asked first."

"'I asked first'? What are we, five? Just tell me what your damn name is." My voice a lot stronger then before. I seem to be regaining my senses, since I start to wiggle my way out of his arms. His strong, strong arms. Not to mention his li-

Focus, Ronnie, focus! This guy can be a murderer! He probably is. He looks like he was built to kill with all that muscle of his.

He ran a hand through his golden brown hair, ruffling it slightly before letting out a little sigh. "I'll tell you, if you agree not to run."

I pause for a moment before answering, "Okay," I nod, though I highly doubt I'll end up staying. I have a feeling I'm not gonna like what he's about to say.

"Liam," He murmurs and seems to grip me tighter in his arms, truly scared I'll run. "Liam Farley."

Liam Farley. Liam Farley. Liam Farley. The name screams itself over and over in my mind. The name is familiar. I search his face for a matter of seconds, before it hits me.

Liam Farley, Portland's number one rogue. Liam Farley the murderer that killed the Sun pack. Liam Farley, the most dangerous rogue in Portland - Non the less, America. Le'ts not forget a murderer!

And here I am, letting him hold me close in his arms, although I doubt he would hurt me. Still, I stumble back, the water sloshing at the back of heels.

He tilts his head at me, looking like a animal examining his prey. I truly feel like his prey at the moment. "You said you wouldn't run."

"That was before I knew you were a murderer," I spat and backed away, swiftly, I go pounding out of the water in a effort to run away from this psycho, but he doesn't allow it.

He catches me and presses his chest against my back, making me feel the rippling muscles. "You know if you run, I'd just catch you. Always."

Something about his words make me shiver. It's because I know he truly means it. Always.

"Is that a threat?" I hiss, and glance over my shoulder to glare at him. He smirks and shrugs.

"What makes you think it's a threat?"

"More like a promise in my book."

I'm about to snap at him when I hear a voice in the distance. "Ronnie! Ronnie, answer me!" Shit. Adam. I had almost forgotten that I'd ran away from the bonfire. From him.

I panic silently. What happens if he sees me with Liam? What would he do to him? Wait, wait, why the hell do I care if something happens to him?

Because whether you like it or not, you know this boy is a lot more then just a rogue to you. You know he's your m-

"Ronnie? That's your name?" Liam's words break me from my thoughts and I wrench myself forcefully away from his hold on me.

"You have to leave," I say and make the best effort to shove him. I fail, miserably.

"Why? Is that your little boyfriend?" He eyes the dark woods, his eyes filled with hatred. I'm scared that if Adam emerges, Liam will kill him.

"No, idiot! Now go! Before he finds you!" I say hastily and make another attempt to push him. He doesn't move. Nor does he make eye contact with me. He just glares in the forest's direction. I know in a matter of seconds, Adam will surely make a appearance. "Liam, you have to go. If he see's you, he'll tell the pack, he'll-"

He cuts me off. "Promise me you'll come back here tomorrow, then I'll go."

My eyebrows furrow and I lick my suddenly chapped lips, "I don't know if I-"

"Promise me or I'll stay. And wait for whoever the hell is calling after you. Smell's like a Alpha, from what I can tell."

I can hear the pounding of Adam's feet, I know he's coming soon. I have no time to think, just do. So I nod rapidly. "Okay, I'll be here tomorrow night. Now go!"

He turns on his heels and make's his way to brush of the woods, before he glances over his shoulder, staring at me with those haunting green eyes of his. "See you tomorrow, Ronnie. Or should I say mate?"

I don't even gasp or anything. It's because I know it's true. I knew it from the moment he touched me. Perhaps by the moment he looked at me.

He give's me no time to reply, since he hurriedly disappears, the dark woods swallowing him up.

I restrained myself from running after him, enveloping him in my arms, and kissing those perfect pink lips of his. I was even tempted to run my finger tips over his scar, ask who did this to him. And I hated it. I knew it was the stupid mate connection. My mate. My true mate.

The more I thought of about it, the more I freaked out. What the hell was I to do about Adam? He wanted me to mate with him. And I didn't understand why. He stopped being my friend. He stopped talking to me. He even stopped looking at me. God, I think that's the thing that hurt me the worse. The fact he wouldn't even glance in my direction. And if he did, it was a look of utter disgust. Like I was trash.

For a while, I believed I was. I had no friends. No dad. No mom. No nothing. I was alone. Not even Anna could understand my problems, since I couldn't tell her. That just frustrated me more. Why did Adam want me around all the sudden? Because I had grown up and turned out to be "pretty"? I wasn't sure. And I didn't think I'd be getting answers anytime soon.

"Ronnie!"

My head snapped to see Adam. He was panting heavily, worry plastered on his face. "Are you okay?"

"I'm fine," I say, making my way up the sand. "Let's just get back before the others come look for us." And discover a rogue has been here. Non the less, been with me. I add, mentally.

Adam doesn't respond. Instead, his eyes roam the area and he sticks his nose up in the air, sniffing. Oddly seeming like a dog. Ironic, really. "That smell.. It's-"

"Probably a animal or something. Are we going or what?" I tug on his arm and pull him into the forest to return to the pack house. He let's me drag him all the way back, but he seems to jump at any small movement in the trees, or any sound, as if he's expecting to jump out of no where and attack us.

We arrive back in the opening where the pack houses are to see everyone still circled around the bonfire, whispering to one another.

They all quiet down once they see me and Adam. I release the grip I had on Adam's arm and start towards my house. Adam, of course, trails after me. "Did you see anything out there?"

"Out where?" I play dumb for the sake of Liam. Even though I may not be pleased Liam's my true mate, I still don't want anything to happen to him. I might have just met him a few minutes - Feels more like hours - ago I was determined to protect him. Because I cared about his well being, whether I wanted to or not.

"Out at the lake. There was this.. scent. A werewolf. A rogue, even."

I stop immediately, causing Adam to bump into my back. I turn and face him, narrowing my eyes at him. "Nothing was out there, Adam. Drop it."

"Why are you being so defensive about it, then?" He pries and at the moment, I feel like punching his face in.

"Excuse me if I'm not in a very cheery mood, It's not everyday someone chooses the life I'm going to live for me. Why, Adam? Why the hell did you pick me? Do you hate me that must that you want me to suffer?" My eyes search his face frantically. I can see him swallow nervously, shaking his head.

"You think being with me is going to be that bad?"

I don't hesitate to nod, "Yes. Because now I'm doomed to this life forever. I don't know if you've noticed, but I have dreams way beyond-" At this point, I'm failing my arms around gesturing to all the pack houses around me. "-This!"

"Ronnie, I'm-"

"Good riddance, Adam." I hiss before turning on my heel and stomping off to my house. I open the door then close it with a slam.

I'm already off to go cuss off my father when I realize he isn't there. I checked his bedroom and all. Nothing. What a coward, he probably ran off knowing I'd come home pissed. A coward, that's the only thing he'll ever be.

I shrugged out of my pants and wet shoes before I fell into bed, staring up at the spinning ceiling fan. I think of what I'm gonna do. How the hell am I gonna get out of this? I don't want to be mated to Adam. Nor Liam, for the matter.

Maybe I could run away. Live in New York. Go to college with Anna. Pursue something I love. It seems to some what lighten the mood I'm in till I think of Liam. His threat. Or well, his "promise" He'd catch me. Always.

Would he really follow me to New York? What if it was just a bluff? What if I'm just psyching myself out?

I knew whatever he meant, lays a lot deeper than the surface. He means that if I even attempt to run off, he'll come after me. He'll find me. Always.

I let out a sigh of frustration and think, how could my life change in just one night?

The next day at school, I'm out of it. Completely. The day seems to go in a blur, and I find myself in a daze. Not even as I sit in Art class can I focus, I say this since I end up painting his eyes. The same green eyes that appeared in my dreams last night.

"Oh, Ronnie, it's beautiful!" My teacher gasps and smiles at me, "Who's it of?"

"No one," I say all too quickly. Ms. Jovovich - Probably one the best teachers in the world - raises a eyebrow at me.

"You know, Ronnie, I was once a teenager before. I know what it's like to have a boy on your mind all the time-" For some reason, when I hear this, I cringe. Sure, Ms. Jovovich is cool, but picturing her as a teenager and with a boy kinda freaks me out. "-Just don't let it get in the way of everything. But I'm happy you've find your muse."

When she says "muse" she means that one person who inspires you. I shake my head at once, thinking, Liam is not my muse. Right?

"When we were you gonna tell me you had a muse, Ronnie?" Anna ask teasingly from her seat next to me. I roll my eyes at her before I look over at her painiting to see she's adding pink to her deformed looking flower. "Do you think this looks weird?"

"Yes," I say without hesitation. It causes her to frown, I quickly add, "But hey, none of us are real professional's here."

"She's right, Annabelle," Chirps Ms. Jovovich. Anna makes another face at the mention of her full name. "You just do your best. And Ronnie, I'd like you to stay after class to talk to you about something." I nod, then Ms. J twirls off to go comment on some other teenager's non-existent love life.

"She's crazy." Anna states, then adds, "And God I hate it when people use my full name."

"She's not crazy. She's nice," I argue. I truly do believe Ms. J is nice, even though she can be a bit spastic, I still believe she's the best teacher in this hell whole they call school. "I like your name. It's.. Pretty. Would you rather have a boy name like me?"

"Annabelle's too sweet. I don't want to be sweet. I want to be sexy and badass, like you are," Now this causes me to make a face. "But who cares about my stupid name, tell me, who's that Green eyed hottie in your painting? A secret boyfriend? You whore, you've been holding out on me!"

I laugh, I can't help it. "It's nobody," I lie, and I'm certainly impressed when I'm able to look her straight in the eye and tell her this without cracking. "I just had a stupid dream."

"A wet one, I bet," She wiggles her eyebrows at me and I gape at her.

"No it wasn't, you pervert!"

She grins and shrugs, "Say what you want but you know you can tell me, I won't judge. I admit I have wet dreams about Adam Beckett, then again, who doesn't?"

At the mention of the name, the cheeky grin I had on my face falls. It's because now Anna, of course unintentionally, has reminded me of the fact I'm supposed to be Adam's mate. I think she notices my dreadful expression, since she frowns as well. "Sorry, Ronnie, I didn't know you liked hi-"

"It's not that." I say, I feel like spilling my guts about everything that happened last night, but I don't. I know I can't. "Anyway, I was thinking maybe this weekend I could come spend the night over at your house."

This makes Anna smile and she quickly forgets about our previous conversation and dives into what movies we're gonna watch, boys, and makeup. I'm grateful when I hear the bell ring indicating the day is over. I tell Anna I'm going to catch up with her after I see what Ms. J wants. She bids me a good luck then she's off, along with the other students who pour our of the classroom.

"So, what's up, Ms. J?" I ask as I saunter over to her desk she sits behind. She smiles at me and leans forward, folding her hands neatly together.

"Well you know how the school plays coming up, I was wondering if you could paint the back drops. I suggested to them that you do it, since you are one the many talented art students here. I also said I'd talk to you and see how you feel about it. It's nothing you can't handle, I assure you,"

For a minute, I'm silent. Before I nod, "Sure, why not?"

She claps her hands together with a even larger grin. "Great! Now we only need one more student to help out. Anybody you have in mind?"

I contemplate saying Anna, but then I think how Anna hates art.. And how she'd probably feel if I volunteered her for it. "Uh, no. Sorry."

"No worries. I guess we'll find someone soon enough. That's all. Thank you Ronnie."

I give her a small smile than walk out of the classroom into the empty halls. I make a quick stop at my locker and spin it out open. I'm actually genuinely happy about doing the back drops for the school's play. It was something that can occupy my troubled mind.

I pop my locker open with a sigh and stuff my books into my locker. I pause once my eyes catch sight of a white envelope. What the hell is that?

I reach out hesitantly for it and grasp the thin paper between my fingers. I open it slowly, as if I expect something to jump out and attack me. I'm slightly relieved when I see it's just a letter, then I think of who it's from.

I pull out the paper and unfold, my eyes scanning the unfamiliar, but neat, hand writing:

I think I know who will be that extra student helping out for the school's play. See you soon, sweetheart.

- LF.

I don't need to think hard to know who, "LF" is. Liam.

I look frantically around me but no one is behind. Nor next to me. How the hell did he get in the school? What does he mean, "I know who will be that extra student helping out for the play"?

Is he some kinda stalker? No, he's not. I know he's doing this to get under my skin.

I crumple it into a ball before I toss the paper aside, onto the ground. The janitor will come by and pick up, so I don't worry.

I walk out of the school and keep my eyes peeled for a certain set of golden brown hair and green eyes. Whether I like it or not, I know Liam Farley is going to be showing up a lot more in my life.

Chapter 3

I don't know what to do that night. I'm torn between going, seeing Liam, or staying home. The more rational part of me thinks staying home is what's best. Then that small, and I mean small, part of me that fancy's him urges me to go.

But I know I can't afford to.

What if I ended up growing close to Liam? He was a wanted man. And if I were to be with him, It'd be like putting a target right on my back. All the people that were after him would use me against him. But would Liam ever really let anyone lay a finger on me? No. He wouldn't.

I knew that from the moment he heard Adam calling after me in the woods. He looked ready to kill. That scared me, frankly. I knew what he was capable of. He could kill me easily if he pleased. Though I doubt he would.

Why am I even pondering seeing him? It's not safe. Everything about him screams danger. Especially that scar above his eyebrow. I still wonder how he got.. Did one of his victims give it to him while fighting back? The thought makes me shiver and ultimately decides I am not going anywhere near him. No matter what.

But as I lay in bed that night, rolling around restlessly, I realize this is gonna be a lot harder then it seems.

I finally push myself out of bed, not bothering to put on any shorts of sorts. I just walk into the kitchen with my clad underwear on and tang top, knowing I'm alone.

Yeah, my father still hasn't come home. It's no shock. He does this multiple times a month, probably going out and spending his time's at bars. Also probably in some women's bed as well.

I push away the though, disgusted at the image of my father with another woman that isn't my mom.

I glance at the stove clock and sigh when I only see it's 12:30 AM. I know I'm not going to be getting a wink of sleep tonight, so I do what I can do. Drag my art stand out of my room and into the living room. I begin to do mindless things, such as mixing colours and creating silly hearts. Somehow, in one of those hearts "L+R" appears.

I scuff at myself, "Really, Ronnie?" I mumble to myself, ready to splatter some paint on it to mask it when a thud sounds in the house. Particularly, my room. What the hell was that?

I'm alert right away. Another sound occurs, louder this time, as if demanding my attention.

I gulp nervously some how finding comfort as I grip my pant brush in my hand. Then I quickly think to myself - What am I gonna do with a paint brush? Paint whoever the hell is in my house to death?

Another thud sounds, this time, I jump. I just need to man - Or should I say woman? - up and find out what's in my room.

I inch forward to my door, letting out small and raspy breaths. I don't even know why I'm so nervous. It could be nothing.. But then again, it could be something.

I stop in front of my door and pull myself together before I reach out and rest my hand on the door knob. I do it all in one fluid motion, not giving myself enough time to panic, and slam open the door. I immediately raise up my fist, ready to punch out any intruder. But there's no one in my room. It's completely empty.

Still, they could be hiding. So I take a hestiant step inside my room. My sharp eyes scanning the area. I even check under my bed too be safe. Nothing. So what made those sounds? My question is answered once I see three of my paint bottles on the floor.

I pick them up from the floor and place them on my desk. I still can't help but think what caused them to fall over.

I sigh, rubbing a hand over my forehead. "It's nothing, Ronnie. Stop freaking yourself out." If I didn't feel crazy before, I for sure as hell do now. Talking to myself? Really? God, I'm losing it.

Though I tell myself it's nothing but a few paint bottles that made the sound, I keep on clutching the paint brush.

I exit the room and make my way to the kitchen, leaning over the sink I quickly splash some water on my face and let my hair down from my bun. I sigh and shake my head. What has gotten-

"Nice underwear. Batman, really? Cute."

I let out a shriek right away and swing around, not even taking the time to try and figure out who it is. I throw a punch right to the face, which the person catches. The next movie comes naturally. I go for the one place that would effect a man.

I send a kick between the legs.

Once I hear the groan and see their hands fall to the front of their pants, I know this is a man. He falls to the ground, rolling and groaning in pain.

I grab what I can find on the counter top, which turns out to my paint brush and topple onto the dude, jabbing it into his chest while letting out a string of cuss words. It doesn't even phase me that I'm trying to stab this guy with a paint brush.

That is till he calls my name out. A normal stranger wouldn't know my name, right? "Ronnie! It's me, Liam!"

I freeze and lean a little closer to him, pulling down the hood on his face. Even though it's pitch black in the kitchen, I'm able to see his features. And most importantly, his glowing green eyes. "Liam?" I pant and tuck my hair behind my ears. What the fuck is Liam doing in my house?! "What the hell are you doing here?" I ask, echoing my thoughts.

"You didn't show up. So I tracked you down." He says and his sentence ends in a groan. "God, is it normal if I can't feel my own dick anymore? I think you killed it!" He cusses under his breath more, leaning his head back onto the tile.

I bite my lip, "I thought you were a rapist! Or a robber! I had to protect myself!" I huff, crossing my arms over my chest. "You don't just barge in on someone like that. You're not even supposed to be here, first off. If Adam or somebody else sees you here, they'll kill you."

"Adam, huh?" He mutters, "Is that the punk that was calling after you the other night?"

I roll my eyes once I see his eyes filled with envy. "That's beyond the point, now-"

"You didn't answer my question." He says, cutting me off. I glare at him, till I see a smirk slip onto his lips.

"What's so funny?" I hiss, and he shrugs. I suddenly feel his rough, but nice feeling, hands on my bare thighs.

"Nothing. But I do like this position quite a bit." He wiggles his eyebrows at me and I gape at him till I realize I'm on top of him. Straddling him. With my hands on his neck and my face inches away from him. I feel his hot breath wash over my face and I shiver involuntarily.

His hands travel further up my thighs. Another shiver ripples over my body and I struggle to swallow down a breathless gasp.

He stops once his hands rests on my waist and he leans to where our noses touch. I know if I make a move, my lips will touch his in a instance. Which isn't a repulsive thought as much as I hate to deny it.

I'm frozen as he runs his lips down my cheek bone, setting every nerve on fire. I hold my breath and feel him lean closer to my ear. His lips brush my lobe, before he nips at it. This time, the gasp leaves my lips and I fist a handful of his soft hair between my fingers while my other hand trails down his muscled chest. The muscles bunch and relax under my touch, causing a small smirk to touch my lips. I have the same effect on him just as he has on me. "Though, just so you know, this is the only time I'll ever allow you to be on top." The comment just makes me grow incredibly hotter. Racy images feel my mind of Liam and I.

I bite my lip and wonder how his hands would feel all over my body.

Hello! Earth to Ronnie! I don't know if you've realized but Liam Farley, one of the most dangerous rogue's, is touching you with his bare hands that he's probably killed with.

Oh my god! What the hell am I doing?

I jump off of him and slam myself up against the counter. "Gross!" I fake horror and disgust as I stare at him, "Say something like that again to me and I'll make sure you go sterile."

He smirkes, amusment clear in his eyes. "You sounded like you liked it when you moaned." I flush right away. It just makes the smirk on his face widen. "And calm down there, Jackie Chan. You just got lucky since I was caught off guard."

I scuff and cross my arms over my chest. "I beg to differ."

He slowly boosts himself up from the ground, rubbing his a hand through his head. "Then try to hit me again. You'll see."

I glare at him and don't even give him a heads up as I throw a punch at him. He dodges and I aim again to kick in his.. reign, when he catches my foot and yanks. Causing me to fall flat on my back. I knew if he wanted, he could have put a lot more strength into that pull. He's being gentle with me. The thought just makes me more angry. Does he really think I'm that weak?

I yank my leg free from his hold and hop back up, swinging my fist towards his face. He catches my bunched fist with ease and twists my arm behind my back and shoves me gently into the counter. He presses himself into my back side. I hear him let out a low chuckle while I let out a sigh of frustration.

It's true. He can beat me so easily. The question is, why hasn't he already?

He has the chance right now. He could break my arm and snap my neck. But he doesn't. He releases me and steps back, giving me my space.

I turn on my heels and stare at - Again, more like up - at him. He just seems to stare right back till his eyes roam farther down my body. I follow his wandering gaze and notice I'm still only in just my underwear. My kiddie, batman logoed underwear.

Oh god.

I squeal and dash around him. I hear his booming laughter as I rush into my room, grabbing the first pair of jeans I can find and tug them on. I also stuff my hair up into a pony tail and exit out of my bedroom, ready to tell him to get the fuck out when I see him gazing at my painting.

I freeze in my tracks thinking about how I did that ridicules heart with both our names in it. Crap, crap, crap.

He glances over at me with raised eyebrows. "And here I thought you hated me." He mocks, smiling while fingering the now dried paint.

I shake my head and swallow down the log of spit that seems to be stuck in my throat, "That L can stand for anything. For instance, that could be referring to... " I trail off, finding I can't think of a decent excuse. I finally just strut over and grip the painting in my hand then place it behind the TV. "Something. I was referring to something that has nothing to do with you. You never answered my last question anyway, what are you doing here?"

"I did answer your question, you just were distracted by my hot body-" I scuff as I hear this and roll my eyes. "-You didn't show up at the lake like you promised I would. So I followed your scent and ended up here."

"Did you also follow my scent to my high school?" I ask, with a edge to my voice. "I got your note."

"Oh yeah?" He raises a eyebrow at me, a coy smile grazing his lips. "Did you like it?"

"No! I don't think stalking me is something I would like! What were you talking about in the note? What are you planning?" I ask all in one breath.

He shrugs nonchalantly and purses his lips. "Wouldn't you like to know?" He sends a mocking grin in my direction.

I glower at him, "You're playing with fire, Liam. And you're bound to get burned." I pause, shaking my head. "Are you so stupid that you don't notice you're not only putting me in danger but yourself? If my pack finds you, they'll kill you. Then probably me."

Liam rolls his eyes as if saying - please, like they could beat me. "They wouldn't bother coming after me, Ronnie. They're not idiots."

"What makes you think they won't kill you? Us?"

"They know I'll get away. They know I could pick off each and everyone of them. How do you think I've gotten around for so long? Most packs don't bother to mess with me. Their all too weak. Just like yours." He says and his eyes dart around the room before they finally land on me. "As for people going after you, I'd kill them before they even got a chance."

His words make me suck in a breath. I don't know whether to feel flattered or horrified.

Flattered because he'd go to any length to keep me safe.

Horrified because I didn't want anyone to kill for me. Especially Liam. It just reminded me of the fact he's a rogue. A rogue that's killed people. Innocent people, even.

Although I fight myself to deny Liam, I know I can't. Even though he's dangerous, everything about him draws me in. The more you fight it, the harder it gets.

"I don't need you to protect me, you know. I'm a big girl. And I don't know about that.. They could hunt you down. Catch you off guard. All I'm saying is that if you show up here again, Liam, I won't hesitate to tell Adam." I surprise myself when I'm able to look him straight in the eye and tell him this huge lie. I beg, no plead, that he won't call me out on my bluff. That he'll stay away, even though I don't want him to.

He eyes me for a minute. He maintains a blank expression, as if he's really contemplating I'll tell my pack that one of the most dangerous rogue's has been hanging around our territory.

I will myself to slow my breathing. To stand straight and not shrink away from his gaze.

Finally, he smiles. And I know he's called my bluff. "You won't do that." He states simply and in a blink of a eye, he's back up close to me, running a rough, but tender, hand down my arm and stops once his fingers brush mine. Our fingers intertwine with one another immediately. "We're bound to one another, Ronnie. You won't hurt me because it'll hurt you. If I go down, you go down with me."

His words leave me speechless. I know it's true. Yet I refuse to admit. Instead, I glare at him and relculantly wrench my hand from his grip. "Don't blame me when you get yourself killed."

He laughs, "I've kept myself alive for this long, haven't I?" He smiles at me before he brushes a loose strand of hair behind my ear. "Good night, sweetheart."

I watch as he turns his back to me and walk to my bedroom. I follow after him and see him open the window in my room, sliding himself out. "Good night," I hiss, walking over to the window and gripping the hinges ready to close it. "And don't call me sweetheart, jackass."

He sends me a taunting grin and wagers a finger at me. "You know, I find it incredibly sexy when you're angry."

I roll my eyes and give him the finger before I shut the window and close the curtains. I can hear his laughter and surprisingly soft footsteps, after about five minutes, all I'm greeted with is silence.

I sigh once he's out of range and fall back into my bed. Suddenly, I feel all worn out.

I shrug out of my uncomfortable jeans and get under the cover, closing my eyes. I snuggle into the sheets and push the thought of Liam being next to me, snuggling him inside of pillow and sheets and fall asleep to the image of him plastered into my mind.

A sound of someone knocking on my door is what wakes me from my slumber that morning. For a while, I just ignore it till they pound harder on my door. I groan and gruggily remove myself from the warmth of my bed, I shove on my jeans from last night and walk to the door, not bothering to even tame my bed head hair.

I swing open the door to see Adam. "What do you want?" I spat, obviously not in the best of moods.

He eyes my attire for a minute before he says, "I wanted to see if you'd like a ride to school."

I narrow my eyes at him. "What's the catch?"

He laughs, clearly amused. "No catch. I'm just trying to be nice considering we're gonna-" He stops once I let out a loud groan and hold up a finger.

"Don't remind me."

"I won't," He says slowly and his eyes twinkle with mischief. "But only if you let me drive you to school."

For a minute, I think of rejecting. But then I think, it's just a car ride. What's the harm? So I nod. "Alright, fine. Just give me a minute to get dressed." I don't wait for him to reply as I slam the door close and trudge my way to my room.

I fine a clean pair of gray skinnies in my drawer and slide them on along with my combat boots and a dark green plain T-Shirt. I manage to get my hair untangled and quickly braid it. I grab my bag and then I'm out the door.

I meet Adam outside, who waits by his shiny BMW. Most people would stop and admire it - I'm pretty sure Adam's use to it, at least, since he has a shocked expression when I just get in the car and wait for him to drive us to school. I was never one to drool over people's possessions, so he shouldn't have been surprised.

He gets in seconds later and starts the engine, pulling out of the drive way and onto the road. I don't even bother to start conversation, I just stare out the window and watch the trees past by.

It's Adam who breaks the silence. "So you know about the up coming formal, right?"

"No." And I hope I won't ever know that one's coming up, nor do I wish to attend one.

The formal is when all the packs in the region get together and dresses up as whatever the theme is intended to be. This year, it's Masquerade. I never did understand why the hell they have them, but I guess it's just to announce big up coming events.

"Well, one's coming up in a week. And you know in about two months, on my eighteenth birthday, my dad will be passing down his position to me. My dad.. He wants me to start introducing you as my mate. So you can mingle with-"

"I'm not going. Pick someone else." I cut him off right away, folding my arms over my chest. I swore at myself mentally. I should have never accepted the damn car ride offer.

"Ronnie, it's a done deal. You're the one I've chosen. You're my mate."

I shake my head rapidly and glare at him, "You don't decide for me who's mate I am and who's I'm not. It's my life. I make my own decisions. And I decided that I don't want to be your mate. Do us both a favor, Adam, leave me alone. Pick someone else. Someone who actually wants this."

His mouth falls slightly a gape at might. He's speechless. And I'm glad for that. I look back towards the road, seeing our school come into view.

"I.. I can't do that. I'm sorry." He whispers as he pulls into the school parking lot and picks a spot.

"You're really gonna be sorry soon, Adam." I hiss and swing open the door, slamming it behind me. This seems to catch some on goers attention since they stop and stare.

I don't even bother with them, I just strut up the steps and head off to my locker. That's when I notice Ms. J is walking right over to me.

"Good morning, Ronnie." She greets with a big smile.

I give her a stiff nod, "Morning."

"I have great news!" She grins, clapping her hands together.

"Oh yeah? What?"

"A new student volunteered to be help you with the painting the back drops!" She squeals, acting like a teenage girl while I stare blankly at her.

"New student?" I utter. Oh god. Oh god. Please don't let it be who I think it is.

"Yes. A new student. He should be joining us in a few days of sorts. Anywho, class should start any minute. See you in six period, Ronnie!" With that, she saunters off. Leaving me to my scattered thoughts.

Chapter 4

I'm distraught and completely dazed through the morning, leading up to lunch. It's because I can't stop thinking of what Ms. J said. What if that new student was Liam? Was he stupid enough to come to a school where my pack went? If he was indeed the new student, he had a death wish, certainly.

Then again, could Adam even take Liam? No. But his father could. Alpha Beckett would probably group the strongest men in our pack and hunt for him. They'd probably tear him limb from limb, cheering that they had killed the Liam Farley. The thought makes me feel sick to my stomach and I'm quick to push it away. I don't want to think about anything but my work in front of me. But I can't even seem to handle that.

By the time the bell rings, my test is still as blank as it was when my teacher passed it out. I couldn't even managed to write my own name down, pitiful, I know.

I walk up to the front of the class and hand it to my teacher, cringing slightly when her eyes rake over the blank test. "Did you not just feel like completing my test, Ms. Mars?"

I open my mouth to justify myself with a decent excuse, but nothing comes out. What excuse do I say? Oh, sorry, Mrs. Salimando. I was just thinking about how my mate, Liam Farley, might be coming to our school. Did I mention that he's a murderer and every pack wants him dead? No? Well, he is.

Instead, I let out a sigh and thank the gods when the bell rings, signifying it's time for lunch. Mrs. Salimando shakes her head a me, a disapproving look plastered on her face. "That's a automatic F, Ronnie. I hate to give that to such a smart girl like you."

I stop myself before I can roll my eyes. I mean, come on! How many times have I heard that stupid lecture? You're a smart girl, Ronnie. I'd hate it all go to waste.

You could say I'm servilely use to it. I just nod. "I know, Mrs. Salimando. I really need to get my priorities straight and stuff.. But with my grandma in the hospital, I just can't seem to." Oh yeah, I'm definitely pulling out the sympathy card.

"Oh? What happened this time? Did she have another heart attack or get in a car crash?" Mrs. Salimando props her head on her folded hands, pursing her lips.

I cuss silently under my breath. Damn it, how many times had I actually use this excuse? Mrs. Salimando recognizes my defeated expression since she laughs. Bitch.

"Go, Ronnie. You wouldn't want to be late to lunch, would you?" She gives me a mocking smile before she grabs a red pen and write's a big, bold, 'F' on my paper. She then hands it back to me. "Get one of your parents to sign that and hand it into me right away. See you tomorrow, Ms. Mars."

I snatch it from her grip and turn away, resisting the urge to punch that mocking little smile right off her face.

I stuff the stupid test into my bag and head off to the cafeteria. Once I walk in, I'm greeted with the sound of obnoxious laughter and loud chatter with the occasional sound of someone chewing with their mouth open, causing their food to make a gross smacking sound. Damn my werewolf hearing.

I make my way to the lunch line and grab a blue tray. It's when I feel eyes burning wholes into my freaking back that I turn and glance away from the disgusting food. I'm met with numerous curious eyes. Are people staring at me? No, you're just being paranoid.

But as I glance around the cafeteria, I see many more people looking in my direction. Some stare and whisper to one another, giggling. My eyebrows furrow in confusion and I scan over the tables to see more people looking at me. What the hell is their problem? Do I have something on my clothes or something?

I face back to the selection of food. I suddenly feel insecure. My actions become stiff and hesitant.

"Are you gonna pick something or what?" Asks the old lunch lady who stares at - Just like everyone else - with her beady eyes.

I point in a random selection and lift my plate. It turns out it was a stale piece of pizza that obviously wasn't fresh.

I pay for my food and make my way to my usual table in the back. I ignore the lingering gazes and take a seat. I pull out my plastic fork and begin to poke aimlessly at the pizza before me. I never bother to touch it.

When I hear the familiar clicking sound of Anna's heels It's what causes me to look up. Her cheeks are flushed bright red and she has this huge goofy grin plastered on her face as she sprints towards me in long strides. She reaches the table and slams her hands down on it, making me flinch. "Is it true?"

I blink, shaking my head. "Is what true?"

"Don't play dumb with me, you lying skank!" She shrieks and shoves me. The bad part is that I'm not playing dumb. I truly don't know what the hell she's talking about.

"I'm not. What are you talking about?"

Her face masks confusion for a minute, before it turns into a frown. "You really don't know what I'm talking about, do you?"

I cock a eyebrow at her, "Should I?"

"Yes! Their's this crazy rumour around that you're-" Anna's cut off when a bunch of girly giggles come from behind us. We both look in the direction of where it came from to see three girls looking at us, erupting in more fits of laughter.

I have a feeling whatever Anna's about to tell me, has to do with the whole situation of why everyone is acting so weird today.

"I can't believe he's dating her," One of the girls whispered. She stares me straight in the eye and doesn't act the least bit coy. It's like she wants me to hear this, to know they're talking about me.

"Who the hell is she anyway?" Another girl asks, a lot louder then the other one. She doesn't seem to care that I'm only sitting a few feet away. Just like the other girl, she keeps her brown eyes on me and a look of disgust crosses her features. "Why would Adam choose her?"

Wait, what?

"I don't know," The third girl chimes. "She must be easy. I just can't believe she's Adam Beckett's girlfriend."

That's when I completely freeze. Dating Adam Beckett? Did they just say I'm his.. Oh god. If I didn't feel sick before, I do now.

I don't even care they called be easy, or ugly, all I can think is when the fuck did I start dating Adam? Nonetheless, when did I become his girlfriend?

"People think I'm his.." I trail off. I can't say it. I can't say the word girlfriend. And I feel so incredibly childish. It's just a word. But it has a big meaning behind it. Then again, mate has a even bigger meaning. I force myself to utter out the word, "Girlfriend?"

"Well, aren't you?" She replies. Her brown eyes search my face. I can tell she's more then confused right now.

I don't even know what to say. So I simply shake my head and avert the question at all cost, "Who said I was his girlfriend?"

Anna shrugs. "I don't know. Sidney told me that Adam was saying that you were his girlfriend."

I stand up right away and don't bother with my tray.

"Where are you going?" Anna asks quickly and she's on her feet in no time, trailing after me. I wave her off with a hand and I'm grateful when I don't hear the clack of her heels anymore. She's no longer following me.

I dart out of the cafeteria room and I begin scanning every single classroom in the building. I know it's stupid, how am I going to find Adam in this school when there are dozens of classrooms? But I don't stop.

I continue you on till I cover the whole first floor. I stop and think of where the hell Adam could be. I know he's surely not in the lunch room. I hadn't seem him in there for three weeks now since play rehearsal started..

Play rehearsal!

I make my way to the audotium and push open the heavy door. I'm greeted with the musky scent that reeks off the stained carpet.

My eyes scan the empty seats and the sage. They're numerous people there, parading around while one older man shouts orders at everyone.

It's complete chaos in other words.

I start down the long aisle and I notice a few familiars faces from my classes. They don't bother to pay attention to me. They're too absorbed in their lines and what the older man says. Once I'm close enough, I realize the old man is Mr. Taylor. He's the one who taught music class and ran the drama club.

I never had a class with him, but I heard a lot about him. How he was insane with perfection. He had even screamed at a girl who messed up a note at the schools annual Christmas show. The girl cried, long story short. She went as far to transfer out as well. Not that I blame her.

"What are you doing, Lacy? Get with the program!" He screamed and I can see the veins in his neck pulse violently. The girl, AKA Lacy, flinched and cowered away from him. She muttered a quick apology before scappering off the stage. Probably to go cry like that other chick did.

I edge to the stage and rest a hand on the old wood. I watch in amusement as one boy marches across the stage dramatically, waving around a top hat.

I have no clue what the play is actually about, but it seems interesting. I'm sure once I start painting the back drops, I'll find out soon enough.

"Can I help you with something?"

My head snaps up in the direction of the voice to see Mr. Taylor hovering above me with a glare. I nod my head slowly. "Uh, yeah. Is Adam here?"

He sighs and rubs his temples. He's obviously read to explode with anger. "We're kind of rehearsing for a play, I don't need you distracting my actors. We only have four weeks to get ready."

"I know," I say, "I just need to discuss.. the back drops for the play. I'm the one painting them."

He raises a think eyebrow at me and brushes a stray of greasy brown hair out of his face. "You're Ronnie Mars?"

"That's my name. Don't wear it out." I joke and do the cheesy thing by pointing a finger. He doesn't seem the least bit amused. I let my arm fall limp to my side. "I'm sorry, that-"

"Adam's in the back. Go before you waste anymore of my time." He says dryly and turns his attention back on all the actors. "Lacy, where are you? Get back here!" He stomps off with that. Probably to scream more at her.

I let out a exasperated breath and walk to the steps, I make my way up and I move to the blood red curtain and wrench it back. I'm glad when I see there are not nearly as many people back here then there are on stage.

Right away, I spot Adam in one of the high chairs, mumbling to himself as his hazel eyes scan over what I can only guess is a script.

I approach him slowly and stop when I'm directly by his side. He still doesn't look up, just studies the print on the paper.

"You're in the play?" I blurt out. I even surprise myself that I don't lash out immediately at him.

He doesn't bother to look up still. "Yeah."

"Who do you play?" I ask, though I'm not the least bit interested to know. He can tell, since he sighs and sets the paper down on the desk before him.

"Gaspard," He mumbles. "He's the main, troubled, character. But you don't really care about who I'm playing, am I right?"

"Not really," I answer truthfully. "That's great, though. Congrats, I guess."

"It's about the rumours, isn't it? I guess I should congratulate you too. I heard you scored head artist of the back drops."

I nod and choose to ignore the "thanks" part of the sentence. "Yeah. Did you start them? Adam, I thought I made it clear that I'm not your-" I pause and glance around, making sure no one is in hearing range. "-Mate. Nor am I your girlfriend."

He shakes his head and boosts himself out of the chair, "I didn't mean for the rumours to start. I was talking to Mandy who was arguing about how I picked you and well, I just blurted out that I was with you now and some freshman heard it. I think you know what happens next."

I let a sigh of frustration, "That's the thing, we're not together. Do you know how many stares I've been getting today? Or what people are saying about me? You have to tell everyone it's not true, Adam."

He pinches his lips together and fumbles with the edge of his script. His face scrunches together and I know he's pondering something deeply. "I.. I don't think I can do that."

I scuff, "You can. But you won't."

"It's not like that Ronnie," He says and looks to his right, probably thinking of a get away. "Look, I need to get back on stage and practice my lines. I'll talk to you later, okay?"

I shake my head and reach out to grasp his arm as he starts to walk away, he dodges and disappears behind the curtain. Why does everyone avoid telling me the truth?

I don't even have time to go after him and demand he tell me what the hell is going on since the bell rings. I hurry out of the back and make my way back to locker. I declare in my head that the discussion between me and Adam isn't over. I'm determined to get some answers and I will stop at nothing to find out what the hell is going on. And also how the hell to get out of this huge mess that's been created in less then a week.

Again, I repeat, how could my life change so drastically?

By the time I get home, It's late. At least six. I stayed after school to cram in a late study session and to finish a paper of mine that should have been done a week ago.

I sigh as I enter my house and drop my bag on the floor. My shoulder and back aches from having to carry around that thing all day.

I groan and reach up to rub my tender shoulder when I hear a shuffle of loud feet hitting the wood floor. I know right away that it isn't Liam. And for some reason, that seems to disappoint me.

I peer around the frame of the door to see my dad huddled over the small coffee table, stacking papers together. He stands up straight once he catches my wondering gaze. "Hey, Ron."

"Hi," I mutter and ignore the fact he's called me by the nickname I absolutely despise. "Are you leaving again?"

"Yeah." He says and collects the papers from the table and rolls them up, stuffing it in his back picket. "I'll be gone for a.. few days, or so."

I lean against the door frame and shrug. "Whatever. Bye."

"Bye," He mumbles and walks over to where I am. He stops and pauses to gaze at me. His eyes bore into mine and I'm slightly surprised to see them holding sincerity. Hesitantly, he reaches out a hand, brushing his fingertips across my shoulder. I'm caught off guard by the unfamiliar gesture.

I move away quickly out of range of his touch and reach up a hand to cover the spot he's just touched. I cradle it like as if I've just been burned badly. "You should go. Wouldn't want to keep the girl waiting."

His face falls before it hardens. "Yeah." He passes me and opens the door, then closes it behind him. I watch from the kitchen window as he disappears into the thick plush of the woods.

My father could be so weird at times. Sometimes he was mean, rude, and stubborn, then the next he almost wanted to rekindle our broken relationship. I don't, though. I think that's what hurts him the most.

I shake my head. I don't care to think of my father's and I's strained relationship.

Instead, I focus my thoughts on taking a shower and getting to bed. And I do just that. I shower quickly and slip into my nightwear, braid my hair in my usual style and settle down.

I'm about ready to let myself fall into a deep sleep when the phone rings. I know who it is already. Anna. She's the only one who had gotten a hand on my house phone number. She must be calling to ask about Adam. I reluctantly get out of my bed and pick up the the wireless phone.

I press the green answer button and press the phone to my ear with a sigh.

"Hey, Anna. I know what you're gonna ask, so I'll come out and say. I'm not Adam's girlfriend. Honestly, I barely like the guy, so why would I date him?" I rant to her and fall down on the coffee brown sofa. "I have no idea how I'm going to convince people it's not true. Or how I'm going to get him to tell people it's not true. Any ideas?"

"Yeah, Liam can kick his ass for you."

I freeze. Their voice is deep, silky, masculine and incredibly familiar. It's also for sure as hell not Anna's chirpy, cheery, voice. I know right away it's Liam.

"Do you always talk about yourself in third person?" I say, "And how the hell did you get my number? This just proves you are a stalker!"

His melodic laugh rings over to the phone, making my knees quiver. I'm thankful that I'm sitting down or else I would have sunken to my knees in awe. "It's called the Internet. Ever heard of it?"

"You looked me up online?" You can actually look up someone online and their information pops up? I knew there was a reason why I hated computers.

"Yup," He says. "It's not all that hard. I just typed in your name and boom! There you were. By the way, I like your Facebook picture. It's.. interesting, by far."

My cheeks heat up and I know I probably look like a tomato right now. It's because my Facebook picture is just horrible. It was from Halloween. And from a year ago when I was a sophomore. Anna had picked out my costume, while I picked out hers. She had chosen me to dress up like a guy with a funny mustache and blond wig. Even though Donald Trump doesn't have a mustache, I resembled him greatly.

Than Anna took that picture and convinced me to put it as my picture. I did. I never logged on ever again onto my stupid Facebook, mainly because I didn't care for it one bit. But now I really needed to log on and remove that horrid picture. "It was a stupid joke," I mutter into the phone. Again, he laughs. "Okay, I'm going to hang up if you keep laughing at me. I should just hang up, anyway."

His laughter dies down quickly at my threat. "Alright, sorry. Changing the subject, what's with the Adam guy?"

"I don't think that's any of your concern."

"It will be when I see you tomorrow at school."

I go silent. All I can think of is what Ms. J said about the next student. Liam is the new student. My worst fears have been confirmed. Oh god. "Are you crazy?" Is what I manage to say. I can just picture him grinning like a mad man because I'm completely lost for words.

"Obviously,"

"They'll kill you. Adam will tell his father and.. and-" I cut myself when I let out a grunt and stand up from the coach. "You have a death wish, don't you? That or you're just plain stupid. I'll go with the later."

"You worry too much," He says. "Your pack won't be touching me any time soon. Trust me."

Something about his words makes a shiver crawl up my back. Your pack won't be touching me any time soon? The tone was incredibly suggestive. As if he knew something I didn't. Maybe he had something up his sleeve. I'm possibly sure, though.

All I know is that the idea of Liam coming to school is nerve wrecking.. And somewhat exciting, as much as I hate to admit it. Exciting because I'd get to see Liam everyday of the week. That I got to peer into those sea green eyes of his. Though my mind objected that all we should be doing is staying away from him. Yet I don't think I ever could.

The nerve wrecking part is how it all plays out. What if Adam kills him on the spot? Would Adam do that? I wasn't sure who Adam really was anymore.. I had no idea what he's capable of and what he's not. The thought scares me.

"Ronnie?" His voice is suddenly soft now instead of humours. It's a nice change, I suppose.

"Yes?"

"Get some sleep." He says, "We both have a long day ahead of us tomorrow."

"I bet," I mumble really more to myself then him. "Whatever. Night."

"Night princess."

Before I can swear at him not to call me that, he hangs up. I sigh and place the phone on the coffee table.

I sluggishly make my way back into my room and fall into my bed, closing my eyes and hoping - No, praying - that tomorrow everything would be just fine.

Though I try to fool myself everything will be fine, my gut tells me the exact opposite. I sigh and force myself into a deep slumber where I dream of Liam reluctantly. Only two days ago I met that boy and he already has me wrapped around his little finger.

The next day I'm incredibly ancy. At first when I woke up I pondered staying home in bed.I thought about how I could bury myself in a cotton fortress of sheets and maybe hide there till my days are done. Obviously, my plan fails when Adam pounds on my door.

He offers me another ride. I decline at first till he agrees to talk to me about the whole "I chose you as my mate" thing.

So again I got dressed quickly in a tang top and a open flannel, along with some jeans and my combat boots along with my signature hairstyle; My braid. Then I got into his car and well, here I sit awkwardly waiting for him to say something. Anything would do. But he doesn't. He just watches the road with a scrunched face that makes him look freaking constipated.

I start to regret ever agreeing to this car ride. He clearly lied about telling me he was going to talk to me about the whole girlfriend rumour and mate thing just to give me a ride to school. But why would he do that? God, it seemed like I didn't know anything that was going on in my own life anymore.

"So," He finally says, breaking the silence. I turn to look at him and watch as he nervously drums his fingers over the leather steering wheel.

"So." I repeat, pressing my lips together.

"How's your dad? I haven't seen him around much." He asks and takes a quick glance at me before he focuses back on the road. I shrug.

"Fine, I guess. But do you really care where or how the hell he is, really? I know I don't."

"I figure It'd be a nice change asking a civilized question before diving into a fight like we seem to do every day now," He says with a sigh.

Again, I shrug. "Maybe you should stop giving me shocking news right after another. What are you gonna tell me next? That I need to get pregnant before you become Alpha or something?" I joke at the end. It's when he stays completely serious that I worry. "I'm not having your baby."

He lets out a low chuckle, "No, Ron, you don't have to have my child. Yet." I choose to ignore the last part. "And I know it's overwhelming, you know, all of this. It's all happen fast.. Too fast, maybe." He whispers the last part and reaches a hand to tousle his blond hair.

"Way too fast," I agree. "Are you going to put the rumours to a end at school? Tell everyone we're not dating?"

"I don't see the point. In a week or so we'll really have to start acting like mates. And introducing each other as that. Letting out relationship be known is just the first part."

I groan, lolling my head to where it rests against the window. "I can't be your mate, Adam. Nor can I be your girlfriend. Don't you understand about what I want?"

He sighs, nodding his head. "I know, Ronnie."

"Why'd you pick me?" I ask abruptly. "Why did you choose to make my life hell? You could have picked Mandy. I'm sure she would have been happy."

I really do wish he would have picked Mandy. I mean, she's not that bad. Right? Okay. Maybe I'm slightly wrong.

Mandy is one of the craziest fan girls of Adam's. She's always hanging around him and sneering at any girl that walks by and dares to take a glance at him. She was probably my death right now. I wouldn't be surprised.

"Mandy's.." He trails off and pinches his lips together. "Mandy's-"

"Crazy?" I offer.

"Ape shit crazy." He says with a laugh, "You should have seen her yesterday at school. I think she was trying to rape me the way she pushed me up against the wall."

I cringe at the mental image that pops up in my mind. I can just see Mandy shoving her tongue down his throat. It seems like something she would do. "Lovely." I say sarcastically, "And are you going to tell me why you picked me or what?"

"Yeah." He answers and stays silent for a minute, before saying, "I picked you because you're not like the others. I remember when we were little kids and how I thought every other girl had cootie's except for you. I even told my dad how I'd marry you one day. And I never meant for us to grow apart or anything. I was just.. confused? I'm not sure." His eyebrows furrow. "I chose you because I know you'll fight for the pack. You're smart, head strong, and god Ronnie, you're beautiful inside and out. All the other girls of the pack want me because they want to be Alpha Female. You don't."

That's because I don't want you at all, I think. But I don't say it. I can't bring myself to tell him I don't want him when he's probably just said the nicest thing to me in my whole life. So I stay quiet and stare out the window. I almost cry out in a joy once we pull into the school parking lot and park. That is, till I remember what Liam said last night.

I scan over the crowd of students through the window of the car. I'm pleased when I don't see a pair of green eyes looking back at me or nothing.

I get out of the car with ease and shut it behind me, knowing I'm safe and Liam isn't here to put himself at risk. Maybe my words really got to him last night and he decided staying away from the school, the pack, and me was for the best.

Or maybe he's just not here yet.

I go with the later.

I give Adam a stiff wave before I go jogging up the steps of the school and head over to my locker. The whole time, I manage to keep my eyes peeled for a boy with golden brown hair and green eyes.

I pop open my locker and stuff some of my un-needed books into my locker, then grab out my Math book for first period.

I jump when I feel a tap on my shoulder and swiftly turn on my heels to see Anna. Talk about Deja vu.

"Good morning, Ronnie!" She chirps with a big smile on her face. I don't smile back and greet her just as cheerily as she did. It's because Anna isn't like this in the morning much. Sure, she's a happy person but not when it comes to getting dragged to school when all she wants to do is sleep.

"What's got you so giddy this morning?" I ask and stuff another one of my books in my locker. I close it to watch her lean against the locker next to mine with a dreamy look on her face.

"I think I'm in love." She states. And I raise a eyebrow at her.

"Oh yeah? You seem to fall in love a lot. What's this.. the fifth time, already?"

She dwindles a piece of her golden blond hair in between her fingers, completely oblivious to the fact I'm practically insulting her. "He's perfect."

I'm really starting to worry now. "Who is he?"

"I don't know his name, but he is a God, Ronnie. He has these perfect muscles and these perfect green eyes. And his hair, wow. He's just..."

"Perfect?" I suggest, though I'm slightly panicking instead. Please don't let it be Liam, please don't let it be Liam. "What else is perfect about him?"

"Everything about him is perfect. The thing I find the hottest? The scar he has above his eyebrow. It just screams bad boy, don't you think?"

I freeze.

There's only one boy I know with muscles, green eyes, and a scar. Liam. He's actually here. He's in my freaking school.

I wonder how many girls have seen him already. And how many have made failed attempts to talk to him. Well, at least I hope they were failed attempts. Were they?

I shake my head and tell myself I don't care. If Liam wants to get himself killed off by the pack, then so be it. I at least tried to warn the idiot.

I manage to regain normal composure and shrug, "Doesn't sound like much to me."

For some reason, I don't like the thought of Anna drooling over Liam. I just find myself getting angrier and angrier as she babbles on about him. About how handsome he is, about how she has dibs, and about what she'd do to him. The thought makes me become uncomfortable.

"I get it, Anna," I say finally breaking through her non sense babbling. "He's hot. So what?"

I grip my bag in my hand, ready to just storm off when I catch scent of something. It's not the usual over applied axe that the boys put on or the strong perfume that reeks off the girls of the school, no. This scent is.. familiar. And by far, not human.

The smell is woodsy with another scent that I can't decipher. Is it mint? Cinnamon? I'm not sure, either way, it's addicting and make's me slightly light headed.

And If I thought the smell couldn't get any stronger, it does. It forces me face Anna again and scan the cluster of students making their way to class.

That's when I catch sight of golden brown hair. Not to mention, bulging muscles. It's not hard to notice him from the crowd of scrawny teenage boys, he sticks out like a sore thumb.

Anna clutches my arm, digging her nails into my flesh. "That's him, Ronnie, that's him!" She squeals.

I know, I think and stare after him as Ms. J falls into step with him. She pushes a paper into his hands and says something that makes him laugh. That silky laugh. And slowly, still with a smile on his face, his eyes land on me.

My breath halts in my breath and I probably appear to be a deer caught in head lights.

His grin - Or well, smirk, - widens at the sight of me.

"Ronnie!" Ms. J calls, beaming at me like a mad woman. "Here's the new student I was talking about! Liam, meet Ronnie."

Liam's features cross into a amused look and he sticks out a hand to me. "Nice to meet you, Ronnie."

For a minute, I just look at him dumbfounded till Anna elbows me in the rib cage, making me gasp out. "Shake the guy's hand, idiot," She mutters to me and gives me a pointed look till she glances in Liam's direction and flashes him a bright smile.

I robotically place my hand in his. I'm hit with small little tingles that travel my arm to my neck, making my hair stand on end. I snatch my hand out of his grip quickly and push my hand into my chest, acting as if he's burnt me. "You too."

Anna gives me a questioning look and practically asks with her eyes, what's wrong with you?

I cower away from her hard gaze and glance to my dirty shoes. I suddenly wish I would have put a little more effort into my appearance today.

"Has the Principal already assigned who's gonna show Liam around?" Anna asks and from the corner of my eyes, I can see her eye rapping Liam. Slut.

What is wrong with me? Did I just call Anna a slut? Oh god, I did. Liam's really messing with my mental state.

"Yes, he did." Ms. J replies.

Please don't let it be me. Please don't let it be, I plead silently and clench my fist at my sides. I manage to keep my gaze averted to the floor.

"I told him Ronnie would be perfect for the job! He agreed to let her show Liam around." Ms. J chirps happily. God kill me now.

I step in quick to object. "Ms. J, I really have a lot on my platter, so maybe-"

"Nonsense!" Ms. J booms, cutting me off. "You guys should get to knowing one another, anyway. You'll be working on the back drops together."

I hate you Ms. J. I really do.

I sigh and force a smile. "Of course. How could I forget?" My eyes dart to Liam and I give him a death glare. I'm quick to conceal it with the same fake smile I had just given Ms. J. "We should get going, yeah?"

"Certainly." He replies, and turns to Ms. J, giving her a heart stopping smile. It even seems to have a effect on her since her cheeks redden. Gross. "Thanks for the help, Ms. Jovovich. I'll see you in six period."

Ms. J nods and Liam takes his place next to me. I give Anna a quick wave and begin to walk away from the two love struck girls who stare after Liam and I. Well, mostly Liam.

Now that I notice, most of the girls seem to be checking him out. I can't help but feel a surge of jealousy.

"I can't believe you came here, Liam," I say deathly low, "You're an idiot. Once Adam sees you-"

"Once Adam sees me he'll kill me. Blah, blah, blah." He rolls his green ques at me and he hurries his pace to catch up at me.

We fall into step with each other. "Like I said before, they won't bother to touch me. Now won't you be a good tour guide and show me to where my class is?"

"Why are you here?" I ask and ignore his previous request. I sneak a glance at him to find him watching me.

I forget my train of thought as I fall into his alluring gaze. I forget that I'm supposed to be cussing at him rather than drooling over him. I find myself focusing on nothing but just him.

Slowly, the curve of his lips pull up into a beyond sexy smirk. Again, my heart seems to speed up and pound loudly against my chest so hard that I'm afraid It'll leave a mark. His smirk seems to widen. I know he can hear my accelerating heart beat.

"I'm here to claim what's rightfully mine, princess. You."

CHAPTER 5

I don't reply to his comment. Instead, I blink and make a face to muster up the best fake disgust I can. The truth is, I'm not the least bit horrified by his comment.

My stomach flips and drops and a rushing excitement courses through me. Just like the feeling you get when you're on a roller coaster. But this feeling is much better.

I don't know what about it causes me to get a surge of excitement, maybe the chase that's to come. I wonder to what heights he'll go just to make me truly his. Yeah, that's definitely the exciting part.

"Speechless, are we now?" He muses as he trails beside me. "I tend to have that effect on women, no worries."

"No. I figured I'd keep quiet then rather insult that cliche line. I was doing you a favor," I say and quickly go to change the subject. "Give me your schedule."

"Say please."

"No." I stop and wrench the schedule from his grip and examine it closely to see all of his classes are with me. How the hell is that possible?

I glance up from the paper to see a smug look plastered on his face. He obviously notices my shock. "Now we get to spend all eight hours of the school day together. Exciting, isn't it?"

I give him a flat look, making it clear I am not amused. "How did you end up in all of my classes?"

He shrugs and innocently flashes me a smile. "A coincidence, perhaps."

"Oh, it is no coincidence, you-"

I'm cut off when the bell rings loudly, practically screaming at every single student to get to class. I sigh and grasp Liam's hand in mine, ignoring the tingles, I pull him along and run as fast I can to class before we both get detention and have to spend more time together.

Then again, that doesn't sound too repulsive. I shake my head to rid myself of the vile thoughts. I will not let myself grow close to him. I will not let myself grow close to him, I repeat over and over again in my head. But who am I trying to fool, me or him?

By the time lunch swings around, I'm happy enough to be able to break away from Liam. And when I get my lunch, I get a surprising offer as well.

"Would you like to sit with us?" Adam asks, a dim smile on his lips. For a minute, I hesitate. And does Anna who stands next to me with her eyebrows furrowed. She's probably more confused than I am.

"What?" Anna says, dumbfounded.

"Would you like to sit with us?"

"What?" She repeats, blinking slowly. I give her a nudge to her side.

"Sure," I answer with a curt nod. It's not like I actually want to sit with Adam. I just know that if I sit with Anna at our usual table, Liam will gladly join us and that would probably just cause chaos. Not to mention, numerous questions from the pack that I'm not ready to answer.

I trail behind Adam and Anna does too, looking like a lost puppy.

Once we get to the round table, everyone their seems to stop what they're doing and just stare at us. I shuffle nervously from foot to foot while Anna just wears a gullible smile on her face. She's obviously snapped out of her confused trance.

"Uh, where do we sit?" I say, darting my eyes between Adam and Mandy, who gives me the stink eye.

"How about over there?" Mandy points one slim finger in the direction of our usual table and flashes me a mocking smile.

I flash a bitter sweet grin right back. "Why would I do that when I can sit with all you wonderful people?" I make sure to add extra sarcasm to the word 'wonderful' just so she gets the point. Knowing how dumb Mandy is, she'd probably think I was complimenting her and her posse.

"It looks like our table is full," Jessica - AKA, Mandy's bitch - inquires. And it's true. All the seats are full. And I doubt they would be moving any time soon to try and make us fit. Anna's tugs on my arm, obviously feeling defeated. But instead of giving up, I wrench my arm from her grip. I look over to Adam, saying with my eyes, make them move, or I'll do it myself.

He swallows hard and I stop myself before I can roll my eyes. He's supposed to be future Alpha, and he's nervous about telling Mandy to back off? What a wimp. "Make space, Mandy.

Better yet, why don't you and Jessica let Anna and Ronnie take your seats. You can get two other chairs from another table, no biggie."

Mandy's nostrils flares with anger and she's about to complain when I speak up, "Get to it already."

She glowers for me before she pushes herself up from her chair and tugs Jessica up. They both spare me and Anna another glare before they march off.

Adam grabs the chair Mandy was once in and pulls it closely to his, then indicates for me to take a seat. I eye it for a minute and final settle by putting my tray down and taking a seat. Anna takes the one next to me and she nervously picks at her food.

Nobody in the table makes us feel welcome as they stare at us as if we've sprouted a second head.

After a few minutes of silence, a girl named Kara finally sparks a conversation that Anna soon gets in on. I don't pay attention. Instead I look around the cafeteria. I already know what - more like who - I'm looking for, but I don't admit it to myself. I convince myself that I'm just looking for Mandy and Jessica to get a laugh as they look for chairs at another table.

Finally, I catch sight of golden brown hair. Liam. Involuntarily, I seem to suck in a breath as his green eyes dart in my direction. We hold our intense gaze for what feels like eternity. But it's sadly broken when a arm slithers around my shoulders and we both look to the source to see Adam's questioning eyes watching me. "Are you okay?"

No, I'm not. And soon you won't be either. My eyes nervously dart to Liam who stiffens at the sight of Adam and I so close to one another. It looks as if he's ready to march right over and pound Adam's face in. His fist clench at his sides and his muscles involuntarily flex at the action. I get lost in the distracting movement for a minute. Every other girl in the lunch room seems to do the same thing.

It's no surprise. It's been happening the whole day. Every where I went with him, girls seemed to be ogling him in desire. I'm not gonna lie, it bugged the hell out of me each time one of them sent a flirtatious grin in his direction. I had to quickly convince myself that Liam wasn't mine. I couldn't just stake my claim on him and tell those girls to piss off.

Just like how I'm not Liam's. Okay, that's another huge lie. I am. But I can't accept that. Me and Liam could never work. We can never be together. The mere thought of never being able to wrap my arms around him, or kiss him, or just anything, sends a sharp pain through me.

Would I really have to be stuck with Adam? Would they force me to be with him, even if I said no? No.. they would never do that. Right? Something tells me that they would. How am I going to get out of this? I could run away... with Liam.

No way! How could I even think of running away with him? If I did, all my dreams of living a normal life would be crushed. We'd have to hide out just because of the fear of someone attacking us. I didn't want to be moving around from place to place. I wanted to have a home. Perhaps even a family, though that's highly unlikely.

I wasn't a girl who wanted to get married or have children, weirdly. I just never saw that kinda stuff in my future. Though the thought of being alone for the rest of my life is depressing.

I didn't need to be thinking about this stuff. All I need to be thinking of right now is getting a way out of becoming Adam's mate.

"Ronnie?" Adam squeezes my shoulders, catching my attention. I glance over to him and then slowly to his arm that's wrapped around me. Hasn't he ever heard of personal space? "Are you okay?"

My eyes, as if they have a mind of their own, land right back on Liam who looks more tense then before. I can just tell he's fuming right now.

Adam slowly follows my gaze.

My breath halts in my throat and just like Liam, Adam's tenses right away. For some reason, he presses me closer against him. As if he's trying to protect me. Does he think I'm some weak little girl that can't defend herself? I wriggle in his grip and glower at him. "Remove your arm before I rip it off and beat you with it."

He isn't even faltered by what I say. He just glares at Liam.

I resort to swatting his arm off my shoulder, and scooting my chair away from him. This catches his attention. "Don't you realize what's going on? That's Liam Farley!"

Everyone in the table snap's their head in the direction of where Liam is. And I can hear the rumble of their menacing growls crawling up in their throat. Anna doesn't look the least bit phased, she just shrugs. "What about him?"

Cliff eyes Anna for a minute, before he glances over at me. "Who invited her?"

"Shut up Cliff," Adam snaps. It's the first time I've ever heard Adam speak with such a edge to his voice, it shocks me.

Cliff cowers away and doesn't say another word. Instead, he trains his eyes on Liam.

Adam abruptly stands up and makes his way over to Liam. I immediately jump right up and follow behind him. Adam doesn't even glance back. He stops right when he's in front of Liam. I do too and stand close to the both of them. If a fight breaks out, I'll be able to stop it, right?

"What the hell are you doing on my land, rogue?" Adam spat and glares at - Well, more like up - At Liam. "You're asking for a death wish."

Liam snorts. "Really? You think you could possibly take me?" Liam steps closer, emphasizing the fact he's a lot bigger. It's then I realize how abnormally big he really is.

Liam towers over Adam's 5'11 frame easily. And he probably out weighs him by another 100 pounds. Not from fat, but from pure muscle. Sure, Adam's got some muscle himself, but nothing compared to Liam.

The look in Adam's eyes falter's for a minute as he takes in just how much Liam over powers him, but as quick as it came, is how quick it disappears. He puffs out his chest the best he can and holds his head up high. "Easily."

Liam let's out a booming laugh that causes Adam to flinch. He stabs one thick finger into Adam's chest and watches him jolt with a amused glint in his eyes. "I haven't even done anything yet and you're already flinching. What kinda Alpha are you?"

Adam grits his teeth and his hazel eyes dart to me, finally noticing that I'm here. "Go back to the table, Ronnie. Let me handle this on my own."

I shake my head and glance to Liam who raises a eyebrow at me. I draw in a shaky breath, would anyone ever really be able to take down Liam?

Some of my worries seem to die down. Adam can't take Liam. He's way too strong.

Adam grabs me and forcefully shoves me behind him, again, acting as if I need his protection. Like he could.

"Don't touch her." Liam warns, practically saying, she's not yours to touch.

"She's my mate, I can if I want to."

Like hell you can! I shout mentally and glare daggers into his skull. It's my body, and I should allow who gets to touch it.

That's when I notice he called me his mate. My face suddenly masks horror and my eyes find Liam's. Weirdly, he laughs. And shakes his head at Adam. "Have you even questioned why I'm here? Wasting my time in this stupid school?" Liam questions and Adam's eyebrows furrowed. No. He hasn't. "I'm here to claim what's mine, dim wit."

Still, Adam maintains a clueless expression. And I frantically search Liam's face. "Don't." I whisper, so lowly that I can barely hear myself. I know he hears me. But just like Adam, he ignores me.

"What the hell are you talking about?" Adam asks, his voice is low and shaky. I can just see the wheels turning in Adam's head; He's slowly piecing everything together.

Liam crosses his arms over his chest and smirks. I know it's way too late to stop him. "Ronnie's my mate. My true mate. Not someone you can choose, Adam, like you've done. She's bound to me, just like I'm bound to her. While else would I waste my precious time in school?"

I close my eyes and intake a sharp breath. Damn it, Liam, damn it! Don't you realize what you've done?

All the lunch room chatter doesn't even matter. I block it out and focus in on them. I can hear Adam's heart thudding violently. "You're a liar." Adam croaks.

"You know it yourself Adam. She's not yours. Admit it."

"I admit to nothing!" Adam shouts hoarsely. It seems to catch the attention of numerous people in the lunch room, since they begin to stop and stare. Adam notices too. And backs away from Liam. He turns and gives me one last glance before he darts out of the cafeteria. Leaving me and Liam to stand in the center of the lunch room together.

I shake my head at Liam. "I can't believe you just did that." I whisper, before turning on my heel and stomping back to the table. Anna watches me with a questioning gaze. I don't bother to tell her what's just happened. It's not like I could. Instead, I slump down in my seat and daze off the rest of lunch. Adam never comes back.

In six period, Ms. J informs me that working on the backdrops begins next Monday. I nod and say "Okay" before dazing back off. Just like I had done for the rest of the day since lunch ended. Adam hasn't spoken to me. He just gazes at me when we pass in the hallway. Probably in disbelief and confusion.

I'm glad that he hasn't. It gives me time to come up with a decent excuse that Liam's lying. That he's just trying to get under his skin.

I don't know how I'm going to convince him, but I'll try, at least. It's not that I'm ashamed to be Liam's mate, but if that gets around, it could be dangerous.

I haven't talked to Liam since. I think it's evident I'm pissed off and talking to him is the last thing I want to do.

Once the bell rings, I'm out the door and making my way into the parking lot. I'm surprised when Adam appears and offers me a ride home.

I don't even think, I just say, "Sure."

The ride home is deadly quiet. I make no attempt to break the silence. I mean, what am I gonna say? I hadn't even thought of a good excuse. Could I? I wonder if he'd even believe me. Or if he deep down he truly knows I'm not his to have.

I sigh and rub my temples as we pull up in front of my house. I quickly get out and a mutter a thanks, then dart up to my door. That is, till Adam calls out to me. "Ronnie?"

Yeah, like a get away would have been that easy. I face him slowly while keeping a hand on the knob of the door. If anything, I could just run inside and hide. "Yeah?"

His eyes search the area around us before he slowly walks over to me and stops when he's only a few inches away. "Is it.. is it true?"

I don't need to ask to know what he's talking about. I open my mouth to blurt out a lie, but nothing comes out. What do I say? No? Yes?

I sigh and my grip on the knob slips. My arm falls limp at my side. "Adam.." I drawl. My actions speak louder then words, and Adam seems to understand.

"Oh my god," He mutters under his breath and then he's off. I don't go after him. I watch as he gets in his car and drives off. Away from his house. Away from the pack. Away from me.

I walk into my house like nothing's happened and drop my bag to the floor before I collapse onto my couch. I glance around to find no trace of my dad here. I'm alone. As always.

Night falls quickly. Still, there's no sign of Adam. His mother stops by to ask where he might be and I tell her I don't know. She leaves without another word.

I take a shower and settle down into bed, closing my eyes and whipping away the events of what happened today. I start to slip from consciousness when I feel my bed dip down and a arm extends out, pressing me back against their muscled chest. I know who it is. But still I mutter out sleepily, "Liam?"

"Who else would it be?" He breathes, his minty breath washing over my features.

"Santa Claus?" I mumble, pressing my face into my pillow with a sigh. "Why are you in my bed? Are you here to rape me?"

"It wouldn't be rape. You'd like it too much." He teases and I groan. But don't make the effort to pull away.

"How old is that line? Seriously, get with the program."

"Someone's cranky." He says. I roll over slightly so I can glare at him.

"Wouldn't you be if a strange man crawled in your bed and started talking to you when all you want to do is sleep? Not to mention, this strange man pissed you off earlier in the day?"

"Well, now that you put it like that-"

"Liam!" I shriek and sit up. "This is not a joking matter. I can't believe you actually did that today! What if he tells Alpha Beckett? Oh my gosh, I'm gonna get slaughtered."

Liam laughs. Yeah, he actually laughs when all I'm doing is freaking out. Aren't mates supposed to be comforting? But no, he laughs. "Adam won't tell. He likes you too much." He says, "And I couldn't hold back. I mean, he acted like he owned you. When he certainly doesn't."

"No one owns me," I gruffly tell him and fall back onto the bed. "So you now how they're forcing me to mate with him?"

"Yup. I spied around here and kinda figured it out. What tools. Is this how your pack is? They force you to mate with people?"

"I suppose." I grumble and he presses me back against him. Out of reflex, I lean into him and close my eyes, inhaling his calming scent. That is, till I remember I'm supposed to be mad at him. Not to mention, I'm not supposed to let myself grow close to him.

I pull myself out of his grip reluctantly and scoot to the edge of my bed. He reaches out for me and I move an inch farther away, when he reaches out another time, I end up tumbling off the bed. Liam chuckles while I flare with anger and glare up at him from the floor. "Need a hand?" He taunts.

"No, I'm fine." I spat and stand up, getting myself out of the tangle of sheets I brought down with me. "Now go."

"Why is your dad never here?" He asks, ignoring my previous request. Or well, demand.

"That's none of your business." I say harshly. "Now get out of here before I kick you in a place where the sun doesn't shine."

He playfully growls. "I love it when you're feisty. You have no idea how much of a turn on it is, princess."

I grab my pillow and smack him in the face with it. "Make another sexual comment towards me and you'll get worse than a hit with a pillow." I cock a hand on my hip with my free hand. "Now get out, really."

Liam grunts and pushes himself up from my bed, "Fine. I'll go. Only because if I stay any longer I'll probably jump your bones."

He makes his way to my window and pushes it open, he gives me a tantalizing smirk. "Goodnight, sweetheart." He jumps out and I watch as he dashes off into the forest without another glance.

I close the window and draw the curtains close, then slip back under the sheets of my bed. I let my eyes drift shut and let the fluttering butterflies in my stomach die out. God, I hate the way you make me feel Liam Farley.

Chapter 6

I haven't spoken Adam or Liam since that scene in the lunch room. They hadn't made the effort to speak to me either. I think they were both just trying to grasp what was going on.

Come to think of it, I hadn't seen much of Adam to even try and talk to him. His parents questioned me further Friday morning when Adam still hadn't returned home.

When I got to school and saw him there, by his locker, I was surprised. We made eye contact for less than a minute before he turned away and walked off.

As for Liam, I saw him around school. He made few attempts to spark a conversation with me, each time, I kept quiet and gave him a death stare till he got the message and scampered off.

Now it was Saturday night and I was over at Anna's, since I had promised her I'd spend the night over at her house. The night started off promising once Anna whipped out the horror movies and sweets. Such as popcorn, candy, and all sorts of energy drinks.

Usually, we wouldn't eat this kinda stuff since Anna's mom was a total health nut. But lucky for us, her mom and dad had chosen to go out for dinner and see a movie, enough time to stash the evidence and cover up the fact we had been eating junk food we were supposed to not touch.

Anna's endless squeals bring me out of my thoughts and I watch with amusement on my face as she thrusts a pillow in front of her face, than peeks over and watches the man in the movie shove the other dude's hand in the drain, than turns on the garbage disposal, and well, we all know what happens then.

"I think we should have just stuck the traditional chick flicks," Anna voices once the scene passes. "Why did we rent horror movies again?"

"Because romance movies suck." I state dryly.

"You know what really sucks? Getting your handed grinded by a device that's meant to grind food up! Who knew it could be such a deadly weapon?" Anna shivers before shoving another load of popcorn in her mouth. "We should have just watched Titanic."

I groan and shake my head at the mention of that movie. "How many times have we seen it? Yeah, okay, it's great the first time or two, but it gets old after a while. And I have no desire to see Kate Winslet boobs another time."

Anna let's out a pain staken gasp, "Are you insulting the greatest movie of a lifetime? How can you be so bitter about love stories and boys when you've got Adam Beckett trailing after you? Sooner or later, he'll change your views on love, you know?"

"You make it seem like I hate the idea of love."

"It's because you do!" Anna shrieks.

I shake my head at her. I don't hate the idea of love, nor do I question if love actually exists. I'm not one of those people who say I won't ever fall in love, either. But the idea of it makes me sick.

I've never been one of those girls who crave a fairy tale romance. I don't want a prince charming like most. I know the perfect man doesn't exist, but most girls fool themselves into believing they do. Like I've said before, marriage and kids is certainly not something I see in my future.

Maybe Liam would be changing that thought soon.

I sigh inwardly at the nagging voice that insists on implying that Liam maybe will change my views on that subject. That maybe he'd be the first guy I'd ever love. But how could I fall in love with someone, when I didn't even know what love was? I was only sixteen years old. And I hadn't even experienced liking a boy before.

Yeah, I was a virgin physically and emotionally. I hadn't even kissed a boy, and here I am, thinking about love. And most importantly possibly falling in love with Liam Farley.

I wondered if Liam has ever fallen in love. Or if he's a.. Well, you know, a virgin.

No freaking way. Have you seen the muscles on that boy? Girls must be lining up in hopes to get a chance to sleep with him.

I don't deny or push away the looming thought. I bet girls were trying to sleep with him every chance they got. My stomach clenches and knots when I think of how many girls he could have been with.

Something about another girl being with him bugs me. And I know why. It's because he's my mate and I can't help but feel possessive over him. That I should be the only one allowed to ever even touch him.

And I really needed to stop thinking about him constantly.

"Ronnie?"

I snap around to see Anna watching me with curious eyes. "Yeah?"

"You did that weird blanking out thing," She says over a roar of screams that comes from the TV. "Am I that boring to talk to?"

"No. I just have a lot on my mind."

"What? About Adam?" She asks and reaches for the remote to the TV, she pauses it then focuses her attention on me.

I sigh, "Not exactly."

"Then what? School? The new kid at our school?" She presses the subject further on, and I realize that's she not going to be dropping it anytime soon.

"Why would I be thinking about Liam?"

"You remembered his name?" Anna raises a eyebrow at me. And I suck in a breath. She knows something's up.

"Well, he's not someone you can forget about exactly." I inquire.

Anna purses her lips. "Perhaps not. It's just weird you made the effort to memorize his name. I remember when I was new to the school you called me Amber for a week."

It's not a lie. When Anna was new in our class freshman year, I made no attempt to even remember her name nor speak to her. When she started bugging me and I realized I didn't even know her name, I took a guess and started calling her Amber.

I can see where she's coming from. It's not about memorizing Liam's name that's leading her to believe something's up, but acknowledging his presence.

"What great memories, huh?"

I than try and go into the whole story of how weird it is that we became friends. It's a pitiful attempt to change the subject. And Anna knows it.

"You fancy him, don't you?" She asks abruptly in the middle of my mindless rambling. I pause and my lips part in an effort to spew out a deny. Nothing comes out.

Anna smirks, obviously in triumph that she's caught on to me.

"It's not like that," I manage to utter out. "I don't. It's just-"

"You like him." Anna states and nudges me with her foot. "You slut, even after I called dibs you still like him."

I don't reply. Instead, I slump against the couch and groan.

"First Adam, now Liam," She laughs, "You naughty girl."

"I don't like either of them," I mutter. "Besides, I would never make a move on Liam. You called dibs."

Again, she lets out a laugh. "Like I have a chance. He was staring at you the whole day, Ron. He likes you too. Most guys do."

I make a face, "What do you mean?"

"You're so gullible," She accuses and sighs. "I mean, look at you. You're gorgeous. Even though you keep your hair in that horrid braid. We're not five anymore, you know? Braids aren't cute." She leans over and tugs my long braid, probably trying to let me hair loose. I swat her hand away and glare.

Anna knows I hate wearing my hair in any other style. The last time I put my hair down was.. well, ages ago.

My mom even use to braid my hair when I was smaller. It's how I learned to do it. She told me how much prettier I looked. That everyone could see my beautiful blue eyes better.

But how I wear my braid, is the least of my problems right now.

"I like my braid," I say, "And I think I would have noticed if boys looked at me."

That's a lie. A terrible one. Anna is right, I'm incredibly gullible when it comes to boys. I had no experience with them, so how was I supposed to know if guy liked me or not?

"No you wouldn't have," Anna scuffs. "Like I said before, you're naive." She sighs and nestles back down into the couch. She yawns and gives me a lazy smile, "But that's okay. I still love you, Ron."

I give her a meek smile, "I love you too, Anna." I get comfortable back again and Anna presses play. For the rest of the evening, we stay quiet and watch as Michael Myers slaughters some teenagers. Yeah, that's definitely going to help me sleep tonight.

Sunday is just as calm as yesterday was. I stay over and have breakfast with Anna's dad and mom, than spend the rest of the day with Anna, bathing in the sun in her backyard. We chat about small events that should be coming up with the school, and I try to render out of it once Anna brings Nick Morrison's party that's next weekend.

I knew where she was going with the conversation when she said, "I bet it would be pretty awesome if we went.."

At first, I objected till Anna got literally on her knees and begged. I finally fell into her trap and agreed. She grinned and informed me once I got down with starting the back drops, that we could go to the mall together. Again, I agreed reluctantly.

At six, once the sun went down, I packed my stuff and gave Anna a brief, stiff, hug. "I'll see you at school tomorrow."

She smiles softly and nods, "Yeah. See you tomorrow, Ron."

"Are you sure you don't want me to drive you home, dear?" Anna's mom voices from her place on the living room couch.

My eyes dart to her to see her looking at me with worried eyes. In a way, Anna's mom is kinda like my second mom. She always worries about me and my well being.

I shake my head, "No. It's cool. My.. dad, called and ensured me he was just a block away. So I'll just walk and meet him there. Don't worry about me, Mrs. S, I'm a big girl."

She frowns at the same lie I've been telling her since we met, but nods, accepting the fact I'm never gonna accept a ride from her. "Okay sweetie, just be safe."

I fake a smile, "Always am." I grasp the knob of the door and swing it open, "Later." I call over my shoulder than close the door.

I trail down the stone path away and start down the side walk. I venture more farther off from sight of Anna's house before I cross the road and enter the dark woods. It's not rare for me to do this, I do it all the time I walk back from Anna's, plus it's nice to shift and just shake off the usual stress from the week.

Once I get deeper into the woods where I'm clear from the lights, houses, and cars, I shift.

I run, dodging tree barks and thick roots. I'm able to clear my head and focus on my pace, and the surroundings around me. It's like my little escape from the world. Besides art, that is.

I'm almost so lost in the feeling of running that I don't notice the black blur that dashes miles in front of me. And the odor they reek. Key word - almost.

I come to a skittering stop and watch as more faceless figure's dart by. At first, I'm uncertain of what to do. Run? Hide? That is, till I smelt the scent they reeked of.

I realize who they are immediately. The Purgatory pack.

I shift back and press myself to a bark of a tree, hoping I can somehow disguise myself. What the hell are they doing so close to our border?

The Purgatory were probably the most dangerous pack in our area. They had always gotten a laugh out of terrorizing my pack. It all turned into something more than just a laugh when one of their members hurt one of ours.

That's when all out war broke out.

I don't remember how it all ended, since I was so young, but I had been informed that they were aren't allowed to cross our boundary. Nor theirs. If found on their land, there would be no mercy. These were the monsters that killed my mother.

That means if they found me, I would be good as dead. Just like mom.

I couldn't myself from letting out a jagged breath. A sense of fear nestled itself into the pit of my stomach and I realized how dim my chance of escaping were.

Bile rose up in my throat once their scents reached my nose. Rotting flesh. That's what they smelt like.

I slap a hand over my mouth to resist the urge to gag. I train all of my thoughts on thinking of way to escape and not get caught.

All else fails after a few minutes when I realize I can barely focus on remembering my name.

I take a peak around the thick bark to see them in now human form. I couldn't make out of their faces, just the shapes of their body.

They talk in soft whispers, so quietly, that I can barely hear them. I only made out few words. Such as - Shift. Enemy. Attack. War.

What were they talking about?

I peer around the trunk more, hoping to catch a glimpse of these faceless, and nameless, men. I make the fatal mistake of taking a step forward, when I do, a loud crunch sounds under my boot. Immediately, one the men look in my direction.

I'm quick to jolt back and press myself against the tree. My nails dig into the bark. I don't even register the pain. I can't. I'm too panicked. Too scared.

"Did you hear something?" A gruff voice asks, and I don't need to look to know his eyes are scanning the forest right now. Probably just waiting for me to pop out.

I squeeze my eyes shut, my breathing comes in heavier. This is it, I think, This is how I'm gonna die.

"No, why?" Another voice replies.

"I heard something. And saw something."

My blood pounds so hard that I can't even hear their words anymore. My heart thumps so incredibly fast that I'm afraid it'll pop right out of my freaking chest.

I try to piece my thoughts together, to be able to think of a way out of this, but nothing appears. I can't think straight when death is being dangled right above my head.

I'm coming Ronnie, don't panic.

Oh god. Oh god. I don't even focus on the fact that I've just heard a voice that certainly doesn't belong to me talk in my head.

Was I going crazy?

That's when I feel something - or someone - grip my hand. A scream crawls up in my throat. My eyes fly open and I'm about to let that blood curling scream out when I see a pair of green eyes. Liam's green eyes.

Was this a hallucination? Or was he real?

Ronnie, His deep voice fills my head and I stare up at him with my lips parted. When I tell you to run, you run. Alright?

If I didn't feel crazy before, I do now. I mean, how the hell-

It's the bond. The more we are together the faster the mating process is. So now we can comunicate mentally to one another. And well, feel each others emotions. That's how I knew you were in trouble. We have to get out of here-

He pauses to gaze around the bark. He doesn't even looked phased as the thud of footsteps near us. Instead, he grips my hand tighter in his grip. As if trying to reassure me everything would be fine. Would it?

-I'm going to distract them. When I do, I want you to run as fast you can. I'll be right behind. Once you cross your boundary you'll be fine. And god Ronnie, whatever the hell you do, don't stop running. Understand?

I nod numbly and he lets my hand go. I watch him lean down and pick up a rock from the forest ground. I watch him with wide eyes as he leans further out, than he pulls his arm back and throws it. I hear a breathless curse from the man who had just spoken moments ago, and Liam runs into plain view.

Go, Ronnie, go!

I don't question his command.

I force my feet to get moving and dart out into plain sight. I don't stay too long to see the scene unfolding in front of my eyes. I run as fast as I can, my braid thumping against my back.

I hear thundering footsteps behind, immediately knowing It's not Liam. I whip my head around to see a boy around my age chasing me. I let out a breathy gasp and force my burning legs to keep going.

But It's not enough.

His foot steps near closer and than, I feel his hand wrap around my long, flailing braid, where he tugs me by. A gasp leaves my lips as he yanks harder, causing me to fall back against him.

I thrash and kick, letting out a inhuman wail. "Let me go!" I land a kick to his knee cap. He hisses a curse and his grip on me falters. I take the advantage to wrench myself from him and run again.

"I'll find you." He rasps, "I'll find you and I'll kill you!"

I don't let the fierce edge to his voice stop me. I pump my legs harder. Even after I've crossed my boundary, knowing I'm safe, I keep going.

Apparently, most of the pack most of heard my scream, since I see clouds of people running into the force. They all call out my name.

I collapse once I get to the clearing. Heaving and gasping for air.

Hands reach out towards me, and faces past in front of my vision, but they're all a blur. They're nameless faces, just like those men in the woods. All except for one face is unfamiliar. Adam.

He falls to his knees in front of me, grasping my shoulder giving me a shake. "Ronnie! What happened? Ronnie!"

I swallow roughly. My throat is burning and I need water majorly, but I need to get the words, "The Purgatory pack," I say hoarsely, "They're back."

They let me collect myself before they decide to question me. Deciding it's best that I arrange my thoughts and what happened so it won't be a onslaught of rasps and curses. What I had been doing after five minutes of finding me.

I settle onto my couch after I drinking a tall glass of water and watch Aloha Beckett, Adam, and the Beta of the pack pace and mumble to themselves. They're always just as puzzled as I am.

After a while of staring at them, I finally clear my throat and tell them I'm ready to explain what happened. I dive into the whole story, and by the time I'm done, they all have a the same expression. Horror.

"The Purgatory pack?" Adam echoes once again for the fifth time. I don't think he can believe it himself - that the Purgatory pack were near our land - but that's okay, because I don't either and I saw them with my own eyes.

"Yes," I mumble. "The Purgatory pack."

"Why would they be so close to our boundary?" The Beta, Clark, whispers. More to himself than any of us, though.

But I decide to answer anyway. "I don't know," I start, "But I heard them whispering. Something about war, and attacking, and.. something else." I mumble the last part, mostly to myself as I go quiet and try to remember it all.

"How'd you get out again?" Alpha Beckett asks. The same question he's been repeating since I started the story.

I told him how I had managed to distracted them than ran from my life. It's not exactly a lie. I mean, they did get distracted, just not by me. Liam did.

Liam.

Was he okay?

Liam said how he could feel my emotions. Feel my fear. Now were we mentally linked to one another?

God, why did everything just get more and more complicated?

"Like I said before, I distracted them long enough to run." I say. Alpha Beckett narrows his eyes at me. He doesn't buy it. "Alright, well, we just have to make sure everyone stays inside the boundary. We can't afford another run in with them." He pauses and eyes me for minute, "Are you sure there wasn't anyone else at there?"

"No," I say. "No one else was out there."

He doesn't say anything for a while, just stares me down. As if expecting I'd break at any moment and blurt out how the Liam Farley had actually saved me. And oh, that he was my mate too. Yeah, he better keep dreaming if he thought that was gonna happen.

"Okay. If you say so. " He stands up and gestures for the Beta to do the same. "I should let you get your rest. Goodnight, Ronnie."

I give him a curt nod and watch as they exit. I don't say anything till I hear the bang of my screen door and I know they're gone.

I face back towards Adam to see him staring at the floor with his eyebrows knit in contemplation.

I sigh and toss the blankets off of me. "You should get going too. School's tomorrow."

"How'd you really escape, Ronnie? Did he help you?"

I don't need to ask to know who's he asking about. Liam.

What should I say? Yes? No? But just by silence, he has his answer. "How did he find you? How did he know you were in trouble?"

"The link," I mutter.

He understands. He draws in a shaky breath and runs a hand through his hair. "I can't believe this."

"Join the club." I retort sarcastically. He narrows his eyes at me, just like his father had minutes ago. But doesn't reply.

He stands and stuff his hands in his jeans, "You know you're going to have to choose. It's Liam or me."

"Then you already know my choice." I say, "Neither. I pick neither of you."

"We obviously know that's not a option. Think wisely, Ronnie. I'd hate for you to make the wrong choice."

I go to say something back, but he marches off. For a minute, when he's in kitchen, he pauses and looks to his side. As if he's staring at something. Or someone. He shakes his head and exits. I flinch when I hear the bang of the screen door, but I still don't feel like I'm alone.

I learn that I'm not when the screen door bangs again. Who was that and had they just heard my conversation with Adam?

The next morning, Adam doesn't offer me a ride. And for that I'm grateful. I walk to school in the chilly morning air, ignoring the fact I can't feel my fingers after five minutes.

Once I get to school, I'm greeted by Anna who asks how I got home.

"Fine," I tell her.

She doesn't seem to buy it exactly, but she nods and continues to ramble on about some paper that's due this Thursday. I nod and make it seem like I'm interested, but the truth is, I'm not. It's because I'm hopelessly searching through the crowd of students to catch a glimpse of Liam. To know he's okay.

Liam? I call out mentally. No reply comes and I feel like an Idiot. I sigh inwardly, and follow Anna to class. Still, there's no sign of him that morning.

That is, till after Lunch, I see him in the hall. Walking to six period, Ms. J's class.

"Hey, Anna, I'll catch up with you later, okay?" I mumble to her, and before she can object, I chase after Liam and catch up to him, clasping a hand on his shoulder.

"Liam?"

"You're alive." He states bluntly.

I nod and swallow harshly, my throat suddenly feeling dry and tight. It doesn't get any better when I lock gazes with his burning green eyes."Thankfully you are too," I retort, "What happened? Are you okay?"

"Yeah. I got away on time. I would have came after you, but once I heard that.. scream, I figured you'd catch your packs attention. I thought something happened to you, though,"

"Why?" It's a stupid question. I know why. Because of that scream I'd let out.

"That scream," He confirms, "You have no idea how many times I heard it in my nightmares." He admits. And his face glazes over in anger. "What the hell were you thinking?"

"What do you mean?"

"I mean, what were you doing in the woods at night? Are you crazy? You could have gotten-" He stops in mid sentence, looks around the crowded hall way and grasps my forearm, yanking me towards the direction of a empty classroom. He shoves me inside before he closes the door and locks it. "-You could have gotten killed, Ronnie."

"You don't need to lecture me," I say, "I know what I did was crazy, and st-"

He cuts me off in mid sentence. "Crazy doesn't describe it! That was incredibly stupid of you! And I know your smarter than that. Do you realize what it would have done to me if you got hurt?"

I glare at him. "I didn't know they were near my boundary. I'm not a psychic. I'm sorry, alright?"

My apology doesn't mean anything to him. He shakes his head and grasps both of my shoulders, looking down at me. "I don't want you ever going to the woods alone without me. Do you understand?"

"What? I can do what I pl-"

"Do you understand?" He repeats, cutting me off in mid sentence again.

"You can't tell me what to do." I snap, and he raises a perfect eyebrow up at me. God, did he look sexy when he was mean or what?

"I can," He argues, "And I will. Do what I say or I'll force you to do exactly what I say."

I know he's not bluffing when I don't even see him a crack a smile. He's so damn serious and angry that I can practically feel his eyes burning holes into my forehead. I know I'm not going to be getting out of this unless I agree.

"Fine," I spat. And wrench myself from my grip.

"Good. Now let's go. We'll be late."

I numbly follow after him towards six period. This is gonna be a long last three months of school, I grumble mentally.

Don't look so down, sweetheart. You're far too pretty to wear a frown on your face.

I glare at Liam to find him looking at me with amusement clear in his eyes. I give him the finger before I push him to where I'm ahead.

Chapter 7

After six period, Ms. J leads Liam and I to the art wing where she informs us we'll be working on the back drops indefinitely.

When we arrive there, the whole room is like my personal haven.

Huge canvas are everywhere, all different kinds of paints, pencils, sketchpads, everything you could ever need. Or well, anything I could ever need.

I take a seat and Ms. J begins to describe to me the whole scene of the play. It's mid-evil like, from what I learn.

I grab a sketchbook and began to sketch what she says, trying to picture it all. Once I'm done, I show them to her and she nods eagerly, grinning, "It's perfect!" She says. And I meekly smile back at her.

When she's done giving us the whole down on everything, she exits, but not before stopping and saying, "And oh, Ronnie, I hope you don't mind but I used that picture you had painted in class and hanged it up in the hall way."

"What painting?" My eyebrows furrow and I take a step towards her, peering out the door to the long hallway that's covered in numerous paintings. All the paintings are so different and.. beautiful. All the paintings are so colorful, and light. So mine's bound to stick out.

I catch sight of it and my eyes widen.

Liam. That's what the painting was of. The one I painted when I was so out of it. Oh god.

"Painting?" Liam echoes and walks over to where me and Ms. J are. Ms. J smiles at him and points it out. But it's not like she needs to me. Mine sticks out like a sore thumb.

I close my eyes and groan lowly, Why Ms. J? Why?

"Wow," He breathes and I open my eyes to look up at him to see his face full of astonishment. He takes a step away from us and makes his way to the painting.

He stops when he's in front of it. I find it slightly humours as the green eyes in portrait stare right back at him.

"It's beautiful, isn't it? Ronnie has some real talent." Ms. J inquires and look over at me a small grin, she reaches out and gently pats my shoulder, "I should get going, anyway. Make sure to lock up when your done." She tosses a set of keys to me and with that, she's gone.

I sigh and toy with the keys in my hand, turning back to Liam. He traces the painting with his fingertips. I suck in a breath when he glances over his shoulder at me and asks, "Is this me?"

I swallow roughly. "No, why would it be you?"

He raises a eyebrow at me and looks between the painting and I. "Then why do we have the same eye colour?"

"A coincidence, perhaps." I mock his words from the other day, "Is it that big of a deal? Come on. Let's get to work."

When he doesn't move, I grip his hand and tug him back into the room. I make him help me out with spreading out the large canvas and grip a pencil between my teeth. I take off my shoes and socks, tossing them to the side before I start to get to work.

I keep my smaller sketch by my side the whole time. I look back to it as a reference of sorts and slowly transfer it all onto the canvas.

But It's not as easy to concentrate with Liam staring me down from his position at a desk. I look up at him multiple times to see him watching me, each time, he keeps his gaze with me. I'm always the one who chickens out and looks away.

I sigh once I'm done with one half of the canvas and lean back to examine my work.

I brush back a stray hair that had fallen out of my braid and purse my lips. "What do you think?" I ask Liam and glance up at him.

His eyes dart to the paper and he examines for a minute or two before he shrugs, "It's nice, I suppose."

"You're really great help," I drawl sarcastically. "What the hell are you doing anyway? Aren't you supposed to be helping?"

"I am," He says, "Supervising is hard work, you know?"

I scuff. How is sitting down with your feet propped up on a desk and leaning back in a chair hard work? "Why'd you even sign up for this if you weren't going to do nothing?"

"So I get to to be with you," He admits. "Don't you want to hang out with me too, princess?"

"No," I lie, "I want peace and quiet. If you're not going to help, than leave."

"What happens if I still don't want to help and won't leave?"

"I'll tell Ms. J you're a lazy, incompetent, egotistical, ass-"

"I get it," He says, cutting me off in mid sentence.

I glower at him, "Do you really?" I thrust the pack of pencils in his direction. "If you do, than you'll get down on your knees and help me draw this."

He stays seated for a minute and I raise a eyebrow at him, challenging him to test me. He stands finally and grabs the pack of pencils - while keeping his eyes on me the whole time - and pulls one out. He kneels down by the edge of the canvas and glumly asks, "What do I draw?"

I smirk in triumph and gesture to the notebook by my side. He places it by his side and we fall into a silence. The only thing that's heard is the pencil scrapping against the paper. I'm able to concentrate enough that I get most of the work down. Once my knees began to ache so much from crawling around on the floor is when I decide to relax.

Liam doesn't rest though. Instead he works on the canvas with knitted eyebrows in concentration and also frustration. He has a death grip on the pencil as he tries to copy my portrait from my sketchbook. He lets out numerous curses under his breath and erases furiously each minute or two. Than the pencil ends up in snapping in half.

"Damn it!" He hisses and chucks the broken pencil along with the others. I don't flinch like I did the first time or two. I watch in amusement as he breaks yet another one and tosses it to the side. I stop him before he can get another pencil and break that one in half too.

"Your strokes are too hard." I tell him, "Hold the pencil a little more lightly. And just let it flow."

"Easy for you to say, little miss Picasso." He mutters and grasps another pencil, again, he breaks it. I sigh and decide not to be heartless.

I move back down the floor and clasp my hand around his much larger one. I press myself to his side, ignoring the tingles that threaten to overwhelm me and lead his hand down to the paper. "Let me help you."

He nods stiffly and surprisingly, he lets me direct his movements. I gently show him how to stroke the pencil properly, and once the picture slowly starts to appear perfectly, I smile lightly. "Beautiful."

"Very." His minty breath brushes my cheeks, causing a shiver to ripple up my back. My breath catches in my throat and I turn slowly to where are noses touch and our breaths mix. "You have a smudge on your face," He mutters and I reach up to rub it away. But he beats me to it.

His fingers graze my cheekbone lightly, even by this small little touch, all my senses seems to come awake and I feel myself suddenly heating up.

He rubs his thumb over the spot where he claims the smudge is and keeps eye contact with me the whole time. I let out a shaky breath when he leans down further and his lips are just a inch away from me. If I leaned further just a inch more, I could catch his lips with mine. The thought is tempting and just like him, we forget about the canvas.

I remove my hand from his, only to replace it by pressing my hand to his face. My heart nearly leaps out of my chest when he turns his head lightly to nuzzle his face into my hand. His lips brush the inside of my palm.

I run my finger down his nose and his cheekbones, just like he had done to me seconds ago, my finger on their on account trail to his forehead where I stare intently on the scar above his eyebrow. I hesitantly place my hand closer to the scar and watch his face for any sign that I should back away, but all he does is watch me with those green eyes of his.

I run my fingers all around it, before I inch closer and touch it. Even though the scar appears to be incredibly rugged, It's not. The skin is smooth as I trace my finger over it. Just how he had traced his finger over the painting of him in the hall way.

He sighs and presses a kiss to my wrist, causing me to shudder. I withdraw my fingers slowly and lean into him again with parted lips, practically begging that he kiss me. We seem to have the same train of thought since his eyes fall to my lips as well.

We lean in slowly, almost too slowly for my liking. And all I can think is, this is it. I'm going to kiss Liam Farley.

Even that thought doesn't snap me out of my trance. I just find myself wanting it more. Wanting him more.

He leans, ready to capture my lips when I hear a shriek. "You skank! This is why you were late! Trying to make your move on Liam."

I gasp and whirl around to see Anna in the door way with raised eyebrows and a wide grin on her face. I flush, I can only imagine how this looks. I'm practically sitting on Liam's lap while he has his hand wrapped around my waist while his other hand is pressed against my cheek.

Everyone's silen't for a minute. We all stare back at forth at one another, probably pondering on what to say. I draw in a breath, ready to make up some stupid excuse. But Liam beats me to it.

"It's exactly what it looks like."

Anna let's out a loud laugh. And I glance at Liam, glowering at him. I wrench myself away from him and stand up, crossing my arms over my chest. "It's not. I can explain, exactly."

"I can too," Liam says, "Ronnie was teaching me how to.. draw. Yeah, that's what we can call it."

Anna laughs harder and clutches her stomach, "Ronnie obviously did a good job. I mean how, I can just feel the sexual te-"

"Were supposed to be going to the mall, right?" I snap, cutting her off before she can blurt that sentence that will cause me nothing more than embarrassment.

Anna nods, "Yeah. We were supposed to leave thirty minutes ago. I was waiting for you, but figured you got caught up with.. something.. so I decided to come look for you," She says, "Are you still up to it?"

No. I want to stay here and kiss that boy senseless, you idiot. "Yeah," I nod and collect my stuff, and shrug on my socks and shoes. I avoid eye contact with Liam the whole time. I grab my beg and put it over my shoulder. "Let's go." I make my way to dart out of the room when Anna grabs my forearm. I look over at her questioningly to see her eyeing Liam.

"What are you gonna do, Liam?"

"I don't know," He mutters and pushes himself from the ground, regaining his composure. "Probably just go home and chill out."

"That sounds boring," Anna chimes and she flashes me mischievous grin at me. Don't you dare- "Why don't you come to the mall with us? We need a guys opinion on the dresses, anyway."

Damn you Anna, damn you!

"Well-" Liam begins, but is stopped when I start to rapidly shake my head.

"No, no. You don't have to. I'm sure you have better things to then go to the mall and watch us shop. Right? Right. Come on, Anna." I tug on her hand, begging her with my eyes that we just leave. She refuses and swats my hand away.

"Nonsense! You coming, Liam?"

Liam doesn't miss a beat. Instead, he smirks and says, "Who's car are we taking?"

We end up taking Liam's car. Which turns out to be a old school mustang. We could have taken Anna's beetle, but Liam could barely fit in there. Because of how freaking tall he was. And how much muscle he was packing.

I was mostly silent the ride. Anna wasn't. She was chattering on and on about Nick's party. About what look she wanted to go for. And what store we should head to as well. I nodded and said a occasional, "Yeah. Cool." along the way, though I was more absorbed in my thoughts. Thoughts about Liam. About how I had almost kissed him.

I find myself banging my head more and more as I think of how stupid I was. I didn't even know Liam, yet I allowed him to get so close to me. I almost let him kiss me. And the worst part is, I wouldn't have stopped him if it wasn't for Anna walking in.

Liam wasn't the only one playing with fire. I was too. And it was incredibly dangerous. But I couldn't help it. I was attracted to him in every sort of way. Everything he did had me hypnotised, like I was under his spell.

I gnaw on my lip, stealing a glance. He watches the road intently with his eyebrows furrow. The same look on his face when attempting to draw.

I look away and slump against the door, promising slightly to never let that happen. To never let him have power over me. Silently, I know that I won't be able to keep that promise. He's just walking temptation.

I shove it all away and plan out the rest of the schedule for my week. Or well, my whole month. You know what my schedule really consists of? Avoiding Liam all the time.

I plan to just work with him for the back drops, get it done quick and fast as I can. I can just talk him when necessary and than avoid him elsewhere at all costs. I vaguely note that I still need to find away out of becoming Adam's mate.

I could run away. It's not the first time that thought occurred to me. Whenever I think of the subject, that's what just comes to mind. I could leave after the year ends. Relocate somewhere else and attend school. Graduate, than do it I wanted to do with my life.

Though it all seems easy putting it like that, it's actually not. Where would I go? How would I survive if I don't even have money?

It's a messy a plan. A highly unlikely one that I would be able to achieve. I can only dream of getting out this god damn pack. Getting away from this stupid town. And most of all, getting away from stupid Liam.

"Are you coming?"

Speak of the devil, I think and glance up to see him out of the car. I look around and realize we're here. At the mall. My god, I am more out of it then ever. I mutter something like, "Yeah," then get out and follow Anna who walks next to Liam. He says things occasionally, making Anna laugh and playfully shove him. I become even more aggravated by the fifth time she does and adds in a hair flip and wide grin.

I walk ahead of them into the booming mall, ignoring Anna's calls to wait up. Instead, I hurry my pace and stuff my hands into my leather jacket.

I take my time scanning the display windows of stores. I stop when I catch sight of a small vintage boutique, and a piece of jewelry catches my eye. I walk up to the display window and finger the cool glass, staring at the necklace.

It was weird, unlike most I had seen. It held no diamonds of sorts, but a pendant that looked like as if it was blown glass. When I look closer, I notice it is blown glass. It's a simple circle with all times of swirling colours like yellow, blue, and green. And maybe that's why I like it. Because It's out of the box and not some stupid diamond necklace.

"What are you looking it?"

I snap my head to the side to Anna looking at me with her her eyebrows raised. I also notice that's Liam by her side, staring at the necklace I had just had my eyes on. "Nothing," I say and move away from the glass. "Let's just go to that place you wanted to go."

"Okay," She drawls, "Come on Liam."

Liam and I follow silently behind her. Once we get to the store she desires, she tugs us both inside with a grin on her face.

Than she gets to looking through the racks of clothes. Meanwhile, I fiddle around with the scarfs on a table in the center of the store.

"Why did I agree to this again?" Liam leans against the table, pursing his lips. I shrug and look around the store, seeing the various females in the store watching our interaction. Or well, just really watching Liam.

I resist the urge to roll my eyes when one girl "accidentally" bumps into him. She apologizes to him and offers a flirty smile, but to my surprise, Liam doesn't care. All he does is say, "It's fine." Before turning back to me and trying to start up a conversation again.

I raise my eyebrows at him once the bimbo is out of sight, "Didn't you notice she was flirting with you?" I question.

"No," He says, "Did you?"

"It's kind of obvious," I mutter and lean against the table too. "Come to think of it, all the girls in here are practically eye rapping you."

"Maybe," He shrugs, "But I don't care."

As much as I hate to it, I'm incredibly relieved at his words. "Why not? You could have any girl in this room. I bet twenty bucks that chick who bumped into you comes back and asks if you saw her bracelet or something because it obviously fell off when she bumped into you. Than she'll start up a conversation with you saying how clumsy she is."

Liam just laughs, probably thinking how stupid I am to believe that.

Ten minutes later the girls comes back. Claiming she dropped her keys and if he's seen them. I watch the whole time with amusement as she dives into a conversation about how stupid she was for dropping her keys. She also tells him her name is Elena.

Finally, as if she's just realized I'm here, she says, "Oh! Hi. I didn't notice you. Are you guys brother and sister or something?"

You wish, bitch. I'm about to say something when Liam's arm suddenly wraps around my waist, thrusting me into his side. "Actually, no. This is my girlfriend, Ronnie. Ronnie, meet Elena. She dropped her keys when she bumped into me. Have you seen them by any chance, baby?"

The girls face falls and I can't help but saying, "No," I then flash her a bitter sweet smile. "Too bad, huh?"

She notices my harsh attitude towards her and glowers at me, she looks over at Liam and gives him the same look, "You know what, maybe I dropped my necklace in another store. Thanks for the help."

"Necklace?" I echo, "Didn't you lose your keys?" I raise a eyebrow at her and she flushes.

"Yeah, right. Keys." She than turns with that and she leaves. I can't help but laugh. Liam simply mutters something about me being cruel before he too turns away and walks somewhere us.

I never found a dress for myself. Though Anna tried her hardest, I turned everything down and just declared I wasn't going to be wearing a dress anytime soon. She then forces me to at least get a pair of jeans, shoes, and cute top since I won't be wearing a dress. I say yes just to get her off my back.

Liam drops Anna back off at the school. She bids me and Liam a farewell, then she's off, leaving me with Satan himself.

Liam doesn't ask if I want a ride home. He drives me there forcefully till he can no longer get any closer to our pack houses without being attacked.

I get out of the car and mutter a thanks, and a "See you later."

I give him no time to chase after me or anything. I simply shift and run the way home. Once I get to the clearing where all the houses are, I shift back to human form and walk to my house. Along the way, I catch sight of Adam sitting on his front porch, staring down at the gravel. He obviously senses my gaze, since he glances up and eyes me for a minute. Pain evident in his eyes. And a warning of sorts. But what's he trying to warn me of? Too soon and too quickly he looks away, gets up, and walks off. Leaving me to wonder what the hell that was about.

My question is answered when I walk into my house and see Alpha Beckett sitting at my kitchen table.

I stop and stand awkwardly near the door frame, staring at him as he places the mug he was drinking from back on the table.

"Hello Ronnie," He greets and flashes me a grim smile, as if everything is freaking dandy. But It's not. Whatever he's here for, I know it can't and won't be good.

"Hello," I reply, and slowly place my bag down. "How are you?"

"Wonderful," He retorts and traces the handle of the mug. "You?"

"Peachy," I say. "I don't mean to be rude, but is there something you want?"

It's a lie. I do mean to be rude. But I obviously can't come out and say that. I stiffly take a place at the kitchen table, across from me.

I watch him fold his hands neatly while rubbing his thumb over a golden wedding band. After a minutes of silence, I start to shift around uncomfortably, the knot in my stomach tightening. I feel like I'm going to be sick. And I don't know why. Maybe it's his presence. Or his intense stare. Either way, I just want him gone.

Something about Alpha Beckett always did give me the creeps. People claimed he was such a friendly, giving man, but when I looked into those eyes of his, the same eyes that Adam has, I just see something that lies deeper, as weird as that sounds.

I believe that Alpha Beckett isn't who he claims to be.

I know in that mind of his, lies malicious intents. He smiles, but it's fake. Incredibly fake.

Yeah, I know he's helped people out in the pack. Smiles, laughs, and is always nice to people, but don't they see it as a act? Is it? Or is it just me who believes that?

As we lock gazes, I notice the same ominous glint in his eyes that Adam had the day of the bonfire. They look so alike that I can barely tell them apart. The same blonde hair, the same hazel eyes, the same bone structure. It's scary. And it just leads me to believe that I will never love Adam like the pack wants me to. Like they're forcing me too.

I find my dislike growing more for this man - and Adam - as I stare at him. Because his eyes say it all. I believe he enjoys the power he has over everyone. That he gets to tell each and every one of us what to do. That he controls our everyday lives.

You're not who you claim to be, Alpha Beckett, I think silently. And I can tell he knows my dislikes for him, since a smile threatens to spread across his face. He thinks It's funny. He finds my hate for him funny.

"What did you come here for?" I ask, lowly and deadly. I'm no longer in the mood for games. And I no longer can contain my anxiousness. I want to know. I don't want to wait anymore to hear the news. I know he's not here to stop and have a little nice chat with me. No.

He laughs softly and leans back in his chair, a grin widening across his face. As if he knows something I don't.

I learn that he does when he says, "Liam Farley, huh?"

Chapter 8

My mouth goes dry and the words I try to say, seem to be stuck in my throat. I don't know what to do. So I just stare.

He flashes me a sly smile, he knows he's caught me. He knows I'm at his mercy now. But I refuse to let him think he's won, so I compose myself. Sit up straight and put a hard expression on my face. "I don't know what you're talking about."

He laughs - more like cackles - before he pushes the mugs towards me. "Do you mind getting me some more coffee, dear?"

I narrow my eyes at him. Biting back the urge to say, get your own damn coffee. I don't need to test him right now. I don't think It'd be the smart thing to do, then again.

I reach for the mug and grasp it in my hand. I stand up and walked over to the pot on the stove and pour some in.

I slowly walk back over to the table and place it down roughly in front of him, causing some hot coffee to splatter across his hand. He lets out a sound and rubs over the spot. I resist the urge to smirk. "Sorry."

"I bet you are," He mutters and takes a sip from the mug, "Most people don't like their coffee without sugar, but I do."

I only stare at him. Questioning silently how he can act so casual. Like this isn't happening. Like he hasn't just announced that he knows about Liam. But he has.

I rest my forearms on the table and convince myself to not leap across the table. To not punch that smile right off his face. I also manage to get my anger in control remarkably. Not because I want to somehow still be respectful to this ass, no way.

If I want to somehow pull this whole act off, I need to act calm. Being angry would just be a dead give away that he's caught me.

Plus, I won't give him the satisfaction knowing he's stuck a nerve. I compose myself and lean back in my chair, crossing my arms over my chest and giving off the airy feeling that I don't care. That this isn't big news to me. Too bad it actually is.

"You do know what's going to happen, don't you?" He asks bemused, placing his mug back on the table.

"Nothing," I say, and he seems shocked by my answer since his eyebrows shoot up.

"What makes you think that, Mars?"

"Because I don't even know what you're talking about," I say calmly, "What about Liam Farley?"

He shakes his head at me, clicking his tongue against the roof of his mouth. "Let's not play dumb here, Ronnie. I heard it all the other day."

It all clicks together quickly and mechanically, surprising even myself, the second bang of my door. That must have been him exiting my house.

I'm screwed. I'm completely screwed. How the heck can I get out of this when he heard it straight from my mouth?

Maybe he's lying. Maybe Adam just told him or something, I think dolefully. But not even as I repeat that over and over again in my head do I come to believe it.

I swallow roughly, and my once calm composure fades. But even then I try to hold it together. "I don't know what you're talking about."

"Well, let me refresh you're memory," He gives me a smile, standing up from his chair and walked over to where I am. I stiffen once he rests a hand on my shoulder. "You said to Adam that Liam came for you. He helped you escape, didn't he?"

"No," I say, "I don't know what you're talking about." I curse silently when my voice cracks at the end of sentence. But I can't help it.

I can only imagine what he'll make me do to ensure Liam's safety. Then again, I could just tell Liam. Maybe Adam or Alpha Beckett couldn't take Liam alone, but the whole pack could.

"You do," He replies, taking his hand off my shoulder. "I'm going to tell you what's to happen now, alright?"

I refuse to reply. I stare straight ahead with my arms crossed and keep a expression of stone. When he notices I'm going to say anything anytime soon, he begins to speak,

"You're going to go through mating with Adam. You'll act like his girlfriend to the humans and you'll attend the ball coming up. Is that understood?"

"I'm not doing any of that," I hiss before I can swallow down the harsh words and refrain myself. "You can't make me."

"But I can," He insists, "You dare cross me and just imagine what would happen to Liam. Perhaps I wouldn't be able to take him down myself, but I could slip a word to Purgatory pack that Liam Farley is in the area. Sure they hate us, but if that gets around, I'm sure they won't care for us anymore."

My breaths halts in my breath and I look up at him, shaking my head. "You wouldn't."

He gives me a sly smile, one that confirms he's not even close to playing around. "I wish I was. But I'm not. Just imagine what would happen, Ronnie. They'd tear him to pieces, that's a nice thought, isn't it? And if word got around that you were his mate.. You'd be dead too. Who's life is more important, yours or his?"

Both, I think weakly. I close my eyes. They're really forcing me to be with Adam. They now I won't refuse because of something happens to Liam, it effects me just as well. It's that mate insists that urges me to protect him. To go with the flow even if it means promising myself to another man.

"And you'd also hate for something to happen to your friend, Anna, wouldn't you?"

I nearly cry out at that threat, or well, promise. They would hurt Anna? I don't doubt it. Anna. Poor Anna. She wouldn't even get the chance to protect herself, she'd be killed instantly. "Leave her out of this." I croak, "She's not even involved with any of this. She's just a human."

"Maybe," He says, pursing his lips. "But accidents can happen, right?"

I open my eyes, my eyebrows furrowing. "What do you mean?"

"I'm just saying she could get in a.. well, accident of sorts. Something bad could happen to her, Ronnie."

"But it wouldn't be an accident," My voice suddenly becomes high pitched, and maybe it's because just the thought of Anna getting hurt makes me panic.

I know when he says it'll be an 'accident' he doesn't mean that. It means he'll make it appear like one. He's practically saying he can kill her and get away with it.

"That's not the point. She could hurt, do you get that?" He asks, gritting his teeth.

I glower at him. I don't care if he's the Alpha. Or if he's freaking Jesus, he's crossing the line. Threatening Anna, threatening Liam, and threatening me.

Again, I rapidly shake my head and shoot up from my chair. I put as much distance as I can between us. I'm afraid if I stay any closer, I'd end up choking up. Though, that's not such a repulsive thought. "Who do you think you are? You have no right to blackmail me into mating with your son! You're pathetic excuse for a life form!"

"I'd lower your tone if I were you." He says calmly, though his eyes burn with anger. "Remember your place. And I think I do. I run this pack and you listen to what I say."

"You're supposed to be running a pack. Not our lives. And certainly not who I decide to be with!"

"Do not raise your tone, Ronnie," He snaps this time, glaring at me. "I suggest you keep in your place or I will not hesitate to have Liam Farley killed! Do. Not. Test. Me."

I fall silent. Glowering at him as imagines of grabbing the back of his head and slamming into repeatedly into the table appears in my mind. I don't even push it away. I welcome it.

I ball my fist at my side, so much that I dig my nails into flesh hard. I don't even wince when I draw blood. I'm too enraged to care. "You're a monster."

"I'm flattered you think so," He drawls sarcastically, "I'd love to say for another hour or so and chat, but I have to get going. Think about what I said Ronnie. And don't do anything rash, yes?"

I don't say anything. Instead I stare him down, hoping he gets the message to leave before I leap over the table and attack.

Lucky for me, he leaves without another word. Nor glance. And for that I'm glad, because I don't think I could take another moment of his taunting smile.

Or the glint in his eyes. I feel sick to my stomach, worse than before. All I can think is how Adam and him look exactly alike. Does Adam know that his father has just threatened not only my life, but Liam and Anna's?

Surely he's heard of his father's plans. Surely he's agreed.

How could he? Would Adam even do that? I don't know. I didn't even know who the hell Adam was anymore. Nor what he was capable of.

Was he as malicious as his father? Would he do anything to his way?

The answer to all those questions are - I don't know. And that seems to be my answers to everything that's been happening.

A week. It's been a week and everything different. Everything's completely screwed up.

And I can only imagine where It'll lead to in the next month. Two months till Adam turns eighteen. Two months till I'm forced to be with a man I don't even like, nor will I ever be able to love.

I shake my head, telling myself I need to stop thinking about. But I can't. His words repeat over and over in my head.

I take a seat and fold my hands over my head. I'm so frustrated. So angry. And so desperate for my life to be semi normal again.

But I know it never will be again. And that's what causes my anger to deflate and turn into sorrow.

Sluggishly, I take a shower, get dressed and bolt my windows shut to ensure Liam won't make an appearance. Though I don't a closed window would stop him.

I crawl and get comfortable under my comforter. I tug the sheets till they're pushed under my chin and stare into the dark room, trying to force myself to sleep.

Once I do, all I have is horrid nightmares. Mostly of Liam's death. And Alpha Beckett's never ending cackle playing over and over like a broken record.

I woke up many times in the middle of the night, mostly screaming Liam's name. Each time I remind myself that Liam is okay. That's he alive. And I intended to keep it that way.

I promise myself to keep him safe and stick to plan. But it's not only because of Liam that I agree to any of it - It's because of Anna as well. If anything happened to her, I don't know what I'd do. I wouldn't be able to sleep at night. Knowing I had a chance to save her, but was selfish and ended up getting her killed.

It goes beyond not be able to sleep. I wouldn't be able to live with myself.

Anna didn't ask to be involved in my problems. I wouldn't make her pay the price. Even if he meant mating with Adam.

I'd go along with it. I'd do it because I'd be protecting both of them.

Somehow, I manage to go back to sleep and get up the next morning. I greet Anna like normally. Make it seem like nothing's wrong.

As for Liam, I avoid contact with him. And that's how it continue's till Thursday.

I keep to my word and make it appear like I'm happily Adam's girlfriend. I sit by him in lunch, though I don't talk. The only thing I do is push around my food and stare glumly at my old table.

Adam at least allows Anna to sit with us, so it's not all that bad. I guess.

The only thing I don't go along with his Adam putting his arm around me or such. Obviously because I don't want to be touched by him nor do I like the feel of it.

I'm not even sure if I had spoken a word to him the whole week really besides, "Yeah" and "No"

I haven't dared to bring up the subject of how his father threatened me. And that just increases the tension between us.

It's weird. How everyone goes from not paying attention to me to now suddenly wanting to be my friend. Probably because I'm now the schools IT boy's girlfriend.

Yeah, it didn't take long for that to spread like a wild fire. I can't even bare to look at Liam. When we go to work on the project, I don't say much. I only discuss the back drops. Though he insists on talking to me.

He throws numerous questions at me, but I deflect them all and focus on the main topic. I don't even let him stand close to me in fear Alpha Beckett will catch his scent and kill him.

When I get to school Thursday morning, I'm bombarded with guys and girls trying to befriend me. I stare at them all in disgust the whole time.

"I heard you're going to Nick Morrison's party, we could totes car pull," One girls says, clinging desperately to my arm.

I shrug her off and pull my bag closer to me, "Not interested. Thanks." I tell her harshly and quicken my pace, pushing my away out of the cluster of people that circles around me.

Of course, I'm not able to catch a breather.

Liam rushes to my side once I'm at my locker. "They're annoying, aren't they?"

"No, really?" I retort, stuffing my books in my locker.

"Yeah, you know that wouldn't happen if you broke up with him."

If only you knew I was doing this to keep you safe, asshole, I think and regret it slightly when I think of the mate connection. He couldn't hear that right?

I glance at him for the first time in days and search his features for any indications that he's heard me. All he does is watch me with his green eyes, pleading with me silently to talk to him.

I resist. And go to turn and walk away when he catches my forearm. I suck in a breath once I feel tingles travel up my arm. "Talk to me, Ronnie. Please."

I stay quiet and direct my eyes on the tile. I don't even tug my arm out of grasp. I'm too weak emotionally to tear away from the first contact I've felt from him in days.

Too soon, he releases my arm. But the disconnection between us is short lived when I feel him touch my cheek. He guides me to look at him.

I look up at him, trying to ignore the proximity of our bodies. I fail miserably when I feel the heat reflecting off of him. "What's wrong?"

"Nothing," I manage to say. "What makes you think that?"

"The fact you haven't spoken a word to me the whole week. Not even a insult," He says, frowning.

"Have you ever thought it's because I don't want to speak with you?"

The words effect him slightly. I can see his eyes glaze over in disbelief of my words before he shakes his head. "I don't believe that for a damn second. What the hell is going on, Ronnie?"

"Nothing that concerns you." I say and reluctantly step back away from him. "It's true what I said earlier Liam. I don't wish to talk with you."

The words are painful to say. But I do it. He gets the point when Adam appears and raps an arm around my shoulder, pulling me to his side while glaring at Liam. "Something wrong here?"

I resist shrugging Adam's arm off of me, hoping that Liam get's the message and backs off. "No, nothing. We should get to class, yeah?" I mumble the last part.

Adam nods stiffly replying with a brief, "Yeah." He tugs me away from Liam and leads me down the hallway.

I can sense Liam's gaze on my back the whole time. I glance over my shoulder to see him staring after the both of us with a burning look in his eyes.

I'm not giving up on you Ronnie. Never.

I shake my head softly at him and turn back to face forward. This is for the best.. right?

The drive home from school is awkward. Just like it has been this whole week. None of us bother to speak. And for that I'm grateful, or else I'm pretty sure I'd snap.

I already was on the verge of doing so.

This whole BS act was getting to me and it hasn't even been a week. I feel like screaming at everyone that I'm not Adam's girlfriend.

I actually did today earlier in class.

It just made people a lot more in school confused about our status. You know what our status really is? Non existent. And that's how I'd like to keep it.

Once we pull up to my house, I jump out, ready to run inside when Adam's voice stops me. "If we're going to be doing this, we should at least get along, don't you think?"

I pause. And look over at him to see him getting out of his car. "Why would I want to get along with someone who's forcing me to be with him?"

He flinches. Obviously because of my words. But I don't even care. Beckett said I had to act like his mate and be nice to him public. He didn't say after closed doors that I had to be. I didn't like Adam one freaking bit, and I wasn't about to start trying to.

"Ron, I'm sorry about.. that, but we didn't think we could get you to agree any other way. So we had to be forceful, I guess. But it's for your best interest."

I scuff, "My best interest? Forcing me to be your mate is for my best interest?"

"It's better then being with Liam. He's a walking target. If you were to be with him, that would make you one too."

"Who says I want to be with anyone? When did your stupid pack get to make my decisions?"

"Our pack," He corrects, "This is for the best. And I know that maybe one day you'll-"

I cut him off immediately, knowing what he's going to say. "That I'll what? Come to want to be your want? Or even love you? You're stupid, Adam." I spat, no longer willing to hold back my crude words. "I could never love the son of a monster."

He winces at my choice of words. "Please, Ronnie-"

Again, I rush to speak. "Don't even go there, Adam. Again, I could never love you like the way your pack wants me to. The way they're trying to force me to. You look exactly like him, I could never.." I trail off, shaking my head. "You'll never get it."

"I look exactly like him? Like my father?"

"It doesn't matter." I say, and open the door to my house. "None of it matters." I slam the door shut with that, locking it shut.

I'm pleased when he walks off and makes no further attempt to talk to me. I collapse onto my bed. I don't think I'll be able to go through with this.

I can't even bare to look at Adam without feeling like I'm looking at his father. It's too creepy. Everything he does reminds me of him. How could I love someone who reminds me of the person I hate most in this world?

Even if he didn't, I never would love Adam. Nor even like.

It just leads me to think I need to get out of this. I need to. Run away and never turn back. But I know I can't. Because they'd probably kill Anna. And most importantly Liam.

They'd probably hunt me down too just to kill me or whatever. The only reason Liam is alive right now is because they need to use him to get me to be with Adam.

My mind wanders to other thoughts and I begin to wonder if Liam will be at the party.

The party. I groan when I think of how I'll have to go. Everything is just total shit in my life right now.

I do the only thing I can do, I paint. And let it take my never ending haunting thoughts out of my head. I simply focus on what's in front of me. Not what's around me.

Chapter 9

I stand before the mirror, smoothing out my blouse and frowning when the girl before me mimics the gesture.

I hate it, I think miserably, I hate this stupid outfit.

I desperately try to tug the shirt down to cover my stomach, but it doesn't budge. Instead it bounces back to where It was before, showing off a uncomfortable amount of skin.

The jeans I have are no better. They're unbearably tight and I feel as if I sit down, they'll bust open. I figured at this stage when I put on the jeans, it couldn't get more worse.

I was wrong.

The shoes were four inch heels. The first time I walked in them and tested them out, I doubled over, landing on my face.

Anna wasn't the least bit concerned for my well being, instead she said, "Great, now how am I gonna be able to conceal that red mark on your face? And damn it, let me do your hair!"

I had agreed to let her dress me reluctantly. I regretted it now majorly as I examined myself.

"I can't wear this," I tell Anna, "I look like a slut."

She laughs from behind me and places her hands on my shoulders, "You look perfect." She argues, she smiles for a second before her eyes fall to my braid. "I can't believe you wouldn't let me do your hair."

"We've gone over this." I grumble and move away from her, I go to snatch up my leather jacket when Anna grabs it and takes it out of my reach.

"You are not wearing this hideous thing," She says. "You won't let me do your hair, fine, but I'm gonna control what you wear."

I glare at her and reach forward, snagging it quickly before she can wrench it back. "I already look horrible enough. I'm gonna wear my damn jacket whether you like it or not."

Anna begins to fuss how I never let her do anything, and I do my best to block at her. Which I succeed when my mind starts to wander to other subjects.

Liam is the main one.

I can't help but wonder where he's at right now. If he's thinking of me. Is that creepy to think that? Maybe.

But I can't help it. He just consumes every ounce of my thoughts. And the more I try to reject him, the worse it gets.

I hadn't been able to focus much on things since I talked to him yesterday. That same night I had dreams of him. That same look that played on his face when I told him I didn't want to talk to him plays over and over in my mind.

When I went to school Friday, he wasn't there.

Was it because of me that he didn't come? Was it because I told him I wanted nothing to do with him?

A small part of me was thankful that he had gone. So he wouldn't have to see me wrapped up in another dude's arms, but another part of me mourned not having him close. Not being able to at least look at him.

But then again, I'm not sure Id hold up quite as well as I did if he gave me that same look he did yesterday.

And it wasn't only Liam I was worrying about.

It was Adam too. He hadn't spoken to me, sure, he went to school but he didn't even put on a show for everyone like he had been doing the whole week. He had ignored me. And honestly, I didn't care one bit that I had pissed him off.

Had I pissed him off? I had no clue. I didn't know about anything anymore these days.

Maybe he's just trying to digest what I said to him the other day, I think meekly. He was probably perplexed about what I said about him looking like his father.

I didn't even know where it came from that line. Maybe because it was so much on my conscious that I finally said it.

I didn't regret telling him the truth, I just wish I would have picked my words a little more carefully. I mean, what if he went crying to his daddy that I had stepped out of line?

I could just imagine Alpha Beckett giving him a sly smile, promising he'd take care of it. I'd probably see Liam in a coffin the next day, no doubt.

Then Anna would be next.

How could Alpha Beckett be so cruel? So cruel to have to force me into mating with his son. Why did he want me so bad to mate with Adam? I'm sure there were plenty of other girls who would have been a much better, and less complicated, choice.

I would think any girl in the pack would jump to be with Adam.

And I honestly didn't understand why. What was so amazing about Adam Beckett that I couldn't see, but everyone else could? Was it his looks? His personality? The power he will hold in the future?

I wasn't sure. But they were all clearly blind to worship him. He was just like his father, wasn't he?

Of course. He had to know that his father was going to black mail me before he did it. I remember the look he gave me before I walked into my house. He knew.

He knew and he hadn't tried to stop it. That just lead me to believe that Adam was no better then his father.

I use to think that was crazy. That they were never alike because the Adam I use to know, was the most kindest boy you could have ever met.

Maybe he was just confused on what to do, I think. And quickly ask myself why I'm trying to justify his reasoning. Maybe because I was still hoping the ghost of my old childhood friend was still there. That he was still the boy who picked flowers for me, the same boy who was loud and care free, the same boy who thought it was funny to throw water balloons at adults.

But he wasn't that child anymore. And I surely wasn't the girl I use to be. I'm different. We're different. And it sucked.

Then again, you can't stay a child forever. And clearly you can't stay friends forever.

Anna brought me out of my never ending thoughts a few minutes later, informing me Adam was outside waiting.

I was slightly shocked that he had shown up, but instead of voicing that, I followed her out the door and loaded into the car.

Adam and I didn't even bother looking at one another.

I looked at the window the whole time, wondering what the night had in store for me.

Clearly, it wasn't going to be good.

Liam's POV

Standing in front of the booming and pulsing house, I question what the fuck I'm doing here. Why had I convinced myself to come to a party where a bunch of drunk and horny teenagers would be at? You could say parties weren't my scene. Mostly because I didn't want to stumble into a local pack of sort and start a riot. But there wasn't another pack here besides Ronnie. And well, now the Purgatory pack.

The Purgatory pack.

What happens if they were in this house right now? It's silly, I know, but I can't help but scan the whole front yard, wondering if they're gonna jump out at any fucking minute and come at me. It wouldn't be a shock, that's for sure.

Why would I care if they were here anyway? It's just the Purgatory pack. I had taken them down more then once. There was no reason to worry. But I was.

Not for me, but for Ronnie.

She had a bad run in with them, and I'm sure they were out for her blood. They were always up for holding grudges. And I knew the extent of it since I was one of the people they held a grudge against till this day.

I shake my head, almost as if to rid myself from the tantalizing thoughts. Instead, I let my mind wonder to Ronnie.

She hasn't arrived here yet. And I haven't seen her since Thursday. When she had told me she wanted nothing to do with me or such.

Honestly, I did not believe any of it. We both knew she didn't have the strength to push me away.

Maybe she was just trying to scare me off. I wasn't sure. But whatever it was, it had to with Adam. And his pack.

I had heard all of how they wanted Ronnie to mate with him. I hadn't meant to, but when I went to go see her, I stumbled across them talking and stayed a little longer then I should have to listen.

It was Adam and his father that were talking quietly. Adam was saying how Ronnie was being reluctant to it all. His father told him he would take care of it.

And I figured he had, since Ronnie was more then ever determined to make me back off. But it's not like I am.

I meant what I said when I told her I was going to claim what was rightfully mine, which was Ronnie. Adam Beckett certainly wasn't going to have her, I wouldn't allow it.

I'd stop it all before he had the chance to mate her. He wasn't even hers to have, anyway. She was mine. My mate.

Adam just clearly needed to get that through his head. But maybe after I beat some sense into him, he'd understand to back the fuck off.

If he didn't.. well, I had killed. I could surely kill him off just as easily with no regret. I was already a wanted man. It's not like I had nothing to lose.

Well, maybe Ronnie. It was her pack. I'm sure if I actually killed Adam they'd come after to her. Kill her.

The thought makes me chest tighten in pain. It was weird how I now had to think about savoring someone's life then my own.

I couldn't be selfish anymore.

I had to think about her. How my actions effected her well being. But It's not like anyway knew we were mates. Only Adam, his father, and Ronnie herself knew we were mates.

The whole universe would know if I decided to kill Adam, though. And the thought isn't that repulsive as I'd like it to be.

I wasn't ashamed Ronnie was my mate, no, it was about her safety. Ronnie was frail, though she would never admit it, she would never be to protect herself. They'd kill her easily.

That's why I had to protect her. In more ways then one. It was time to stop playing stupid and think over my options. My actions.

If something happened to her, I don't know what the hell I'd do... That's a lie. I'd know what I'd do exactly. Kill every person who had hurt her. Pick them off one by one and enjoy doing it.

Maybe even laugh when they begged me for mercy. Was it sick that I thought of that? Perhaps. But I wouldn't have to kill anyone. Because I'd keep Ronnie perfectly safe and sound.

No one would ever hurt her.

A guy bumps into me, making me snap back into reality. "Watch where you're standing, asshole." He spat, he attempts to shove me but fails. I don't even jolt.

The kid cowers once he realizes I'm a lot taller. And I'm packing a lot more muscle then him. I give him a intense glare. He doesn't even give me time to say something back. He scampers into the house, glancing over his shoulder, as if thinking I would be chasing him.

I wait till he disappears from my vision before I start up the steps of the house. People stumble in front of me, chucking up whatever they previously had in their stomach.

I frown when I enter the house and I'm greeted by the stench of alcohol and sex.

I can only guess why when I glance to the dance floor and see a mass of people grinding, kissing, and swallowing down loads of vodka.

One girl even makes a attempt to drag me out into the chaos, but I shake her off and make my way into the kitchen.

I don't bother touching any drinks of sorts. I'm afraid I'll get roofied if I did.

For a while, I hang around. People come over and try to converse with me, but I usually just shrug them off. I wasn't here to chat and get drunk. I was here for one reason, and that was Ronnie. But after thirty minutes of waiting, I question going home.

Why would Ronnie even come to a place like this? She didn't exactly fool me for the kind of girl that loved to come out and go to parties.

I'm not even sure if Ronnie's ever even picked up a drink. I doubt it.

But since she's apparently "dating" Adam, he'd force her to come. And maybe even her human friend Anna, would force her to come to the party.

I lean against the door frame that gives me a direct view to the door way, for a while I watch kids come in and out, before I start to really contemplate leaving.

I could always see Ronnie at school, and for the project.

I collect myself and I'm ready to go when I catch a familiar scent. I know immediatly who it is when a shiver ripples up my skin.

My eyes drift throught the sea of kids till I come to the door and see Adam, standing right in front of Ronnie.

He seems to do the same thing as me. He scans the room till his eyes land on me. His face turns hard then and I give him the same look right back.

He turns around and whispers something along the lines of, "Avoid Liam tonight, Ronnie."

Avoid me? How could she avoid me when I was her mate?

I clench my fits involuntarily at my side. I restrain myself from going over there and yanking her away from him, and I probably would if it weren't for all the human teenagers around here.

Surely I'd cause a massive fight if I did do that.

I watch as Adam steps out from in front of her, finally. I'm almost happy and over joyed to see her, but when I see what she's wearing, I only frown.

I mean, what the hell was she doing wearing that barely fitting top? And those jeans? And those.. heels? When had Ronnie ever worn heels?

I clenched my fists harder, feeling my nails dig into my skin and draw blood. Was Adam making her change? Was he making her become a different person she surely wasn't?

Maybe I was jumping the gun, but I couldn't help but assume the worse. She even seemed uncomfortable in her own skin.

She twiddled her usual braid, (The only thing that seemed like her tonight) and looked around. She looked so innocent and out of place, I almost wanted to grab her and take her out of this place.

She seemed to notice me since she glanced at me and her lips parted, in surprise? I wasn't sure. But I had the biggest urge to press my lips right to her smooth and soft ones.

I remembered the almost kiss that happened not too long ago. I got goosebumps from just remembering how her fingers felt running over my skin.

Especially over my scar.

I reach up and run my own fingers over it, rubbing it. She seems to notice I'm thinking of the day we almost kissed while working on the back drops, since her cheeks turn red and her blue eyes widen.

I smirk at her and she quickly averts her eyes to her friend, Anna.

Anna eagerly tugs on Ronnie's hand and whispers, "Look! It's Liam!"

"I can see that," Ronnie replies, her voice low and cold. Ronnie tugs her hand from her grasp and goes to dash away when of course, Adam just has to stop her.

"Where are you going?" He asks, and before Ronnie can say anything, he quickly shakes his head. "It doesn't matter. Let's go dance, okay?"

He doesn't even give her a choice. Instead he tugs her into the crowd of people and guides her in front of him.

Ronnie seems like a fish out of water as she scans the crowd of people, trying to mimic their motion. But she fails quickly. Adam doesn't really seem to care. All he does is pull her unbelievably closer and stare at me the whole time, just saying, she's mine now.

Like hell she was.

Before I register what I'm doing, I'm making my way through the sea of people and grabbing Ronnie, pulling her to my front while I glower at Adam.

Ronnie stares at me in horror, "What are you doing?" She asks hoarsely.

"Getting you away from this jackass." I mutter lowly to her and grip he hand in mine, tugging her away from Adam. He calls after her but Ronnie doesn't make any attempt to pull away from me and go back to him.

She lets me guide her out of chaotic crowd and out of the house.

But I don't even stop when we're out of sight. I pull her away further away from the booming house and hand her my leather jacket along the way when a guy whistles at her.

Ronnie has to convince me to calm down because I was incredibly tempted to go after that fucking guy and pound his face in for looking at my girl.

I was so damn tired of guys going after her. That's why I intended to get the memo out that Ronnie wasn't for anyone's touching but my own.

And I also intended to get to the bottom of why Ronnie was with Adam. She obviously didn't like him with the looks she was giving him the other day.

I stop once we reach a empty park and I command her to take a seat. She obeys reluctantly and collapses onto the bench, tugging my jacket closer to her.

I don't bother with chit chat. I get straight to the point and say, "What are you doing with him?"

She doesn't need to question me to know who I'm talking about. "I'm his girlfriend. That's why I'm with him."

"Don't say that," I growl out unintentionally. I can't bare thinking about Ronnie with Adam. And being his.. girlfriend.

She scuffs, "Don't say what? The truth?"

"But that's not the truth," I argue. "You don't even like him. I can see that everytime you look at him."

"I don't need to justify myself to you. Or really justify why I'm with someone." She says and crosses her arms over her chest definitely.

"Yes you do," I say, "I'm your mate. The only person you should be with is me." I hate to make myself out to be a possessive ass, but I couldn't help it. It'd only been two weeks and I was tired of seeing Adam and other guys hanging around her.

She doesn't reply. All she does is stare at the ground, probably unsure of how to reply to that. I fall down next to her and groan, running a hand through my hair. "What is going on? What's happening? Are they forcing you to date him? Did they do something to you? Tell me." My words come out in a slur, and I don't mean for them to, but I just want to get to the bottom of this shit and find out what the fuck is going on.

"No," Her voice is hoarse and dry. "They didn't. I'm dating him because I like him. Why can't you just accept that?"

For a minute, I believe her before I glance at her and as corny as this is gonna sound, but when I looked into her eyes I knew it was a bluff. Ronnie did not like Adam. We were bound to one another, it was impossible to have stronger feelings for someone that wasn't your mate. "I don't believe that for a minute. I know when you're lying."

She stands and glares at me. "I don't need to sit here and listen to this bull. This was a stupid idea anyway," She mutters the last part to herself, "Why the hell would I even go to a party?"

"Because that douche Adam made you come?" I prompt. Ronnie sighs and begins to walk in the opposite direction of the house.

I fall behind her, though she tells me many times to get lost.

We go the long way into the woods and Ronnie even attempts to out run me many times, but fails when she realizes I'm not easy to shake off. I catch her everytime.

It's when we're only feet away from her house that she whirls around, "Get lost, Liam!"

"I will if you tell me why you're with Adam. The real reason."

Ronnie huffs and widly flails her arms around, "Because I don't like you! Because I don't want you! Did you ever think of that or are are you so big headed that you don't realize that not every girl wants you?"

It's my turn to go silent and stare at her. I'm actually kinda shell shocked. Ronnie's says some rude things, but this seems to hit home the most when an unfamiliar pain attacks my heart.

And here I thought I didn't have a heart.

"That's what I thought," She hisses cruelly. "Now I'm leaving. And don't follow me, idiot."

And with that, she stomps off. Leaving me bewildered.

Ronnie's POV.

I feel guilty. Incredibly freaking guilty.

It's been an hour since I told Liam off and stormed home. Anna had made many failed attempts to call me, even Adam, but I never answered. And I didn't want to.

This night had been horrible. All it consisted of was fighting. Even on the ride over to the party it was non stop arguing. Mostly with Anna.

She demanded to know why I wasn't happy and all that stuff.

I never answered her.

I just wanted to be left alone in peace. I wanted people to stop questioning my actions. Mostly, I wanted people to stop trying to control my life.

Though I felt guilt I told Liam off, It needed to be done to trail him off. Though something unsettling nestled itself into the bottom of my stomach. I knew nothing good could come out of it and I knew Liam was more furious then ever. And I didn't know who with. Me or Adam.

Probably Adam.

And another thing I knew was that Liam wasn't going to lay off because of my words. No way. He was too much of persistent basterd to give up.

Plus, the way he acted tonight was.. a whole new side to him. I wasn't sure if I liked his possessive side or hated it.

One thing I was sure I hated was Alpha Beckett.

I fell asleep that night just thinking over my harsh words before. Faintly I could hear his soft mummers through our connection telling me he was going to win me over.

Chapter 10

The weekend passes surely but slowly. Saturday and Sunday, I lock myself away in my room and just paint. I don't even answer the door when someone knocks. Instead, I turn up the music louder and ignore the fact my whole world is collapsing around me.

Okay, maybe that's a little dramatic to say.

The world wasn't ending. And if it ever did, it wouldn't be over boys. I always use to insult girls who only worried about their boy problems, but now I was becoming one of them in a matter of only three weeks since Liam invaded my life.

When had both Adam and Liam became my life to even dare to declare my world was crashing down around me, anyway? Both of them were messing with my head for two incredibly different reasons.

Adam because, well he was forcing me to practically be with him. If that wasn't clear enough. The more I thought of actually mating at him, the more disgusted I became. I needed to find a way to get out of it, but the only solution I could come up with was Liam.

He could surely get me out of it, couldn't he? Then again, he was the reason I was in this whole "be-with-Adam-or-else-I'll-hurt-Liam-and-Anna" problem. If I wasn't his mate, I could have gotten out of it by now. Right?

I don't know. I wasn't sure of anything anymore these days.

I could barely focus on one thing without my thoughts going back to Liam.

Liam.

What had he done to me? Put me under some type of spell? He seemed to invade not only my life, but my thoughts, actions, and dreams.

Yeah, I could barely sleep without him appearing in my dreams, beckoning me to tell him the truth. He also promised to help me. To love me, even.

Each time I woke with a start, glancing around frantically and wondering if he was there. He never was.

I couldn't help but wonder if it was because of what I said. How I told him I didn't need him. It was such a lie, because now only two days without even being able to see him I was going crazy. How was I suppose to bid him from my life if I couldn't go two days without his presence?

I couldn't. I would never be able to get rid of him. He'd always be on my mind. He was sinking into me like poison, tainting me.

When Monday morning comes around, I get dressed quickly in a pair of black jeans and white V-neck. I shrug into my usual boots, braid my hair, then I'm out the door for the first time in two days.

I see Adam momentarily for a moment, though his back is to me.

I don't give him the chance to spot me. I hurry my pace, jogging slightly to the main road. I stop and resort to walking once I'm far away from the pack neighborhood.

I do what I did Saturday and Sunday, I put on my headphones and turn the music up till my headphones are literally pulsing.

Once I get to school, I manage to get through the crowd and make my way to the locker. By now, I should be comfortable with the stares I get, but I'm not.

Especially not when the girl next to me doesn't even open her locker, instead she just watches me, titling her head.

What a freak, I think and do my best to ignore her, though it's hard when someone is watching you so boldly.

I pop open my locker and stuff my Science book in while fetching my math one. I sigh, and close my locker, ready to walk off when I'm suddenly whirled around slammed up against the lockers. My eyes widen in surprise and I come face to face with a angry looking Anna.

"Thanks for calling me and letting me know why you left the party." She says sarcastically, glaring at me.

I part my lips, my jaw slack and my mouth dry as I try to come up with a excuse. But after a few moments of silence, I realize I'm not going to get out of this. I do the cowardly thing and say, "Sorry."

Anna isn't pleased the least bit by my pitiful attempt to apologize, but she backs off and releases her death grip on me. "You have no idea how worried I was when I didn't hear from you the whole weekend. I thought Liam ended up murdering you like he almost did Adam."

My eyebrows furrow at her words. Like he almost did Adam? What was she talking about? Before I could ask, loud gasps and whispers catch my attention. My eyes flicker through the crowd until they fall on Adam.

I can't resist the shocked sound that leaves my lips, just like everyone else, I peer closer.

Adam has a black eye. Along with a busted up jaw and numerous bruises and cuts covering his arms. He even has one long jagged cut across his cheek that makes me wince just by looking at it. That one looked like it hurt the most to get.

Who had done this to him? Liam? My question is answered when one boy laughs, "Look who got his ass whipped by Farley!" He hollers, and slowly, people join in with the laughter.

"Shut up, idiot." Adam hisses, venom leaking from his voice that the kid who was once laughing, flinches. And I didn't blame him.

That was the same tone that Alpha Beckett used on me.

My throat tightens and I reluctantly turn away from the scene, and stuff my headphones that had fallen out of my ears back in.

I dodge Anna's out stretched hand and dart around her. For the first time in my life, I'm eager just to get to class.

Liam is surprisingly here. At school. I hadn't expected it all, since I thought he'd ditch out again. But he's there.

He doesn't make any attempt to talk to me, or even look at me. I don't know what hurts more.

Then again, this is what I was asking for, wasn't I? For him to leave me alone? I did. But then why now did I crave his attention? His persistence?

I found myself looking at him every time I got the chance. At one point, I almost reached out for him. To at least to make sure he's real, that's he actually here.

When the bell rings signaling it's lunch time, he doesn't glance at me even then. He just walks out of the classroom, hands stuffed in his pockets with a calm expression.

I trail behind, following a whole crowd of kids into the lunch room. Somehow, I end up by Liam's side in the line to get food. We make no attempt to talk to each other. Instead, we focus on things that are happening around us.

But I couldn't stand it anymore.

I look to him and study the side of his face. He notices my stare, since he tenses, his muscles bunching and he holds a tight grip on the blue tray in front of me.

My eyes trail down and to his bruised knuckles. Bruised Knuckles?

I suck in a shaky breath and my eyes flicker back up to see he's now facing me. His green eyes glazed over with hardness. It hurts to know that it's all directed at me.

Make up your damn mind, Ronnie. Do you want him to love you or hate you?

The true answer was that I had no clue. But the hate I was getting right now, didn't feel so good.

He didn't hate me. He couldn't. Right?

What had I done? I question silently. I don't even care how the rumours of him beating up Adam are true. All I care about is Liam. And how he might potentially hate me.

Then again, if he hated me, why did he pummel Adam? It made no sense. Nothing did.

"It's true, isn't it?" I whisper softly, aware to the fact people our watching our every movement. Our every word.

They're probably so curious to why suddenly Liam Farley is talking to me, Adam Beckett's supposed girlfriend. I cringe mentally at that.

He doesn't answer. He just turns away and slides his plate to the cash register, he pays and leaves, not sparing me another glance.

I watch after him helplessly. This is how Liam must have felt after I screamed at him and marched off.

I pay and depart, finding my way mechanically to Adam's table. Anna's already their, talking to some girl that I don't bother to know.

I set my tray down, catching everyone's attention. Even Adam's who once sat picking at his food. Nobody says something for a minute. The tension is immense.

Finally, Anna says, "Hey Ron."

I stiffly give her a nod, my own way of saying hello. Then they dive back into conversation. I don't talk much, instead I mimic Adam and start picking at my food till I can no longer take it and turn in my seat to face Adam. "Is this the part where we breakup because of what happened with Liam?" I ask lowly and my eyes dart to the rest of the table to see them too involved in a conversation to care.

"No," He replies, "This is the part where we pretend it never happened."

"But how?" I press the subject further on, refusing to just 'pretend it never happened.' "Your father surely won't forget. So why should I? We?"

"You'll forget about it because I tell you to. Understand, Mars?" He says it so composed. So relaxed. There's no hint of frustration or anger at all.

Mars.

That's what his father had called me when he was threatening me. More and more reasons to believe he was just like his dad. A monster.

The sentence replays over and over in my head. The more I hear it, the angrier I become till my blood boils so badly that I clench my fist that are rested on the table.

He notices it, since he glances at me with raised eyebrows. I glare at him in response.

He think he can tell me what to do, I think, he think he can control me.

It 'causes me to say, "No." My voice is loud and filled with hatred. And it's all pointed at him. It also catches everyone's attention. The conversation between them stop and they all look at me.

"What?" Adam's jaw clenches, and I shake my head at him. So much like his father. He's so much like his father. My chair scraps loudly against the marble flooring as I scoot back and stand up, ready to launch off when Adam catches my wrist and holds me in place. "Ronnie, you need to under-"

"I don't." I snap, already knowing what he's going to say.

He's going to tell me I need to understand. That I need to listen to him. But I refuse to. I'm not going to become his little servant like the pack wants me to. I'm not going to let him drag me through the mud because of my fear of what he'll tell his father.

I already knew Alpha Beckett was going to do something major since Liam had attacked Adam. I figure if I tell him off, it won't effect the decision he's going to make.

That's why I wrench away from him, though he shouts after me. Telling me to forget about it all if I knew what was good for me. I scuff at that, like he really knew what was good for me?

"I know what's good for me," I say harshly, earning numerous gazes from nosy on lookers. "And it's certainly not you."

Adam gives me a hard glare, "This is not the place for this discussion, Ronnie."

I huff and shake my head."Go screw yourself." With that, I walk off. Out of the lunch room, and out of the damn school. Away from damn Adam.

But I don't head home.

I choose to distance myself away from the water and run to the place where I spent most of my childhood at. The lake.

When I get there, I stop and collapse near the shore. Not even caring when the water touches my knees.

I sit there for hours. Recalling it all when I use to come down here with Adam. And I don't even grimace, surprisingly.

I just wonder what exactly went wrong with him. Why he's different. Why's he changed.

But I don't let the current of events that played out today mess with my head like I usually did. Maybe that's why I was having problems with thinking of a plan to get out of all of this.

Then again, I was sick of always thinking about Adam. Or Liam.

I lay back in the sand, ignoring the scratchy and uncomfortable feel of it against my skin. My breath falls shallow and soon enough, my eyes close and I fall asleep from there, no longer wishing to dwell on today's events.

When I open my eyes, I don't expect to see it's night time. Nor the fact a pair of haunting green eyes are staring down right at me.

I don't need to question who they belong to. I know it's Liam. I could sense it. Sense him. Talk about freaky.

I stare right back at him, my lips slightly parted. I shiver when a cold water brushes my legs and I jump up with a start at the feel of it, bumping foreheads with Liam.

That surely didn't feel any better.

"Ouch!" I hiss and grip my head as I push myself to my feet.

Liam mimics my movement and grips his head, "What is your head made out? Steel? Damn it," He mutters.

I roll my eyes at him, "Oh please."

"Now I'm gonna have a huge bump on my forehead. Thanks." He drawls sarcastically.

I scowl him, only a little pleased that's he finally talking to me. Though it consists of sarcasm and perhaps insults, I'll take it. "At least it'll take away the attention from your ugly face."

He laughs, surprisingly. And probably because of that lame comeback. At least it'll take away the attention from your ugly face? Really Ronnie?

I grimace, but don't even try to justify myself. That'd just be digging myself a even bigger hole.

"Ugly face?" He taunts, and laughs louder. Weirdly, I join in and laugh too. And again, I repeat, it's really freaking weird how we were ignoring each other today and suddenly we're laughing. I didn't understand why. But I go with it. Because it's better then fighting, right?

"That was a pretty stupid insult, huh?" I muse, pressing my lips together, silencing my laughter.

He nods, "Very."

I sigh and rub at the forming lump on my head before I drop my arm and let it fall limp at my side. We're silent after that, unsure of what to say.

Somehow, I end up blurting, "I shouldn't have said those things to you yesterday."

"Regretting it already?" He teases, a smile playing at his lips. But it's really not funny. Maybe I shouldn't have said those things, maybe they were a little too harsh.

It's not a maybe. It's definite.

I could only imagine Liam saying those things to me. I'd probably feel incredibly heartbroken. Though I don't know where this little spark of niceness has come from, I continue on. "Really, Liam. I shouldn't have said those horrible things. I'm not sure if I meant it or not. But I'm just.." I pause, looking for the right words. "I'm just trying to protect us both before we both get hurt."

"Before we both get hurt?" He echoes. I nod, gnawing on my lower lip.He steps closer to me for the first time in a few days and rests his hands on both of my shoulders. "No one is going to hurt you, Ron." He steps another step closer to me, his hands sliding up from my shoulders to my face. He cups my cheek tenderly, his thumb brushing across my skin. "I'll never let anyone hurt you."

I draw in a shaky breath and reach up, placing my smaller hand on his much bigger one. I brush my fingers lightly across his bruised knuckles. He makes a sound in the back of his throat. "It's not me I'm worrying about, mostly."

His eyebrows knit together and his lips part in silent questioning.

I make sure to emphasize the it by brushing my fingers over his knuckles, lingering on them. Still, he watches my with the same expression. "It's not only Adam that's out to hurt you, Liam." I whisper and I fear I've said too much when his face changes into something masking shock.

"What are you trying to say?"

"Nothing," I answer in a monotone. "Just think that over. Okay?"

He shakes his head at me, leaning down to where our noses touch. It breaks me back to our intimate moment back in art room. Only this time there's no one to interrupt us. "I shouldn't have hit Adam, right?"

"You shouldn't have." I confirm. And not because I care about Adam and I'm trying to protect him from Liam coming after him again, no. I'm actually trying to protect Liam. Trying to protect him from Alpha Beckett that will surely come after him if he pushes too far.

"And why not?" He question, his voice dangerously low in anger.

I smile sadly at him, running my hand from his to his shoulder and over the planes of his muscles through his shirt. My fingers linger near his neck and I hesitantly rest them there. The whole time I keep my gaze locked with his, unable to glance away from his burning green eyes. "Bad things happen to bad people, Liam."

"Are you saying I'm a bad person?"

"No," I whisper. "But others think that. They think you're bad."

"I don't care about what the hell others think about me," He says. "I only care about what you think of me. I care about you only."

"Don't say that." I shake my head at him, "I don't think you realize what's happening Liam."

"I do," He argues in a gruff voice. "I get the fact that you and Adam aren't going to happen. I won't let it happen. Never."

"You're an idiot." I mutter bluntly. And he really is if he thinks he can stop it when the odds are all against him. The odds are against the both of us, clearly.

"But I'm your idiot," He replies, a smile twitching at his lips. "Just like you're mine."

"Are you calling me a idiot?" I question, making a face at him.

"Yes," He says honestly, "Because you underestimate me. Just watch Ronnie." One hand leaves my cheek and instead he brushes his hurt knuckles across my jaw. I shiver involuntarily, lost in the feel of him.

I can't find the strength to pull away. Instead I only pull closer, pressing his knuckles against my lips. I press a kiss to each one, watching his facial expressions.

He doesn't even flinch when I press my lips down harder. All he does is watch me with those green eyes of his.

"Well," I drawl. "What even makes you think I am yours?" I question teasingly, a taunting smile finding my lips.

He chuckles at me, drawing me close and pressing my to him. He brushes a stray hair out of my face, leaning down and pressing a scorching kiss to my cheek. One that makes me tremble and exhale a shaky breath.

His lips drag across my cheekbone as he nears my ear. He stops, letting his hot breath blow across me. "You've always been mine Ronnie. And you always will be."

I manage to get away soon after that statement. I tell him how it's late and I need to go. I dodge any further questions when I detangle myself from him and jog off.

The whole time I walk back to the pack houses I wear a huge goofy grin on my face. Though I tell myself what I've done and said is stupid, I don't care frankly.

The feeling of having Liam close is too good for me to care about everything. Even Adam and stupid Alpha Beckett.

Still. I worry. About how I've just given Liam a massive hint of to why I'm acting the way I am. I must seem so bi-polar to him. How one minute, I'm pushing him away, then I'm being all sweet and even touching him.

I was confused by my actions myself. I just couldn't help but want to be close to him every chance I got. Was that such a crime? Apparently.

Once I near the pack neighborhood, I let the smile slip from my face and instead turn into a hard one. I'm glad when I do because when I immediately walk into the clearing, I see Alpha Beckett and Adam outside. Talking in hushed tones.

I see Alpha Beckett brush a hand down his son's face. His eyes hardening at the sight. His gaze flickers to me and I tell myself not to flinch when he glares at me coldly.

I read it all clear in his eyes. What he's trying to tell me,

Someone has to pay for this. And that person is going to be you.

Chapter 11

God, kill me now.

That's all what does through my mind as I stare at the colorful flyer before me. My stomach clenches in dismay when I realize this is the formal Adam was talking to me about in the car. This is where he's supposed to introduce me as his mate to all the other packs.

Why was everything happening so damn fast?

It felt like only hours ago that Adam had declared he wanted me as his mate. It also felt like hours ago that I met Liam. Now here I am, three weeks later staring at this flimsy piece of paper that just represented my doom.

"I don't want to go." I repeat for the sixth time this morning. I push the paper away from me, glancing up at Adam under my lashes. "I'm not going."

Adam sighs and rests his forearms on the table. "Ron, you-"

"Ronnie." I correct him quickly, "I only let people I like call me Ron."

He grimaces and his jaw clenches in anger at me. Yeah, we're still fighting even after yesterday. I wouldn't talk to him without giving him attitude and well, he obviously didn't like that.

But he didn't fight with me like he did at lunch.

Instead he takes it and carries on, probably afraid I'll have another out break. And I would if he did. But this time, I would punch him straight in the face rather then just saying, 'Go screw yourself.'

"I already told my mom you would meet her after school," He says, letting out a frustrated sigh at the end of his sentence.

"Tell her I'm not going." I say calmly with a small shrug. I know I'll end up getting forced to go, but I can't help fighting back with him. I didn't want Adam getting the idea that he could walk all over me.

But then again, I was playing with fire here. Adam at any minute could run to his daddy and tell him I was refusing and then Liam would end up six feet under. Or even Anna.

The thought makes my stomach clench painfully.

"I don't want to fight Ronnie," He mutters and stands up from his seat. "Just please go after school and do what she wants. She'll only most likely get your size for the dress her tailor is making for you. And probably talk over colors and such."

I frown, like I would even want to talk about that stuff. "I have the back drops to do after school. You know, for your play." It's not a lie. Today I really do I have to really get going on the back drops and finish them in about three weeks before the play. Three weeks of being stuck in a room with Liam. All alone.

"Fine. What time will you be done?"

"I don't know, around five or so." I reply with another one of my signature shrugs.

"Okay. I'll tell her you'll be there at six then. You can even have dinner with us, sound good?" He asks, and makes a b-line for the door, already opening it.

"Not really." I say flatly, "Don't hold your breath. I might just not show up." I follow him to the door, picking up my bag and putting it over my shoulder.

"You should.. you know how my dad would get if you didn't," He mumbles, his eyes flickering to my face as if expecting I'll snap at him.

It's a warning.

He was just like his father, warning me not to do this or that or they would surely drop hints of what was to come if I disobeyed. God, they were complete, heartless, jerks.

I just remain with a hard expression. Mainly at the mention of his father and his unspoken threat. "Whatever. I'll be there."

He claps his hands together and smiles. "Great! See you then." He begins to jog off to his car and then turns, asking, "Are you sure you don't want a ride?"

"Nope. I'm perfectly fine." I turn on my heel and make my way to the main road, muttering under my breath how I desperately need to get a car.

And how I was going to be late. I only had ten minutes till class began, and that's when I broke into a run.

God, I hate school!

Not even my running could save me from the bell. I had gotten to school three minutes and had to get a stupid slip. While also getting a scowl from my teacher and how I needed to be on time.

Liam was simply amused by it all, clearly, since when I sat down he laughed, shaking his head at me.

I gave him the finger before turning and paying attention to the board.

And the day seems to fly by fast, because before I know it, I'm in the art room, laying out the canvas while arguing with Liam.

"I don't know, I think we should go with light blue instead of a dark blue." I say, pursing my lips and staring down at the canvas.

"Who cares? Let's just paint the stupid canvas." Liam grumbles and tosses me a paint brush and a bottle of light blue paint.

I narrow my eyes at him and huff, "If you think it's so stupid why are you even here? Like I need your help, anyway."

"I figured I'd stick around and bug you," He says, clear amusement in his green eyes. "Personally I like the dark blue better."

I glower at him and clench the paint brush tightly in my hand. He's doing this on purpose just to give me a hard time, I think. "We're going with light blue. End of discussion." I turn away from him and uncap the bottle of paint, ready to dip my brush into it, but I can't, since Liam snatches it away seconds later.

"I want dark blue." He argues stubbornly, wearing a small smirk on his lips as he watches me fume.

"No, we're going with light blue." I say, gritting my teeth together and reaching to grab it. Of course, he does the childish thing and decides to hold it above his head, laughing like a mad man as I jump and claw at his arm.

"Give it to me, Liam!"

"Oh don't worry, I will soon enough, princess."

It takes me a minute to understand what's he's meant, then I get it suddenly. Pervert! I feel my cheeks warm and I realize that I'm blushing.

Blushing at a disgusting remark Liam has just made. What was wrong with me? I shake my head as if to shake myself from the thoughts and step back, quickly masking a face of horror than flattery. "Like I'd ever let you anywhere near me. You disgust me."

"You weren't saying that yesterday at the lake." He grins bashfully and my jaw falls slack, my lips part in disbelief before I turn away from him and avert my eyes to the ground just so he won't see me blushing. Again.

"I was clearly out of it," I mutter and desperate to change the subject, I say, "Okay. We'll go with the dark blue, whatever."

"You must really want to change the subject, huh?" He muses.

I let out a sigh of frustration, "No. I want to get this canvas done so I can go home."

Liam frowns. Obvious that I'm in no mood to joke around today. And I'm honestly not. I have far too much on my mind.

Like spending time with Adam's mom and having dinner with them. It makes it seem like it's official now. Like this is really going to happen. That I'm going to be Adam's mate.

The thought makes my stomach churn.

"I didn't mean to upset you," He mumbles, lowering the bottles of paint and thrusting me into my arms. "I was just trying to make you laugh. You do know what that is, don't you?"

I sigh and put the bottles on the ground, kneeling in front of the canvas, I shrug. "Of course I do. I'm just not in the best mood today."

I don't know why I say it, but I do. Secretly hoping that he'll ask, that I'll at least be able tell someone what's happening and how I feel.

But he doesn't say anything at all to my dismay. He just stares me, probably tossing around the idea in his head if he should ask or not.

I sigh after a few minutes and decide it's not best to tell him anyway. He'd probably just go beat Adam to a pulp again.

So I quietly get to work, stroking the brush gently against the paper. It's after a few minutes of doing so that Liam says, "You're good at that. You know, painting."

My eyes flicker over to him briefly before they land back on the canvas, "It's the only thing I'm good at it."

I don't need to look to know he's giving me a questioning gaze. "What do you mean?"

"I mean painting is the only I'm good at," I drawl slowly. "I can't seem to do anything else right. Like, oh, dancing. I have no rhythm at all."

His eyebrows furrow, "Really?"

I nod, leaning back on my heels. "Yeah. I remember my middle school graduation party. I tried dancing and I thought I was doing okay, till I tripped over my feet and crashed into the punch bowl. Talk about fun."

Liam laughs. Loudly at that. Probably just imaging it all. "How painful was it?"

"The physical pain wasn't the worst part," I say. "The social pain I suffered was immense. I think someone even caught it on camera."

"Really?" His eyes widen, before a slow smile curves onto this lips. "Do you think they could make me a copy?"

I laugh. For the first time today, I actually laugh and a smile slides onto my face. "Not likely, but I'll try."

He laughs a long with me and shockingly, he gets down onto the floor and stops next to me picking up a brush and saying with a small smile, "Let's get started, yeah?"

I stare him in bewilderment for a few seconds, wondering where his sudden mood change had come from. I had just shared a brief fact about me, and he was jumping for joy. And laughing. We were both laughing. And it felt good.

It felt a lot better then constantly fighting or discussing my obvious issues. Maybe Liam wasn't as bad as I once concluded.

Maybe there is another layer to him. Something that lies underneath that hard exterior he has. The real Liam.

Though Liam and I were complete opposites, I understood what that was like. To put up so many walls. And I still had mine constantly up.

But right now, I could feel and hear those walls cracking. And I wondered if he could hear them too.

I smile at him, tucking a stray of hair slowly behind my ear, "Yeah," I say, nodding jerkily. "Let's get started."

Liam and I maintained light conversation. Surprisingly, we talked about all sorts of things, like music, and past funny stories that we shared. Or well, mostly I did. I even dared to breech the subject of his past. His life.

He really didn't talk about it. And he tensed if I brought it up, but shrugged it off like it was nothing before turning the subject back around on me.

I was more then just disappointed.

I wanted to more about him, where he came from, and why he did the things he did. Yet he refused to tell me.

I didn't know what had suddenly sparked my sudden curiosity to know him, but I went with it. Though it was stupid.

I guess I was just too tired to keep pushing everyone out of my life when I desperately needed someone to lean on. And to tell my emotions and thoughts to before I burst.

So, I talked to him. And it felt pretty damn good, I'm not going to lie.

It was just foolish telling myself that maybe Liam and I could grow close. That maybe there was more to him then being some murderous rogue.

And perhaps there was. But it wasn't best to dive down deep into it. And certainly not safe heading into the unknown.

Then again, I was heading into the unknown right now. Adam's house.

I sigh, absentmindedly fixing my clothes as I walk over to their front porch. I don't what to do it. I don't want to spend time with Adam's mom, him, and most importantly Alpha Beckett.

I brace myself though as I walk up the steps, raising my hand to knock on the door when it swings open, revealing's Adam's mom. "Ronnie!"

My eyebrows fly up at her excited squeal, "Uh, hi Mrs. Beckett."

"Come in, come in!" She says, but she doesn't even give me a chance to. Instead she grabs me by my forearms and yanks me into the house. "Adam! Ronnie's here!"

I wince at high pitched scream, causing Mrs. Beckett to glance at me with questioning eyes. I manage to fake smile at her. And she smiles back, perhaps a fake one of her own too.

I take the time to glance around their house, seeing that it's so.. different, then it was before. They completely repainted the house beige and clearly insisted on mahogany furniture everywhere. It was so plain, and I could only imagine that Adam's mom had done it.

I wasn't going to say anything. I was at least happy that Mrs. Beckett remembered my name.

"Hey Ronnie,"

My eyes flicker to the large staircase and I see Adam perched at the top, giving me a brief wave. I mimic the gesture slowly.

"What kinda greeting is that? She is your mate." Mrs. Beckett scuffs, "Come giver her a real hug and kiss."

My eyes nearly bulge out of my head at the horrible suggestion. Did she mean a kiss on the lips? I felt sick to my stomach just at the thought. I didn't want Adam touching me. Even if it did have to be just a hug or anything, no way.

And I certainly did not want Adam to be my first kiss.

"Um, we're not a huge fan of PDA, mother." Adam says with a shrug. "Maybe next time. When we're more comfortable with that idea."

Mrs. Beckett frowns, shaking her head. "Well you're going to have to be for the formal ball, you know that, don't you?"

Adam goes to say something else, but I quickly beat him to it. "We know. And we figure it'll be more special for the first time kissing there. In front of everyone. It'll be the best announcement and sure to make a splash. Don't you think?"

Mrs. Beckett jumps right on board with this idea, since she nods and smiles like she's won the freaking lottery. "Of course! That'll be the only thing everyone's talking about the whole evening!"

"Yes, very exciting." I give her a bitter sweet smile and once she turns away, I quickly scowl her. Though she's too moronic to notice I am.

"Well then, we should get going to get fitted for your dress," Mrs. Beckett reaches out again and grapes my arm, tugging me along. "Let's go!"

Reluctantly, I follow after her, silently asking for a miracle. To somehow get out of this. And how to travel back in time and take my words back about me and Adam kissing at the formal ball.

Now his mother was never going to forget that. And it's all because of my big mouth.

Save me. Please.

It's about two hours later that the tailor and Mrs. Beckett have finally agreed on a color. I say them, because I really had no pick on it.

They picked gold, since it would with my mask or whatever. I just nodded and smiled at everything they said. I figured the quicker I agree, the quicker I could get out of here.

I don't even care if the dress turned out hideous because I practically said yes to everything. All I wanted was to head home and wallow in my pity. Lovely, I know.

"The dress is going to turn out so great!" Mrs. Beckett says, re-entering the room since she had lead the tailor out.

"No doubt." I nod and turn away from the mirror with a sigh, brushing back a piece of my hair that had fallen into my face.

I glance up when I realize it has gone incredibly silent for the first time since I've been with Mrs. Beckett, only to see she's smiling softly at me. Which 'causes me furrow my eyebrows at her expression.

"I can see why Adam likes you so much," She says. "You're absolutely beautiful."

"Um, thanks." I mutter, feeling slightly awkward that Adam's mom has just told me I'm beautiful.

"He talks about you a lot," She continues and this time, she truly catches my attention. "It's never ending."

"What do you mean he talks about me?" I ask.

She laughs, "You didn't know?"

I shake my head slowly, "Should I?"

"Well, yes," She replies, "That boy is crazy about you. He has always been talking about you since you two were kids. He told us stories about you guys at the lake, also. He still does talk about you a lot, mostly to me."

My lips part in disbelief, "What?"

"Yeah. He says how he occasionally swings by the art room and checks out your paintings."

I'm left to stare at her dumbfounded. What? Adam dropped by the art room and looked at my paintings?

And he also talked about me? Why was that? Adam didn't really like me.. Did he?

Oh my god, I think, What if he actually does like me? Was that why he chose me to be his mate because he said some school boy crush on me?

My stomach does flips and I feel as if I'm gonna hurl. No, no, no. Maybe this was all just a joke. Adam didn't like me. There was no way.

But what if it were true? What if Adam really did have feelings for me?

Why am I even thinking about this? Of course he doesn't like me, I convince myself by repeating that line over and over again.

Still, I can't help but wonder. Wonder if Mrs. Beckett is telling the truth. If Adam really does talk about me.

It was just weird. I had treated him so sourly these past weeks and he still talks of me.

I glance over at Mrs. Beckett to see her with raised eyebrows, as if she expects me to say I talk about him too. If I have feelings for him.

But that would be the biggest lie I would ever tell.

I didn't have feelings for Adam in that way. I'm not even sure if I liked him as a friend. Perhaps not, since he proved to be just like his father these past weeks. I'm so confused. So confused about everything that's happening around me.

"That's.. nice," I manage to utter out. She doesn't say anything, just stares at me, making me twitch and fidget at the awkward conversation. I'm desperate to get out of this, so I say, "We should get going to dinner, right?"

Slowly, Mrs. Beckett nods. "Right," She mutter then gestures me out the door. "We should go before the boys start without us."

I follow her out the door, keeping my head bowed and my eyes focused on the floor. It's too weird to talk to her after what she said. I was afraid she was going to question me on my feelings for Adam, and I wouldn't know what to say.

If I lied, that would just resort to the worst. And Adam's mother would probably get a crazy idea, like to speed up the mating or something.

Then again, I couldn't tell her the truth either. That I really didn't like Adam. I bet she'd go running to her husband or something and tell him that.

It'd be like setting my own death wish.

Mrs. Beckett was nice, I guess, but I didn't think she was trustworthy with secrets and stuff. She reminded me of the girls in high school who spill your secrets just to get attention for it.

I did not want to be one of her victims just for her entertainment.

Plus, I didn't even want Adam knowing I had that conversation with his mother. It would be make things.. well, weird. More weird between the two of us.

And I'd be forced to talk about it, most likely. I wasn't ready for that. I wasn't ready for any of this, then again. The mating, the ball, the pack.

My life had truly become so damn complicated.

I liked it better when all I had to worry about was what flavor of ice cream I was going to get on Saturday night and what movie I was going to watch with Anna.

Anna.

I hadn't even spoken to her today. For lunch, she went and sat with Adam and stuff, while I remained in the art room, talking with Ms. J about the back drops.

Even when I got out of there, we hadn't talked for the rest of the day. It was weird. And I was scared I was losing my best friend to Adam and his posse.

Anna wouldn't do that to me. She wouldn't ditch me for them. I knew her better then that.. I knew her better then that.

I sigh out loud on accident, catching Mrs. Beckett's attention. "Everything alright, dear?"

"Yeah," I mumble, "I'm fine."

But I'm really not. And it doesn't help my mood when we round the corner and I see Alpha Beckett and Adam at the dinning room table.

Right when they see us, the conversation they were having stops, not even giving me a chance to perhaps ease drop on them.

"There you two are." Alpha Beckett says, with a wide grin on his face. "Adam and I were just about to go find you guys."

My eyes flicker over to Adam at the mention of him, and instead of wearing a fake cheery smile on his like his father has, he just sat there. His expression hard and his eyes glassy. With tears? With anger? With worry? I wasn't sure.

But when he glances right back at me, I realize it's pain. Evident pain. Not physical pain, but emotionally.

What had his father said to cause that expression? The last time I had ever seen him with look, was when he favorite toy. I remember being with him for hours, promising him it'd turn up. It never did.

But this time, he didn't have that expression because he had lost a toy. It was something much deeper.

And I had a feeling I'd find out soon enough.

"Take a seat, Ronnie."

My eyes dart in the direction of the voice and I see Alpha Beckett is gesturing me to sit down. Mrs. Beckett already is, and I hadn't even noticed it.

I slowly inch my way to the table and I end up sitting to Adam, since both Alpha Beckett and Mrs. Beckett gesture to it.

"So, how was the fitting?" Alpha Beckett asks, as if he really cares.

I don't say anything. Instead Mrs. Beckett dives right into it, telling him everything. And he pretends to look interested, which he pulls off marvelously.

He's even a better liar then I thought.

And she carries on like that for a while. Enough for the food to be done and served. I pick at it the whole time, scared that they may have poisoned it or something.

"Are you not hungry?" Adam whispers to me and I glance over at him briefly, shaking my head.

"I'm just not feeling good. Must have been something I ate earlier."

Adam shrugs before he turns away and focuses back on his food. I sigh, resting my head on my hand.

"Are you excited for the ball, Ronnie?" Alpha Beckett asks and inwardly, I groan. Could they not tell I was in no mood for talking?

Then again, I was never in a mood to talk with Alpha Beckett. I force a bitter sweet smile, one that he can so clearly see through and say, "Of course."

"And I'll bet you'll be even more excited when we announce you two are to be mated, right?" He taunts, though he doesn't make it evident. Instead he wears a great big grin, as if he really expects me to be.

My hand tightens on the fork in my hand and for a minute, I contemplate stabbing it right through his hand. "Yes," I say through gritted teeth. "I'm just ecstatic."

Mrs. Beckett laughs, "You should be. Oh, it's going to be exciting!"

I smile and agree, nodding my head. Maybe I should just stab myself with this stupid fork and put myself out my own misery.

Luckily for me, the night pasts fast enough. Though Mrs. Beckett insists I stay a little longer, I decline and tell her I really need to get a good night's rest for school tomorrow.

As if I really care for school.

I'm about ready to walk out the door when Mrs. Beckett says, "Adam, be a gentlemen and walk Ronnie to her house."

"Oh, he really doesn't have," I say all too quickly, causing Mrs. Beckett to raise a eyebrow at me. "I mean, my house is just right there. No biggie."

Mrs. Beckett shakes her head at me, "Still, Adam should go with you. And he is. So go on Adam, walk her to her house."

Adam sighs and boosts himself up from his seat on the couch, "Whatever."

He seems really happy, I think sarcastically and open the door. He walks out and so do I. Then we start off to my house in silence, and before I can really register what's going on, I'm at my door.

I sigh and unlock my door, "Thanks for walking me home, I guess." I'm about to walk, but his words stop me.

"Did my mom say anything embarrassing?"

I stiffen for a minute, before I turn and face him. "No," I lie, shrugging. "Nothing really. All we talked about was the dress."

"Then why do I feel like she did?"

"Maybe you're just being paranoid," I mumble. "It's late. I should get to bed."

"Yeah, you should," He nods and bites his lip, almost nervously. "Good night, Ronnie."

"Night Adam." I say, giving him a small wave. He smiles back sadly and turns, walking off and shoving his hand in his pockets.

For some reason, I frown. The old Adam wouldn't have done that. He would have kept asking, bugging me and making me laugh until I actually told him.

So much had change. But that was okay, because I had changed too just as much. I wasn't like the old me. I was a lot more serious. And sarcastic.

I watch his back as he walks, and even though he stills looks like the old Adam, he doesn't feel or sound like him.

He was like a stranger.

He was just somebody that I use to know.

Chapter 12

Anna had told me that someone had caught the fight that Liam and Adam had at the party on their camera.

And that they had uploaded it on the web.

Of course, I was so curious to see what happened. What they said, and how badly Liam really kicked Adam's ass.

And here I lay, at 3 AM, contemplating turning on my computer and watching the video. I wouldn't even have to go out of my way and search for it, Anna had already emailed the link to me.

It's stupid. But the temptation grows for the next thirty minutes, then I can't take it anymore and I spring up from my bed and walk over to my computer.

I take a seat and sigh, rolling my mouse and watching the computer hum to life. I'm partly blinded by the bright light that floods the room, but I ignore it quickly and click right onto the Internet.

I go to my email to find the mail Anna was talking about, I roll my eyes when I see the message above the link.

Have fun drooling over Liam as he pummels Adam's face in!

xx, Anna.

I type back a quick reply and press the link. It pops up to a whole different website and I watch in awe as Liam and Adam appear on the screen.

I can barely make out their words to one another when all I hear is the hollering from the crowed screaming, "Fight!"

But finally, everyone goes quiet when Liam shoves Adam.

Adam stumbles, and catches himself before he can fall down. "So what? You're gonna beat me up just to somehow impress Ronnie and win her over? Looks like you have way bigger problems then I thought."

"You have no idea." Liam sneers and I'm shocked to see how angry he looks. With his face twisted in anger, his muscles clenched and ready to fight, and his eyes.. his eyes are different. They aren't the welcoming green I'm use to.

They're dark, though I can't make out the exact color since the camera shakes massively. But I'm able to see Liam draw his fist back and send a punch right to Adam face.

That's when all chaos breaks out.

Everyone shouts, screams, gasps. But the sound that really catches my attention, is Adam's guttural screams of pain.

And the satisfying crunch that sounds when Liam lands a blow to Adam's nose. But it doesn't stop Adam's never ending remarks. "You don't deserve her," Adam rasps. "You don't deserve Ronnie."

This doesn't calm Liam's already raging anger. Instead it only propels him forward with the beating he's giving Adam.

Liam hurls Adam up from the ground, grabbing him by collar of his shirt and slamming him up against a near wall, his eyes narrowed and hard. "Say her name one more time and I'll break your fucking arm."

His words - even though they're not directed at me - make me flinch. Especially since it's the first time I've ever heard him talk so.. sadistic, I suppose.

Adam doesn't even seem phased by the statement, He smiles, blood dripping down the side of his mouth and splattering against the floor. "Why? Are you jealous that she's mine? That she can never be yours?"

Liam jerks Adam away from the wall, only to slam him against it twice as hard. I'm pretty sure I can even hear the wall crack. "She's not yours," Liam says quietly. So quietly and lethal that it's much more scarier then him screaming. "She's not yours to have. Nor will she ever be," Liam pauses, pressing his lips together. "If I see you touch her, I'll make sure to not only break your arm, but every fucking limb. We clear?"

Adam doesn't reply. He simply shrugs, wearing the same taunting smile. Liam obviously has every intention to wipe that smirk clear off of his face. He does when he whines his fist back and sends one last fatal punch at Adam's face.

One that probably caused that massive black eye.

Adam slumps limp against the wall, now only with a grimace coating his features. Liam's pleased by this, since he backs off, leaving Adam to support himself.

But Adam can't. He's obviously in too much pain, since he falls to the ground with a groan. People, - really only girls - go sprinting to his side, shouting his name.

And with that, Liam turns, not sparing Adam another glance and walks off. He doesn't even have to shove his way through the crowd. They all part and let me walk to the door smoothly, probably to afraid to stand in his way.

Then Liam disappears out the door and the last image that you see is the blood on the floor. Adam's blood.

Then the screen goes black.

And I'm left to stare it with parted lips and a mask of confusion. What just happened?

I have no clue. No exact clue. I can't even seem to comprehend the fact that Liam just kicked Adam's ass. And all because of me.

Maybe Liam really did live up to his name. He was dangerous. And I bet if he wanted, he could have easily snapped Adam's neck.

I could imagine he would if it weren't for the group of humans watching the scene intently. That would surely make national headlines the next day.

"Teenage boy get's his neck snapped and all because of a girl!"

That would just be lovely.

I groan and shake my head as if to rid myself of the thoughts, then I slowly drag myself back to bed, tugging the sheets up under my chin with a sigh and closed my eyes.

I don't get a wink of sleep that night. Or well, those three I attempted to sleep.

I would doze in and out of consciousness, each time awakened by a new dream. Or nightmare. Mostly they consisted of Liam, the fight, and Alpha Beckett. Yeah, he even threatened me in my dreams too.

And when morning comes, I'm in no mood to go to school. Yet I get up, get dressed, braid my hair, and suddenly before I know it I'm on my way to school.

Though I grumble how I hate my life the entire time.

When I arrive with minutes to spare, I rush to my locker and yank out my books, ready to turn and run to class when I see Anna.

Though, what's different about her today, is that she isn't coming over here to come talk to me. Or even nag at me about my clothes.

Instead she walks with Kara and Mandy, throwing her head back and laughing at something Kara says.

Anna doesn't even like Mandy, I think meekly, watching her past me down the hall without even looking in my direction.

She just loops arms with both girls and practically skips off to class with them, smiling.

I can't ignore the pang of pain that echoes through my chest and without even noticing what I'm doing, I reach up and cover my hand across my chest, just over my heart.

What was Anna doing with them?

Had she really just ditched me for the popular group? The people she had only just really talked to a week or two ago?

That wasn't the part that confused me the most. It was the fact she was hanging out with Mandy.

Mandy, the bitch who made snarky comments about the two of us not too long ago. Had she forgotten about that?

She was just like everyone else, I think, all she ever wanted was popularity. Not to be my friend.

I swallow roughly, and push away the thought. Anna wouldn't do that to me. Anna was my friend. My friend for two years.

She wouldn't just ditch me for Mandy and Kara, girls she just met two weeks ago, right?

The scary part was that I honestly didn't know the answer to question.

Maybe I was just over reacting, I mean, she can have more friends then just me. It's not a crime. I just wished she would have picked another group of people to be friends with rather then my pack.

I didn't even know why Mandy and Kara were hanging out her. Last time I checked, Mandy didn't even like to hang out with humans. Especially at school.

She was probably angry. Angry that I had "stolen" Adam from her. Now she simply wanted to repay the favor, by stealing Anna, my best friend, away from me.

I bet once they accomplished that, and Anna stopped fully talking to me, they'd dump her.

I just hoped Anna wouldn't put herself in that situation. She was smarter then that. Right?

Again, another question I couldn't answer.

I just pray I won't lose my best friend.

Sighing, I close my locker and head in the opposite direction of where Anna had gone, the feeling of betrayal setting in my stomach.

The morning seems to drag on. And it's probably because of the fact the whole time Liam and I seem to be having some sort of stare off with one another.

We don't say anything to one another. All we do is exchange nervous glances and coy smiles. Though he's mostly the one who sends me a smile, I just stare at him with parted lips.

Now that I look at him, I just imagine seeing that same hate-filled expression on his face like he had in the video.

And it's not like I can help it.

I just find myself questioning who Liam really is. And why he was claimed to be a murderer. My mind lingers on to the thought to why he had even come here.

I mean, he had to know the Purgatory pack hung around here. It was like asking for trouble. Though I'm pretty sure Liam's middle name was trouble.

I guess I just wanted to know his motives behind it all. I wanted to know who Liam was, but that would mean growing close to him.

And I couldn't afford to that.

It'd be setting myself up for heartbreak. In just two months, I'd have to mate with Adam - that is, if I can't get out of it - And if that were to happen, It would be painful. Even more painful if I really knew Liam then and liked him. Perhaps even loved him.

Love.

When had that come into my vocabulary? I would never love Liam. Because I wouldn't get to know him.

I would get out of my mating with Adam, run away, and never look back. Never give Liam the chance to win my heart.

And that was final.

With a new sense of determination and promise, I make my way to the lunch room slowly and find my place in line.

I quickly pay for my food and scan the cafeteria, seeing Anna at Adam's table. Though this time she doesn't ignore me.

She sees me and feverishly waves me over with a smile. As she does that, Mandy and Kara give her a look of disapproval.

And as much as I would love to go over and sit with them, I don't. Especially when I see Adam there. After that conversation with his mom, it's far to awkward to talk to him without feeling uncomfortable.

So instead, I shake my head at her and turn away before she can respond. I walk over to our old table and hesitantly sit down, eyeing the scrawny boy that sits there as well.

Minutes past and I contemplate heading over to Adam's table, since the kid just stares at me the whole time. Or well, more like stares at my chest.

I knew I shouldn't have worn a V-neck, I think meekly and try to causally cross my arm over my chest. His eyes never waver.

And it doesn't help when I can feel everyone's eyes on me, practically burning holes into my freaking back.

I bet they're just questioning if Adam and I have "broken" up. Since I had told him not too long ago to go screw himself. I can only imagine.

I manage to gather up the courage and look around; the first thing I see is Liam. Standing just at the lunch line, paying for his food.

And immediately when he turns away after he pays, his eyes land on me.

I suck in a sharp breath, taking in his flawless appearance. Though he's dressed casually, just in a pair of jeans and black shirt, he still amazes me.

He appears as if he's some type of model, and I wonder why the Gods had paired me up with him. I wasn't strikingly beautiful, nor was I ugly, I was just.. Ronnie.

And Liam was just bloody breath taking.

And he was walking over here.

I panic slightly when he starts to make his way over; I abruptly turn and reluctantly face the scrawny boy.

I cross my arms over my chest - Clearly not helping by taking the kid's attention off of my breasts - and tuck away a loose strand of hair, almost nervously.

Maybe I should get up and leave.

I really do contemplate getting up and making a run for it, mostly because I could only imagine what people would say if they saw me with Liam, but I can't. I don't even get the chance since Liam drops his tray right next to me.

I don't look at him, instead I sightly raise my head up enough to see the boy - which name is now Perv, since, well he is a perv for staring at my chest - is shaking madly. I'm not surprised when he I notice he's not watching my chest, but Liam.

My eyes dart to Liam for a minute to see he was fiercely glaring at Perv. Why is Liam glaring at the kid? Perv isn't really competition. Nor someone to be jealous of.

It isn't even minutes into the stare contest that the kid scampers off, not sparing another glance towards the table.

Though I'm glad he's gone, it still leaves me with Liam.

The first thing that comes into mind once the kid is completely out of sight is, run.

And I try to, really, I do. But it's as if Liam sees my intentions, since he clamps his hand down on my thigh, keeping me in place.

I swallow roughly at the sudden contact. I can just feel the heat of his hand burning through the thin lair of denim.

I squirm, hoping he'll get the message and release me, but he doesn't. He leaves his hand there, obviously not the least bit annoyed because of moving around.

When I notice it's not going to work, I clasp my hand over his, ignoring the tingles and trying to yank his hand off relentlessly.

Not once does his grip on my thigh budge. I whip my head around to glare at him, only to realise he's been watching me this whole time with a sly smirk twitching at the corner of his mouth.

I narrow my eyes at him and pull at his hand. He knows that I want him to remove his hand, yet he doesn't do it.

Probably because he finds me getting angry funny. Jerk.

"Remove your hand," I manage to utter slowly.

He shakes his head defiantly, now with a full blown out smirk on his face. "I'm afraid if I do you'll try to make a run for it."

"Obviously," I say, with an edge to my voice. "I'm not one bit interested in chatting with you."

"That's a shame," He murmurs, "Because I wanted to talk to you. About the formal ball."

I stiffen slightly at his words, "How do you know about the formal ball?"

He doesn't reply, instead with his free hand, he digs into his back pocket before placing a folded up piece of paper in my hand.

My eyebrows furrow and I glance up at him for a minute, before for slowly unraveling the paper to see it's the flyer.

The same exact one Adam had showed me. "How did you get this?" I ask, rubbing out the creases in the paper to see it more clearly.

"I got it from your bag." He says it so casually, so composed, as if it's the most normal thing ever. But it's not.

It was invading my privacy, I mean, who goes through someone's bag without their permission? "You went through my bag?"

"No," He replies, leaning back in his chair. "I just simply put my hand in your bag and pulled that flyer out."

"That's called going through my bag." I say, shaking my head at him.

"Not really."

"Yes it is!" I screech, "Either way, you had no right to look through my stuff!"

"It's not like you had anything personal in there," He shrugs, "Just sketches. Who's the girl on the front page?"

I frown, why had he gone through my sketch book? Why had I even left it in my bag?

I shuffle around in my seat, suddenly feeling a little too hot for my liking. And it didn't really help my nerves with him touching me.

I don't reply. I don't think I can. Mainly because that girl on the first page of my sketch book is my mom. And I can only imagine the following questions that will come after if I did tell him.

My mom wasn't my favorite subject, that's why most people didn't even know she was dead. And that's how I intended to keep it.

I didn't want anyone's pity. Nor did I want them to question how she died, mainly because I couldn't even tell them the real reason.

It had to do with the pack.

Another problem that Alpha Beckett had caused, I think bitterly.

I'm reminded that I'm not alone when I feel Liam squeeze me thigh, 'causing me to look up at him. He wears a questioning gaze, lifting a eyebrow at me. "Well?"

"It's no one," I mutter, "And what about the ball? Are you planning on crashing it?"

"That'd be like a death wish," He replies.

"Because of all the packs that are going to be there, right?" I ask.

"Yeah," He nods, a smile playing at his lips. "Maybe I should go just to see what happens."

I scoff, shaking my head. "That would be incredibly idiotic," I say, "Then again, you're practically the definition of idiotic. So good luck."

I knew Liam was just joking, yet I still worried. Liam was unpredictable, and I wasn't able to read him. Maybe he wasn't joking. Maybe he was serious.

No way, Liam couldn't be that stupid. I mean, he was the number one rogue in all of America practically.

He must have to think out all his actions in order not to get caught, right? Obviously. If he was stupid, he would have been dead by now.

Liam was definitely more than just a pretty face.

"And you're the definition of rude." He counters, "Besides, I always love crashing a good party."

His words make me think of the video I had saw just last night. The fight. The look on his face. I shudder involuntary, "Yeah, I noticed."

He doesn't even need to question me on why I've suddenly become stiff or anything, instead he says, "So you saw the video?"

"Yeah." I mumble and focus my attention on playing with my leather bracelet.

My answer doesn't waver his attitude. He keeps his eyes on my face, making me squirm further. "I didn't mean to lose control like that. Your words just.."

"Made you angry?" I suggest, my eyes darting to him. It's then I realize how close we are. And how comfortable it all feels.

I can't find the strength to tell him to back off. I'm scared if I do he'll get up and walk off, leaving me confused. Like he practically always did.

Liam was a mystery. And I really wasn't one of those people who would want to take their time slowly unraveling the truth. I didn't want to be around the bush, I wanted answers.

"Yeah," He replies, his eyes slowly dragging away from mine to stare at a invisible spot on the wall. "Those were the same words someone I use to know said to me. It struck a nerve, I guess."

"Someone else said that to you?" I ask, titling my head and examining his face.

His jaw clenches, his muscles bunching and his eyes hard. "It doesn't matter."

"It seems like it does," I prompt, pressing the subject further on. "Who said that to you?"

"No one," His voice is hoarse and dry, "Forget I said anything. It was stupid."

I notice it's not best to carry on this conversation. Especially not with everyone's eyes on us, so I nod and whisper, "Okay. I'm sorry."

"For what?"

"For screaming at you that night at the party," I drawl and bite down on my lip, "I'm just frustrated. Everything around me is spiraling down wards and I don't know how to control it."

"You can't really control the unexpected." He says, "All you can do is live with it."

I nod, though I cock a eyebrow at him. "When did you become so deep?"

He laughs softly at that, bowing is head and 'causing his unruly brown hair to fall into his green eyes. I suck in a breath at his appearance, meeting his gaze. "I'm not exactly sure." He replies, though I'm not really paying attention to his words.

He was a complex man.

Just from that small conversation, I felt as if I knew him better. Yet I really didn't. It didn't answer any of my looming questions, well, all except one.

Liam had definitely been hurt. I mean, what did he mean someone had said to me what I had that night of the party?

Someone else had told him they didn't like him. Need him. Want him.

I just wondered who. Whoever did, obviously made a big impact on his life. And I wanted to know what about this person made Liam tick.

I just wanted to know Liam, period.

I couldn't fight the attraction I felt towards him, it was literally impossible. Especially because of our bond.

Sure, I told myself I wouldn't let myself grow close to him, yet I was. And I didn't - couldn't - stop myself from it happening.

The temptation was too much. And could anyone really blame me?

"I should go," Liam says, bringing me out of my thoughts. "I needed to swing by Ms. J's room anyway."

My lips part in questioning, but he ignores it. He pulls his leg off my leg and stands up. Before he walks off, he shrugs off his leather jacket and throws it to me. I catch it clumsily, my eyebrows furrowing.

I don't get the chance to ask him what the jacket is for, since he says, "I don't like people looking at what's mine."

I'm utterly confused and he seems to be okay with that, because he walks off a minute later. With a frown, I turn and stare down at my plate.

What did he mean?

I rake my brain for possibility's, till it suddenly dims on me. The kid! Perv!

Liam had given me the jacket so I could cover up my chest and ward off anymore guys like that pervy kid. That's why Liam was glaring at him as well. Because he had also noticed the guy staring at my chest.

I shake my head, a small smile sliding onto my lips. "Liam, you jealous idiot."

Later that day, when I went to the art room, I noticed how two things were missing. First, Liam, and my painting of Liam.

It had been completely removed off the wall and I wondered what had happened to it. I asked Ms. J and she quickly replied, "You'll see soon enough, dear."

Her words made me worry. Mainly because I had no idea what was to come.

She had also informed me that Liam had to go do something, so today I was working by myself. I simply shrugged and said, "Whatever." As if I didn't care. But secretly, I did.

Now that I had that conversation with Liam, I wanted to speak with him more. Perhaps even casually. Though I doubt it, our conversations were never normal.

Probably because neither Liam nor I were normal.

I quickly finished up in the art room and made my way home at five. I took my time, seeing as I really didn't want to face Alpha Beckett or Adam. But I couldn't avoid them any longer, and I didn't intend to. I didn't want to show them I was afraid or that they had some sort of power over me, so I braced myself as I walked into the clearing.

Lucky enough for me, none of them were in sight.

My joy is short lived when I hear the slam of a door. I flinch and turn in the direction of the sound to see Adam and Alpha Beckett right behind him storming out of their house.

"You can't do that, dad! That's taking it way too far!" Adam screeches and stops, turning his father. Completely oblivious to the fact I'm standing only a few feet away.

"I can and I will!" Alpha Beckett retorts angrily, "She crossed the line. That rogue crossed the line. So one of them has to pay for it. Don't you realize that?"

She crossed the line?

I know who they're talking about. Liam and I. My throat suddenly feels tight and dry as I stare at the both of them. One of them has to pay.

And I knew who that person was going to be. Me.

"Don't do it," Adam pleads, "Tell them it's not true. Tell them you lied."

"No," Alpha Beckett says, with a simple shake of his head. "Besides, everything will go according to plan. Don't worry."

"But I am!" Adam yells, failing his arms around madly. "This is Ronnie we're talking about! The girl I-" He cuts himself off, pressing his lips together while shaking his head. "Don't do it."

Alpha Beckett doesn't show mercy on him. Nor me for the matter. All he does is stare down at his son before his eyes dart to me, suddenly aware of my presence.

And Adam follows his gaze.

His face masks horror as he watches me. I gaze back at him with narrowed eyes, making it obvious I've heard.

Slowly, my eyes cast to Alpha Beckett's, who stares at me with a blank expression on his face. I glare at him.

I hate him. I hate him so much.

And all this just confirms it. Adam is just like his father. His first words give it away, that's taking it way to far.

He had to know about his father black mailing me. He had to know all these weeks of what his father was forcing me to do.

I just wondered what suddenly made him declare that his father was taking the situation too far. Personally, I thought blackmailing me was already "taking it too far".

"Ronnie-" He begins, but I don't give him the time of day.

I turn and walk off to my house, not giving him another word, or look.

And that's how it remains. I lock myself in my house the whole night, refusing to even glance out my window. Adam nerves comes to try and explain what I had witnessed. Instead he leaves me in the dark.

Honestly, I wasn't sure if I wanted to know.

I was secretly scared of what was to come. Whatever it was, I would take it and deal with it. Because I had no other choice, right?

I did. I could tell Liam. He could help me.

It's a stupid idea, yet I ponder it. I had a brief conversation with him for what, twenty five minutes and now I was questioning telling him this?

I shouldn't anyway. I was afraid Liam might snap and go after Adam and give him another beating. Then surely Alpha Beckett would put me in a casket.

Or perhaps Liam.

Or Anna.

My chest tightens at the thought and I know right then I can't tell him anything. I have to keep quiet for not my own sake, but Anna and Liam's.

Just because Anna had ditched me today to chat with Mandy and Kara, didn't mean I was about to turn my back on my best friend. And I was sure Anna wasn't about to do that either.

She wouldn't ditch me for them. Anna wouldn't throw away two years of friendship for Mandy and Kara. Anna was smart. She'd realize they were using her soon enough.

Besides, It's not like she'd been ditching me the whole weekend or week for them or anything. We talked practically daily.

One day of hanging out with someone else doesn't mean anything. I just needed to stop freaking out about everything.

But I definitely needed to find a way of getting out of Alpha Beckett's wrath.

That night, when I try to sleep, I can't. And it seems to becoming a major habit of mine. I toss and turn and eye Liam's leather jacket that laid on my desk.

Finally, after about a hour of not getting any sleep, I slip out from under my sheets and grab the jacket. I bring it up slowly to my nose and inhale it's woodsy scent. The exact scent Liam always had.

I rub my hand over the cold leather before I finally slide it on. It's big, mainly because of the height difference and muscle difference between the two of us, but it's still comfortable.

I don't even feel stupid for wearing it. I simply slide back into bed, wrapping the jacket fully around me and closing my eyes with a content sigh.

Goodnight, Princess.

It's his voice that I hear through our connection. I'm too tired to jump or scream at the sound of his voice. But I really did forget we even had that mind link or whatever it's called.

Goodnight Liam, I reply. And then I drift off to sleep, completely forgetting about today's events.

And what's to come in just a matter of days.

Chapter 13

I spend the next two days mostly with Adam's mother, since she claims she wants me to apart of the dress making process fully. And she had even insisted we design my own mask as well. Grudgingly, I agreed and stuck through it.

Though all I wanted to do was sprint out of that damn house.

I also yearned to speak with Adam, about what I saw, but he seemed to be avoiding me. Every time I came between a five mile radius he'd run off in the other direction.

I just wanted to prepare myself for what was going to come, but clearly, Adam didn't.

And my days at school weren't any better. Liam wasn't around, while Anna still hung out with Mandy and Kara. But she had stopped by a few times to chat with me, but I just wasn't interested. So I guess it was my own fault.

I spend most of my time painting at home and when I'm not doing that, I find myself at the lake. I'm surprised that the past two nights Liam hasn't appeared out of no where and tried to converse with me. As much as I hated it to admit, I missed him being around.

The sad part was it had only been two days and I wanted to see him again already.

I mean, when had I become so clingy?

I wasn't sure, but the more time I spent apart from him, the more ancy I grew. And it was completely stupid.

It's not like I was with Liam. And nor had I come to accept we were mates, but I just couldn't help but worry about him.

I knew Liam was a rogue, though I didn't know the full extent of what he did to others. I had seen him fight with Adam, but I never saw him really lose it.

I hadn't seen the monster everyone claimed him to be. And I couldn't avoid it forever.

Wednesday morning comes around way too quickly. And I'm incredibly reluctant to get out of bed, but I manage to push me way up and get dressed in a pair of jeans, a long sleeved teal shirt, and my leather jacket, though I stare at Liam's for a minute or two.

I kick it aside, shaking my head and grasp my bag. I walk outside, just in time to see Adam speed off in his car.

I sigh and continue my way down the gravel path to the street. I walk slowly to school, figuring I'll already be late when I get there, but surprisingly, when I get there I have but minutes to spare.

Though when I walk into the school, I do get some stares, but I learn to shake them off. Recently, a new rumour has emerged.

That Anna and Adam are now dating.

Of course, I knew it wasn't true, but I cringed when I heard it. And I questioned if Anna would really date him after I supposedly was. Then again, I never confirmed if Adam and I were together. So I thought maybe Anna went for it.

I didn't care, either way.

I seemed to be in some sort of slump since I wasn't even making an effort to be pain to others. Instead I just grumbled and groaned whenever someone tried to talk to me or whatever.

It wasn't all that bad of a method. Mainly because most of Adam and Liam's fan girls left me alone once they saw I wasn't going to answer any of their questions.

And for that, I was incredibly grateful.

I pop open my locker, letting out a string of cusses once all my papers and books all fall to the ground. I immediately scurry to pick them up once the bell rings, but the kids around me don't bother to help. Instead they walk right on by. Some even step on my papers and books.

It's not till I see a flash of blonde hair that I realize I'm not alone, I glance up fully to see Anna helping me by collecting my paper and books. "How did this happen?"

"It all came out of my locker when I opened it," I mutter, standing up and thrusting all of it back into my locker. "Why aren't you in class?"

"I was late," She says, "I just got here."

I frown, when had Anna ever really gotten late to school?

She hadn't ever from what I recall. Anna's mom was really hard on her, but only because she wanted the best for her. It had been like that for a while. I remember once that Anna forgot to do a report for English and her mom totally flipped. She was grounded for a month. I could only imagine what would her mother do when she discovered she had come to school late.

I knew she probably didn't know right now. Since Anna's mom went into work early. She would probably hear about it when one of the teachers called and tell her that Anna has detention for being late.

I wasn't any better off, though. I too would probably get detention. Though I had no one to care if I did get in trouble or that I didn't. So perhaps I was luckier then Anna who would probably get the punishment of her life.

"Over slept?" I ask. Anna nods.

"Yeah, I guess I just had a long night," She mumbles, tucking a strand of her blonde hair behind her ear. She opens her mouth to say something when she suddenly pauses, reaching into the mass pile of papers and pulling out a white envelope. "What is this?"

My eyebrows furrow and I reach out, pulling it from her grasp. I flip it around to see my name neatly printed right on the front.

I peel it open and pull out a single ticket. I frown, not exactly understanding what it means till I pull out a small slip of paper that reads;

Come with me to the Young Artist exhibit. I think you'll find some of their works there interesting. - L

I roll my eyes and stuff the ticket and note back in the envelope before I place it in my bag.

"I didn't get to see it. Why are you being so secretive?" Anna questions, raising a brow at me.

I roll my eyes, "Why are you being so secretive?"

Anna makes a face, "What do you mean?"

"I mean about your 'long night' excuse," I explain slowly, "You're never late for school and I'm just saying it's a little weird."

"You never know, I could have just been doing homework and I stayed up late finishing it. That equals a long night." She crosses her arms over her chest, her eyes averting to the floor.

It was possible. But I wasn't buying it. Especially since she wouldn't meet my eyes, almost nervously she scanned the hallway. "You suck at lying."

She doesn't say anything for a minute till she mutters, "Really? I thought it was good."

"Not really," I shake my head, "Especially since you couldn't look me in the eye and say it. Maybe then I would have believed you."

"Oh, forgive me Queen of Lying," She rolls her eyes with a laugh.

"Only if you tell what you really did last night." I say, waggling my eyebrows at her, "Were you with a boy?"

Her cheeks immediately turn a shade of pink and I know I've caught her in the act.

"Oh my gosh!" I gasp, "You dirty skank. What did you do?"

"Nothing!" She squeals, burying her face in her hands to block me from seeing her blush, "I didn't do anything."

"Then why are you blushing so bad?" I tease, "Did you do the deed?"

"Ronnie!" She screeches.

"Oh my gosh, you so did!" I accuse, pointing a finger at her. "You used a condom, didn't you?"

"Ronnie!" She repeats, swatting my arm. "Shut up. I did not have sex."

I can't help but laugh at her obvious embarrassment. And it feels incredibly good that we're finally talking again without the awkward silence. Honestly, I wasn't expecting to even make an effort to talk to her. Nor anyone for the matter, but I couldn't help but taunt her once I heard her lame lie.

I was too curious to know who this boy was as well. "Whatever you say," I retort, "Just tell me who he is."

"You promise you won't tell anyone?"

"Who do I have to tell? I only talk to you," I roll my eyes at her and Anna quickly shakes her head.

"You could tell someone by accident. Or maybe you could-"

I cut her off, "Stop stalling and just tell me who."

She bits her lips, before whispering, "Cliff."

My eyebrows shoot up at that. "Cliff? Adam's friend, you mean?"

She nods, "Yeah. Him."

I can't help but stare at her with shock. I mean, what was Cliff doing hanging around Anna anyway?

I didn't know Cliff personally, but I had heard enough to know he had no interest with human girls but to sleep with them. And if they hadn't slept together, why was Cliff even bothering with her?

He had been rude to her at lunch too. What was Anna thinking?

What the hell was Cliff thinking? He was a bloody werewolf while Anna was just a human! He was putting himself more at risk of her finding out our secret then me!

"Cliff?" I repeat in disbelief.

Anna nods again, "Why is that so hard to believe?"

"I don't know," I say, though I really do know. Cliff is a jerk and he wouldn't spend his time on a human girl. "I just thought he wasn't your.. type."

"Why wouldn't he be my type?"

"Because," I begin, raking my brain for some kind of excuse. "Because he was pretty rude to you at lunch. He seemed like a jerk."

Anna waves me off, "He was just asking who I was. Not like he was insulting me."

"It's just weird," I mutter, frowning. Anna doesn't seem to like my reaction, since she scuffs at me.

"Why can't you just be happy that I found someone?"

"I am!" I protest, "I am happy for you. Cliff's just.. different from who I expected you to be with."

"Yeah, well, I didn't have much of a selection to pick from since you took the two hottest guys out of the league," Anna's tone is playful, but it still 'causes me to cringe at her words.

She didn't really think that, did she? That I was taking away every guy she liked?

Anna wasn't like that. She wouldn't get upset and let stupids boys get in the way of our friendship. Would she?

"It's not like I asked for it," I mutter. And it's the truth. All I really wanted to do was tell Anna the complete truth at that time.

This was practically eating me up inside and I just wanted someway to out my emotions. But I couldn't do that without spilling my secret that I'm actually a freaking werewolf. I'm sure Anna would never believe that, anyway.

"I know," Anna says lowly, "Besides, I have Cliff now. So I'm happy." She shrugs, "Hows things going with Adam?"

"Non existent," I reply, "Like it's always been."

"And Liam?"

"Same." I say, grabbing the rest of my papers and stuffing them in my locker before I close it abruptly making sure they won't fall out again. "I should get to class before I get any later. See you in dentition?" I joke. Anna laughs with a nod.

"Yeah, see you later Ron."

I give her a curt nod and turn on my heel, shoving my hands in my pockets while walking to the office. Though I'm glad Anna and I have finally talked, I'm still not so sure I really wanted to know about her and Cliff.

It just added to my list of things to worry about.

The morning drags on once again for the third day. Then again, I did spend half of my morning with Anna..

Either way, the morning goes by slowly and it's another agonizing day of teachers nagging at me. It's no surprise when I get detention for being late and not completing the homework assignment.

By the time I get to lunch, I'm ten minutes late for that as well. Though it's not my fault. It was my teacher's instead who decided it would be fun to lecture me on being responsible. I didn't listen to half of it. I only nodded and pretended to care.

All I really have on my mind is talking to Adam at the moment. Mainly because I'm desperate for answers.

I don't bother getting lunch since the line is too long by now. I make my way over to Anna who sits with Cliff closely by her side, giggling at something he's said. I interrupt when I say, "Have you seen Adam? I need to talk to him."

Anna scowls me, obviously annoyed I've stepped in on their conversation, though she replies, "No."

My eyes slowly drag over to Cliff, "Have you?"

"I heard he was rehearsing for the play," He says with a shrug. Mandy glares at him from the corner of her eyes, probably upset that now I know where Adam is so I can talk to him. What a jealous idiot.

"Thanks," I give Cliff a nod and Anna one as well before I jog off out of the lunch room, down the hall, to the theater. I swing open the heavy set of doors to see Mr. Taylor yelling at everyone once again.

I don't need to ask him where Adam is, since Mr. Taylor sees me first and says, "He's in the back. Make it quick."

"Sure thing," I mutter and find my way into the back, though I have to dodge a string of dancers who are performing once I get up on the stage.

I hurriedly yank the curtain back and find Adam sitting at his high chair, mumbling to himself while playing with his fingers.

I could only bet that he was rehearsing his lines.

"Hey," I say, catching his attention. I can see him stiffen and shift uncomfortably in his chair.

"Hello," He responds in a monotone, keeping his eyes on the sheet of paper before him.

"Cliff and Anna, huh?" I muse and take a few steps closer to where he is, resting my hand on the desk in front of him and staring at his reflection in the long mirror.

I can see his jaw clench and he gives a jerky nod, "Yeah."

"What's your father got planned?" I blurt, unable to hold it in any longer. Though I've only been here for what, three minutes? And I'm already dying of anxiousness.

Adam doesn't reply. Instead, he stands and makes a move to get away. I don't give him the chance when I grap his elbow and wrench him back to me. "Don't walk away from me."

"You've done it to me plenty of times, why can't I?"

"Your life isn't on the line, isn't it?" I shoot back. He goes silent at that and I release my tight grip on him, glaring at the back of his head. "I didn't think so."

"It's not my fault you don't listen to my father," He spat, turning to face me with burning eyes. "If you listened, you wouldn't get hurt."

"I'm not about to be anyone's lap dog," I say and clench my fist at my side. "I'm not going to follow your orders nor your fathers. I'm not a coward. I'm not a coward like you."

"I'm not a coward," He says it so calmly, so lowly, as if he's trying not only to convince me that he's not a coward, but himself.

"You are," I prompt, "If you weren't, you wouldn't have stopped being my friend because of what people said about me. If you weren't, you wouldn't have left me when I needed you most. If you weren't, you wouldn't let your father do this to me, Adam. You wouldn't."

My voice is thick with strain. And it's almost painful to force these words beyond my lips. It's because I've never voiced them before. I've never voiced how much it hurt when he left me in the dust when I needed him most.

Again, Adam greets me with silence. And it only seems to anger me. Why can't he give m a answer? Why can't he just tell me why he truly stopped being my friend?

Then again, why did I care? I didn't need him. I didn't.

I bit down painfully on my lip to keep down the scream that's building up inside of me. I force myself to bite down my harsh words. He's not worth it. He's not worth my breath, my time, nothing.

Still, I can't help but whisper brokenly, "You were supposed to be my best friend."

Though the feeling is light, I can sense the thin line of blood that runs down my lips. And soon enough, I can taste my coppery blood in my mouth.

"You're right," He admits slowly, "I'm sorry."

"Sorry doesn't cut it," I reply harshly, pushing away the pain that tightens in my chest. "You have to help me, Adam. You have to tell me what he's going to do."

"I can't," He shakes his head, and I'm ready to object when he says, "The night of the formal ball. Be careful and don't do anything stupid. Maybe it won't happen then."

"You have to tell me so I can avoid it," I say, "Tell me. Please."

"I can't, Ronnie," He repeats. Though this time his voice is stronger. "Just be careful, alright?"

I don't reply. And he doesn't give me the time since he's off. I don't chase after him. Instead I stand hopelessly watching him walk away. Just like he had done four years ago.

I stay majorly late after school. Since I have both detention and the back drops. Lucky for me, I managed to worm my way out of detention half way and got to go to the art room.

I worked alone, painting in silence, which wasn't that bad. Because it gave me time to focus. I bet if Liam was with me, all he'd do is distract me. Still, I missed him.

And I sat staring at his normal seat for a few minutes with a frown, as if I was just expecting him to suddenly appear.

I just wanted to know where he was right now. What he was doing. And that might seem a little stalker-ish, but I was worried. Could you blame me?

I mean, what could be more important than coming to school the past two days? Never mind. That was a stupid question.

Anything was way better than coming to school.

But he had been here most of the time to annoy me, and now that he wasn't here, it was just weird. The suspense was killing me, and I couldn't resist thinking, what if he was hurt?

Then the worst thought occurred to me, what if he was hurting someone else?

As much as I liked to believe that maybe meeting me had changed him, I doubt it. He couldn't change his ways in such a short period of time.

And if he did, it definitely wouldn't be because of me.

He was so damn secretive, yet I didn't know if I liked it or hated.

I rid myself of the thought soon enough and carry on with what I'm doing. That night I walk home in cold night, and my thin leather jacket does me no good.

It's not till I'm about half way home that I take a detour into the woods, mainly because of the fact I didn't like the tinted window cars that passed by and always seemed to slow down once they saw me. I bolt off once the third car does that.

I shift into wolf form easily, trotting slowly, keeping me eyes peeled for any weird movement. Though I shift back once I know I'm close to the boundary that will directly lead me to my home.

I'm almost there when I hear a ruffle of leaves not too far away from me. I immediately spin around and with my sharp eyes, I scan the woods looking for something. Anything.

But there's no one in sight.

Maybe I'm just being paranoid, I think meekly. Though I can't shake off the feeling of fear. Especially when I see a figure flash right be me.

And then crash right into me.

The scream builds up in my throat and it seems to stuck there as I stare up at the man above me wide eyed. He looks familiar. So incredibly familiar.

I scramble away from him, staring wide eyed at the man before me. He seems to do the same. He's stiff, as if he's expecting me to attack him or something.

"It's you," He croaks.

I don't understand him at first, till I recognize the familiar scent on him. The one that reeks of rotting flesh. The only odor the Purgatory pack possesses.

Horror masks my face and I'm ready to launch off when he reaches for me, his finger tips brush my arm before a large figure comes pounding from behind a thick tree bark and crashes right into the man.

And before I know it, I can see another figure immerse behind from a thick bark of the tree, and they come barreling down into him.

I can't recognize who it is, since they're in wolf from. But I also know this scent.

I watch in complete utter silence and horror as this large, brown wolf claws at the man's face. All I can hear is the man's blood curling screams. He pleads for mercy, he begs for mercy. Yet it all fails and the mysterious, but familiar, wolf isn't having any of it.

Instead, it wears somewhat of a human smirk on his face. As if it's laughing. Laughing at the fact he's taking the guy's life.

The man's screams soon die out once the wolf clamps it's teeth down on his neck and decapitates him.

A scream rips from my throat before I can stop it. This catches the wolfs attention and I find myself staring into a pair of green eyes. Liam's green eyes.

He transforms slowly back into his human form, racing his hands and taking a step towards me, as if he's trying to assure me he won't hurt me.

Though I tell myself he won't, I can't help but stare at the blood that coats his hands. The man he's just killed blood.

I'm up and running by then, looking over my shoulder as my feet thud against the forest ground. I can hear his calls for me, but it only causes me to push myself faster.

I swallow down the scream that crawls up my throat, Liam is a monster. Liam is a monster. Liam is a monster.

That's the only thought that goes through my head. And it's completely and utterly true.

I had just witnessed Liam kill a man. And the worst part of it all, is that he felt no remorse. Though, yes, the man was apart of the Purgatory pack and I'm sure the man deserved it, I can't shake the feeling that rises in my stomach. The sickening feeling.

He didn't even show guilt when the man pleaded with him. Instead he just looked like he enjoyed it. But what I had expected? Liam was a rogue. Is a rogue. Killing what was he known from. But it still felt like a huge shock.

Mainly because I never really wanted to believe Liam was the monster everyone said he was. I wanted it to be all fake.

Yet it was all true. All true.

And It was only just a preview of what he really is capable of.

CHAPTER 14

I run for what feels like hours. I run till my legs burn massively and I can no longer go on, no matter how loud Liam's footsteps are behind me.

Instead of running to the pack houses, I run in the opposite direction in fear that Liam will be foolish and reveal himself to the entire pack.

I knew he was frantic enough to speak to me right now. And yes, I had seen him just take another man's life, but I wasn't about to let him get himself killed. Especially not by Alpha Beckett.

So that's why I find myself lost in the forest. No idea where I am. And the worst part is, I can't even feel, nor hear, Liam after me anymore.

I guess I had managed to lose him all a long the way. Though I bet he would find me in a matter of minutes. Seconds, perhaps.

I collapse shortly after, breathing heavily while pressing a hand to my chest, as if to prevent my pounding heart from flying out.

"Ronnie!"

My head shoots up in the direction of his voice. He's close by. I can tell now because his shouts start to get closer and closer. And so does his powerful footsteps.

I force myself to my feet, screaming at myself to keep going. That Liam is a monster. But I can't bring myself to.

Instead, I stay and watch the trees ahead of me, waiting for him to emerge. He doesn't disappoint when he appears only seconds later.

He stops only a few feet away from me, staring at me with glowing green eyes. Neither of us say anything for a while, the only sound is my ragged breathing.

Even if we did speak, I wouldn't know what to say. This was a new side of Liam that I wasn't familiar with. How do you speak to someone's who's just killed another person, anyway?

Sure, the man was in the Purgatory pack, but it's still scary. Scary to a point where when Liam advances towards me, I have no choice but to step back.

"Ronnie," He breathes, holding out his hand to me, but I quickly back up and stare at the crimson blood that coats his hand.

Now that I look closer at him, I can see blood on his clothes as well. And some on his face too. Though I don't know if it's his or not.

The thought makes me shiver and I truly wonder if that man he slaughtered in front of me was really the only man he's killed tonight.

I tremble uncontrollably and my lips part, words and questions stuck in my throat. I don't know whether to run or stay.

To hear him out. But was there really a good enough excuse to killing someone?

There wasn't.

I needed to stop being a foolish girl and open my eyes and see Liam for what he really is. A murderer.

"Ronnie," He repeats, his voice is strained, "Come here. Please."

I shake my head faintly, so you can get me in your grip and kill me? No thanks.

Liam flinches. He's probably heard what I've just thought, but I don't care. I'm completely in a state of panic and shock, and I can't seem to shake myself out of it.

Liam would never hurt me. He wouldn't. He cares about me, I have somewhat of a mini battle with myself. One side agrees that Liam would never hurt me, but the other side doesn't.

I don't know what to believe and what not to. I was running on instinct right now and Liam, currently soaked in blood, wasn't helping with my panicking.

He takes two steps towards me. I take two steps back.

He continues towards me, his hand out reached for me. Eventually, I collide against a tree bark and I'm caged there when Liam stops in front of me.

He looks down at me with thoughtful eyes, while I tremble helplessly underneath him. He reaches forward to cup my cheek, but I surprise not only him, but myself, when I muster up all the strength I have to give him a shove.

He doesn't even jolt.

"Don't touch me," I manage to utter. Though my voice is shaky.

His eyes flash with something I can't read and dreadfully, he lets his arm fall limp back to his side. "I would never hurt you."

And as if to reassure me, he places his hand on my arm. I quickly wrench it back, "Stay away from me!" My shout is hoarse and dry. I attempt to get away but Liam grasps both of my shoulders, keeping me in place.

"Let me explain, Ron," He says gruffly, "Let me explain."

"No!" I flail around in his arms, "Let go of me! Let go!"

His hands travel up my arms and to my face, where he cups both of my cheeks, forcing me to look at him.

Though I've always loved his touch, this time I don't. Mostly because his hands are wet. Wet with blood that is now on my cheeks.

"I did it to protect you. I did it because I was keeping you safe. I did it because I-"

I cut him off when I send a kick to his 'area.' He immediately releases me with a pain stricken gasp and a string of profanities.

I don't run. I reach up and rub my cheeks raw to get the tainted blood off of me, but all it does is convert it to my hands.

I wail in horror as I stare down at me my hands that are now covered in the man's blood. I almost feel like crying, but I don't. I can't.

I let out sounds I can't decipher. All I know is that they're full of horror and shock. Mostly importantly pain.

That's when I run again. This time, I run straight back home. Desperate to get there where I can hide under my cotton fortress. Where I can block out the world and pretend this night never happened. But it did. And I can't erase it from my memory no matter how hard I try.

I almost want to turn around when I hear Liam's strangled screams for me. They're so pain filled and.. animalistic as he pleads with me to come back to him.

I don't give in no matter how much I want to.

I continue on going until I reach the clearing, luckily, no one is outside to stop me. I go pounding into my home, sprinting towards the sink, turning on the water and scrubbing my skin raw with soap. No matter how much I try to remove the crimson blood from my hands, it still leaves a thin coat of red on my hands.

It's probably barely noticeable to most, but It's not to me. Especially because I know the story behind it.

When I realize it's not going to come off, I slide down the wall, burying my hands in my hair and shaking my head, as if to rid myself of the memories.

It doesn't work.

Especially when I go to sleep that night and I'm awaken by numerous nightmares. And I relive the feel of blood not only my hands, but everywhere.

Though the victim in my dreams isn't the man Liam killed. It's me. And Liam is the one who makes me his prey.

It's always a new place where the scene takes place. At first, it was the woods. Then it was my home. Then it was my school. And so on.

But it contains one event that is always in my nightmares.

My death.

I'm completely restless the next day at school. I'm like a zombie as I walk down the halls. Many people try talking to me, including Anna, but all I do is stare at the ground.

It's stupid, I know.

But I can't manage to put a smile on my face. Especially not when Liam appears at school.

I avoid him at all cost and try to blend in with the crowd. Though that won't save me either. Maybe I was taking this a little overboard.

And maybe I wasn't.

I had seen Liam kill someone. Was that really overreacting if I was shaken up by it? I had a good reason to be.

Hours drag on till lunch, and I immediately sit with Adam and Anna. Along with Cliff, Kara, and Mandy. I may not like them, but I definitely was not going to bait myself to Liam sitting alone where he could talk to me.

"Ron?" Anna's voice brings me out of my trance. And I'm glad, since I was honestly starting to get a head from thinking so damn much.

I lazily glide my eyes over to her, giving her my acknowledgement.

"Are you okay?" She asks quietly. I nod stiffly and look away, no longer being able to stand the sight of Anna and Cliff's entangled hands together.

I just couldn't get over the fact they were now dating. And how Cliff gave me the creeps.

I didn't trust him one bit. And certainly not with Anna.

He always looked at me with a smirk, one that he seemed to be doing even more today, as if he knew something I didn't.

I couldn't help but wonder if Anna had told him something she wasn't supposed to. She was practically wrapped around his finger, so I wouldn't be shocked.

Then again, why did I care? My life right now was a living hell with Alpha Beckett. Cliff couldn't make it any worse with the little secrets Anna had told him.

If her telling him those secrets about me kept them together, then so be it. I rather they not break up and Anna is left utterly heartbroken.

She wasn't one to take break up's lightly. When Anna fell for someone, she fell hard and fast. Just like she has for Cliff.

That was the difference between the two of us.

I was a lot more cautious about who I let around me and who I didn't. As much as I hate to say so, I get hurt sometimes too. I'm not emotionless. Though Anna thinks so because I've never once cried in front of her.

I didn't like crying. And besides, my life wasn't that bad that I was about to become some sniveling fool.

The only thing I've ever cried about was my mother's death. And I wanted to keep it like that.

"Are you sure you're okay?" The question comes from Adam this time who sits next to me. And I guess we're on speaking terms now.

"I'm fine," I reply and keep my eyes trained forward. I discover it's not so great of an idea when Liam comes into sight.

I meet his eyes for a brief second, but it's long enough for me to see he's pleading at me to speak with him. To make it evident, he says directly through our link, don't block me out.

My eyes immediately avert to the food in front of me and I study it for a while, feeling Liam's burning gaze right on me. But I don't look up. No matter how much I want to.

The day go slowly and quietly. For most of my classes, I stare out the window, watching the black clouds swirl and flash with lightening.

Soon enough, it's raining and it only brings me deeper into my depressing state.

Luckily for me, the day ends. And I'm free. Well, slightly, seeing as I still have the backdrops for Ms. J to finish.

And Liam is actually here today, so of course, I can't avoid having to do the backdrops with him. I sluggishly make my way to the art room and brace myself before walking in, already seeing Liam there in his usual seat.

He looks up once I enter the room, catching my curious gaze. We don't say anything for the longest while. All we do is watch each other for a numerous amount of minutes till I finally manage to say, "Are you ready to work?"

Liam nods. And I quickly grab a brush or two and a few bottles of paint before I settle down and start. Liam numbly follows my lead.

We paint in silence and for that, I'm grateful. Because I honestly don't know what to say after out little episode together.

Not knowing what to say at all was starting to become an annoying habit of mine, clearly.

We work for hours, so much that by the time night time falls, we've completed two full back drops. Which is pretty crazy if you ask me.

I lean back on my heels and wipe my hand across my forehead, in the process smearing paint on my forehead. But I don't care.

I get back to work shortly after and we're half way finished when Liam grunts and tosses the paintbrush to the side. "What are you doing?" I ask hurriedly, watching him roll his wrist and hearing a faint crack.

"My wrist hurts like a bitch," He mutters, "We've been going at this for hours. Can't we take a break?"

"No," I reply, "We need to have these finished in two weeks. We're never going to get there if you want to take breaks. Well, I don't think we will since you're always disappearing anyway."

Sometimes I really wish you'd disappear for good and stop playing with my heart, I think faintly. And I know he's heard me since he tenses at my words.

"I'm sorry," He says lowly. And I figure there's a double meaning behind his words. Not only is he apologizing for the fact he hasn't helped me at all this week, but probably for what I saw in the woods the other day.

"Sorry doesn't really work with this situation," I whisper, pausing with my brush. With a shake of my head, I continue on slowly painting and filling the canvas with colors.

Liam puts his hand over mine, quickly halting my movements and causing me to look at him. "Maybe explaining will."

"Liam, I really don't have-"

"Talk to me," He somewhat demands, "Insult me or anything but don't block me out."

"I can't do this right now Liam." I close my eyes, letting out a sharp breath. "I have to finish this. And I'm honestly in no mood to fight."

My voice is weak and barely above a whisper. But it's true. I don't even want to talk. Because that would just bring back the memory of it all.

I want to forget about it all. I know I can't, but a girl can hope and dream, can't she?

I force myself to remove my hand. He let's me. And he get's up at the same time, grabbing his jacket from the chair and shrugging it on.

"Where are you going?" I ask. No reply comes except for the long bang of the door as it closes. I flinch and stare at the blue door that Liam is just behind.

I almost want to get up and chase after him. I want to hear him out. To forget about Adam, Alpha Beckett, and the ball. I want to get lost in our own little world. But that will never happen. No matter how hard I shut my eyes and wish that this was a different time. A different place. Where Liam wasn't a rogue and I wasn't promised to another guy.

I was confused. Confused about my feelings and my thoughts and I just felt like this helpless little girl. And I guess I was.

I was weak. And stupid. And torn over a stupid guy.

I shake my head angrily, I needed to focus on the more important things in my life then Liam Farley. And that's exactly what I did. Well, at least for the weekend.

I spend it mostly with Adam's mother, preparing for the ball which is next Saturday night. My dress is completely finished and I try it on for the first, a long with the mask.

Everyone tells me I look beautiful. As if I'm some type of princess. But I certainly don't feel like one.

I manage to muster up a smile for them and give my thanks, saying how brilliant Mrs. Beckett was for helping me out with it.

Though Mrs. Beckett is nice, she got on my nerves with her constant nagging. She constantly picked at every little flaw and made it her job to correct them all.

Like my posture. Or the way I spoke. Or what language I used. By Sunday, I was sick of it and decided to spend time with Anna.

I briefly did for a while, but it became too much with Cliff constantly around and them sucking face. I depart from them and find my way home.

Adam is around, but not much. He seems to be preparing for the ball just as much. It's a shock Monday after school that he appears at my door step.

"Can I help you?" I ask, raising a brow at him as I open the door.

He nods stiffly, "Uh, yeah. We got ballroom dancing classes right now and we kinda need you."

"Ballroom dancing classes? I didn't agree to that," I frown when he grabs my hand and starts to tug me away from my house. I shut the door to my house and I let myself be pulled a long for the ride.

"That's because my mother didn't want to scare you off." He replies and we enter the house quickly, where he leads me to the dining room.

They've pushed the table to the far right wall that it gives us enough empty space to well, dance, I guess.

And in the center of it all stands Mrs. Beckett with a large grin on her face. "Oh, this is going to be so exciting!"

"For you, maybe," I mumble, earning a hard nudge to the ribs from Adam. "What? I was being honest."

"No, that was rude, Ronnie. Manners, sweetheart, manners." Mrs. Beckett says, not even phased by what I've just said. But she's gotten use to it these past days she's spent with me. I've actually been quite rude to her at times. Each time she simply corrects me.

I grunt, "Kill me now."

"Be careful what you wish for," Adam gives me a grim smile and thrusts a pair of black heels into my chest. "Now put those on."

"I have to wear these?" I twiddle around the heels in my hand, as if I'm expecting them to magically disappear. I was kinda hoping they would.

"Obviously. You can't wear those horrible boots to the formal ball," She looks down at my feet and her lips curl in disgust. "God, they are awful."

I grimace, but comply, seeing no way out of it. I slip off my boots and chuck them aside, nearly laughing when my dirty boots collide against her shiny floors and she cringes at the sight.

I have to balance myself with holding onto Adam's shoulder as I slip on the high heels. Once I've strapped them on, I stand, only to have Adam grasp onto me tightly so I don't fall on my face.

"Now, Ronnie, place your arms around his neck." Mrs. Beckett commands. I really don't want to, but I suck it up and slowly wrap my arms around his neck while he places his hands on my hips.

It feels weird. Really, really weird. And wrong. It doesn't feel the way it did when Liam wrapped me in his arms, I think faintly, swallowing roughly and meeting Adam's eyes.

I can't look in them for long because I just see Alpha Beckett's face flash before me. I almost recoil back, but I remind myself this isn't Alpha Beckett. This is Adam. The boy I'll never love like the pack wants me to.

The music begins to play, bringing me out of my daze and I'm forced to focus on my feet rather then my thoughts. Not that I'm complaining.

"Let him lead, Ronnie," Mrs. Beckett says, "He is the man. He leads."

"How sexist," I mutter and Adam purposely steps on my toes for that. "Ouch!"

"My bad," Adam gives me a sheepish grin with amusement clear in his eyes.

I glower at him silently and press my lips into a thin line to resist insulting him. I follow Adam's lead like Mrs. Beckett says. Of course, I decide to get revenge so when Adam twirls me, I step on his foot. Digging my heel into his shoe.

He winces, though his grim smile never wavers. I return a bitter sweet one of my own.

This continues on for a while till Mrs. Beckett get's to frustrated with my constant tripping and falling that she dismisses.

And that's how it continues on for the rest of the week leading up to Thursday. It's almost a routine that I get back from school and directly head over to the Beckett's for dancing lessons.

I don't really get better, but I somewhat progress to where I can stand on my own. And that's probably the best I'll get to, seeing as I can't dance to save my life.

The week is slow. Not that I'm complaining.

I honestly don't want the date of the ball to come around. I just don't really want Saturday to come around, mainly because I discovered the Young Artist exhibit that day too.

I can't help but wonder if Liam is expecting me to show up or something. Even if I did, he probably wouldn't be there.

He had been absent the whole week and when I went for runs late at night, he never appeared like I was secretly hoping he would.

Had he been absent from school because he was trying to avoid me?

Maybe. I wasn't sure. Then again, I wasn't sure about anything anymore. All that was really on my mind was the ball.

And how I'm going to have to act like Adam's mate. That's all that swirls around my head Friday and to make myself forget, I swing by the art room to get some work done on the back drops, knowing it'll take my mind off of things.

To my surprise, when I walk in, I see Ms. J there too.

"Ronnie!" She squeals with a smile, "Aren't you excited?"

I frown, tossing my bag on a chair. "For what?"

"The Young Artist exhibit! You must be, you're apart of it!"

My eyebrows furrow, "What are you talking about? I'm not apart of it. I don't even know what you mean by that."

Now it's Ms. J's turn to frown. "Liam hasn't told you?"

"Told me what?"

"That he sent your painting there and talked to them about show casing it," Ms. J says slowly, "They loved it, so they put it apart of the show."

My lips part in disbelief, Liam sent my painting to the Young Artist exhibit? That was practically the hardest show to get in for upcoming artist who wanted a chance at the big time stuff!

"Why would he do that?" I mumble, mostly to myself. But Ms. J answers.

"That boy is just crazy about you," Ms. J shakes her head, "I may be old, but even I can see it."

I cringe. It was weird enough hearing it from Anna that Liam 'liked' me, but hearing it from Ms. J, a teacher, was even more weird.

And I still didn't understand why he wouldn't go through all of that just to get my painting show cased. Maybe he did care, I think meekly.

Maybe he was just look out for me. Maybe he was just trying to protect me because he cared. And all a long I had been cruel and blocked him off.

Perhaps Liam wasn't a monster. I guess I was just seeing it all wrong and he was trying to show me truth. But it was all blurred with all the lies.

That night, I return home and look at the ticket Liam had given me. I tell myself It's stupid to contemplate even going, but I can't help but want to.

I stuff it in my drawer, out of my sight and out of my mind. I slip into bed that night, thinking about tomorrow and the ball.

I can't sleep at first till I pull up Liam's leather jacket. It's not till I press my face against it and inhale his soothing scent that I seem to drift off.

But my looming fate of what's to come tomorrow still hovers in the back of mind. And I was so not ready for it.

Chapter 15

The ball's today. And I'm so not ready for it.

The morning started off seemingly normal, and I really tried to shake off my nerves, but I couldn't. Especially when Mrs. Beckett came around and chatted about how many people would be at the ball tonight.

She told me I had to make a pristine impression. Since, I was the Adam Beckett's mate. I nodded the whole time, though I wasn't really paying attention.

After about three hours of discussing of how I'm going to walk, talk, and act, it's about 1 PM when Mrs. Beckett decides to get to work on me.

I sit quietly through most of it, till she gets to my hair and starts to tug my braid loose. That's when I grip her hand and still her movement. "What are you doing?"

Mrs. Beckett grunts and yanks her hand from my tight grasp, "I'm taking out this braid. You can't wear that to the ball."

"Why not?"

"Because you're not twelve years old anymore, Ronnie. You're a young lady." She says this perfectly and calmly, not giving me another minute to reply as she threads her fingers in my hair and pulls it all apart.

I let out a frustrated sigh, she sounds exactly like Anna.

I don't say much after that, nor do I protest when she begins to put makeup on me. I figure I have no absolute say in any of this.

I manage to break away after she's finished with my hair and makeup. I made up some stupid excuse that I needed to go to the bathroom.

I was aiming to perhaps get out side and get some fresh air, but I fail miserably when I end up lost in Adam's huge house.

I peek into the rooms as I pass. Most of them are empty and each one leads to another dead end.

That is, till I peer into a room that looks oddly familiar, yet different at the same time; I stop and despite the voice in my head that tells me to turn away, I can't help my curiosity.

I push the door open a little more to where I can see a bed and a wooden desk. My eyes scan the room, taking in the blue walls.

Before I can convince myself to turn around and walk away, I go into the room slowly, glancing over my shoulder to see if anyone is coming.

The room is big, though much of the space isn't really taken up. Besides the bed and desk, there isn't much else but a TV plastered on the wall and numerous photos on the wall.

I realize it's Adam's room when I spot a picture of him on one of the walls. It's one of him when he was young, smiling goofy at the camera with tomato sauce smeared all over his face.

I smile faintly at the picture and look to see more photos of him, mostly with his friends and pack mates.

I halt in front of his desk, fingering his objects on the desk which is really just a colon bottle, a lamp, and what appears to be a book of sort.

At first, I tinker around with the colon bottle, running my fingers over the glass. I give it a sniff too, only to cringe in disgust when I realize how strong it smells. I settle it down quickly, resisting the urge to sneeze.

I look around for a while, my eyes constantly darting to that small black book on his desk. I itch with temptation and I can't stand it for long.

I give in and grasp the thin book.

Once I confirm that no one is coming, nor looking for me, I peel it open hesitantly. Immediately as I do, something falls out from the tiny book.

My eyebrows furrow as I pick up what fell from the book. I discover it's a crumpled photo when I flip it over and it reveals my smiling face that stares right back up at me.

My breath catches in my throat at the sight.

I'm not the only one in the picture. Adam's there too. And we're much younger, probably ten years old from what I can tell.

I have my arms wrapped around Adam while he has his arms around me too. Instead of beaming at the camera like I am, Adam is gazing at the side of my face with a smile of his own tugging at the corner of his lips.

I slam the picture down when I can't look at it any longer. Why does he have a picture of me?

MRS. Beckett's words replay over in my head; when she was telling me that Adam talked about me and how he liked me.

My stomach clenches tightly. Adam doesn't like me. It's just a stupid picture, I tell myself this repeatedly. But it doesn't help one bit.

"What are you doing?"

The familiar voice makes me jump and I hurriedly whirl around, only to find Adam practically two feet away from me. "Adam," I breath shakily, "Hi."

"What are you doing?" He repeats and tries to push me out of the way, but I keep firm.

"Nothing." I reply with a small shrug, "Why? Scared I found your porn stash?"

Adam grunts, "No. I just don't like people going through my stuff." With that, he dodges around me and swats my hand away that's clamped on the picture. He speedily grasps it and the small black book.

Adam doesn't say anything as he stuffs the picture back in the book. And neither do I. But now that he knows I've seen the picture, I want to ask him why he has it.

But I don't.

Instead, I stare at him silently as he looks down at the book.

We sit in silence for a while till Adam faintly whispers, "It's nothing."

"It didn't look like nothing," I manage to utter, "Why do you have it?"

"It's just a stupid picture I kept over the years, okay?" His voice is cold. Venomous. And obviously not willing to continue on with this conversation.

I sigh, suddenly wishing I would have found his porn stash instead. Though it would still be awkward, it wouldn't be like this. And that's probably really weird to say.

"Yeah, because keeping picture of girl's you use to be friends with totally isn't weird." I mutter sarcastically.

"Aren't you supposed to getting ready for the ball?" Adam asks abruptly, moving away from me and to his dresser, where he stuffs the book in. "It's only two hours away."

"What time is it?"

"Four," Adam replies.

"Aren't you supposed to be getting ready for the ball, too?"

"Not really," He shakes his head, "All I have to is get dressed. But I can do that five minutes before we go."

"Lucky you," I mumble, "Your mother has been terrorizing me for the last three hours."

"Well, you look nice, if that helps."

I frown, still wondering about the picture. But I decide I'm not in the mood for fighting over it right now. All I want is to get this day over with it. I'm about to reply when I hear Adam's mother shouting my name.

I groan and pinch the bridge of my nose. Adam laughs at my obvious misery. "Did you run away from her?" He asks, his lips twitching up into a smirk.

"Maybe," I answer with a slight shrug.

Though Mrs. Beckett chooses to scream at that moment, shouting, "Ronnie, come back this instance! We have to get your dress on!"

"You should go," Adam says, "She'll get angry if she thinks I've been hiding you this whole time."

I nod stiffly, "I guess."

But I don't even have the time to get out of Adam's room since Mrs. Beckett appears at the door, looking flustered and frustrated. All because of me, probably. "There you are!"

"Sorry," I begin quickly, "I got lost on the way to the bathroom. So I ended up in Adam's room."

Mrs. Beckett rolls her eyes and waves me over with her hand, "Sure you did. Now come on, we have only two hours."

I sigh and walk over to her slowly. Immediately, she grasps my wrist and pulls me off, nearly pulling my arm out of the socket at the same time. I don't complain, though. I just let her drag me off, considering I have no say in any of it.

Once we get back, she hurriedly shoves me in the dress and does all my touch ups. It's about thirty minutes till we have to leave that she stands me up and makes me face the full length mirror, wearing a grin on her face. "What do you think?"

I'm breathless for a minute as I stare into the mirror. I watch the girl in the reflection mimic my movements as I reach up and touch my mask. And I just can't come to believe that this girl is me. Not because I'm overwhelmed by my beauty or such, but because I look so different.

I have a floor length golden dress on, two slits up the side showing off a daring amount of skin, and a long golden train leading right behind me. I'm afraid if I walk, I'll trip on it and go tumbling forward.

Not to mention the mask I have on doesn't help.

I can still see through the small holes where the eyes are meant to be, but I'm constantly having to readjust it so it won't come sliding off my face. I'm worried that while I'm walking, I'll have to adjust it and in that short period of time, I'll fall.

And these stupid heels didn't help either. It's like Mrs. Beckett was setting me up for disater. And I had a feeling this night was going to be a complete mess.

"And what do you think of your hair? Pretty, right? Much better than that ugly braid," She mutters the last part to herself, running a hand through my sleek waves.

I make a face at her and swat her hand away from my hair. "Yeah, great. Now aren't you supposed to go get ready?"

Mrs. Beckett glares at me from the corner of her eyes - Probably because I had hit her - but sighs, giving me a curt nod. "I suppose you're right. I'll go get dressed then I'll be back. Stay put."

I roll my eyes at her, "Whatever."

"Manners, Ronnie!" She calls as she struts out the door, finally leaving me alone. I nearly cheer once she's out of sight, that is, till I remember I'll be sending the whole evening with her at the ball. She would be constantly reminding me how to talk, walk, and act the whole time there, no doubt.

I turn back to the mirror, running my fingers over the white and gold mask that sparkles whenever my face finds the light. I stare into the reflection, though this girl looks beautiful, she doesn't feel like she is by the dull look in her bright blue eyes.

This is definitely a new side to me. And I'm not too sure if I feel it or not. I wasn't use to dressing up and playing someone's fake mate. I was kinda hoping I never would.

I can't help but let my thoughts draw back to Liam. If he's going to the Young Artist exhibit and waiting for me to show up.

I don't think Liam was that stupid, then again. After what I'd seen, he couldn't possibly think I'd be totally cool with it and go to the event with him.

At this moment, all I want is to disappear from sight. Perhaps spends hours painting and to stop worrying about everything around me. But was pretty cowardly, wasn't it?

Wanting to hide away from the world. From your problems. And mostly importantly, away from Alpha Beckett. Who had decided to dictate my life.

But that's what I am. A coward. Because I let Alpha Beckett control my life and my fate.

He was threatening to kill the only two people you care about, Ronnie, A small part of me argues, you put them before you. That's being self-less.

I try to believe this. Really, I do. I even repeat it over several times, hoping at some point I will come to think it's true. But as minutes past, which feel like hours, I can't.

And maybe that's why it was wrong of me to call Adam a coward. Because I'm one too.

I should be standing up to Alpha Beckett. I shouldn't let him control me. I've become something I've never wanted to be in my life. I've become just like my father.

Meaning, the pack's lap dog. Or well, more specifically, Alpha Beckett's lap dog.

And here I was, thinking I was strong. But that was a facade. A stupid facade that slowly withers away. Underneath it all, I'm weak. A weak, helpless, girl. Another thing I never wanted to become.

I ball my fist tightly at my side, my nails digging into my skin. I shake my head at myself, as if to rid myself of these painfully true thoughts. I tell myself to stop throwing myself some ridiculous pity party. The world isn't ending and I shouldn't cry over my feeble problems.

I look myself in the mirror, straightening my back and managing to appear indifferent instead of defeated. Like I really feel inside.

"Ronnie?"

I turn at the call of my name, facing the door way to see Adam there. Dressed in a black tux and his hair smoothed perfectly back. He smiles, an odd smile that I've become in-familiar with over the years.

"Yes?" I reply, suprised when I don't sound weak. Or shaky. I sound actually quite sullen. And I realize I'm a lot worse at hiding my true emotions then I thought.

His smile dims a bit, but he quickly recovers it, mustering up a fake smile. "The car's out front," He says, "My mother told me to come find you."

"Oh," I mutter, "Are they riding with us there?"

It may be a stupid question, but silently I pray that I won't get stuck siting in a car for God knows how long, staring at Alpha Beckett.

"Of course," He nods, "Why wouldn't they be?"

"No reason." I say with a slight shrug and walk over to him carefully, making sure I don't trip on the hem of my dress. Nor my heels. "Where's your mask?" I ask suddenly, finally noticing he doesn't have one on.

He reached into the pocket of his blazer, pulling out a small black mask and swiftly putting it on. "I don't know what you're talking about."

I roll my eyes at him and don't reply. We exit the room and walk down the empty hallway, the only sound to be heard is the click of my heels against the marble floor.

I'm sure Adam is too sucked into his thoughts to talk, anyway. He has this far away look in his eyes as we head off to car.

I wonder if he really wants to go to this ball. If he wants to put on a show for everyone and try to convince someone we're mates. And that we're so gleeful about it.

Surely not.

Adam wanted someone who really liked him, didn't he? A mate that would actually cherish him? It didn't seem like it. Since he had chosen me, the most difficult and stubborn girl in the whole pack.

The talk with Mrs. Beckett floats around in my head again. About him liking me. I swat it away like some annoying fly and instead, focus not on falling flat on my face.

We turn at a corner, passing many other family photos and vases of floors. Though the house is so nicely decorated, it still feels empty and sort of hollow.

And that's how it felt back at my own home as well. As if this wasn't where I belonged. And maybe it wasn't.

I don't have time to dwell on it for long, since we reach the stairs leading to the front door of the house. I climb down slowly and hitch up my dress. Adam walks in front of me, though he looks back at me frequently, as if afraid I'll come stumbling down and crash right into him. Then again, I might.

I'm grateful for when I'm on flat ground again, but that only lasts so long when I see Alpha Beckett's beaming face.

He grins madly at the two of us, appearing to be just that. A mad man. "Don't you two look wonderful!"

"Thank you. You look good too, dad." Adam gives him a sad attempt of a smile and Adam's eyes dart to me then his father, obviously indicating I should say thank you and probably give him some fake compliment.

"Thanks," is all I say. Quite harshly too.

"Smile, dear, smile. That's what you'll need to do tonight at the ball." Mrs. Beckett chirps and I finally realize she's standing right next to him.

Mrs. Beckett looks nice, I guess. She wears a form fitting black dress, black heels, and her makeup neatly applied.

"Right," I nod jerkily, "How could I forget?"

Mrs. Beckett gives me a grim smile, smoothing back her ashy blonde curls. "Well then, we should get a move on, shouldn't we?"

Alpha Becketts nods, wrapping his arm around his wife's waist. They both turn and walk out the already opened door. Adam and I quietly follow behind, briefly stopping to make sure the door is closed.

I'm not shocked when I notice an extremely nice black limo outside, though I think it's kinda cheesy. This isn't some stupid prom.

Of course it's not. Because this is much worse.

We reach the car and slide in. I take a seat as far away as I can from Alpha Beckett, though I end up sitting next to Adam. Still, I'm at least grateful I didn't get stuck with Alpha Douche bag.

The ride is nearly silent. Even Mrs. Beckett, who nearly talks all the time, is quiet. The only thing that is exchanged is nervous glances and fake smiles.

At one point, I find myself directly looking at Alpha Beckett. And he does the same. An emotion I can't detect dancing in his eyes.

Perhaps a warning. Trying to remind me that I shouldn't step out of line.

I look away once that leaks into my mind. I'm afraid I'll end up doing something drastic like strangling Alpha Beckett if I think about it any longer.

It's not a long ride. I know that since I saw the location on the flyer. But it's still in downtown, rather then the outskirts of town.

I stare out the window for most of it. I nearly stop breathing as we past the Young Artist exhibit. How I know that it's the exhibit? Mainly because of the flashy lights and huge red banner that broadcasts it.

My painting is actually in that exhibte, I think meekly, and I'm going to miss it.

I sigh inwardly, resisting the urge to fling myself right out of this car and go bounding up those steps.

We drive a few blocks over till we reach another building. One that I know is the ball's location. I see numerous people out in the front, all wearing masks and extravagant dresses.

I swallow roughly as we pull into some sort of carline that leads into the front of it. I watch as one man stands in the center, opening the car doors and gesturing the people down some cliche red carpet and into the fancy hotel that has probably been rented out for this special event.

It's our turn shortly, and that man I saw before opens the door, grinning wildly at us as he says, "The Beckett's! I was starting to think you weren't going to show up!"

Alpha Beckett laughs, "Of course we would. It wouldn't be a party without us."

The man quickly agrees and ushers us out of the car. Though when he reaches his hand out to me to help me out of the car, I don't take it.

I climb out easily by myself and proceed with trailing behind Alpha Beckett and his mate. They walk slowly, waving and exchanging words with others that walk by. As if they own the place.

Adam falls into step beside me as we enter the massive hotel, one that's filled with laughter and people, all with flashy dresses and suits. But it's not even the people in it that leave me in aw, but the hotel itself.

You can tell it's made for upper class people with the high crystal chandlers and the marble floors that radiate.

I feel like I've traveled back in time as I examine the vintage furniture. It's completely breath taking.

I've noticed I stopped to marvel at it all when Adam slips his hand into mine and pulls me a long, reminding me where I am.

I let him keep a hold of my hand while traveling deeper into the hotel. I know that it's time to start acting like we're some sappy mated couple.

We round a corner, one leading into a huge room filled with people who laugh and chatter loudly. I inhale sharply, taking in all the unfamiliar scents. Though it's easy to tell I'm in a room full of werewolves.

Adam grips me hand tight and I let him, since I'm aware of the numerous stares that linger on the both of us.

"Don't be shy," Mrs. Beckett calls to Adam and I, glancing over her shoulder, "Start mingling!"

"Right. Mingling," Adam says under his breath, barely audible.

Soon enough, we're being swung around the room, stopping to talk to many people who congratulate us about finally settling down with a mate.

They also tell me how beautiful I look. As if I'm some type of princess. I do my best to smile and speak politely. It's surely not my forte, especially when one man makes a snarky remark.

"So this is who you chose, Adam?" One boy, the same age as us, says. He looks towards me, raising his brows and raking over my body as if I'm some piece of meat. "Ain't much."

"I can tell you don't have much of a brain," I snap, drawing people's attention who are close by.

Adam laughs nervously, pulling me to his side while wrapping his arm around my waist and squeezing me to a point where it hurts. "She's kidding."

"Yeah," The unnamed boy scuffs, "Keep her on a tight leash, bro."

He walks off without another word. And I'm glad. Because I'm sure if he stuck around any longer, I'll lose it.

"What do you think you're doing?" Adam hisses to me, turning to face me with angry eyes, "Do you know who that was?"

"No, and I don't give a damn who he is frankly." I spat back and try to wrench myself from his grip, but all it does is make him tighten his hold on me.

"Marius is the next line in for Alpha, and I honestly don't want to piss off his pack." Adam says, glowering at me.

I look away from, my blood boiling. I try to focus my eyes on anything but Adam's burning eyes, but I can't seem to. Especially when I meet Alpha Beckett's eyes. He eyes me thoughtfully, calmly, even. But this time, the threat is clear in his eyes. Follow a long or something will certainly happen.

I don't say much after that. I follow Adam around reluctantly and take up dance offers with many strangers. Though I obviously don't want to. Adam does no such thing to help. All he does is insist on me dancing with them.

And I bet it's just so he thrust me on something else and get rid of me for a while.

The ball is just as dreadful as I knew it would be. Some are kind, some are sceptical, and others are just plain rude. Or quite perverse as they make dirty remarks about my appearance.

I find myself thinking of Liam the entire time. What he's doing right now. If he's at the exhibit. Or if he's off somewhere else.

I weakly try to contact him at one point threw our link. I don't get a reply.

My stomach tightens when he doesn't. Why he is angry at me?

Why did I care if he was, anyway? There was no reason to be mad at me. I wasn't the one who had killed someone. He had to understand I was completely freaked out by all of it.

Maybe he was angry because I hadn't heard him out when I should have. I bang my head on the subject practically the whole night, wishing I was with him, instead of a room filled with fake people who only like me for my status. Or my looks.

For the moments I'm not dancing, I spend with Adam. Chatting with people who I don't care about one bit.

Adam doesn't talk to me directly. Only if he needs to somehow get me involved in a conversation and appear to care about what's happening around me.

He sometimes shoots me what seems to be guilty glances. I'm pleased that he's actually conveying some type of emotion that shows he's not an emotionless robot.

And truly, I want him to feel gulity. For putting me threw this. For making me pretend like I want this when I really don't.

Then again, I wasn't quite sure of what I exactly wanted in my life, but whatever it was I did want, it surely didn't involve Adam.

It's only I decide to listen when Alpha Beckett appears on stage, eagerly calling Adam and I's names.

I don't want to go up. To make a fool of myself. But I'm forced to when Adam drags me up the steps and in front of a hundred or more judging eyes.

We take place next to another couple and I learn the boy that had insulted me previously, is Dash. He has picked his own mate, though she looks like a complete bimbo with bright orange, spray tan, skin and crumpled brown hair. A long with a face caked with makeup.

She oddly resembles those people from the Jersey Shore.

They introduce them and celebrate the fact in just a month Dash will be crowned Alpha of his pack. They kiss and cheer themselves, then are led off the stage.

I notice the same pattern continue on with the same other couples. They laugh at some corny joke Alpha Beckett tells and then kiss.

I become aware all too quickly. That this is the moment Mrs. Beckett has been waiting for. For Adam and I to finally kiss.

And frankly, it's sort of creepy. For one, his mother wants to see us kiss and all these strangers do too.

It'll be my first kiss as well.

Adam keeps me in tack when he notices I now know what's going to happen. It's either I do this or I don't. I know if I don't play off I'm some happy girl who's been chosen to mate with the Alpha, I will face the wrath of Alpha Beckett.

Still, I debate running right off this stage. Perhaps running off and never returning back home. Home.

Was this really my home?

My mother use to say to me that your home is where the people you love are. And I didn't love Alpha Beckett, Adam, or any one of these people in these room.

But I loved Anna. Or I think so. I'm not sure if I love my father. But how could I when I didn't know who he was anymore?

I hadn't seen him since that night he told me he was going to be gone. I wonder if he went somewhere, leaving me to fight for myself.

And then there was Liam.

I certainly didn't have a clue on what my emotions were towards him. But I knew I had a pull to him that went far deeper before just being mates. It was something I couldn't explain.

It doesn't feel forced like this. Or artificial like it does here. With Adam.

The question I wonder the most is if these people love me.

"Ronnie?" Adam nudges me softly, "It's our turn to step up." He tells me. Barely just above whisper.

I look into the sea of people, all to notice they're watching us. Waiting for us to make a move.

I suck in a sharp breath, exhaling shakily. I force my feet to move to where I stand directly next to Alpha Beckett, who holds a microphone with a large grin on his face. "And last, but not least, my son and his mate, Ronnie Mars."

They all clap, hollering congralulations to us. Adam waves and plasters on a bitter smile, acting as if he's the freaking president.

Lucky for me, the introduction doesn't stop there. And Alpha Beckett buys me time.

He dives into some heart felt speech about how he watched his son grow up to be the man he is now. The whole time, he speaks with a certain glint in his eyes. Another emotion I can't decipher.

I almost buy into it. That Alpha Beckett cares about the both of us and our happiness. He speaks so truthful, so sincere. But I know better.

Under that kind and giving act lays something much more deadly.

I realize I'm playing with something much more here then just fire. I'm playing with my life and the one's around me.

And it's all for me to mate with Adam.

"I knew he was going to grew up to such a well young man the minute he was born," Alpha Beckett says, glancing back at his son lovingly. "I love you son. And I am so proud of you."

For the added effect, Alpha Beckett steps forward and embraces his son in an hug. When Alpha Beckett pulls away, he wipes at some non-existent tears. The perfect ending to his speech.

He claps, and the crowd joins in. Soon enough, they are hollering, "Kiss, kiss, kiss!"

"Yes, let the crowd see a kiss!" Alpha Beckett agrees feverishly, stepping back and giving us space. Though it doesn't really help.

Adam grips my hand, making me face him. He seems nervous too. He licks his lips nervously, his eyes darting between the crowd and me.

They're quiet now. Obviously in anticipation.

"Let's get this over with, okay?" He whispers so lowly that I barely catch it. I know it's for my ears only to hear.

I nod, despite the screaming voice in the back of my head.

He removes my mask and his too. He tosses them to the side and takes a step closer to me, cupping my cheeks in his hand while I awkwardly rest mine on his chest.

We stare at each other in silence and I silently plead with him to stop this. Perhaps to stop everything.

His eyes tell me that his sorry. Especially when they darken into a deeper shade of brown rather than the regular hazel.

But that's all. There's no reassurance of sort that he's actually going to do something. Adam's just as weak as me, clearly. We both don't want to stand up and say something. I wonder what his reasons are.

My mind screams at me to turn away. To do something. It increases further when he starts to lean in, heading straight for my lips.

Turn away, Ronnie! Run! I can't ignore it. The feeling that makes me stomach churn and my palms sweat.

I don't want this. I don't want any of this.

I don't want to be kissed by Adam Beckett, I don't want to be his mate, I don't want to be controlled. I want none of it!

And I was sick and tired of being manipulated. This time, things were going to far. Would they force us to actually... really, really mate? As in to do the deed? It's what normally happened after being marked. And it was almost a seal of love.

If I couldn't handle a kiss, there was no way I would be able to do that.

This has gone too far. I've let it get out of hand while foolishly convincing myself I'll find a way out. But I know if I do this right now, my fate will be determined. I will become Adam's mate if I do this.

And the thought is scary. Because how can I be with someone who I don't love? Who I'm not even sure I like anymore?

I can ever hear Liam's voice. Telling me himself not to kiss Adam.

I don't object. Because I honestly don't want to do this myself. It feels wrong. Nothing like when Liam almost kissed me back in the art room. The way his hands felt on mine.

Adam's hands feel different. They're cold and make a shiver ripple up my spine as he leans ever so closer. So close that our noses touch and his breath fans over my lips.

This all is too weird. Too forced. And the more he approaches to press his lips to mine, the louder my mind and body scream at me.

I can't do this, I think, shaking my head causing Adam's eyes to meet mine and confusion masks his face. I can't do this, Adam. This is wrong!

Without thinking for another second, just as his lips are about to meet mine, I roughly shove him.

He staggers back, a look of surprise crossing his face. The crowd equally seems surprised since they let out tiny gasp.

"Ronnie-"

I shake my head jerkily, stepping back, "No. I don't want this." I turn and bump right into Alpha Beckett. Who's eyes don't hold that glint like they previously did. Instead, they are filled with anger. If looks could kill.

I don't have much time to react as he reaches out and clutches my arm tightly in grip. I know it will leave a bruise in the morning. "What do you think you're doing, Ronnie?" He asks threw gritted teeth, his nails digging into my skin.

I don't wince.

I glare at him, letting all the anger I've let build up inside of me reach the surface, threatening to burst. "Leaving." I say simply and wrench my arm free.

I run off the stage with that, kicking off my heels in the process and sprinting threw the crowd of people.

I can hear the furious shouts from Alpha Beckett, demanding that I come right back. I don't listen.

I propel my legs to go faster and burst right out the entrance of the hotel. I see the man before who had opened our car door there. He gives me a wide eyed look, but he doesn't try to stop me.

The train of my dress and hair fly behind me as I run, my bare feet slapping hard against the pavement.

My blood pounds hard in my ears, my heart thudding in a rhythmic beat, practically about to explode right from my chest.

It's not long before that I can hear the sound of footsteps behind me. I glance over to see a group of unfamiliar trailing after me as I run across the street, hopping to escape the cold night and them as well.

I don't know who they are, but I surely know Alpha Beckett has something to do with.

I dart around many cars and buildings, trying to get them off my tail. It doesn't work. Desperate to get away, I spot down an alley way a later. One that leads up to a row of apartment buildings. I could go there and crawl threw a window. At least if I did, there would be people around. And these men surely wouldn't snatch me with witnesses, would they?

I hold onto the brief stray of hope and do probably the stupidest thing I've done in my life. I run straight into an alley way.

I hurry down, stepping in a puddle a long the way. Once I get in front of the later, I yank it down. The later let's out a screech, but comes down without much of a struggles. I climb the first step. Then the second. And then third and I can already get to the top. I'm almost there when I feel someone roughly tug on the hem of my dress.

I peer back to see it's a man with flaming red hair and black eyes. His lips are raised in a snarl as he attempts to pull me down.

I don't need to guess long for me to know who it is. The Purgatory pack.

Without a second thought, I slam my bare foot right into his nose as hard as I can. I hear the sick crunch and he immediately releases me.

I climb up, hearing their gruff voices below me. I know one of them is after me when I hear the later whine at the weight it's carrying.

I reach the first balcony of the emergency stairs, that lead to another row on them and stairs that must lead to the roof.

Once I reach it, I try desperatly to pry the window open. But it never budges. And with the man approaching me, I don't have much time to think.

I bolt up the stairs, gripping tightly onto the railing as I bound my way up, climbing higher and higher until I indeed reach the roof.

I climb up, seeing a doorway that leads directly into the apartment. I run there, twisting the knob, and pulling as hard as I can to open it. But it's locked shut.

I become frantic when I see a head emerge from where I've just come from and I know they're close. Unable to resist, I pound my fist on the door. "Somebody help me!" My voice sounds inhuman as I screech and even slam my body against the door, determined to get it open. No such luck.

The man with flaming red hair and black eyes is on the roof. Coming right towards me with crimson blood that runs from his nose over his lip.

There isn't anywhere else to run. I'm trapped. Completely trapped.

This was a real good plan.

I make a feeble attempt to run to the edge, though I'm not sure why. I can't do anything. If I jump, I die. If I stay here, I die.

My options aren't looking good right about now.

I stare down at the racing cars on the street, wondering if they will hear my screams as I'm murdered by the Purgatory pack.

"Got you!" The man says, a cackle following as he grasps my forearm and pulls my back to where I hit his chest.

I can't help the scream that builds up in my throat. Without thinking about it, I bellow the first name that comes to my mind. The first person that I know will possibly risk my their life for mine. "Liam!" I wail loudly. I don't know how this will save me, or if he will be able to hear me, or feel I'm in danger, but all I can do is hope. "Liam!"

"Liam," The man behind me echoes thoughtfully. "Do you think he'll show up?" The man twirls me around to face five other men I'm not familiar with.

"Of course he would," A man with blonde chair says. "He killed Trice. In the woods. Her scent was there and I'm sure he did it for himself and for her."

A man with black hair nods, and they all agree with mutters.

I thrash madly against the hold he has on me, "Let me go, you creep! Liam! Li-" I'm earned with a hard blow to the face. One that's so powerful it fills my mouth up with blood.

The man with blonde hair catches my shin, his fingers squeezing to a point where I'm scared my jaw will break. "Your boyfriend can't help you. Your own pack won't help you."

"How do you know that?" I say, cringing when I fully taste the coppery blood in my mouth.

"How do you think we found you so easily?" He retorts, "Your Alpha gave us a lead. He knew we were pissed about Farley killing Trice. And he also knew if he gave you up, we'd lay off his pack and not break out little 'agreement.'"

I squeeze my eyes shut. Trying to block out his words. This can't be true. This can't true.

But it is. Alpha Beckett has sold me out. He warned me if I crossed him, I'd get punished. And this was how it was going to happen.

"Maybe you should have listened," The man taunts. And I spit the blood that fills my mouth right at his face, unable to contain my anger. My anger at Alpha Beckett. At Adam. At the world.

That's when the real chaos starts.

It's all mainly a blur as I'm thrown on the floor. I receive numerous kicks and punch, all leaving me to let out a blood curling scream one after another.

I want to shift. To be able to get away. But as the blows continued to be deliver and I actually feel and hear a crack in my side, I know I won't be able to.

So I do the only thing I can do. I scream Liam's name. Earning taunts and laughter from the six men. And I know if I can't fight, or can't get help, they will shift and end it.

The only reason none of us had was because we were in a city. Surrounded by lights and cars and people.

But if we really were, why wasn't anyone hearing me? Why weren't they coming to rescue me?

My side aches and so does my face and just about every other body part. The blonde man, who seems to be the leader of the group, commands them to stop.

They do, but I know it's not over.

He leans down, digging his bloody fingers into my hair. He tugs painfully on and lifts my head to where I'm only inches away from his face, his rotten breath fanning over my face. "I got places to be tonight. So, let's end this quickly, okay?"

I shut my eyes, waiting for the fatal blow, heplessly calling out in my mind, please Liam. Please come and help me. Please.

"What should the finale be?" The blonde man asks casually, peering at the others. They all chime in horrifying ways on how to kill me. And I wonder if this was apart of Alpha Beckett's plan. To kill me.

I highly doubt it. Alpha Beckett wanted to keep me alive for the main purpose of mating with Adam. I know he hadn't intended for the Purgatory pack to really kill me, and knowing how foolish Alpha Beckett is, he probably believed some foolish lie they told him. Like they'd only give me a good beating then leave.

What an idiot.

I cough, blood running down the corner of my lip, with hooded eyes, I stare up at the man that will take my life.

And I'm positively scared of death at this moment. Because I'm not ready to die. Not one bit. I'm sixteen years old. Just a kid who's still trying to find herself. And I would never get that chance.

"Are you excited as much as I am?" The man whispers, trailing a finger down the side of my cheek.

Another cough rakes my body and it sends currents of pain threw me. I'm sorry Liam. I'm so sorry for not hearing you out.

If I'm going to die, I might as well die with some sort of pride. So I do the most foolish thing yet, I croak, "Go to hell."

He doesn't even get angry. He remains composed as he says, "Not today. But maybe I'll see you there when my time comes, sweetheart."

Without another word, he wraps his hand around my throat. His nails growing and piercing my flesh. He picks me up, lifting my limp body. If I could scream, I would. If I could fight, I would. But I'm numb. Numb with pain. So all I do is rest my hand on top of his, weakly trying to peel his fingers away from my throat.

Ronnie!

The familiar voice sneaks it's way into my hazy thoughts. And then it's there again. Screaming and telling me to hold on. That they're going to save me.

I can't tell who it is. My brain isn't working and neither is my body.

My arms fall limp to my side, my vision dotting with black spots. And I think this is it. That I am going to die.

I still hope for the cliche moment that someone will burst out of nowhere and save me. It doesn't happen. And this is the way I'm going to die. What a way to go.

Just as my vision begins to fade to black, and I think it's all over, I can hear something. Something in the distance that sounds like a scream. Like my name.

"Shit," One man cusses, "It's Farley."

Farley? My mind is sluggish as I try to process it all, but I manage to make it out threw all the rest of my blurry thoughts. Liam! It's Liam!

The blonde man drops me abruptly, making me land on the side where I heard the crack. I gurgle an inhuman scream. The sound is ear piercing. And I can barely believe this is coming from me.

The air fills my lungs, though I still contain a heavy amount of blood in my mouth. I gasp and choke, pressing my hands tightly against the cement, as if I'm trying to anchor myself into reality.

"We need to go." One man hoarsely shouts, "Come on, Carden, we need to go!"

I watch with hooded eyes as one man tugs furiously on the boy with flaming red hair's sleeve who's name I know now is Carden.

Carden grunts, shoving his pack mates hand off of him. "No. I'm not running. I'm not a coward, not like you-"

He's cut off when a large figure I can't make out slams right into him. The other men don't hesitate and they turn, sprinting off in the opposite direction and into the night.

I hear the snap of bones and snarls and growls. Then follows whimpers and howls of pain. I know Liam's got this guy when I hear a sickly crack and then a loud thud.

I can hear Liam's foot steps, his heavy breathing. And I realize he's back in human form when he presses his warm fingers against my cheek, letting me know he's here. "Ronnie?" He rasps, his voice husky, "What did they do to you?"

He runs his fingers across my cheekbones, leaving a tingling sensation mixed with pain. I can't speak. Can't answer him.

I know I'll really die if I don't get help at this moment.

"I'll kill you!" He shouts loudly in the direction of where the men ran off, "I'll find you and I'll kill you!" And he turns towards me, whispering incoherently.

Or well, I can't make any of it since the familiar black dots fill my vision. And my eyelids begin to droop.

"Ronnie?" He says, "Ronnie, keep your eyes open. Ronnie!"

I try. I really do. But I can't. I'm so tired. So tired and all I want to do is sleep, not really caring about if I close my eyes right now, I might get sucked into darkness forever.

I feel something wet splatter onto my cheek. And I don't know if it's rain or what. Or if it's my own tears. I can't tell.

My breathing begins to slow, and I stare right into Liam's glowing green eyes. I muster up everything in me, just to whisper, "I'm sorry."

For what? I'm not sure. For putting him threw hell. For not letting him explain. Everything.

He says something again, but I can't make it out. I let my eyes close, aware to the fact he's shaking me, willing me to staying awake.

Before I can shake myself out of it, I'm swallowed up into darkness.

CHAPTER 16

It's incredibly dark.

So dark that I can't see anything in front of me.

I blink many times, trying adjust my eyes. But not even with my werewolf sight, I can't see. I question for a moment if I actually died, but that's silly. Especially when I run my hand across the plush comforter that's draped up to just under my chin.

I wiggle my fingers, rubbing them across the silk sheets and confirming I'm not dead. I really get a confirmiation when my head begins to throb and pain floods my entire body. It hurts to even move. Which I attempt to do weakly.

I don't even let out a grunt of pain. I can't. My throat feels so dry, a long with my lips. I probably look like I've come back from the dead.

And now that leaves me with where I am. I'm certainly not at the hospital. I discover that when a loud flash, presumably thunder, lights up with the room.

I'm nearly binded for a minute before I focus my eyes long enough to get a glimpse of the wooden walls. Wooden walls?

Was I in some sort of cabin?

Another flash of thunder eliminates the room, this time, I peer around long enough to realize the only thing in this room beside the bed, and of course myself, is a lone chair that's positioned directly next to me.

My eyebrows furrow. Who else was here?

My heart quickens at the thought. So hard that my blood pounds in my ears and I suddenly grow painfully hotter than I like.

It's at that moment that I can hear heavy footsteps and then the squeal of a knob being twisted.

I shut my eyes tightly, pretending to be asleep. Though I highly doubt I'll fool anyone with the rate my heart's going at.

Or the smell of my fear.

I mean, what if those guys came back and did something to Liam? What if they got me and dragged me to their head corridors where they could torture me?

Just like they had in my dreams.

It's true. Most of the time I was passed out, it was all a sea of black. Then there was times where I would dream horrible things containing those exact six men. But what happens to me this time is much worse. And I'm not the only victim.

Liam was in those nightmares too. And Anna. Even my father who I wasn't sure knew of my existence anymore.

Most of the time, they'd make me watch. Their cruel laughter filling my ears a long with Liam's, Anna's, and my father's screams.

I remember one dream in particular. One where I laid in not my own blood, but Liam's. I remember him whispering to me as he died, the same sentence playing like a broken record; "Why didn't you save me Ronnie?"

I could never speak in these dreams. My mouth felt like it was full of cotton each time.

I wanted to tell him I was sorry. That I never meant for this to happen.

The scariest part was that I could never wake myself from these dreams. I was stuck in an endless pit of despair.

But now I'm not. This is real. This isn't a dream. And whatever happens right now, is real.

I can hear the squeak of the door as it opens, letting in a cold draft and a light that ulimates everything just beyond my eyelids.

I'm tempted to reach up and cover myself from the brightness that itches at me. I don't. I remain as still as possible, not even daring to draw in a breath.

I hear the person sigh, and then their breathing. I know they're standing over me when I can feel the immense heat that's radiating off of them.

That's how I know they're a werewolf. And that's it's not just anyone, but Liam.

It's evident when he presses his fingers to my face, reminding me of right after I was beat senseless by the Purgatory pack.

"You can stop pretending your asleep, Ron," He rumbles, his voice unnaturally husky, as if he had just woken up. "I know you're awake."

I open my eyes slowly, meeting his tired green eyes. I'm apalled by his appearence.

He's not the perfect looking Liam Farley I'm use to seeing. Or, well, hearing about it.

His hair is messy, sticking up in many directions while black bags rest right under his eyes. He also appears paler than usual.

My lips part slightly, "What.." I trail off, not able to finish the sentence when the burning returns in my throat.

He gives me a lazy grin before he turns on his heels and disappears out the door. I want to follow after him, or at least ask him where he's gone, but either one is practically useless in my situation.

I slump back against the pillows, a weird sound stirring at the back of my throat. One that slightly resembles a grunt.

I glance around the small, stuffy rooms. Then down at myself.

I'm not wearing my dress. I notice that when I manage to lift the sheets. The only thing I have on is a overly sized gray t-shirt. Obviously Liam's by the size and the smell.

But that's not even what really catches my attention. It's the purple bruises that covers my legs.

With a gasp, I raise the blanket off of me.

Everywhere I look, to my arms, stomach, and legs, I'm covered in bruises and cuts. Though some appear to be healing, I can't help but cover a hand over my mouth to contain the wail that's crawling up my throat.

I should be healed by now. I'm a blood werewolf for crying out loud!

I naturally heal faster than humans. I shouldn't feel this sore,

Then again, these marks weren't caused by humans. They were caused by my own kind.

I can only imagine how my face looks right now. And my hair. I probably look twice as worse than Liam.

And in all honesty, Liam still looked just as good even if he did look dead tired. I wonder if he looks so distraught because of me.

My chest tightens at the thought.

The creak of the floor boards causes me to look to the doorway, only to see Liam there with a glass of water, staring at the numerous bruises covering my legs.

He's eyes meet mine before walking over and grasping the blankets. He drags it up to my chest and tucks me in tightly. He then presses the cold glass to my lips, commanding me to drink.

I do, just hesitantly.

After a minute or two, he pulls the glass away and smooths back my hair. "How are you feeling?"

I lick my dry lips, "Fine." I lie, and quickly ask, "What time is it?"

"Three AM." He replies and takes a seat down on the chair by the bed.

"Oh," I mutter, "What made you wake up?"

"I wasn't asleep," He says.

I frown at his monotone, "Are you okay?"

"Shouldn't I be asking you that instead?" He chuckles, a smile grazing his lips though it doesn't meet his eyes.

"You already did." I counter, "Besides, you don't look so hot."

He shrugs, "I've had a lot on my mind."

I swallow roughly and out of habit, I lick my lips again. They feel like sandpaper. And that's probably what they look like too.

I honestly feel like I've just been ran over by bulldozer.

My face throbs madly and so does my body. Numbly, I reach up and graze my finger tips across my lips, to right under my eyes. That's where it hurts the most. I can't help but ask, "How many bruises are there on my face?"

Liam shakes his head, "Does it matter?"

"Yes," I say and then try to add some humour into the situation by adding, "I just want to know if they did any permanent damage to my beautiful face."

Liam doesn't laugh. Instead his eyes darken with an emotion I can't read. Mostly because he doesn't give me the time to.

He glances down, staring into glass.

His face scrunches, almost as if he's in pain. After a long strong of silence, he utters, "I'm sorry."

I shake my head, confused. "For what?"

"For not getting there sooner," He mutters, setting the glass down and digging his fingers into his hair. "It's all my fault."

I roll my eyes, "Please don't tell me you're one of those people who blames themselves for every bad thing that happens around them."

"No, Ron, I'm not one of those people." He spat, more harshly now. It takes me back for a moment. "This is actually, really, my fault."

"Why?"

"Because I killed their pack mates," He states, his eyes darting to mine. "Remember?"

I nod stiffly, "How could I forget?"

"They got me back for it. They went after the only person they knew I gave a damn about," He mumbles, "You."

"It's not your fault. Trust me," I mutter the last part. Mostly to myself.

I contemplate telling him for a minute about Alpha Beckett. About how he's been black mailing me this whole time. But I fear if I do, Liam will go right after them. And probably murder Alpha Beckett.

Then again, that's not so much of a repulsive thought.

"I just wish I could have got there sooner," He whispers, almost brokenly.

This is a new side of Liam. One I'm not familiar with. Mostly because this is the most vulnerable I've ever seen him. And frankly, it surprises me. Liam has always been so head strong. Daring, even. How can someone like him ever feel weak?

Then again, just because we're werewolves, doesn't mean we're unstoppable. We all have our moments.

I shuffle uncomfortably in my place, clearing my throat, "So, how long have I been out?"

"Three days, tops."

"Three days?" I screech, "Does anyone even know where I am?"

"I told the school you were sick," He says, "They buy it. Anna does too."

"And Adam?"

He shakes his head, "He doesn't know anything. He keeps demanding to know what's happened to you."

Was that true? I think silently, pinching my lips together.

I don't think Liam is lying, I think Adam is. I mean, wasn't he the one who warned me in the first place? Wouldn't he know what his father had planned for me if I disobeyed?

I don't dwell on it for long. Mainly because the thought of Alpha Beckett makes me blood boil. "And what's my injuries, doc?"

He laughs softly, a real laugh this time at the nickname. "Nothing that won't heal. Though I'm worried about your side. I think you broke something."

"You think?" I inquire, "A blind person would be able to tell I broke a rib. You're not a very good doctor."

"That's because I'm not actually a doctor." He rolls his eyes, "Besides, you're not dead. So I did a pretty good job with patching you up."

I glance down at myself, playing with the collar of my shirt. Or well, his shirt. "How did this happen, exactly?"

I don't need to elaborate on what I mean. He get's it by the amusement that lights up in his green eyes. But just to tease me, he says, "Well, you see, I first start by putting the shirt-"

"Shut up," I grumble, rolling my eyes. "You know what I mean."

"I put my shirt on you. It's as simple as that."

"Yeah, I noticed you put a shirt on me," I huff. "I'm just curious.. did you.. well... you know, look?"

"Yeah," He nods. "Nice underwear."

Blood immediately rushes to my cheeks, "Are you serious? You looked? Liam!"

He let's out a roar of laughter, shaking his head while pressing a hand to his stomach. Though I'm not comfortable with the conversation, it's better than before. When he was feeling guilty about what happened when it really wasn't his fault.

"No, I didn't look." He finally says after his fit of laughter ends, "You're so innocent."

"Yeah, yeah."

He gives me a meager smile. "You should get some sleep," He inquires. "It's late. Tomorrow, we'll get some food into you and maybe I'll move the TV into here so you aren't so bored, okay?"

Though I honestly don't feel like sleeping anymore, I agree reluctantly. "Okay. You should get some sleep too. You look horrible."

"You're very blunt," He comments and stands up.

"I know," I say, "Now go sleep."

I almost ask him to stay with me. To actually sleep in the same bed with me and hold me, so he can ward the nightmares off.

I mean, just these few minutes speaking with him he's made me forget what's happened. My dreams, most importantly. And the image that's burned itself into my mind. The one of me holding him in his own pool of blood.

"Okay, okay," He grunts. "If you need anything, just call, alright?"

He reaches out, tucking a piece of my hair behind my ear. I smile weakly at him, "Yes sir. And Liam?"

"Yeah?"

"Thank you." I say, sincerely. I catch his hand in mine for a minute, giving it a squeeze before I release it and lean back.

He smiles tiredly back at me, "You're welcome." He leans and presses a kiss to my forehead. He shuts off the lights without another word. Though he leaves the door open.

It gives me a sense of security, knowing that he's just across the hall. I close my eyes with that, somehow, I fall asleep within a matter of minutes.

The next three days I spend my time in bed. Most of the time watching TV or chatting with Liam.

He tells me how this is his cabin. And how he discovered it months ago and decided to fix up the place.

He spends every moment of every day with me, getting me anything I need. And though I want to tell him I'm getting better, I don't really feel it.

I'm still in pain. So much that attempting to stand up hurts. I haven't tried it since.

I can't do much but lay in bed, eat, talk to Liam, and watch stupid cartoons. And when I'm not doing that, I'm over thinking. About Alpha Beckett. Adam. Anna. And my father.

Mostly my father. Which is weird.

I can't help but wonder what he would think if he knew. Would he care? Would Adam care? Or even Anna?

I highly doubt it. Anna was too busy with her new boyfriend.

Liam tells me that she spends most of her time with him at school. And Mandy.

I almost feel jealous that Anna was more caught up with Mandy then worrying about me being supposedly sick.

And though I tell myself that Anna is my best friend and that of course she cares, I don't buy it. I had seen the way Anna acted with boys before.

The news didn't get any better when Liam told me the teacher's were starting to get suspicious. If I didn't show up by next week, I knew something drastic was going to happen.

But how could I show up to school with a black eye and cut lip and explain that?

Yeah, I had a black eye. A long with a busted up lip. It took two days of convincing for Liam to finally let me look into the mirror.

The first time I did, I cringed at my own reflection.

I certainly did not look as extravagant as the night I went to the ball. My once sleek waves were tangled and knotted, a long with a patch of dried blood in my hair.

My body, of course, was no better. I was sporting many bruises, though they were starting to go away.

And my side, wasn't getting better. I coudln't turn without hissing in pain. I had definitely broken something, and I knew it would take more than a stupid week to heal.

I was stuck to rot in bed. In my own fiflth. I probably smelt like a dumpster.

I wonder how Liam could stand by me without shuddering in disgust. Nonetheless, look at me.

He was my rock, really. There were many times those three days that I would wake up in the middle of the night, completely hysterical by the same dream that haunted me every night. Not the one about me being beat to almost death, but about Liam. Anna, and my father.

I told him about them. How I was scared.

He did his best to comfort me. To reassure me that nothing would ever happen. But I didn't buy it. I couldn't. Not when something like this happened.

I still didn't know when was the right time to tell him. Or if I was going to tell him at all.

I couldn't go on like this forever. What if I disrespected Alpha Beckett again, and something happened? What if I didn't get lucky and actually got killed that time? What if Anna died? What if my dad died? What if Liam died?

There were so many things to take into consideration. I almost wanted to ask him to run away. That we could get Anna and run away where the Purgatory pack, nor Alpha Beckett, could ever touch us. But that was silly. I couldn't leave my whole life behind. And I certainly wasn't going to let Alpha Beckett believe he had gotten to me.

I had too much pride, anyway. And I'm sure Liam did too.

He wouldn't leave this place till he got his revenge. That's for sure.

Many times, I would catch him looking at some map. One that he explained had marked out all the wolfs in our distance.

"Why does the Purgatory pack have a red 'x' over their location?" I remember I asked. Liam didn't reply. His jaw simply clenched. That answered my question.

He was planning something. Something that might end up getting him killed.

And the more time I spent with him those three days, the more I find myself depending on him, when I knew I shouldn't.

But as weak and needy as I sounded, I needed him. I needed someone to lean on so I wouldn't fall further than I had the years I spent by myself.

I never realized how much I missed someone's hugs, kind words, or even appreciation till I spent those days with him.

It made me think of the past. And why I've ended up the way I am today.

I wondered about my mom. Was she proud of me? Was she proud of who I had become?

My mom told me she'd always love me no matter who I was with, who I was, and where I was.

I would myself missing her company more and more. I missed someone looking after me when I was sick. I missed everything about her.

Her laugh, her smile. It made those feelings I had pushed away so long ago emerge. And I could hear the walls around me that I had built up for so many years cracking. I think Liam could hear it too.

Today was the fourth day I had been here. Or well, the fourth night. It was the middle of the night and I couldn't sleep.

Memories of my mother haunted me. More than those six men that had nearly killed me.

I always told myself that I didn't miss her anymore. That I didn't need her and I'd be perfectly fine on my own. Because I was strong.

I could only imagine it was worst for my father. The one who had spent half of his life with her, creating memories that could go on forever.

That didn't excuse his actions, but I understood what he felt.

I stare up at the ceiling, the soothing sound of rain drops hitting the window. It's been like that for the last few days. Gloomy.

It didnt' help how I was feeling.

I suddenly hate the fact that I've been throwing myself a pity party. That beating wasn't a life scarring reason. It was just a bump in the road and I needed to grow up. To be strong. Just like I had told myself to be when I was twelve years old.

Over come with a new sense of determination, I push myself to the edge of the bed and throw the blankets off of me.

I plant my bare feet on the cold wood flooring, slowly beginning to push myself up. I stand up wobbly, pain shooting up my legs and side.

I don't feel as strong as I did just moments ago.

I fall to the ground, right on my injured sound with a loud wail right on impact. My own cry rings in my ears and surely throughout the cabin.

"Ronnie!" Liam immediately calls out, and the door is thrown open. I don't even flinch when the door slams loudly into the wall.

I'm too busy wailing in pain.

Liam rushes to my side, calling my name, "Ronnie, what did you do? Ronnie, what happened? Ronnie!" I don't reply, making him become more frantic. "What do I get you? What do you need? How do I stop the pain? I'm so sorry, Ron. I'm so sorry."

I shake my head at him. I don't question my next move as I throw my arms around his neck.

He immediately sets me right into of his lap, wrapping his arms around me, tightly, but I don't mind. All I want is for him to hold me. I want him to hold me together when I know I can't. I want him to do what he's done for days, I want him to be my rock. To tell me nothing will ever happen to Anna. My father, or him.

I want him to be strong for not only him, but me. I need him to be.

I press my face into the crook of his neck, ignoring the pain and whispering, "You. I just need you."

Chapter 17

There was nothing left to be said after my breakdown. And I was perfectly okay with that.

After I had told him I needed him, he simply pressed a kiss to my temple and placed me on the bed, tucking me in as if I was some small child that just had a nightmare.

If I would have been acting normally, I would have told him to stop. That I was a big girl and I didn't need to be treated like a child.

I wasn't strong enough to push him away at that moment. It was true what I said. I needed him. And the realization of that was daunting.

It was all so unfamiliar. The gentle whispers, the comforting touches, and most importantly, the feeling of needing someone. And them needing you.

He sat in the chair next to my bed the whole night. Pressing kisses to my face and gripping my hand tightly in his.

But that was all I really needed to calm down. It was his presence that soothed me into a dreamless slumber.

I wondered what had happened to my master plan to stop Liam from ever getting close to me. To stop the feelings that were trying to creep up on me when I let my guard down.

But did I ever really believe I could keep him away? We were mates after all. Mates.

Now that was something I would never get use to.

I still worried about Alpha Beckett. I questioned what he would do if he found out that I had been staying with Liam.

Alpha Beckett had become too unpredictable. Just like my life had.

It's when I wake in the morning that I sit and think about telling Liam. Maybe, we could come up with something to end this madness.

Though I'm sure Liam's plan would be to kill Alpha Beckett.

And it's not like I was against that. I wasn't. I just wanted to be careful. What I should have been that night of the ball.

I can't bare the thought for more than thirty seconds before those faces of the six men appear in my mind.

I can still feel the imprint of the blonde man's - who appeared to be the leader - hands wrapped around my throat as he tried to strangle the life out of me.

I remember all their words. How they chimed in ideas of how to kill me.

"Why not have some fun with the girl?" One man with black hair whispers sadistically, "I've been dying to cut her pretty little face up."

I shivered involuntarily as the words replay over and over again in my head. I imagined a horrifying scene too. Of the man with hair as black as night, looming over with me with a knife in his hand, slowly bringing it to my face.

I bet he'd laugh while I screamed and cried for mercy.

I wonder if they're all plotting not only my death right now, but Liam's.

Indeed, Liam had killed Caden, but I was the cause of it. Nonetheless, I was the weaker link and I knew for a fact they wouldn't give up till I was buried six feet under.

They'd do the cliche thing and capture me, perhaps. Drag me back to their lair and then coax Liam into being heroically stupid. He'd fall perfectly into their grasp.

And then, when The Purgatory pack had him, they'd sit him down and make him face the worst torment known on this planet. Watching the person you care for die.

Liam decides to wake up at that moment just when the horrifying scenes start to leak into my mind. He asks how I feel and so on.

The morning mostly consists of him trying to coax some food into him. And each time, I tell him I'm not hungry. He doesn't listen. But that's nothing new, then again.

Liam carries me around his cabin, since I started to whine once he tried to put me back in bed. And obviously, after last night's events, he's not willing to take a chance with me trying to walk again. He takes me to his room, giving me another spare change of clothes before he rests me on the couch in front of the TV.

He departs then, and takes a place at the kitchen table and pulls out some sheets of papers and sorts, though I don't see what's so special about that.

I decide I've bugged him enough, so I sit and watch dumb soap operas for an hour or two before I start to become restless.

I twist myself around as best as I can to get a look at Liam, resting my head on my arms.

Liam doesn't seem to notice that I'm staring straight at him. All he does is keep scribbling down on the long paper that's splayed across the small, white table.

I give time to notice me, but he's completely oblivious. That's when I finally voice, "What's that?"

Liam finally glances up at me, meeting my questioning gaze. He's quiet for a minute. Then he shrugs, "Just some papers."

"Just papers?" I raise a brow at him, "Doesn't seem like that. You've been working on them for hours."

"Jealous pieces of paper have my attention and you don't?" He teases, obviously trying to turn the subject around on me. Typical.

"No," I roll my eyes. "What are on the papers? Are they that much of a secret?"

I push myself up slightly and manage to catch a peak of what appears to be map. One with many 'X's covering it. I also see a name a recognize.

Riverwood.

Riverwood was some stupid little hang in the other side of town. It was pretty much a venue for all things bad. I had heard of it from Anna, who was very much so eager to even be able to get a glimpse of what happened over there. I was for a while, until I learned who exactly hung around there.

I knew werewolves lurked there. I had heard it from Adam a few months ago at some pack meeting. That's where they believed The Purgatory pack was hanging around at. They were trying to recruit more rogue's.

The Purgatory.

Was that map full of their locations? Was Liam marking it down so he could take them out?

Well, it surely isn't a map of America, I think sarcastically.

Liam tries to cover it up, throwing countless books on top. But I've already seen enough.

"It's nothing, Ronnie," His voice is gruff and cold. "Drop it."

"No," I shake my head frantically, "Are you thinking about going to Riverwood? That's a death wish!"

"How do you know about Riverwood?" Liam asks, his eyebrows furrowing.

"I heard about it from Adam," I say, "But why-"

Liam cuts me off, "What did he say about it?"

I don't reply. I'm afraid if I do, Liam will do something incredibly stupid. Like go over there looking for trouble. But by the looks of it, Liam is set on going. It was practically the only location on the map without a red 'X' over the name.

I could only guess that those X's stood for the locations that Liam already cleared out; It didn't make sense.

Like a angry hive of bees, erratic thoughts swarm around fill my head. All consisting of, why did Liam have a map of the Purgatory? When did he make it? And how long has this been going on?

Was it possible that Liam was hunting the Purgatory pack before he even met me? Sure, the Purgatory pack was bad, but there was plenty of other packs that were just as worse. Why did Liam take an interest in them?

He must have a motive of some sort. One that didn't only include me.

Did it have to do with Liam's past?

Has I ever really thought of why Liam had ended up in Portland? No, I hadn't. Maybe I just always pushed the lurking question into the back of my mind. I guess I just assumed it wasn't important.

But now it was.

What if Liam hadn't stumbled across my town on accident? What if he was looking for something, or more particular, someone?

I swallow roughly, looking up to meet Liam's intense gaze. He's practically warning me not to ask. To not bring up the subject.

He should know by now I'm not the type to drop a heavy subject easily.

"What do you want with Riverwood?" I breathe shakily and shift my eyes to the map on the table.

If only I could get my hands on it.. I think warily, and as if he can read my mind, he snatches it up and disappears into another room.

I hear the shuffle of his feet, his slow breathes, and then the slam of a drawer. He appears again moments later and heads off to the table, clearing off the rest of the papers. "Never mind. Just forget I asked. It's not important, anyway," He says nonchalantly.

I don't reply. I simply stare at this man I know absolutely nothing about. Who is Liam, really? Where did he come from? And well, did he have a family? Friends?

Curiousity itches at me. But I force it go away. Forget about the map, Ronnie, I think with a shake of my head, you have enough problems.

Liam keeps the rest of our conversations casual the rest of the day. Mostly consisting of what I want to eat or what I want to watch.

And though I tell myself to forget about what I saw, I can't.

I ponder it for most of the day. None of it really adds up. And that's what frustrates me the most.

We sit currently on the couch, silently watching some TV show I'm not the most interested in.I still keep my eyes on the screen. I don't want to arise any more questions from Liam about how I'm feeling.

He already knows. I'm completely confused and I honestly have no clue about what's going on around me anymore.

Who is there to believe, anyway?

"I never did understand why girls loved this movie so much," Liam suddenly says. I glance towards him with furrowed eyebrows before I look back at the screen to see the Notebook playing.

"Yeah, me either." I retort slowly. We fall back into silence until I can't take it anymore and I blurt, "Do you have a family?"

"Doesn't everyone have one?"

"Yeah, but, do you know yours?"

He shrugs, "Do you?"

I pinch my lips together. I know he's just trying to turn this around on me. Like he always does."Yeah, I do."

"I don't see your dad much over at your house."

Now it's my turn to shrug, "He's.. busy, I guess."

"And your mom?"

My throat suddenly feels tight. And I can only imagine this is how it must feel when I ask Liam questions he's not comfortable with answering. Now I've just witnessed a piece of my medicine.

It's been four years. The subject shouldn't bother you anymore.

I agree silently. Though I still suck in a shaky breath before I say, "She's gone."

Liam eyes me hazily. But as always, I can never guess what he's thinking. "Mine too."

His reply takes me by shock. Mostly because Liam has never shared something so personal with me before. But I guess it's a start.

Maybe I'm not the only one who guards themselves. And maybe, Liam isn't only breaking down my walls, but I'm breaking down his.

An unfamiliar feeling rises in my chest. I don't know what it means, but something about Liam trusting me with this information makes me.. happy.

But that's what is. The beginning of us starting to trust each other with foreign feelings, secrets, everything. And though it may take a while to get all the answers I want out of Liam, I'm willing to wait. Because I know that's what he would do for me.

I don't need all the answers right now. It's like I said the night before. All I want and need right now, is Liam.

And coming to terms that I can't get through everything alone is crazy. But exciting, in a weird way.

A smile creeps it's way onto my face. And when I look at Liam, he returns my smile with one of his own.

The next few days are peaceful.

Liam and I spend practically every moment together. And slowly, he helps me with walking again. By the second day of practicing, I can stand on my own. And the bruises covering my body, are starting to heal.

We talk somewhat. Really at night when we both settle down. It was on Thursday that we had both taken a seat on the couch and he begun to dive into his childhood.

"I use to climb trees a lot," He told me once the credits of a movie we just watched rolled onto the screen. "I would climb so high that I could see all the houses in my neighborhood."

I softly laugh, "Must have been dangerous."

"It was," He nodded and then said, "My nickname use to Squirrel."

"How lovely," I replied, quite sarcastically.

"Didn't you have any weird habits as a child?"

I shook my head, "Not really. But I remember painting a lot when I was a kid."

"So not much has changed then, huh?" Liam mused. And again, I shook my head.

"No, I guess not."

He continued on about that. Asking questions about my painting, while I asked about his childhood obsession with climbing.

The days continued on like that, with simple and subtle conversations. And I never questioned him again about The Purgatory pack. I liked how things we going just then, and I didn't want to ruin it.

On Saturday, I can fully walk again with only little pains. Nothing I couldn't handle. And that's when Liam declares that it's safe to go back to school.

"No," I say for the millionth time. "I still think I need more.. practice."

Liam laughs, "You don't need anymore 'practice'. You can walk perfectly fine."

"Really?" I make the effort to trip, of course, once I attempt to do so, Liam grasps my arm and sits me down.

He turns to me with raised brows, "Okay, so tell me, what are running from?"

"Nothing," I retort defensively. My tone is harsh. "I just don't think I'm ready."

"Is it because of Adam?" He presses, pursing his lips. When I don't reply, he quickly nods and points an accusing finger at me. "It is!"

"It is not!" I spat, "Why would I be running away from Adam?"

"Aren't you supposed to know that instead of me?"

I roll my eyes at him with a huff, "You're an idiot. And I'm not scared of facing Adam."

I'm not. I repeat over and over again in my head. But I never seem to believe it.

Why would I be scared to face Adam? Well, maybe I'm just scared of what he'll Alpha Beckett.

Liam's scent was all over me. It didn't take a lot to put together that Liam had been helping me. And I worried that once Adam caught his scent on me, he'd run to his daddy and tattle. Then, something would happen to Liam. And I couldn't allow that.

I owed him.

Liam had helped me and I was in his debt. And the only way I could repay the favor is making sure Alpha Beckett didn't hurt him.

I still hadn't made up my mind if I was going to tell Liam about what was going on. About how Alpha Beckett was black mailing me.

For now, the only I could do, was keep Liam safe.

Sunday night rolls around all too fast. And though Liam has brought up the pestering subject about me going to school tomorrow, it's still in the back of my mind. Just like the rest of my problems.

"I'm going to have to go tomorrow, aren't I?" I mutter as I climb into bed. I glance behind me to see Liam leaning against the door way with his arms crossed.

"Well, do you want to go?" He asks. I roll my eyes.

"That's a stupid question," I say, "Obviously not. But I can't run away, can I?"

He shakes his head, a frown tugging at the corner of his lips. I let out a pathetic whimper. Immediately, Liam flutters to my side like he has done this whole week. "What are you scared of?"

"Everything," I reply.

He doesn't question what I mean. He simply tugs me into his arms. I don't push him away like I usually would.

I know I should spare myself the heart break. I can't keep Liam by my side for long. And he can't keep me either.

But for now, I'll take what I can get.

With a sigh, I rest my head on his chest. Molding my smaller body into his much bigger one. And as corny as it sounds, I feel positively safe right now in Liam's grip.

I hear the thumps of his heart beat where my head rests. I take comfort in it, but of course, I can't shake the thought of tomorrow.

I can only wonder what's to come.

Chapter 18

Breathe. Just breathe.

I stare into the crowd of people, watching them sprint across the parking lot to their friends, laughing and smiling in the process. As if they don't have a care in the world.

Most flutter up the steps of the school, arms looped with their companions and ready to brace the day. Some others stay behind and make up - with what I presume is their girlfriend/boyfriend - those precious moments of the weekend they've been away from one another.

I feel sick just watching as they whisper to one another and press brief pecks to their partners lips. I almost envy them. That they're so gleefully happy while I'm miserable. I realize it's incredibly childish once they disappear from my sight and up the stairs to our high school.

I've never been more tempted to run away till now.

It's because I'm not ready. As cowardly as it sounds, I don't want to face the never ending questions on what happened. And why it looks like I've been ran over by a truck.

I don't want to tell Anna some stupid lie. I don't want to face her while she's with her new found friend's and boyfriend. I don't wan't her stupid pity. I don't want her to pretend like everything is completely fine when it isn't. I don't want any of it.

The thing I actually do want is to go home. Crawl under my bed sheets and hide away from the world.

And maybe I would've. That is, if it weren't for Liam.

He had made me to get up this morning, even as I made horrid excuses. Such as I had suddenly contracted swine flu.

I pretended like it hurt to walk too. Liam was incredibly heartless, really. He didn't fall for any of my acts.

He told me to face my fears. So I am. Or well, being forced to.

I kinda resented him for it.

Because of him, I'm going to have to see Adam. That's what's really been haunting my thoughts lately. Though it's no shock.

I'm anxious. To see what he says, does. Everything.

I had even formed up some silly speech in my head. About how I'd tell him off and call him a monster. And maybe, for dramatic effect, I'd slap him. God knows how much I would like to do that.

I had convinced myself I was done with wagging a finger at him as if he was some naughty child. I was going to take action. No matter the consequences.

I go to push open the door, to burst through with my new found coinfendence, but just as quick as it came, it goes.

"I can't do this," I say with a shake of my head. "I'm not ready."

I turn to Liam who sits in the driver's seat, completely composed and appearing nonchalant. I almost want him to panic like I do so I won't feel so alone. And well, weak.

"Yeah, you can," He replies firmly and yanks his keys out of the ignition. "And you will."

"But what if-" I begin, but Liam quickly cuts me off.

"Don't you want to rub it in Adam's face that not even what happened could get beat you down?"

I make a face at his choice of words, "Is that supposed to be a pun or something?"

"Sorry," He grimaces. "Poor choice of words, I know."

I shrug softly. It's not exactly my biggest issue at the moment. The only thing I'm worrying about is how I'm going to get through the day. And all the questions.

Then again, I don't have to answer. It's none of their business but my own.

"Yeah," Liam mutters, "Now let's go."

I have no room for objection as Liam hops out the car and comes around to my side, opening the door for me.

I meet his eyes and bite down on my lip. I silently plead with him not to make me do this.

Liam sighs at my obvious attempt to derail him and leans closely to where I can feel his breath on my lips.

He reaches out hesitantly and carefully cups my cheek, awake and aware of the black eye I still have.

I rest my much smaller hand on top of his, letting out a shaky breath as I stare into his green hues. "It's going to be okay," He assures me, "Don't worry."

For the first time ever, I can read Liam easily. I can actually decipher what he's feeling at that moment. And it's because he allows me to see it. So I know I can put my trust in him.

I nod and manage to utter, "Okay."

Liam releases me and steps back. I take the chance to get up before the urge to slam the car door and lock myself in over powers me.

I walk beside Liam in silence.

The few stray kids in the parking lot glance at us, but they dismiss us both shortly after. They obviously don't care.

I can only pray that's how it stays.

Luck is on my side.

Through the whole morning, I keep under the radar, only talking when needed. Of course, some ask what happened, but when they realize I'm not going to answer, they turn away and go back to their own business.

I also get to talk to Ms. J about the back drops. She stresses that they need to be done in two weeks, and how I need to get on it immediately, or else she will be forced to assign the project to someone else.

And even though I have no desire to linger at school, I tell her I will work on them everyday after school.

Besides that little scare, everything goes perfectly fine.

That is, till lunch come's around.

I'm at my locker when I spot Mandy and Jessica calling to someone across the hall, shouting and hollering at the person to hurry up.

And though the hall way is crowded with people - all fighting their way to get to lunch - I still hear that familiar girlish giggle ring in my ears.

Anna's face come's into view just then, too.

She wears a broad smile on her face, her eyes twinkling at the sight of her new friends and boyfriend, who suddenly appears out of the doorway of his last class.

She's embraces Mandy and Jessica, then Cliff, who she gives a swift kiss to the lips before he wraps his arm around her shoulder and leads her to the lunch room.

With that, she is gone from my direction.

I stare after her. I almost want her to look back at me and actually acknowledge my existence.

And I know I'm completely contradicting myself - once saying I didn't want to see her and have to make up some lie - but now I almost want to, as weird as it sounds.

I suddenly realize I'm wrong.

The thing that really hurts the most is when you're gone, and you wonder if those people cared enough to notice that.

Anna hasn't.

But that's what I asked for. To simply avoid all pity filled questions, comments, conversations, everything between the lines.

Now here I am. Silently sobbing over the fact Anna doesn't care. But I had the right to be, didn't I? Anna's my best friend. In order to have the title, you have to be in the other person's life and care about them, right?

Was the same thing that happened with Adam going to repeat itself?

Once this horrid thought leaks into my head, I can't seem to get it out.

It's happening again, I think frantically, Anna's leaving me behind. Just the way Adam did.

I'm no longer in the mood to have lunch.

I turn and head on down to the art wing, where I find my place in front of the huge canvas. I spend half of my time painting, then the thoughts from earlier seem to consume me and I end up throwing the paint brush across the room.

I lean against the wall and pull on the loose strands of hair. I think about Anna more. And how I'm not ready to lose her. Not like the way I lost Adam.

I contemplate marching over to her and demanding answers on why she ditched me for her new, fake, friends. I realize it's silly after a few minutes.

If anything, Anna should be the one demanding answers from me. I've lied to her about everything in my life practically.

About my parents, about where I live, about what I am. Everything.

I don't blame her for just leaving me like that. I'm sure Mandy and Jessica are more suited friends for her, anyway.

They love the same things. Boys, makeup, clothes. Now that I think of it, Anna and I didn't have much in common. But we still got a long. We still befriended each other when we had nothing.

She had told me things that she hadn't told others. Like she secretly thought her family was falling apart, or that sometimes she hated what she saw in the mirror. She trusted me with her deepest secrets, and though I was restricted of what I could and couldn't tell her, I would talk with her about how I felt alone.

About how I wasn't sure if I really knew who I am. Or what I want, exactly.

And even threw all of that, she had thrown it aside and ditched me.

As I think this, I so desperately want to be mad at her. But I can't bring myself to be.

If anything, I'm mad at myself. For letting someone get to know me and giving them the chance to make me feel a stir of emotions. All consisting of hurt and betrayal.

They make me feel weak.

And I don't like to feel weak. Though I'm pretty sure I've established that more than once.

But I'm in the same place again. The same mix of emotions and before I can stop it, the imagine of Adam telling me that he couldn't be my friend anymore plays in my mind.

"I can't be your friend anymore, Ronnie," Adam blurts suddenly.

I blink a few times, looking at him as if he's sprouted a second head. "Huh?"

"I can't be your friend." He repeats, his eyes shifting from the lake to me. "The rest of the pack is.. getting on my case about hanging around you."

I shake my head and my eyebrows furrow together. "Why?"

"Because of your dad," Adam explains, "And how he... well, you know, just dropped out of being the pack's guard."

I swallow roughly and shake my head, "But that's not my fault. He's just down because.." I trail off when I can't bring myself to utter the words. That I can't justify the fact my dad is in the dumps because of my mom dying. It's too painful for me.

The mere mention of her makes me want to cry. And I promised myself I never would again. "I thought we were friends forever."

"I thought so too," Adam whispers and runs a hand through his short blonde hair. "I'm sorry, Ron."

I feel weak. So weak.

"You can't leave me behind," I whisper brokenly, "I need you." My voice breaks. "I need you because you're the only thing I have left. My dad won't talk to me, the pack won't talk to me, I need you because you're my best friend. Because we're always supposed to be their for each other. Right?"

Adam's eyes are glossy and his lips are parted, "Ron-"

"Right?" I echo, cutting him off. Adam is silent.

The tears build in my eyes to my dismay.

I don't want to lose him. I don't want him to slip from my finger tips the way my mom did.

I reach out for him, to grasp his hand, but he steps back, shaking his head at me and muttering useless apologies.

And then he walks away. He walks away from the lake. From me. And our friendship.

The worst part is that I let him go.

His words were like knives.

I spent all the weeks alone. Passing him in the hall, seeing him with his new friends. It hurt. And that's why I promised I'd never let anyone have that advantage over me.

It made me cold in a way.

I push away the emotions that start to overwhelm me.

I need to stop reminiscing with the past.

Once the bell rings, I exit the art room and find my way to class. Liam doesn't bother to ask me where I've been. He understands I don't want to talk. And that's probably why he hadn't come to find me.

At the end of the day, instead of going back to Liam's, I choose to head on home. Alone. The way I want to spend the rest of the night.

We drive in silence.

When we arrive, I bid Liam a goodbye and that's it. I run home and lock myself away in my room for hours.

I snuggle up under my sheets and clutch my pillow tightly to my chest. I feel like I'm twelve years old again by doing this.

And just as I'm about to fall asleep, a knock sounds at my door. I don't react to it at first. That is, till it becomes more urgent.

I stand up from the bed, annoyed and frustrated, and make my way over. I swing it open, ready to tell the person to piss off. But I'm stuck in my place when I see it's Adam.

He has his hands tucked in to his pocket as he rocks back and forth on the ball of his feet. He gazes at me almost shyly. "Hi," He breathes.

I jerk my head in a nod and knit my fingers together while I stare at him. I watch his timid expression morph to horror. About time he noticed.

"They got you, didn't they?" He questions. I don't know how to reply.

That speech I had made up earlier just isn't coming together in my head properly. And just like that, I completely forget it and instead, stare hopelessly lost at the boy in front of me.

So much for telling him off, I think gloomily.

Once Adam realizes I'm not going to reply, he says, "You've been gone for a while. Where were you?"

"Places," I reply monotonously. Adam frowns and he seems to go frustrated by my sudden cold shoulder. I guess he was expecting me to scream at him or something when I saw him. And I thought I did too.

But as I stand before him, I'm too weak and tired to fight with him. Because where will it get me? Nowhere. My angry statements never seem to hit him as hard as I wanted them to.

All I want is to curl up in my bed again and to remember her.

I'm ashamed to say her face has become a blur to me, somehow. I remember her eyes and hair, yes, but I don't quite remember everything. Not her smell, her smile. It's all mixed up.

It's because I've pushed away the mere thought of her for too long. It'sick, really. How can you forget about someone who raised you half of your life? I'm not sure. But maybe it's because I've forced myself to.

I wanted to erase her from my life. As if she had never been there to make an imprint. It's stupid and pathetic, I know.

It was the only way to cope with her death. It still is the only way to cope with the fact she's gone.

Adam abruptly cusses and rubs his hand over his face, "Ron, I-I'm sorry. I never wanted that to happen to you. God, I should have warned you. I should have told you!"

I sigh. I don't want the same conversation to play over like it always does. I don't want a sorry. I've heard too much of it.

I go to close the door, but Adam stops me and reaches out for me. This time, I'm the one to step back.

A look of pain crosses his face.

"I don't want apologies," I say lowly, "I just want you to go away."

"Ron-"

I cut him off, "I want you to leave. It's not that hard for you to do," I mumble. "You did it four years ago."

Chapter 19

There is no room left for argument after that.

Adam left immediately, shooting me one last look of despair as he trudged his way home.

Alpha Beckett was on the porch. It seemed he had been watching our whole interaction. How I knew? It's because of the look Alpha Beckett had in eyes.

He was angry, obviously that I had disrespected his son. And probably also because Adam let me talk to him that way.

I didn't understand Alpha Beckett's crazy obsession on why I had to mate with Adam. I mean, there were plenty of other girls in the pack. Who we actually willing to be Adam's mate. They were pretty, kind, obedient.

Everything I really wasn't.

Maybe Alpha Beckett just wanted to watch me break. Maybe he wanted to see me wither in fear of him.

Either way, I knew a lot more hid beneath the surface.

Alpha Beckett had a bigger reason for tormenting me. I just didn't know why. But I knew I'd find out sooner or later, whether I wanted to or not.

It's a bad thing I hate suspense.

I seem to toss and turn endlessly in my bed the next two nights.

I think it's because I'm losing my mind.

I haven't really spoken to anyone since the encounter with Adam. I just wasn't in the mood.

Liam was upset about that. He spent all his free time pestering me with phone calls and notes, and well, everything.

I never did answer.

And it's cowardly, I know. But pushing people away is my coping mechanism. It's how I keep myself functioning.

Well, how I use to keep myself functioning.

It was clearly driving me insane the past few nights. I didn't sleep.

If I did, I'd have nightmares. One's filled with blood, screams, and memories I'd like to forget. So I avoided it. By not sleeping and making myself delirious.

I'd sit on my couch in the middle of the night and watch stupid movies and shows. Sometimes I'd just sit and stare at an old picture of my mom that I had thought I'd toss to the garbage a long time ago.

Guess not.

I was starting to realize a lot of things I hadn't done. Like getting over her death.

Every time I glanced at that picture of her, that familiar ache would rise in my chest. The same ache I felt just days after her death.

The more I thought about it, the more I realized that it's incredibly like deja vu.

The not sleeping, mourning over my mother's death, and over all, being pathetic.

It's on the third night that I have a guess arrive in my monologue of weakness. Surprisingly, it isn't Liam who catches me in the act, but my dad.

It's late, probably around 3 AM when I hear the creak of the door and heavy footsteps.

I don't jump, I don't scream. I just stare numbly at the photo of my mom in my hands.

He's obviously shocked that I'm still awake, because when I glance to him, his lips are parted and his grey eyes are wide.

I don't try to conceal the tears that build up in my eyes.

Usually, I'd tell him to go away so he couldn't see me cry or whatever. But I'm too weak to care. He can watch all he wants. It's not like he'll be here after tonight.

My dad only comes home to collect money, minimal clothes, and then he's gone. Probably because he doesn't want to deal with me.

I bite my lip at the thought.

My one alive parent can't even stand me, I think gloomily. I look down and close my eyes before he can decipher my pain and lonesomeness.

And though I crave for comfort from another, I make it obvious I want to be left alone when I pull up the thin white comforter and lay down on the couch, pretending to go to asleep.

Normally, my dad wouldn't bug me anymore. He'd do the smart thing and walk away. Ignore me, even.

He decides to take a different route this time.

I hear the creak of the floor boards under his weight and then the couch dips. Then he calls faintly, "Ronnie?"

I don't reply. I keep my lips pinched tightly together.

Go away, I plead mentally, just go away and let me wallow in my pity in peace.

He takes me by surprise when he get's off the couch and instead kneels right in front of me. It's only then I open my eyes and stare at the man who has become another stranger in my life. My own father.

He looks more a mess than he did the last time I saw him.

He looks sickly with dark black bags under his eyes a long with his stringy black hair falling in his dull grey eyes. They are more lifeless than before. He is more lifeless than before.

He raises his hands gently, his fingers extending towards me till they are only inches away from my cheek.

I flip over right when his fingers are about to reach my face.

I can hear his shaky exhale of breath. And then, minutes later, he is gone. Leaving me alone.

I squeeze my eyes shut at the minute and cradle the picture of my mom to my chest. I hold on to the last thing I have her desperately.

I force myself to sleep shortly after.

The next day, the sky is full with grey clouds. There is not an ounce of sunlight.

It makes me sink further into depression.

Reluctantly, I get changed in a pair of dark wash jeans and an over sized sweater, a long with a beanie.

I bid my father one last look before I walk to store just as it begins to drizzle. I start running then.

I reach the school in a matter of minutes and make my way up the steps. I repeat my usual schedule.

1) Go to my locker and get my books. Check.

2) Glare at anyone that looks my way. Check.

3) Rush to class. Check.

4) Avoid Liam and don't talk. Double check.

And I know that's really cruel to do. I know. Mainly because in some sort of way, I owe Liam. He saved my life and cared for me when no one else did. He at least deserved to be treated with all the utter most gratitude and respect from me.

I had said to myself that I'd stop running from the inevitable. But I'm an indecisive coward, really.

So I don't talk to Liam. Nor just about anyone else.

As I said before, this is they way I cope through my pain. I don't talk, I don't sleep, I don't care. Because it's easy that way.

I just hope Liam understands that somehow and someway.

Lunch come's faster than I thought it would. Though I'm not complaining.

I get my usual slice of pizza and find my way to Anna's and I's old table. I sit there alone for a while, picking at my food with a white, plastic fork.

Anna.

We obviously haven't made up over the past three days. She knows I'm here, since I've caught her glancing over at me. She sometimes makes a move to come over and converse with me, but one of her new friends always stops her and drags her off. Somewhere far away from me, most likely.

I still feel incredibly bitter about the whole Anna situation. But honestly, it's the least of my concerns. If she didn't want to be my friend anymore, she should just tell me then make me wonder about wonder if we still were.

And as for Adam, yeah, that's another lost cause.

Things are extremely awkward between the two of us. We can barely make eye contact without twitching and shifting around uncomfortably.

I didn't regret saying what I said to him, though.

I was glad that I had finally managed to strike Adam's emotions. Because I was starting to question if he ever had any in the first place.

Pretty much, I'm not talking to anyone.

With that sad thought, I peer around the lunch, catching sight of Liam who's paying for his food. As if sensing my gaze - which he actually probably did - he looks over to me, his green hues meeting mine.

I suck in a sharp breath at his appearance.

He looks better now. Better than when he was taking care of me at his place.

The black bags under his eyes are gone and he no longer looks so oddly pale. His normal skin tone has returned. A subtle tan.

His hair isn't sticking up like it was before either. It's a perfect mess of golden brown hair that lays on his head. Everything about him is perfect.

Man, compared to him, I must look like a complete disaster.

With my hair, my clothes, my black eye, and my black bags. It makes me wonder how I got stuck with someone so.. well, handsome, I guess.

I look away for a minute, ashamed by my appearance. But the temptation becomes too great and I glance back at him, biting down on my lip and watching him from under my lashes.

But then the view is ruin when a body come's into sight.

More particularly, Anna's body.

For a minute, I question if Anna is really here. If she's actually standing in front of me. Mainly because Anna hasn't left her new friend's side in.. well, practically ever.

"Hi," She breathes and tucks a strand of blonde hair behind her ear. "How are you?"

After not talking to me for god-knows-how-long you only ask me how I am? Really?

I grit my teeth in annoyance. My streak of silence has ended. "Just peachy. And yourself?" Every word is filled with bitter sarcasm. And that's exactly the way I want it.

Anna is taken off guard by tone, clearly, since her face contorts into confusion about why I'm being so harsh.

But I think it's easy enough to figure it out.

I know I said I could care less, but with her now before me, it's different. Because those emotions are now starting to rise up in me again.

The one's filled with hate and betrayal and just about everything bad.

"Are you okay?" She asks and motions towards the bruise on my face. "What happened?"

"Nothing," I say with a shrug and then mutter, "Why do you care?"

"Because you're my best friend," She protests and takes a seat next to me, despite my un-welcoming attitude. "I'm worried about you, Ron."

"You don't seem like you are." I answer bluntly.

A small part of me wants her to disagree with me on what I've just said. I want her to say she's sorry. So I can say it too. And then we can go back to way things were. Inseparable.

Another part of me just wants her to leave me alone. I'm trying to make the second time around losing a friend a lot more painless.

She should just turn away right now. Walk away and save us both the hurt. We can slowly drift away from one another and avoid the awkward goodbye's and 'I'm-sorry-I-can't-be-your-friend' speech.

Anna isn't up for that, since she continues on, "Yeah, well, you didn't even call me to tell me you were okay. It's not entirely me my fault," She retorts and looks over to Liam, "But you told him what was going on, didn't you? He told the teachers you were sick. Even got your homework for you. Tell me, were you with him those days you were gone?"

My throat feels dry at her accusation that's she made sound like a question. She doesn't need me to confirm it to know that the answer is yes.

Anna scoffs after a long string of silence from me. "Exactly. So who are you to get mad at me?"

Something inside of me snaps.

"I have every right to be mad at you! You didn't even make the effort to talk to me once you got a boyfriend!" I shout and shake my head frantically at her.

"Yeah, well, I've heard some things about them from you, Ronnie." She spits angrily, "I have my reasons."

"And you believe them over me? Your supposed best friend?" I screech, "You believe a boy who've you met only a month ago, rather than me, who've you known for over a year?"

"It's not like I can ask you about these things!" She argues, "You don't tell me anything! They do! They tell me about their pasts, their families. You don't." She swallows roughly and shakes her head, "I don't even really know who you are, Ronnie."

I look away from her and pinch my lips together. I can't believe she's saying this.

She never brought this up for before. She never cared about this till she started talking to Mandy and Jessica, and her new found love, Cliff.

Another person has been taken away from me because of my stupid pack.

I stand and begin to walk away, ignoring Anna's demands for me to come back and talk to her properly. I don't want to hear it. I don't want to talk anymore. I want to go home and pretend that I can rewind time. Rewind back to when my mom was alive. To when things were so much easier.

And as stupid as it sounds, it feels like the world is crashing down around me. And I'm desperate to escape in anyway that I can.

With that thought in my mind, I run. I run because it's the only thing I know how to do.

I run out the school door into the poor raining, not even caring as the cold seeps into my skin and makes me feel numb with cold.

I block it all out and I run to the woods, frantically trying to find my way home when my sight is blurry in more ways than just literal.

Over the roar of thunder and rain, I hear footsteps behind me. It makes me panic.

The Purgatory Pack, I think, fear immediately coursing through me, they're back!

I pick up my pace, my breathes comes out in heavy pants as I swat away the wet hair that get's into my eyes.

I glance to see they're catching up to me. And quick.

And in those short seconds of glancing back, I manage to trip and fall straight on my face. That's when they reach me.

They reach out and grab me. And I thrash madly, screaming profanities and telling them to let go of me. They don't and hold me tightly against them.

But the stiff muscles in their body feels familiar. And that's when I realize it's the Purgatory Pack, but Liam. And though I feel some sort of relief that I am not going to have to dance with danger, It still doesn't make the situation any better.

I twist my body and look up at him.

His once neat hair now sticks to his forehead. And his eyes are more green than ever. And even like this, he still the most beautiful sight I've ever seen.

"Why did you chase me?" I ask and wipe strands of hair out of my face. "Why can't you just let me run away in peace for once?"

"Because I'm sick of it," He replies. "I'm sick of you running away and not letting me know what's wrong. I'm sick of you not trusting me."

"That's because I can't just put my trust and faith in you, Liam."

"Why not?" He rasps.

I don't answer.

"Why not?" He echoes. "Tell me!" He demands.

"Because I don't want to get hurt anymore!" I tell him and I can't conceal the tears that surface in my eyes. "I don't want to let another person in so I can lose them. I don't want to lose you like I lost my mom." I say, "It'll hurt so much more if I lose you, because I know I could have stopped. I can stop it. Don't you see what I'm doing is what's best for us?"

"That doesn't even make sense, Ron," He whispers almost inaudibly and cups my cheek, bringing me closer and making me rest my hands on his chest. "Pushing me away isn't what's best. Letting me help you is what's best. Let me in, Ronnie. Let me in."

He shakes me hard and I ball my fist in his shirt, shaking my head for the hundredth time today. I want to say no. I want to tell him to leave. But I can't when he's so close. Not when he's holding me so close and his breath is on my lips. Not when temptation is only a inch away.

I hold my breath as he wraps his arms around my waist and pushes his hips against mine while sliding his other hand into my hair and drawing me forward to where our lips nearly touch. A jolt of pure pleasure over comes me.

My mind screams at me to back away, but I don't listen. I don't want to.

I drag one hand away from his chest and and to his bicep, my nails digging into the rock hard muscles as I hold his heated gaze. He has an emotion I've never seen anyone look at me with before.

Desire.

And though I'm drenched with water, I don't feel cold anymore. Mainly because of Liam's body heat and the fact that we're so utterly close. I don't care about anything right now.

I can't when my brain isn't working right.

I stare into Liam's green hues as he whispers, "Let me change your mind."

And then he kisses me.

CHAPTER 20

I immediately freeze up once Liam presses his lips to mine.

Mainly because I have no clue on what to do.

I have never kissed anyone before. Maybe when I was a ignorant child and I thought it would be fun to kiss a boy. Naturally, I didn't know what to do. So it would resort in chaste and silly, short pecks that left us giggling afterwards.

Those were simple pecks that didn't require much effort, though.This does.

What do I do?

I consider pulling away and saving myself the embarrassment. But just as I ponder this, Liam grips me ever so tighter. It makes me believe that he's anticipated my actions before hand. Figures.

He slides his hand down from my cheek to my chin, where he tilts my head upwards and slowly maneuvers his lips on mine, silently showing me what to do.

I squeeze my eyes shut and remain still under his movements.

It takes me a while before I finally gain up the nerve and begin to kiss back. My kisses start off clumsy as I nervously fumble my lips with his, but soon enough, with Liam's guidance, I respond more eagerly and smoothly.

And once those nerves that I felt before are pressed to the back of my mind, I start to notice faint sensations that are beginning to creep up on me.

Like the shiver that ripples up my spine and the feeling that arises in my chest and makes warmth flood through my whole body.

And though this is completely weird and foreign to me, I determine it's the best sensation I have ever experienced yet.

I drag my hand away from his chest to his neck and I note vaguely that his skin feels oddly hot under my fingertips and the way Liam tastes of cinnamon and something else that is sickly sweet.

And I simply can't get enough of him.

We break apart briefly, catching our breaths for a minute or two before we kiss again. This time though, the kiss isn't soft or gentle, it's needy and urgent.

As time passes, I end up pressed against a tree with my legs and arms and just about every body part wrapped Liam. He has me wrapped up in his arms too.

I don't feel the cold anymore. Not when the tree is protecting us from the rain and the fact that Liam is huddled over me, protecting me with his broad body from the stray raindrops that find their way through the leaves and branches above us.

He pulls away shortly after this thought occurs and leans his forehead right against me. He examines me silently and wondrously, wiping away wet strands of hair that stick to my face.

The corner of his lips tug up in a smile and hesitantly, I return it. He let's me down despite my slight protest and wraps his arms around me. "Let's get you inside before you get sick."

I roll my eyes at him, but I don't argue. Mainly because I'm still dazed about what just happened.

Liam and I kissed, I think dreamily.

And the worst part is that I liked it. Loved it.

Because what the hell happened to never-let-Liam-get-close-to-me plan? Wasn't I supposed to cut all strings with him? Wasn't I supposed to cut strings with everyone? Yeah, it was.

I was supposed to skip town and run away from my problems. Away from Alpha Beckett, Adam, Anna, my dad, and well, Liam.

But who was I trying to fool? Them or me? I couldn't leave. Not as easily as I wanted. I have connections here. People who I care for, I guess. Like Liam.

Yeah, I can run away from my problems, but not fate. And I surely couldn't run away from my emotions.

I tried when my mom died. That certainly didn't work. And it won't with Liam.

Ending up where I am right now with Liam was bound to happen. Sure, I fooled myself that I would never come to grow close to Liam, but that was also really stupid.

It's so cliche. Kissing in the rain, the whole love/hate relationship with Liam. My fear of loving someone. God, my life has become a teen fiction romance.

The only problem is that I won't have a happy ending with Alpha Beckett on my case. And the mating ceremony looming over my head.

The mating ceremony is only three weeks.

The thought hits me suddenly. It feels like a punch to my stomach and like the wind has just been knocked out of me.

Because I don't know what to do. Because I don't know how to avoid becoming Adam's mate. Because I'm scared I'm going to be forced to be with someone who I don't even love. Who I don't even like.

Yeah, unlike those teen fiction romance's, I certainly won't get my fairytale ending.

We arrive at Liam's place about fifteen minutes later. Immediately when we get inside, Liam tosses me a pair of shorts and a shirt that fits me like some ridiculous dress. I toss him back the shorts when I get out of the bathroom.

I help him with wringing out the water of our clothes since Liam doesn't have a dryer in his small cabin. We hang them over the fire and take a seat on the couch where we sit in silence, listening to the fire crackle.

The silence isn't awkward, though. Well, at least not for me. I'm too busy replaying the kiss over and over again in my head to even pay attention.

I just can't get it out of my head.

I'm left wondering where Liam and I now stand. Are we friends who kiss? Are we a couple? I'm not sure. And I'm too embarrassed to question him on it. It'll make me look like an idiot.

I also don't ask because I'm not sure where I want us to stand. I don't know if I want to forget the kiss or if I want to remember it. I don't know if I'm grateful if it happened or if I regret. It's all so confusing.

Liam notices my obvious distress and twists around to face me. His eyebrows furrow at the sight of me gnawing on my lip and twisting my fingers together. "Are you okay?" He asks.

I don't reply for a minute. I simply bite down harder on my lip till I taste blood and the familiar coppery taste fills my mouth. I ignore the pinch of pain that follows and continue pressing my teeth down on the cut that I've just re-opened that was caused by the Purgatory pack.

"Is that blood?" Liam eyes widen and he leans forward. I'm sure he's got his confirmation because he shoots up and rushes to the kitchen, wetting a paper towel and coming back.

"I'm fine," I say when he tries to press the wet cloth to my lips. I push his hand away and wipe at the blood with my fingertips. "Just a cut."

Liam swats my hand away and forces me to be still when he grasps my chin. I resist the urge to thrash and let him do as he pleases.

When he's done, he pulls away and discards the paper to the side, shaking his head at me as if I'm some naughty child that has been caught with their hand in the cookie jar. "What'd you do that for? You opened up the cut again on your lip that was starting to heal," He frowns, "Do you always that? Bite on your lip till it bleeds?"

"It sounds bad when you put it like that," I mutter and reach up to touch my lip, but Liam, again, swats my hand away.

"It'll start bleeding again if touch it."

I roll my eyes, "It's just a little blood." When I say this, Liam makes a face of distaste and before I can swallow down the words, I blurt, "Does it gross you out? It shouldn't, you've probably seen more then enough of it."

I regret it once the words tumble beyond my lips.

Because it brings up the memories of the fact Liam is a rogue. And indeed that he has killed people. He had even touched me while he still had blood on his hands from another man he had just murdered.

The memory makes me cringe at the image that pops up into my head. With Liam and the blood that felt hot and sticky on my face.

Surprisingly, though, Liam doesn't frown or wince. He simply sucks in a breath and mutters, "Harsh."

I shake my head and look up to meet his gaze, "I'm sorry, I didn't-"

"It's okay," He says, cutting me off. "I've heard worse than that."

"That doesn't make me any less guilty," I reply, "You don't deserve that. You've done so many nice things for me."

"Just a few kind actions doesn't over shadow the rest of the bad stuff I've done," He shrugs casually. "Are you thirsty or hungry? I don't have much here. Only microwave soups and water."

"Yeah, but-"

This time, Liam's words don't cut me off, but his actions as he nosily starts rummaging through his small fridge.

I frown and stand up from the couch to see him squeezing his broad frame half way into the fridge. Normally, I would laugh at something like this, but I'm more set on the fact of why Liam so simply shrugged off the previous conversation. As if he's trying to avoid. And maybe he is.

He probably doesn't want to talk about his past. Or how I want to know so badly why he has killed people. And how he ended up in Portland.

I want answers that I probably don't deserve. But he wants answers too, doesn't he?

He appears again out of the fridge carrying a old-looking jar or pickles. Immediately when he uncaps, the whole area is filled with this stench that makes me sick. "Gross! How old is that?" I shriek.

Liam shrugs and sniffs it with a thoughtful expression. "I'm guessing about.. seven months old. Maybe this was in here before?"

"Didn't you ever clean the fridge out when you got here?"

"Not really," He retorts and places the cap back on the spoiled jar of pickles. He tosses into the trash. "I just started back up the generator and got the place working again."

"So you didn't clean out anything?" I make a face at him, "That's nasty."

"I swapped out the mattresses and the sheets," He objects, "But that's about it." He resorts to shuffling around the cabinet and pulls out a pack of dried noodles. "Looks like ramen noodles are on the menu tonight."

"I'm not hungry," I tell him. "But thanks."

"Suit yourself," He mutters and peels off the lid of the cup and fills it with water before popping it into the microwave and setting it for three minutes.

I take that chance to return back to the couch and flip around till I stumble across a movie that's good enough for me.

I curl up on the couch and clutch the blanket that Liam had tossed me earlier and drape it over me. Liam joins me a little while later with a steaming cup of soup.

He kicks his feat up on the coffee table and we fall back into silence. Well, it's mostly silently except for Liam's chewing and the soft whispers of the people in the movie.

After a few minutes, Liam nudges me and I turn to face him to find him handing me a fork. I stare at it for a few seconds before I sigh and take it. Obviously he's going to keep bugging me if I don't eat.

I scoot closer as much as I can without really leaning on him. Liam isn't pleased by this since he places the cup down and nestles me against him properly, then he picks it up again and holds it directly in front of both of us.

I scowl him but decide not to pester him about it.

Though he decides to pester me.

"Is it safe to ask about what happened with Anna?" He asks.

I don't freeze up, though. I simply shake my head. "It was nothing."

"It didn't seem like 'nothing,'" He says, "I caught some of what she said. It was harsh."

"You were ease dropping?"

"No," A smirk tugs at the corner of his lips. "It's not ease dropping when you're practically screaming across the cafeteria for everyone to hear."

"I wasn't screaming," I mutter.

"Yeah, you kinda were."

"Aren't you supposed to be offering kind words about it instead of mocking me?"

"Maybe," He replies, "But I've learned that when I anger you, you give me answers much more easily."

I scuff, "You're unbelievable."

"And you're avoiding the conversation," He declares. "Was it that bad?"

I pinch my lips together and let a dreadful sigh leave my lips when I realize Liam isn't going to drop this. And I should probably just answers to get him off my case. "Of course it's bad when words like that come from your best friend."

"Haven't you guys fought before?"

"Not really," I frown, "The weird part is that the things she said.. she never brought it up before it any of our conversations or whatever."

"What'd she say?" He questions, his eyebrows furrowing.

I knit my fingers together and shrug, "Stuff about how she's heard some things about me and how I don't tell her anything."

"It's probably those girls she's been hanging around that's influenced her to think badly of you," He says, "What are her friends names, anyway? Bitch One and Bitch Two?"

"Something like that." I laugh dryly, "Don't forget her boyfriend."

"Yeah, Clifford, right?"

"Cliff," I correct, "He's Adam's best friend, I guess. Though I don't really see them talk much."

"They probably don't even know each other's favorite color." Liam retorts with a snort, "Isn't he the next in line to be Adam's beta?"

I nod jerkily, "Yeah." And I'm next in-line to Adam's mate.

"Have you talked to Adam?"

I let out a shaky breath and lie straight threw my teeth when I say, "No." I don't want to talk about Adam anymore. I don't want to talk about Anna either. I just want to forget about it all. Liam isn't going to allow this, clearly, since he presses on the subject.

"You're lying. I can tell." He says. "I won't get mad if you did. I just don't like the creep."

"At the moment, I don't either." I mutter and blurt out stupidly, "We use to be friends when we were younger."

"Yeah?" He raises a dark brow at me, "How did that happen?"

I shrug, "He was.. nice back then." I glance down at my knitted hands. "I don't know, but he made me smile and laugh. Especially when we had our water fights down by the lake."

He shuffles around a bit uncomfortably on the couch and finally places the cup that he had been holding in his hand down on the coffee table. He hesitantly asks, "Why'd you stop being friends?"

"My mom's death." I reply bluntly and focus my gaze on an invisible spot on the wall.

Liam wraps an around my shoulder and sighs, resting his chin on my head. "So you stopped being friend's with him after she died?"

"No," I say, "He stopped being friends with me. Because of my dad." I don't know why I'm telling him this. Why I'm suddenly so insistent on telling someone my life story. But I clearly have a very bad case of word vomit because I continue on with my stupid rambling, "We fell to the bottom of the pack because my dad quit his guard duty. No one wants to be friends with you in the pack if you're not at the top of the food chain.

The whole 'We're-a-pack-and-we-stick-together' is bull. But I think you know that by know. I can see why people go rogue."

Liam sighs, "Being a rogue isn't all that great."

"Why not? You don't have to answer to any Alpha or anything." And you certainly don't have to forced to be with someone if you don't want to be.

"Yeah, but it get's lonely not having a pack. My old one.. we were, close, I guess you could say."

I don't bother asking. Mainly because Liam won't answer. If he wants to tell me, he'll do it by himself. And it's made evident that he's not going to tell me anything since he remains silent. I'm the one who breaks by saying, "Your mom passed too, right?"

Liam grows tense for a minute before he relaxes and stiffly nods.

"Does it get any easier?" I ask timidly. "You know, to think about her without wanting to cry?"

"Not really," He replies, "It's been seven years since she passed. It still hurts."

"How'd it happen?" I whisper and angle my head to where I can look up at him. He doesn't meet my eyes, though. He stares straight ahead like I had done moments ago.

"She was attacked."

I give him a grim smile. "Mine too."

Liam glances down at me when I say this. He offers me a look of sorrow. Something I have never liked people to do, but instead of angrily telling him to stop, I let my grim smile blossom into a sincere one, silently letting him know I'm okay and he doesn't need to be sorry he didn't cause.

And then we're back to what we were minutes ago. Silent and lost in thought. Or well, I think he is by the look on his face.

Before I can help myself, I reach up and smooth away the worry lines that crease between his brows.

He does what he did earlier and angles his head down, leaning his forward against mine and letting his warm breath fan over my lips. I'm tempted to press my lips to his once again, but I restrain myself and watch as he lazily traces over my facial features with his other hand that isn't wrapped around me.

He traces around my eyes, then my nose, then my eyebrows, and then my lips, where his fingers linger.

A smirk suddenly appears on his face. "Did I change your mind earlier?"

I can't help but shift uncomfortably and roll my eyes at him, "Shut up."

"What? It's about time we talked about the kiss."

"First you have to tell me something about your past. Something that plays a crucial part of your life." I say and quickly add, "And I'll tell you one of mine."

"Okay, I'll tell you something of my past, if you'll answer one question that I have. You don't have to tell anything of your past. Just answer my question."

"Fine," I breathe, not knowing what I'm fully agreeing to. "But you first."

"Alright," He says. "What do you want to know, exactly?"

"About your family. Did you have any siblings?"

He nods, "Yeah. I had one. My younger sister, Flora. She was six."

"Did she look like you?"

"Not really. She had my mom's blonde hair. But her eyes were green. We both got that from our dad. His name was Ben." He tells me, "We look exactly a like. Except he has darker brown hair and he's a little more tan then me. But I'm taller. Flora thought I was her jungle gym by the way she gripped onto my legs and climbed all over me."

I laugh, "She sounds adorable."

"She was," He smiles, "She would force me to take her to the library and everything. She liked daises. I know because she was always putting them in her hair. My mom and her were both very much alike." He's quiet for a minute or two before he says, "She died when I was twelve."

I pinch my lips together, unsure of what to say. Instead, I rest my hand on top of his and squeeze.

"She was attacked too. I didn't get there on time."

I know Liam's feared he's said too much since his brows furrow and look crosses his face. One of regret.

I resist the urge to bite my lip. "And your dad?"

"I don't know," He replies and he seems to shake himself out his trance since he turns to me with a grim smile. "But now it's my turn to ask you something."

I figure he deserves an answer, so I nod eagerly. "Shoot."

"I want to know about Adam. Why you were... with him... if you guys didn't talk. And I also want to know about your dad."

I stiffen and debate on not replying. Maybe even running off and making up some dumb excuse. But it's futile. Because I can't run away from this long awaited conversation anymore. Especially not if the supposed mating ceremony with Adam is only three weeks ago.

Liam is my only hope to get out of it. And clearly, after this kiss we've shared today, he isn't intent on keeping himself or me at a distance. We are bound to grow close together and to share secrets we would never tell anyone else. There's no longer any point of running from it.

So I speak.

"I don't know who my father is anymore," I tell him honestly. "I haven't known who he was for a long time. We don't talk. And we don't see each other very often. He's out. With other women." I say, quite numbly. "He's not over her, though. My mom, I mean. He keeps a picture of her in his wallet and there is always one stuffed under his pillow.

I think he get's with these other women to maybe forget about her. I tried to forget. Just in a different way. By ignoring the fact she was gone and refusing to cry. I convinced myself I was over her for a long time."

"But you're not?" He utters softly.

I snort, "I wish. But you can't just get over someone who made that big of an impact on your life."

"And Adam?"

I let out a shaky sigh before I say, "It was.. staged."

"What?"

"It was staged," I repeat. "The relationship. It wasn't real. We did it because.." I trail off. I press my lips together. Don't say it. Don't say it. This isn't being smart, Ronnie. You're going to get Liam hurt.

My indifferent expression betrays me and soon enough, I am fighting back the tears of frustration.

I don't want Liam hurt. I don't him to slip through my fingertips the way my mom did. I don't want to lose him. And I certainly will if I tell.

I shake my head and glance to Liam who gives me a bewildered expression, "Ron?"

"I'm sorry," I blurt, "I can't.. I'm-I'm not ready to talk about it. Okay?"

Liam's face contorts into anger. For a minute, I think it's directed at me, but he quickly asks, "Did he do anything to you, Ron? Did he force you to do anything?"

I squeeze my eyes shut and shake my head more rapidly. "Just-"

"Did he touch you? Did he-"

My eyes fly open at the sudden slur of accusations about Adam, "No! Liam, you don't-"

"He touched you! He obviously did something if you're about to cry right now!" Liam jerks away from me and stands up, incredibly furious now. Probably at the thought of Adam touching me. The thought makes a disgusted shiver trace up my spine. "I'll kill him. I'll kill him for laying a hand on you, Ronnie."

"Do you hear yourself right now? You sound like a mad man!"

"He has no right to touch what's mine!" Liam snarls and goes to stalk past me, but I reach out and grip his powerful forearm.

"Don't," I say, "Don't go and do something crazy. Don't!"

Liam turns back to me. He looks more intimidating than ever. His muscles are bunched and his eyes are hard, and crazy, too. "And why shouldn't I? He probably laid his filthy hands on you. I'll break his fucking arms. I'll laugh when I do it too as he screams for his daddy who won't be able to save him." He sneers and he walks off to the door, ready to slam it open and go hunt after Adam. But my words stop him. And probably leave him bewildered in more ways than one.

"Adam never did anything to touch me or harm me or whatever," I breathe shakily and raggedly. I swallow roughly before I say, "But Alpha Beckett did."

Chapter 21

Before I can really comprehend what's happening, I am pushed up against a wall, Liam hovering over me. He stares down at me, his green eyes drawn narrowed. All filled with anger and craze. His eyes are wild as he let's out shallow breaths.

He's obviously misinterpreted my previous statement. And it's probably by the way I phrased it. But I can't find my voice to quickly object and explain thoroughly about what I mean.

Instead I gaze up at him, feeling incredibly small and weak under his burning eyes. I swallow roughly when his forearm presses against my throat. And I know he's not doing this to hurt me. Mainly because he doesn't apply any sort of pressure. He's just trying to lock me in place.

He can't risk me running away when I have said something like this. When I have dropped my biggest and darkest secret that I have been trying to conceal for a month now.

Though I know Liam won't hurt me; panic still creeps up on me. Because I feel so incredibly confined between the wall and

Liam's broad body. Almost trapped as if I'm some deer in head lights. But I guess I kinda am.

It's funny, really. Just a few hours ago I was in between a tree and Liam's massive body and I certainly wasn't feeling as claustrophobic and trapped as I am now.

I realize that's exactly why he has me in this position when I begin to squirm. It's futile. I can't move my arms or my legs or just about anything. It's because of the weight Liam is putting on me and the current position I'm in. He wants to lock me into place. He wants to ensure I won't run just like I have too many times before.

He's tired of me running. And honestly, so am I.

"What did he do, Ronnie? Did Alpha Beckett hurt you? Did he touch you?" Liam spews sporadically, all at once. My head spins at his questions that sounds more like accusations.

I manage to shake my head. Liam obviously wants a real answer since he removes his forearm from across my throat and instead grabs me by the shoulders, lowerng his face down to mine. His top lip curls over his teeth with a deep and frustrated growl. "Explain, Ronnie."

My throat feels dry and taught at his sudden demand. I am silent for several minutes. He forces me to look him in the eyes when I shamefully avert my eyes to the ground. He hisses a lethal, "Answer me."

The the grip on my shoulders tighten to a point where I register a pinch of pain. But it doesn't matter, not right now. Besides, I've had worse.

And it was because of Alpha Beckett, a small part of me whispers, tell him. Tell him so he can make sure Alpha Beckett will never harm you again.

I want so badly to simply spill the secret that I've been holding in for too long. But there's another part of me that argues if I do say, I could be putting Liam at risk. I could lose him.

And I'm so incredibly scared for that to happen. Because I don't want to lose him. I don't want him to slip away from my grasp the way my mom did. I have the chance to protect Liam. I have the chance to preserve his life. The way I never got the chance to do with my mother's life.

Either way, if I decide to tell or not, I'm still putting the both of us at risk. It's either let Alpha Beckett keep manipulating me as if I'm some puppet, or put a end to it before Beckett puts an end to the both of us.

I know I won't comply to the mating with Adam. I'll end up stupidly disobeying because of my morals. Because I can't be with someone who I don't love. Someone who I can't even look in the eye anymore.

And when I don't follow orders, Alpha Beckett will kill Liam. Then Anna. And maybe me if he decides I am of no use anymore. But I'm more scared for Liam and Anna's death than I am mine. Mainly because I know Alpha Beckett won't let it be a merciful death. He will make it slow and agonizing. He will make me regret for not obeying his demands to be with Adam.

Maybe I haven't been protecting Liam and Anna. Maybe I have been setting us up for disaster.

I suddenly realize I was incredibly stupid for making myself believe that I would actually go along with Alpha Beckett's demands. Or that I could possibly run away.

I couldn't run away. Not when I knew I'd be leaving behind Liam and Anna. I had too many connections here. Too many memories to simply discard.

The only way I can escape this whole mating with Adam is if I tell Liam. It's worth the risk. Even if it does end up getting us killed.

So I manage to utter weakly, "Alpha Beckett has been black mailing me to be with Adam."

My statement doesn't do any justice to suppress Liam's budding anger. "Why?" He asks throatily. His eyes flash darkly as he tilts his head at me, examining me like his prey.

"Because he wants me to mate with Adam," I whisper so faintly that it's barely audible. I know he catches it when he presses down harder on my shoulders. It makes me wince.

"What are you talking about?" He says, a growl stirring in his chest that makes his eyes flash again.

I begin to wonder if I've done the right thing by telling Liam this. I'm concerned he will go incredibly ballistic and do something irrational. Like running off into a war zone with my pack and end up getting himself killed.

I'm quickly wrenched from my thoughts when Liam grips my chin roughly and forces me to look him in the eye. "Look at me," He sneers. "And fucking answer me."

"I told you, Alpha Beckett black mailed me so I'd mate with Adam. That's why I was with him."

And that's when he loses it.

He detaches himself from me and begins crazily ranting about how I could keep this from him, and why, and then he throws in some profanities.

"I just wanted to protect you," I argue at one moment when he declares that I was foolish for keeping this vital source of information from him.

"Protect me? From what?" He let's out a sinister laugh that makes me flinch. "From Adam? From your stupid Alpha?"

"Yes," I mutter. "If I didn't go along, they would hurt you. Or Anna. Or my dad. Or even me. I had to take those things into consideration," I pause for a minute, then say, "It was stupid of me, I know. I should have told you the moment after I actually did get hurt from-"

"Wait, what?" He cuts me off. The angry scowl on his face disappears for a minute or two. It's replaced with confusion. "When you actually got hurt? Are you talking about the Purgatory when they attacked you?"

I nod stiffly and suck in a shaky breath, "Yeah. That attack.. It wasn't caused because of you. It was because I didn't go along with the kissing Adam at the-"

Liam - again - interrupts me when he hears the word 'kiss' and 'Adam' in the same sentence. The angry scowl returns along with a gleam of jealously in his eyes. "Kiss? When the fuck did you almost kiss Adam?"

"If you let me explain, I'll get to it."

"How long has this been going on? Have you kissed Adam before? How could you go behind my back like that?"

"I haven't kissed him!" I spit, "And go behind your back? We weren't even a couple."

"It doesn't matter. You're mine. You're not supposed to go around playing house with other guys!"

"I didn't have a choice! I did it to keep you safe!" I seethe and shove at his chest when he attempts to grab on to me. "The Purgatory came after me when I ran off from that night of the ball after I refused to kiss Adam. They went after me because Alpha Beckett gave them a lead. He knew they were angry about you killing a pack member. So they chased me and well, you know what happens next."

He is quiet for a mere amount of seconds before he breathes a profanity and slams his fist into the wall. And then again. And again.

He does it until his knuckles become bloody.

That's when I step in and grasp his shoulder, trying to still his jerky movements. But he simply shrugs me off. I try to ignore the subtle pain that arises in my chest at his action.

"Stop it," I demand feebly, "Liam, stop-"

"I'm going." He declares abruptly. He quickly snatches his leather jacket from above the fireplace and shrugs it on, not even caring that it's still wet.

"What? Where?" I ask as I follow him out the door, into the musky night air. I don't even care when I feel the dirt and leaves sink in between my toes. The only thing I'm concerned about right now is what rash decision Liam is about to make.

But he doesn't answer.

He shifts into wolf form and takes off. Leaving me behind.

I'm tempted to run after him and somehow convince him to calm down. To tell him I'm sorry. But I don't think that's particularly smart when Liam is battling his anger. And I certainly don't want to get into the middle of that.

So I decide to let him cool off. And pray to God he doesn't go attack Alpha Beckett without thinking it through.

Yeah, I want Alpha Beckett gone, but it's too.. well, risky. Everything is at risk right now. Most importantly, our lives.

I know that Liam likes playing fire. He always has, clearly.

I just hope he doesn't get burned.

The next three days are long and agonizing.

The only thing I do is wake up, eat, go to school, eat again, go home, sleep. And though this is just events of my everyday life, it's still weird. Mainly because for those three days, everything is peaceful and quiet.

There is no one to pick a fight with me. No Alpha Beckett. No Adam. No Anna. And no Liam.

They haven't been around much. Anna and Adam maintain their distance. It's only during lunch that we acknowledge each other's existence with chaste glances at one another. We always turn away after and pretend to be incredibly engrossed with our food. That's it.

As for Alpha Beckett and Liam, they are a no show. Alpha Beckett is gone from the pack territory. Mrs. Beckett tells me briefly that her husband has gone away to discuss business with other packs. When she tells me this, I can't help but flinch and wonder if one of those packs Alpha Beckett might be associating with is the Purgatory.

I ponder that thought at night. But I quickly convince myself when imagines of Alpha Beckett and those five men who attacked me pop into my head with a scene of them talking about plotting my death.

Besides, I'm grateful I don't have to listen to his stupid commands for the next three days. It's almost like my normal, lonely life before being chosen to be Adam's mate has returned.

Hence, the almost part of that sentence.

When I had no Liam around to constantly fill my thoughts, when Adam and I were simply strangers with memories. When Anna and I were friends. When my dad wasn't around to even wish me a happy birthday.

Things have really changed.

Because Liam does constantly fill my thoughts. Adam and I are supposed to be mated. Anna and I aren't friends. And my dad is around.

So much for normal.

Then again, you can't really ever have a normal life if you're a teenage werewolf.

Mostly the thing that is the most shocking about all of what I've just listed is that my dad is around. He hasn't left.

We don't talk or really look at one another, but he's still there. And for some reason, it bugs me. Probably because I'm not use to his company and because I don't know why he's here. It leads me to believe he wants something.

The last time my dad stayed for more than a day,it was because he had no cash. He begged me for money when he got tired of being around. At first, I told him to piss off. But I finally got fed up enough to give him the money I had raised just a summer before.

I was planning to spend it on more art supplies, but it was made obvious that even if I had gotten my supplies, I wouldn't be able to paint with his constant nagging in my ear.

It's not until Saturday night that my dad finally speaks to me.

"Are you hungry?" He asks timidly. He stands awkwardly at the entrance of my door while I remain seated on my bed and file through my homework for the weekend.

I glance up from my English assignment. My eyebrows furrow. "Uh, why?"

"I was gonna go head out for a pizza. To Accuardi's. You remember that place, right? We took you as a kid."

I reconciliation with my suppressed memories of my childhood at the mention of the oddly familiar name. I remember it mostly because Accuardi's was the only thing I ever ate as a kid. I refused anything else.

My parents gave in when they realized that. It was after mom's death that I stopped going. Because of the fact many of my memories with my mother lie in that place. And because It's more into the town while the pack lives on the out skirts. It takes too long to get there with human walking. And I don't suppose I can just go jogging into town in wolf form without people screaming for their lives.

The last time I went town is when I got beat by the Purgatory.

Good times, I think sarcastically before I state blandly, "That's in town."

He clears his throat, "Um, yeah. I got my car from the shop the other day. It shouldn't take us too long to get there, if you want to come, that is."

I'm silent for a minute or two. He must have done something really bad if he's offering to go get dinner with me.

I realize whatever the reason he has been sticking around these past few days must be pretty serious. I'm bound to find out sooner or later. I rather find out what this is about from him then the stupid pack gossip.

I sigh, "Alright."

I place my homework on my desk and slip on my leather jacket, along with my combat boots. I don't bother doing up the laces.

I follow him out the door and out to his polished truck. My eyes widen at the sight, since last time I saw his truck, it was all beaten up with scratches and dents. Now it's perfectly painted with a sleek coat of black and there are no traces of previous abuse to his poor car. He notices my facial expression and gives me a grim smile.

"It looks better then before, huh?" He asks as he runs his hand over the hood of the car. "It took about a year for the engine to get fixed. Took another year just to get all the dents out."

"Cool," Is all I say. Then I hop into the car and he starts the car. We drive in silence. But it doesn't bug me. I simply gaze out the window the whole time and watch as the town's over due Christmas lights come into view.

It's no where near Christmas, but clearly, they don't care. They leave it up all year. It somehow bring's life to the dull brick building's and makes the town seem so much more warm and friendlier then I remember it being.

There are also soft glows of light coming off from the other shops and when I step out of the car, the air smells of warm pastries. I realize it's coming from the bakery down the street. I make a mental note to stop by after we get done at Accuardi's.

We drift into the warm and small restruant that smells equally as good. I can't help but stare as one girl walks carrying a platter of pizza that is topped with goey cheese and pepperino.

It's not long before a perky hostess takes us to a table located in the back and hands us our menu's. She wishes a nice meal and then skips off.

The waitress stops by between tables and takes our order. It's only when our food is in front of us and I've already scooped up a slice of hot pizza that I say, "So, what's up?"

My dad shrugs and brushes a stray of inky black hair back. "Nothing. Why?"

"I don't know. I just figured you wanted to tell me something."

He frowns, "What?"

"I mean that you obviously have something to tell me if you offered to go out to dinner with me. What'd you do?"

My dad scuffs, "I got arrested for robbing a bank."

Though it's evident he's being sarcastic, I still say, "You serious?"

"Have you always been such a smart ass?" He mutters. I barely catch it, but when I do, I snort.

"Of course. So what is it?"

He draws in a shaky breath and places his pizza down, leaning back in his seat with a hard look on his face. I decide this must be pretty serious and place my food down as well. I don't want to choke when he announces whatever the heck he feels the need to tell me.

He mumbles something. Something so quiet that I can't even catch with my werewolf hearing. "Huh?" I say, my eyebrows furrowing in confusion.

He covers his hand over his mouth and repeats it.

It's comes out incredibly muffled. The only thing I catch from the sentence is the word 'met'. I roll my eyes. "I don't speak idiot, sorry."

He isn't even phrased by my insult.

His silver eyes flash to mine and he suddenly blurts, "I met someone."

I don't necessarily freeze or go into panic at his words. I just stare at him like he's grown a second head.

Met someone? What did he mean met someone? As in he met a girl that he found special? The thought makes me uneasy for some weird reason. "You met someone," I repeat blankly. "So?"

"Well," He drawls, "It's a woman. Her name's Tara and well.." He trails off and bites down on his lip nervously. "We've been seeing one another for a while. I didn't bother to tell you because I didn't think it was important. But things have gotten serious."

"Does she know about me?" I blurt. He nods.

"That's why I'm here. She wants to meet the infamous Ronnie Mars." He jokes lightly, obviously just trying to ease the tension. It doesn't work.

"Why? Is she gonna become my step-mom or something?"

The nerve-wrecking part is that my dad doesn't laugh when I say this like he probably would before. My dad has had plenty flings. One's that he hasn't concered himself with telling me. His relationship with this chick must be getting serious. And if she's in her late thirties like my dad is, I bet she's expecting a ring on her finger pretty soon.

Just the mere thought of my dad getting married to another woman is.. weird. And almost feels like betrayl. To my mom, that is.

She was his mate. His other half. Once your other half is gone, that's it, right? You don't look for another. But my dad has. He's found someone. And I can't help but feel angry.

He wasn't over mom. How could he date another woman? How could he be in a relationship when he was still mourning over the death of his wife?

It's wrong. So wrong.

But why should I care, anyway? If she was human, they could never live together. Never marry. The pack wouldn't allow it.

It's not until I look up that my dad has been ranting the whole time. I've just been to tuned out to listen. I break his rambling when I ask, "Is she human?"

He nods jerkily and I watch his adam's apple bob.

"You know the pack wouldn't allow you guys to marry or anything, right?"

"I know. If it comes down to it and we do decide to take the relationship a step further, then.. I'm ready to give up the pack if that happens."

I gape at him. Oh, so now he's willing to ditch the pack for a girl, but not when the Alpha's son picks me as a mate and I don't want it?

Then again, dad had given them the permission for Adam to pick me. He had gladly thrown me to the side for his convince.

I don't say anything. I simply nod and fall into silence. That's how it is for the rest of the meal. Once we've finished eating, he pays and we exit the restaurant. I'm ready to get into the car and drive home, but dad has other plans.

"Hey, I'm gonna go stop by the shop and take to a pal there, you mind?" He asks timidly as he points in the direction of the auto shop.

I quickly shake my head. "Uh, no. That's fine. I'm going to go walk around. I'll meet you back here later."

"Okay," He says and gives me a brief wave. "See you later."

I return the gesture and turn away, digging my hands into my pockets and walking off. I wander around for a while. I even stop by the bakery and get a latte along with an oatmeal muffin. I finish the muffin at the bakery and then I walk off with my coffee in my hand and somehow find my way deeper into town where the Art Gallery lays.

When I arrive at the front, there are no flashy lights. Just a soft glow coming off from the tall building. I try the door and find that it's unlocked. I don't even have to question myself if I should be doing this. They're obviously open if the door isn't locked.

I walk down the long halls to see many paintings. All ranging from moods of happiness, despair, love. They all seem to tell a different story each. I wonder if the people behind the piece of art also have a story to tell.

Whoever they are, they're seriously talented. And I silently wonder how my painting got in with all of these. Sure, I think I'm good, but I'm not as great as these people behind the rows and rows of art work.

I bet they have bright futures ahead of them to do with art while I'm stuck with my stupid pack. That's the only bad part about being apart of a pack.

You're supposed to stay together. Forever. And it's very rare for someone in the pack to branch off. Mainly because if you do, it comes with consciences.

If you leave the pack, you're immediately considered an outsider. An enemy. You'll be a rogue. And most packs find rogue's as a threat.

It makes me think of what I would have done if I hadn't been picked to mate with Adam. If I hadn't met Liam.

I probably would have made the decision to leave the pack. I probably would have applied to the art school of my dreams and if I had gotten accepted, I know I would have left in a heart beat. I would have created a new life for myself, no doubt.

I wonder if that path would have been chosen for me, would I have met Liam? Would I have ever really found somebody to love?

Maybe. Maybe I would have met Liam and we wouldn't have anything stopping us from being together. We could have moved into our own little shoebox apartment and chase our dreams together. The thought makes a smile linger on my lips.

But it quickly disappears when I know none of that will ever come true. I won't be able to chase my dreams. I won't be able to become the person I have always intended to be.

Most people would say being a werewolf is incredibly amazing. It has it's perks, yeah. But if I could just be normal, I would pick it.

So I wouldn't have any pack to obey. I wouldn't have to be careful about what I'd say. I could be carefree.

I push away the thought shortly after and continue my journey down the hall until I rear the corner and find my own painting.

Immediately, I stop in front of it and stare at the shiny gold plaque that sits underneath my painting.

Ronnie Mars, 16

Portland High School

I lean forward and finger the plaque with a feeling of pride rising in my chest. And then I collapse down onto the bench directly in front and I can't help but feel proud that I've actually managed to get into a gallery. I can check that off my non-existent bucket list.

Too bad there's no one to share this accomplishment with, I think pitifully. And I feel like some stupid little girl right after this thought occurs. Still, that quick prideful moment is gone and now I feel somewhat hollow when I realize that everyone else has someone while I don't.

Anna's got Cliff. Mandy and Kara at least have each other and their boy toys. Alpha Beckett - the cruelest man I know - has Mrs. Beckett. And my dad has this new Tara chick that he's trying to replace my mom with.

I know I shouldn't care even if he does have some new woman in his life, but I do. Because that's exactly what he's doing. Trying to replace my mom. And apparently he want's me to meet her and play buddy-buddy with her.

And I'm so incredibly angry about that. But you know what's the worst thing? When your anger turns into pathetic tears.

That's what happens. I sit there with tears that drip down my face and onto my coffee cup. A sob breaks from my lips at some point.

And that's when I hear a voice softly call my name.

I turn and I'm not shocked to see Liam standing there. He stands there looking perfect with his perfect golden brown hair and his perfect clothes, along with his perfect beautiful eyes. And here I sit, probably looking like a mess.

Pull yourself together, I tell myself urgently. But then another sob wrenches itself from my throat and I can't stop the next overflow of tears.

Liam doesn't make an attempt to run over and sweep me into his arms. But that's okay. Because honestly, I don't want the stupid pity or whatever.

I just want someone to listen. That's it.

So when he takes a seat down on the bench, I tightly wrap my hands around the warm coffee cup and say, "He met someone." I shake my head, "He met someone and now he's trying to replace my mom. How can he just do that?"

Liam doesn't reply. All he does is stare at the side of my face while I angrily wipe at the falling tears and continue to blabber like the stupid idiot I am, "He said he'd leave the pack for her. He said if it came down to it and they wanted to marry, that he'd leave for her. Why didn't he offer to leave the pack when I made it clear I didn't want to mate with Adam? Why'd he choose a girl who he's only known for a few months over his own flesh and blood?

I know I've said I don't care about my dad. Or that I'm not even sure who he is anymore. But I-I oh, I don't know. I just don't know a-anymore." I stumble over my words and even out my breathing before I whisper brokenly. "All I question is, how can he love her more then me?"

I glance over at Liam. He gives me a sad smile. "I don't know, but I bet she's a bitch."

I shake my head and I can't help but laugh dryly when I realize Liam is trying to comfort me by saying this. "You suck at comforting people."

He shrugs, "I'm a better listener." He says, "What's her name?"

"Tara." Her name taste bitter in my mouth.

"Definitely a bitch," He mutters.

"He wants me to meet her," I state sourly. A frown etches on Liam's handsome features.

"Are you going to?"

I shrug, "I don't know." I wipe at the stray tears on my face before I ask, "What are you doing here?"

"I figured I'd find you here. I wanted to talk about the whole Alpha Beckett situation."

I stiffen slightly but nod, "What about it?"

"I wanna take the bastard down."

"You mean you didn't try to murder him?"

"Oh no," He shakes his head. "I did. But he wasn't at his house. Where is he?"

"No. Mrs. Beckett said he went off to go attend to business with other packs or whatever," I reply. "Where were you these past three days?"

"Around," He answers half-heartedly. "I was pretty angry after I found out about the whole Adam thing.. Especially about the kiss." He spits the last word out. I frown.

"Adam and I didn't kiss. I ran off before that could happen," I mutter the last part. But I know he can hear me perfectly fine.

"So you never kissed?" He questions with a raised brow. I shake my head with a sigh. That's when Liam pulls me into his lap and wraps his arms around my waist. "I still don't know what were gonna do about Beckett."

"Make a plan, I guess," I murmur lowly and twist around slightly so I can face him. "I just can't go through with the mating."

"You're not," He states sternly. He then deadly whispers, "I swear, Ron, I'll kill Beckett. And those Purgatory fuckers. I promise you."

I rest my hand on his cheek with a grim smile, "I believe you."

"We should really start thinking of how to take Beckett down. The mating is in a little, right?"

I nod stiffly, "Yeah." I place my free hand on his bicep and place a real smile on my lips, "But at least we'll be taking Alpha Beckett down together."

"Together?" He murmurs and leans closer to where our lips brush. "Does that mean you're mine?"

I nod, tightening my grip on him and whispering, "Yes. I'm yours and you're mine."

Chapter 22

It's after we break away from another heated kiss that we finally realize another presence in the room. We gaze at the short and plump man, who scowls us. He swiftly warns that the museum will be closing in five minutes and to start on heading out. We comply and stand to leave, when he irritably stops us and asks if we've stolen anything.

I bite back the urge to make a sarcastic remark about how I don't think I'd be able to stuff a entire painting in my pocket. Instead, I shake my head no and so does Liam. He brings me closer when we start making our way to the exit and glances over his shoulder, making a loud and obnoxious comment that he obviously wants the man to hear.

I can't help but let out a laugh and look over my shoulder as well to witness the stubby man's reaction. He turns a bright shade of red that I never thought existed before he spins around on his heel and marches off in the opposite direction, mumbling on how he hates teenagers.

And then we run off. Hands intertwined and letting out laughs and rude remarks on how the man appeared to represent a tomato.

It isn't till later on in the night that we split and I ride home with my dad. The car ride is silent. Probably because he's absorbed in his thoughts and so am I.

Mostly about Liam and I, and my dad's confession.

That's the only thing that seems to be on my mind as the next two days pass. I visit Liam's place frequently, and also the art room at school, where I hurry to finish the canvas. Liam helps me as best as he can.

He also tries to bring up the discussion of what I said to him at the art museum. About my dad and Tara. I refuse to acknowledge it though. I made the decision I wouldn't speak of it that night I arrived home from dinner with my dad.

But that wasn't really a surprise to Liam, I imagine. Because usually when I'm confronted with a problem I'm normally not able to deal with, I ignore it. Though that really doesn't stop the pestering thoughts about the whole situation.

I find myself wondering about my dad's new women he's trying to replace my mom with. I don't know who she is, but I've come to a conclusion that I don't like her.

My dad had asked the next day when I had some free time to perhaps go and have dinner with him and Tara. I didn't respond. I simply shrugged and swallowed down a sneer at the mention of my dad's new lover.

I mainly resisted acting mean because of the way my dad had been acting. He was so.. happy, lately. He would smile and laugh and spend hours on the phone like some love stricken teenager.

It made me sick.

But I couldn't find it in me to rain on his parade. Because in those brief two days I saw the old him. He had even returned to his previous routine. Getting up early, making breakfest for the two of us and putting in effort around the house. Even his behavior changed towards me.

He would try to converse with me. Nothing too significant, just questions about my day and how school is going.

I never did respond. All I did was stare at him with narrowed eyes and wonder if he'd go back to his old ways after this new woman broke his heart.

It wasn't too long after that I felt some sort of guilt leak into my conscious at the cruel thought. I should be happy, right? That my dad was finally functioning again? But I wasn't. And I don't think I'd ever be.

I decided it wasn't good to linger on the thought and so I focused on other things. Mostly with the whole canvas.

In fact, I had only the next two days to finish it since the play would premier this Saturday. So that's why directly that Thursday, after failing another one of Mr. Matthews math test, I start my journey down the hall and to the art room, where I hope Liam is already located.

Of course, I try to convince myself the only reason I hope Liam is there is so we can get to work. But it doesn't work. I know I've been acting like some love sick puppy the past two days, by savoring every touch and kiss that we've been sharing since the art museum.

We haven't completely talked about our relationship status, but it's safe to say we are no longer.. well, friends, I guess? Then again, Liam and I were never friends. I'm not quite sure what we were. But whatever it was, it's done now. And I guess Liam is my boyfriend.

Which feels incredibly weird saying. Or well, thinking. I haven't exactly told anyone about it. I didn't have anyone to tell first off, and second, I couldn't tell anyone even if I wanted to. We had to do our best to keep the relationship secret as possible. Mainly from Adam and Alpha Beckett.

We still weren't sure how we were going to handle the Alpha Beckett situation, anyway. Everything sounded so stupid and irrational. And I mean, we had our lives here to take into consideration. We had to think about it long and hard.

Though we didn't have much time. The mating ceremony was scheduled in about three weeks, and Mrs. Beckett was freaking out about it. Every time I passed Adam's house, she'd come scurrying out and asked if I preferred a pink dress or white. Or if I liked tulips more then sunflowers. Or if I wanted my hair straight or curled. Each time I'd give her a grim smile and tell her to pick. It seemed to satisfy her, since she'd squeal and clap. Then dash back inside, miraculously not tripping in her high heels.

She was taking the whole thing way over the top. Acting like it was some type of wedding. Then again, mating ceremonies were sorta like a wedding.

I mean, in the eyes of the pack you were married. And then directly after you did complete the ceremony, you were expected to, well, consummate. And then give birth to a child shortly after. That's how it worked with my parents and why my mom had me so young.

I honestly don't know why she would even comply to that. She was only sixteen. The same age I am. How could she possibly be ready to mate and have a child when you're so young? Didn't she want more to life than just a pack?

Then again, I don't think my mom would even have argued against it. She was always so soft and gentle and.. understanding. Angelic, really. Everything I never grew up to be.

Though, yes, I resembled her greatly with looks wise, I didn't have a ounce of her personality. I was like my dad. Hard headed, sarcastic, and quite frankly mean at times. That's why I can't just sit back and accept the fact Adam and I are supposed to mate. Someone who I knew I could never come to love. Nor have a child with.

But I guess my mom and dad knew they were going to inevitably fall in love. They were true mates. Something so hard to find today. Mainly because your mate could be on the other side of the world and you'd never know. Never get the chance to find them, either.

I admit, I'd taken Liam for granted at first. I was scared. I still am. I mean, what person wants to accept the fact that someone else is going to intrude your life and discover all your flaws? And maybe that's where my mom was brave. Another thing I exactly wasn't.

I mean, I ran away from every little problem that I encountered ever since I was twelve. It was my coping mechanism. So was confining all my emotions in and putting on a strong front. Though that lately has been crumbling away. And I hated it.

Yeah, I am a coward, but I don't want the world to know. I want to be strong. I need to be strong to hold myself together.

Though sometimes my conscious nags at me that Liam can do that for me. Just like I can do it for him.

The thing is, I don't want to rely on Liam. I mean, what if something happened? What if... Liam did actually get hurt in the process of taking down Alpha Beckett? What if I lost him like I'd lost my mom?

Man, God knows I can't just simply accept the loss of someone and move on. I think that's been obvious since I'm still grieving the death of my mother who passed away four years ago. Going on five soon.

Basically, what I'm saying is, I don't want to set myself up to get hurt. I know I'd lose it if Liam actually died. Maybe I wasn't bound to keep Liam. Maybe he wasn't bound to keep me.

I mean, we had the whole force of the world working against us. With Alpha Beckett and Adam, and just about Liam being a rogue. Once it was made evident Liam had a mate, there would be a target painted on my back.

As dramatic as it sounded, we could both lose our lives. Lose each other. That was one of my biggest fears. Along with not being able to keep Liam.

The thought was toxic. And once it leaked into my brain, I couldn't get it out. It had blurred my whole hope of somehow getting out of this situation I was in with Adam.

Before I can think about any longer, I push away the venomous thought. Just like I'd been doing for a while now.

I turn down the hall that leads to the art room with a sigh, digging my hands into the pockets of my jacket and wandering into the art room, where I see Liam hunching over the canvas with his face twisted into a puzzled expression.

I laugh. It causes Liam to glance over his shoulder at me. "What's got you looking so constipated?" I question and drop my bag by the door, edging closer to where he is.

He gives me a grim smile, rather then laughing like I thought he would. "Nothing. Just deep in thought. What took you so long?"

"It must not be nothing if it's got you looking so distressed," I say, ignoring his previous question. "Thinking about Beckett or something?"

He shakes his head hesitantly. "No. Just something else. Don't worry about it."

"Why would I waste my precious time worrying about you?" I say, in somewhat of a playful tone. Though I'm curious about what's got him so hung up, I decide not to push it. He'll tell me when he wants, I guess.

I'm glad when a smile breaks across his face at my remark. "Because you're my girlfriend."

I hate to admit it, but just at the world 'girlfriend' my chest tightens and I suck in a sharp breath.

I quickly determine I'm just having some bad heart burn and unattractively snort, "Don't remind me."

Liam chuckles and yanks me down onto the floor with him, quite roughly, before situating me on his lap, "Will you ever stop being rude to me?"

"No," I tease and edge my face closer to his, titling my head with a small smile on my face.

He smirks and leans closer to me, his minty breathing fanning over my lips. I meet his intense gaze and brush my lips with his, unconsciously closing my eyes and savoring the heat of his skin on mine. Something that I had quickly come accustomed to in just two days.

His lips brush against mine ever so faintly, just a ghost of a kiss, and I'm about ready to surrender and just press my lips to his. But the moment is undoubtedly ruined when Liam dumps me off of his lap and onto the spread out canvas.

"Then you don't get a kiss." He states firmly and then turns away. I glare at the back of his head and kick him in the calf.

"Jerk," I hiss and sit up.

He looks back at me and smirks before grabbing a paint bottle and tossing it to me. "Yeah, yeah. Now get to work."

That's how we spend the next day. Constantly teasing and arguing over the stupidest things while working on the canvas.

I'm somewhat disappointed when we finally finish the last canvas, mainly because we won't be spending any more time in the art room together. Somehow, it's become our little sanctuary.

But I'm also incredibly relieved that I don't have to work on the canvas anymore and not have the stress of completing them over my head.

On Saturday, Liam and I fold away everything that we previously touched in the art room. And once I spot Ms. J, I reluctantly hand her over the key and bid her a farewell, ready to take off with Liam back to his place, but Ms. J clearly has a change of plans.

"I know this is incredibly sudden, but do you mind helping hanging the canvas, Ronnie? We're short on helpers."

From beside me, Liam grunts. I'm far more polite, so of course I resist the urge to let out my groan of distaste. "Sorry, Ms. J but we got-"

She quickly cuts me off, pushing up her glasses from the bridge of her nose with a frantic look in her eyes. "Please, Ronnie? If you help out, I'll let you have access to the art room whenever you please. Besides, you put it to more use than the other students."

Ms. J really knows how to win me over. That offer is just too tempting to pass up.

With a sigh, I glance over at Liam who is frowning and nudge him in the side, catching his attention. "Head on back to your place. I'm gonna stay here for a bit and help out."

Ms. J squeals excitedly and grasps my arm, tugging me in her direction. "Come on! We're on a tight schedule!"

I send a fleeting glance to Liam as Ms. J yanks me off with her. I expect Liam to pop up once I arrive to theater, but I'm surprised when he doesn't even make an appearance. He knows Adam is in the play. Of course he does. He's been intervening in my life since day one.

I decide not to give it much more thought and instead resort putting my energy into my work. With help from a few other guys, we manage to hang the canvas and set up the props. Though I didn't agree to that part of helping. There wasn't much room for argument when Mr. Taylor swooped in and started demanding why we were taking so slow.

It wasn't too bad. Just because of the fact I got to watch Mr. Taylor yell at the actors and actresses in the showcase when they - in the smallest way ever - messed up their lines. It even resulted in one girl, who looked no older then six - who was playing some orphan or whatever - running off the stage and crying. Mr. Taylor didn't care though. He muttered about the young girl being a diva and adjusted his pony tail. Then got back to screaming.

That's when I stopped enjoying watching the actors cringe at Mr. Taylor's venomous shouts of frustration. It was starting to give me a headache about how loud he was. And the toddler's cries from back stage.

I breathe a sigh of relief when I gather up the last prop and set it at the corner of the stage. I glance over at Ms. J who nods in approval at the set up, "Perfect! You're dismissed. But you're free to stay and watch the play. Won't it be exciting seeing your canvas' up there?"

I shrug, "I guess. But I got things to do tonight. Maybe if someone takes a picture or video, I'll catch it online."

Ms. J frowns, but doesn't argue. "If you say so, dear. Have a safe night."

I nod and blandly wish her a good show. I walk off the stage to collect my bag, only to be stopped when I see Adam perched on a high chair, grasping his script tightly in his hand while mumbling the words softly to himself.

It feels like Deja Vu.

I stiffly make my way over to my bag and hoist it on my shoulder, ready to walk off. But nothing ever goes smoothly in my world.

"Ronnie?" I inhale a sharp breath and look over my shoulder to see Adam with a bewildered expression on his face. "What are you doing here?"

"Helping with props," I reply blandly, "I was just leaving."

"Oh," He replies.

"Yeah," I say, "Break a leg." Literally, I think spitefully. I turn on the ball of my heel, ready to launch off when Adam grasps my arm, pulling me back.

"Look, just stay for the play, please." The desperation in his eyes is enormous. But not even his pleading tone and look can't get me to stay.

"I can't. I'm busy."

"With Liam?"

I tense, but shake my head. "No. It's none of your business, anyway."

"You're right, it's not," He says, clearing his throat. "Just please stay. That's all I ask."

I frown at him and attempt to wrench my arm out of his grip, but he keeps a tight grasp on me. Obviously not about to waver anytime soon. Not even when Mr. Taylor shouts for him to get on stage.

When Adam doesn't comply, he begins screeching at everyone. My headache returns again and I dreadfully huff. "Whatever. Fine. Just go."

It's an evident lie, but Adam seems pleased by my reply. "Great," He nods, a smile etching across his lips. "And you better stay. Or I'm running off that stage and following you."

"Okay, I get it," I reply. "Now go."

He releases me and dashes off to the curtain. But Mr. Taylor's screams are only silenced when the red curtain drapes back and the whole cast is revealed. That's when I hear the actors begin to recite their lines.

I exit the stage by taking the stairway off in the corner. I'm immediately shocked by how fast the seats filled up. Now the whole theater is packed with families who whip out their cameras and intently watch the play, obviously waiting to see their child appear.

I glance at the stage to see Adam spewing words in some highly overrated British accent as he scoffs at a couple that walk by, gazing into each other eyes. He fixes his black top hat before turning to the kid I know from Math class. "Look at those love struck fools. Pathetic."

I only look away from the stage when I feel someone faintly brush their arm against mine. I glance to see Ms. J with a broad smile on her face. "So you decided to stay."

I shrug and gaze back at the stage to only see Adam talking again. "I was kinda forced."

"I'm glad," She states bluntly. "Would you like to come sit with me?"

I nod. No point in arguing. "Sure."

I follow her to front row and take a seat next to her. I sit there for the next hour, completely bored out of my mind. I don't really pay attention to the play. Mainly because play's and musicals don't interest me. The only time I ever glance up at the stage is when they change the scenery and reveal another canvas Liam and I have worked so hard on. Or well, a canvas I've worked so hard on while Liam annoyed me half way through.

I can't help but wonder what's got him so tied up that he hasn't made an appearance the whole night. Right after that thought occurs, though, I push it away just as quickly as it came. I am not about to become some clingy freak.

I'm sure he's at his place, pigging out on food. The whole time we worked today he had been complaining about how hungry he was and how he was going to die if he didn't eat. I scowled him and told him to man up. That earned me a glare.

At least he get's to be at home and not be stuck at some play, I think pitifully. I sigh and shift around in my seat, about ready to grab my bag and leave when I suddenly hear my name.

Confused, I turn towards Ms. J and say, "What?"

But she obviously isn't the one who called my name. Since all she does is stare up at the stage and mouth Adam's lines.

I tense and look up at the stage, watching as Adam repeats my name. Though he isn't directly talking to me. Instead he's grasping some redhead's hand and repeating my name.

"I've told you million times not to call me that nickname, Gaspard." The redhead scowls Adam and then glances around nervously, "If my father hears you, he'll have a fit. I'm supposed to be the prime and proper Veronica Marital."

Immediately, I whip around and nudge Ms. J, bringing her out of her daze. She turns to me, furrowing her eyebrows at me. "What's wrong, dear?"

"That girl's name is Ronnie?"

"Well, yes, her nickname is, at least." She nods, "It's sweet, isn't it? Adam helped co-write the production with Brody, another talented prodigy like yourself."

"Huh?"

"Yes, very talented. I mean, I couldn't believe it when Adam was kind enough to base his love interest off of you. I find it so..."

I tune out the rest of Ms. J's words. Instead I watch Adam as he professes his feelings for this Veronica girl.

"I never meant those words I said, Veronica," Adam whispers breathlessly to the redhead as he cradles her cheek, bringing her closer. "I was a stupid and careless child. I never wanted to lose you, Ronnie."

The play isn't only based off my name, but Adam and I's past?

I learn that it indeed is when he dives back into his history with this Veronica girl. Just like Veronica's supposed love interest - the dude Adam's playing - he abandoned her as a child and left her in her time of devastation to grieve her mother's death alone.

That's when I decide I can no longer sit here and watch this.

I hurriedly gather my bag and stand up from my seat, sprinting off to the door, hearing the echo of my name in my ears. I don't know if Adam's legit calling after me, or this other Ronnie girl or whatever. Either way, it doesn't matter.

I run off. My feet thudding against the tile and I instantly find my way outside and into the depths of the forest. Heading for Liam's place.

I don't know where else to run off to, anyway. I didn't know how to deal with this. What did this mean? Is what Mrs. Beckett said true? Did Adam have feeling's for me and this was just his way expressing them for me?

No, no, no, I repeat over and over again in my head. Adam doesn't have feelings for you. It's a coincidence. A mere coincidence.

But I know it's not. Ms. Jovovich had even said this Veronica chick was based off of me. And frankly, that was weird and creepy and somebody wouldn't do that unless they liked you. Or even worse, loved you.

The thought makes me cringe and I pick up my speed, determined to get there faster and hysterically fling myself into Liam's comforting arms. I don't know what I'll say, but honestly, I don't care.

I'm too caught up in my thoughts and confused emotions that I don't realize the figure that is running in my direction too. It's too late before I can somehow skid to a stop.

So we collide. Quite hard, too.

I go flying off my feet and land on my side - the one where I fractured my ribs - the air whooshing out of me as I release a breathless gasp and involuntarily clutch at my side. I only manage to register a pinch of pain.

I squirm around on the ground like some fish out of water, trying to get the air I've just lost back. And when I finally do, I realize the person is who knocked into me is still in front of me, hurriedly shuffling to get back onto their feet.

I prop myself up on my hands and come face to face with a girl who looks no older then me. But from what I can tell, she's incredibly small with pin straight dark brown hair and vicious glint in her dark brown eyes that appear to be nearly black.

She doesn't say a word. She simply raises to stand and so do I. That's when I notice how small she really is. Sure, I'm not the tallest person, but she's even shorter then me, standing only at 5'2.

I don't even get the chance to demand who she is. She runs off. Her long hair fluttering behind her as she hops over a fallen tree.

It's not until I look towards Liam's house that I realize she was running from that direction.

And that she reeks of the Purgatory pack.

CHAPTER 23

"Ronnie?"

The familiar voice calls for the fifth time. I ignore it. Instead, I focus my undivided attention on the plate in front of me, pushing around my untouched eggs with my fork. It's what I've been doing for the last fifteen minutes while my dad tries to make me talk.

He's been pestering me the whole morning since I got up. Asking me about Adam, how was the play, and other things I have no desire to discuss.

I'm too caught up in my thoughts to care.

All I can seem to think about is that girl from yesterday.

I mean, who was that girl? Why hadn't I ever seen her before? Why was she running from Liam's direction? And does Liam know her?

When this last thought occurs, a twang of jealousy strikes me quite forcefully. Mainly because I don't like the idea of another girl hanging around Liam. Just how he doesn't like me hanging around another guy.

But it doesn't make sense. Why would Liam be associating with a Purgatory member? He hates them. For what reason? I don't know. I don't know a lot of things about Liam. And though I said I'd remain patient, I'm starting to get sick of all the secrets he's keeping.

I bet this is how Liam felt when I dodged all his questions about Adam and I. And man, it sucks.

I'm the kind of person where I need to know what's going on or I'm positively sure I'll go insane. Basically, suspense isn't a fond company of mine.

And so, naturally, I just assume the worse. Like Liam is seeing another girl behind my back. It's stupid, I know. But what other conclusion is there?

But on the other hand, maybe Liam doesn't know she is. Maybe he's just as clueless as me. Maybe he had no idea that chick was running on his territory.

Then again, Liam does keep a tight watch on the Purgatory pack for more reasons then one. Wouldn't he know the members of the pack and stuff? I'm sure Liam could detect a Purgatory member from miles away. So he'd know of her. And he'd take the chance to kill one, I'm positive about that.

So why hadn't Liam bursted through the clearing last night, searching after that girl? I remembered standing there for several minutes. Simply gazing at that same exact spot the girl had disappeared off to. That was more then enough time for Liam to arrive. But he didn't.

There's another chance he wasn't even home. Perhaps he was in town, getting a pizza or whatever. Or perhaps I'm just driving myself insane.

After I had bumped into the girl last night, instead of going to Liam and simply asking who she was, I chose the hard way. By going back home and doing exactly what I said earlier. Driving myself insane with curiosity and confusion. It resulted in insomnia, seeing as I stayed up half the night, wondering when my life got so complicated.

Oh God, it's too early in the morning to try solving pointless rittles.

With a sigh, I push away my plate and stand up, reaching to grab my bag and head out the door when my dad suddenly stops me by asking, "What time are you free?"

I look over my shoulder and raise an eyebrow, "What do you mean what time am I 'free'?"

"I mean for dinner," He drawls slowly, "With Tara."

I blink. "Dinner with Tara?" I echo stupidly.

"Yeah," He frowns, "I told you she wanted to meet you."

"Right," I mutter and press my lips together. "Well, I'm busy. So I don't know when."

My eyes flicker back to the door, unable to meet his stare while I scowl myself internally for that lame excuse of a lie. Busy with what? Breathing?

But to my surprise, even though it's evident I lied, my father doesn't press on it. Nor does bother to point out I have nothing to be busy with because I hardly have a social life. It's oddly nice of him when he says, "Oh, um, okay. Maybe another time."

I nod, but don't glance back at him. Without another word, I pick up my bag and exit, flinching when the door slams behind me.

I start my way down my usual path to school, kicking aimlessly at rocks and being lost in another swirl of thoughts. But this time, of my father and Tara.

And how there was no way in hell I'd ever meet her.

I was not about to let another unwelcomed visitor enter in my life. I wanted nothing to do with her. And I wasn't surely going to pretend I did just for the sake of my father.

Even if this chick is perhaps changing my dad for the better. He isn't moping around anymore. He isn't going out and disgustingly finding comfort in another woman's bed. Instead he's at home. With me. Trying so hard to rekindle our ghost of a relationship before mom died.

I wonder when he'll be able to see that it'll never happen. We'll never be the same as we were before. Because we've both changed in more ways then one.

I've grown bitter. Spiteful. Sarcastic. While he dwindled into this pathetic state of permanent sorrow. I forced myself to move on. I forced myself to be strong. I forced myself to believe that I didn't need him. And that he didn't me. Even if he is my father.

Before my mother's death, we weren't all that close, anyway. We butted heads, of course. Mainly because we were both so much alike. But he still cared for me. Like I did for him. He would nurture me and comfort me in my time of need when I was crying over the littlest of problems in the world. Like why wasn't Spongebob real.

He still loved me. And I still loved him, nonethless. That's obviously not the case now.

I'm pretty sure our compassion for one another died along with mom.

Like always, I push away the thoughts that trouble me the most and I continue my way to school. When I arrive, it's no surprise that everyone suddenly looks over at me. I can only guess it's because of the play and how Adam creepily named his love interest after me. And how it described our past.

It's humiliating. Especially when girls swarm around me and coo about how sweet Adam is. And how I should take him back.

It get's worse when the guys supposedly start to imitate Adam and I by gazing at each other and dramatically claiming their love for one another in high pitched voices. It makes my blood boil with agitation.

But I swallow down the profanities and screams of annoyance. Even if I did give them a piece of my mind, it wouldn't matter. It won't stop the fact Adam has publicly embarrassed me. Nor will it stop the endless gossip.

So I continue on like any other day. Sharing glares with strangers, getting told off by Mr. Matthews, and failing tests I didn't even know we were having in class.

It's no shock when I discover Liam is missing from school today. It just adds to my level of suspicion. Which is already reaching it's breaking point.

To take my mind off things, for lunch, I head on down to the art room and occupy my thoughts on what colors I should use.

I don't really paint anything. I pass the time by swirling colors together and watching them change into another. And I'm perfectly amused and content with that. Until someone decides to interrupt me.

Though it's not Adam or Liam. But Anna.

I only take mark of her presence when she clumsily trips over a canvas and falls flat on her face. She lays there for a few seconds before she reaches down and rubs her swollen ankle. I can hear her softly cursing herself for wearing five inch heels today.

I glance over at my half empty soda that's just as cold as when I got it from the vending machine. I don't realize what I'm doing till I stand up and grab it and hand it over to her.

She stares up at me, her eyebrows furrowed, but instead of protesting or questioning why, she takes it and places it against her throbbing ankle. She sighs contently at the relief.

And I'm left to awkwardly shift in my place and wonder if I should make a break for it before Anna starts to discuss our argument that we had just a week ago.

The one I'm still not ready to talk about.

Mainly because I still can't wrap my head around what we fought about. I'm still bewildered about all the things she said. And all the things I said.

How she claimed Cliff, Mandy, And Jessica had told her things about me, but then just minutes ago said she was my best friend and was worried about me.

Then again, I did initiate the fight with the snarky attitude I had, A small, and I mean small, part of me argues, she's your best friend. Apologize and don't lose her like you lost Adam.

I'm too stubborn to listen. So I go to collect my stuff and leave, but nothing ever goes as I want.

"I saw you run out last night at Adam's show." Anna blurts suddenly. I miss the awkward silence not even a minute later after she's said this. It's too embarrassing to even mention right now.

I don't reply. I'm hoping she'll get the message and realize this is a bad start to our first conversation after our fight. Obviously, Anna wants to take the chance to bathe in my humiliation since she says, "It must have been a shock when you found out the girl had the same name as you."

I have my back turned to her, so all I can hear is the rustle of the canvas and her unbuckling her shoes.

"Yeah," I mutter. It's the only coherent response I can think of to say. Anna doesnt' mind, though. She's already use to my vague answers. She continues to ramble on.

"He based the story off of you guys, right? So that means some of it was true?" She asks softly, "Like him leaving you after your mom died?"

I swallow roughly and instantly tense. I tightly grasp the wooden handle of the brush in my hand like it's my lifeline. "No, none-"

She cuts me off. "You're lying. Cliff already told me it was true."

"Then why bother asking?" I spit bashfully, turning to gaze at her. She flinches.

"I wanted to see if you'd lie to me again," She whispers faintly. "I thought you'd tell me the truth this time around me. For what reason? I don't know. You never tell me anything. Like about your dad and how you always lied to my mom about how he was coming to pick you up."

Cliff told her about my dad now too?

I narrow my eyes at her, "Cliff told you about my dad too?"

She scoffs, "Someone had to, because you wouldn't."

"It's no one's business-" Again, she cuts me off by standing and pointing an accusing finger at me.

"No, it's not only your business! Because I thought we were best friends, because I thought we told each other everything, like how your dad is some drunk and how your mom is six feet under-"

I cut her off when I throw my brush on the ground and step forward, seething with rage. "Don't you ever, ever talk about my mom. You have no right to even mention her. Not my dad either. You know nothing about them!"

"Then help me understand!" Anna shouts, "For all I know, all the things you bothered to tell me could have been lies too. Were they lies, Ronnie?"

I'm silent. Mainly because I'm shell shocked at the question that sounds more like an accusation. And by the tears in her eyes. That's when I know this isn't just another one of our petty fights that we'll get over.

Because Anna never cries. Never. She's always cheery and happy and forgiving. She only cries when it's about something serious or she's hurting. In this case, it's both reasons. And I can't help the ache that rises in my chest with just seeing that I've caused her pain.

"I thought we told each other everything," She echos from earlier, much softer now. A tear slips from her eye as she says this. "I thought we were truthful and could find trust in each other because we were best friends. So when I found out you were lying to me, I got angry. And I said some hurtful things. But I won't take them back, Ron. I won't apologize. You lied. You lied about Adam and Liam. You lied about possibly everything."

She let's out a shaky breath and wipes away at another onslaught of tears that pound down her face. "All I ask is why? Why did you lie?"

My throat feels dry and tight. I don't know how to respond. I can't, even if I wanted to. The only reason I lied to her was for the pack. Because that would expose me and them too. It is a law, you know. I wasn't even supposed to begin hanging out with Anna. Because she's human and that would only risk our secret.

I can't tell her anything right now either. So I remain silent and wonder what to do. She doesn't give me enough time.

She shakes her head at me and smiles sadly with glassy eyes. "I don't know why I bother. You obviously won't say anything," She laughs humorlessly. "You're right. I don't know anything about your parents. Guess I don't know anything about you either."

And for the first time ever, I'm not the one to walk off and leave the other person behind. Anna does it. She picks up her shoes and bag and she leaves, not glancing back at all. It hurts more then ever.

For the millionth time that day, another sigh leaves my lips as I stir around my latte and numbly pick at the oatmeal muffin that has gone cold.

I've been doing this since I arrived at the small bakery, occasionally sharing a half-hearted smile with the fray old women who runs the place. She comments every now and then, saying how muggy it's been outside lately. I only nod and mutter an agreement. She turns away when she realizes my mind is in another place and I don't want to be bothered. I'm grateful for that.

My troubling thoughts seem to consume me. Like always.

So all I do is stare out of the foggy window, watching my dad kick rocks and talk on the phone, while replaying Anna's words in my head.

Like any other problem I don't want to deal with, I try to push them away and simply forget about this evening. And Anna's shouts of frustration. But I can't. Her words and tears are burned permanently into my mind. It's because I know this isn't just some stupid fight.

Anna and I have fought before, surely. But it hasn't been about anything serious. Just about what clothes I should wear and how I need to be more social, and other things that Anna forgets about the next day. We've always made up. Mainly because Anna is the first one to apologize and gush about how she should of never forced her beliefs on me so strongly. I accept her apology each time and she makes me promise that we'll never fight again. Though we know we will.

We laugh it off either way. And then the next day we're okay again. Talking and laughing, with Anna briefly commenting on how cute Adam's butt is. Was it weird to say I was gonna miss that?

Anna won't apologize. I know that. She had said it herself. And I know she doesn't expect me to suck up my pride and tell her everything.

I can't even tell her I'm sorry. Because she'll expect an exclamation I can't give. And I've never hated Cliff more for telling.

I'm so tempted to march right over to his house and pound his face in. My life is none of his business, and he shouldn't go around telling people. Not even Anna.

I hate Cliff, I hate Mandy, I hate Jessica, I hate-

Wait.

Who is that?

My train of thought stops as I watch a tall figure - who appears to be a girl by the long hair flowing behind her - running across the street and straight into my father's arms.

He wraps his arms around her the moment she leaps onto him and wraps her lean legs around his waist. She buries her head in his neck for a minute, then pulls away and presses a chaste kiss to his lips.

I'm pretty sure my heart stops right then.

Without even thinking, I stand up and rocket out of the bakery to get a better look at this chick.

I cross the street, ignoring the honks of the cars and the shouts for me to get off the road and how I'm going to get myself killed. I don't care frankly.

Once I near close enough, I stop and simply watch in horror as she get's off of him, but keeps her arms latched around his neck and presses another kiss to his lips. He doesn't object, of course. He instead tangles his fingers in her golden blonde hair. And I suddenly feel sick.

It get's worse when she pulls back and exclaims excitdely, "I missed you!"

My dad chuckles as he gazes down at her. "I saw you two days ago."

She flashes him a beautiful smile, about to say something when she glances over in my direction, her light eyebrows furrowing in confusion.

My dad follows her gaze.

Though he doesn't look shocked or confused. He actually smiles. Smiles. "Ronnie, there you are."

"Ronnie?" The women echos, now putting space between her and my father. "This is your daughter?"

My dad nods and grips her hand, pulling her along until they stand before me. And now that she's so up close, I realize just how pretty she is with golden blonde hair and kind green eyes. She's like a super model. Tall, skinny, beautiful. And I ultimately decide I don't like her already.

"Yeah," My dad finally answers her previous question. "Ron, meet Tara Billard. Tara, meet Ronnie Mars."

Tara.

I probably should have realized that this was the Tara my dad was talking about when she threw herself on him, but whatever. I was too panicked at the sight of my father kissing another women that wasn't my mom.

"Ronnie, it's so nice to meet you." She sticks out her hand to me with another, stupid, breathing taking smile. All I do is stare at her out stretched hand.

She reclines her arm when she realizes I'm not going to shake it and be as polite as her. My dad clears his throat awkwardly. "Well, now that we're all here, why don't we have that dinner we were talking about?"

Tara is perfect. Bloody perfect.

Perfect to the way she laughs, smiles, talks, even eats. She's perfect with education. She perfect with looks. Perfect, perfect, perfect.

The whole time during dinner I try to pick out some flaw I can at least hate her for. But no. She's flawless.

She's kind and funny, and she never once gave me an ugly look or anything. Instead she flashes her perfectly white teeth at me and grins just about every second.

She talks about her job for some part of the dinner. Explaining how she's a second grade teacher and how it has it's perks. She also discusses her family and briefly the story of how her and my father met.

Apparently, they met in a bar. Real romantic.

I snort, quite rudely, when she tell's me this. Of course, right when I do, a frown etches her pretty little face while my dad simply shakes his head and tell's her to continue. She quickly recovers her smile and continues on, though I'm not the least bit interested.

I find that I can't her. Not even if I tried real hard. Because there's nothing to hate her for. I mean, she's a second grade teacher for God sake! She even tutors kids with down syndrome on the weekend!

As said before, she's perfect. And loving. And compassionate about other's feelings. And it makes me feel sick.

The whole time I find myself comparing her to my mom. Which really isn't good. Because my mom never tutored the mentally challenged. Nor did she go to Church every Sunday and pray to be forgiven for her sins like Tara does.

I find that Tara and my mom are two completely different people. It's not what I expected.

I thought my dad might chase after a women that reminded him enough of my mom. Maybe to ease the pain that way. But clearly not.

And it get's worse when I notice that my dad has fallen deeply for this women. You can see it by the way he gazes at her, and the way she gazes at him. Like their having their own private little conversation. Basically, I'm the awkward third wheel here. Though Tara does her best trying not to make me feel that way. By asking me subtle questions. Never getting to personal.

That is, till it comes to college and what I want to be.

"What do you think you'll major in? Have you figured out what college you want to go to?" She asks.

I shake my head hesitantly. Even if I wanted to, I can't go to college because I might possibly be mated to Adam and stuck in this horrible town.

Of course, I can't say this, so I resort to a simple, "No."

"Oh," She mumbles, "Well, do you have any hobbies?"

"No."

My dad scoffs, "Yes you do."

I send a glare in his direction. "No. I don't."

My dad ignores me, though, and shifts in his seat towards Tara. "Ronnie paints."

"Paints?" She repeats, her green eyes flickering over to me. "So you're an artist?"

"No. It's nothing." Nothing I wanna share with you, anyway, I add mentally.

"Yes she does," My dad nods with a coy smile. "She's good too. She got into a exhibit, actually. The Young Artist one."

My eyebrows furrow, "How'd you know that? I never told you."

"Adam told me."

I tense immediately at the mention of Adam. And the fact that my dad and Adam actually talk to one another. Not even when Adam and I were friends did my dad acknowledge his presence.

For some reason, this sparks Tara's curiosity. "Adam? Who's he?"

"Ronnie's.. boyfriend." My dad answers awkwardly. Tara beams.

"You have a boyfriend?" She questions, "Oh, I should have expected that. You're such a beautiful girl!"

I shake my head and narrow my eyes at my dad. "Adam's not my boyfriend."

Now Tara is confused.

"Of course he is," My dad argues.

I shake my head and blurt, "Adam's not my boyfriend. Liam is."

My dad freezes at the name and extracts his arm from around Tara's shoulder, leaning closer to the table and staring me straight in the eye. "Liam? As in Liam Farley?"

I don't reply. Instead, I avert my eyes to the ground and wonder why I said anything. I should have just went along with Adam being my boyfriend. But I couldn't help. Just the word 'boyfriend' and 'Adam' in the same sentence creeps me out. As badly as the word 'mate' and 'Adam' too.

We're all silent for a long period of time. Until Tara chirps, "Well, who's up for dessert?"

I'm overwhelmed with relief when my dad drops me off by home and I'm able to return home solely. So I don't have to deal with the onslaught of questions I know my dad is dying to ask.

I had a feeling Tara was saving me from that when she asked if he'd like to come over back to her place and watch a movie. He was reluctant at first, mainly because he wanted to have a private conversation with me, but agreed when she badgered him about it.

I trudge my way home slowly, not even beginning to rush when the cold somehow finds it's way into my jacket and chill's my bones.

By the time I see my house in sight, I'm shivering.

I tug on my beanie as I round my way to the steps, only stopping to glance over at the Beckett's house. I do a double take when I see something move out of the corner of my eye.

I find that it's Alpha Beckett. Who stands with his arms behind his back as he gazes at me with cold and calculating eyes. A shiver ripples up my spine. And I'm sure it's not from the cold.

And then there's this emotion that I can't read in his eyes again. Though I'm sure it's not good when he suddenly turns and enters his house. The door slams loudly behind him, echoing into the once silent and almost peaceful night.

I move into my own home as well, quickly tugging the curtains closed and about ready to lock myself in my room when I spot a mug on the table.

The same white mug that Alpha Beckett had drank from when he blackmailed me. The same white mug that I was so sure I discarded the moment right after he left.

I edge closer to the table and find myself staring right into the pure black coffee in the cup. And then I swat if off the table. Not even flinching the mug shatters loudly and the coffee taints the once clean floors.

I find out exactly why Alpha Beckett was in my house the next day. Why he glanced so ominously at me just the night before.

It's when I arrive to school that it becomes clear.

There's sirens and horrific screams and cries of pain when I enter the parking lot. And for some reason, I find myself in a blur of panic as I fight my way through the crowd. Only to catch a glimpse of long blonde hair and oddly twisted and bloody limbs.

The police officer tell's everybody to get back, but I'm not listening. All I can do is stare at the familiar girl on that stretcher as they load her into the back of the amubalance.

For a brief second, my eyes find Adam's somewhere in the crowd. They hold so much pity and sorrow and grief. And I know immediately who has caused this. Alpha Beckett. He's caused this because he knows about Liam and I. He knows.

A hoarse cry breaks from my lips and I try to fight my way to her. I thrash and I scream her name at the top of my lungs. Many students try to restrain me, but it doesn't work.

Nothing does.

I manage to get close enough to see her again.

Her brown eyes are wide and open as they stare into nothing. They're vague. Blank. Lifeless. And it makes me scream at the top of my lungs in horror.

Because she's my best friend. Because she's the girl I swore to protect from Alpha Beckett. Because she's the girl who trusted me with her secrets and insecurities while all I gave her was lies.

It's Anna.

CHAPTER 24

Two days had passed since Anna's accident. And there still hasn't been one word spoken about it.

For all I knew, Anna could be dead. Her funeral could be being planned right now and I wouldn't know it. Or even worse, she could already be six feet under. Or that other thing they do to people when they die... cremation?

The mere thought of Anna's body being burned makes my stomach twist, forming a tight knot that I know isn't going anywhere anytime soon.

Then again, the mere thought of Anna dying makes me feel sick. And the thought that I could have been the cause of her death makes me feel even worserer. Though I'm sure that's not a word, at the moment, I don't care.

For the past two days, the whole town has been quiet. Even the pack. Surprisingly, Adam hadn't come to bother me at all. Nor Alpha Beckett. And for that, I was grateful.

I don't think I could handle looking into the eyes of Anna's killers so soon. Or well, her supposed killers.

I had found out minutes after the scene what had truly happened. Some girl who had witnessed the horrific tragedy came babbling to me about it, claiming how a car had come crashing through the parking lot and had hit Anna.

Immediately after hearing this, one thing rang in my mind. Alpha Beckett.

The name of the monster who had ruined my life kept on ringing in my head the whole way home when my dad picked me up from school.

I had tried convincing him to take me to the hospital. I had begged and pleaded and did about everything I could to somehow take me. But he argued that whatever was happening with Anna was between her and her parents. That we would just have to wait to find out what the verdict was.

But I couldn't wait to find. I just couldn't. So the next day, I went banging on Anna's door. Though no one answered and I quickly realized it was stupid of me to do so, seeing as Anna's parents or really Anna herself wouldn't be home.

For some reason, I didn't leave the house immediately. I had sat on their porch practically all day, praying that Anna's parents would return home. To at least maybe catch up on some sleep or something, as silly as it sounded. But it never happened. And it was stupid of me to think they'd really come home to catch up on some sleep when their daughter was on the brink of death.

I wanted to go to the hospital. But I knew I couldn't. The nearest hospital was two hours away from our small town and I couldn't reach it without crossing into Purgatory territory. And I couldn't risk attracting their attention and ultimately drawing them to Anna nor her family. So I had to stay put, for the sake that they wouldn't discover my other weakness beside's Liam.

Then again, perhaps it wasn't Alpha Beckett who had killed Anna. It could have been the Purgatory for all I know. Maybe they were just doing what Alpha Beckett was doing. Targeting the people closest to me just to strike me down. But how would they know about Anna? They couldn't. They didn't know anything about me besides the fact that I was Liam's mate.

But maybe - just like the night of the ball - Alpha Beckett could have given them a lead. A lead to Anna so he wouldn't have to get his hands dirty and actually kill her. Most likely that was the case. Either way, I knew I'd find out sooner or later, if I wanted to or not.

That first night of not knowing what happened to Anna, I had drove myself insane with the thoughts that were slowly eating away at me.

And that's why, on the the second night, after gaining up the courage, right after my dad had fallen asleep, I had shifted and dashed off as far as I could before I entered the main town. From there, at twelve AM in the morning, I caught a bus to the hospital.

The only thing I did for two hours was watch as people got on and off the bus. With the occasional hobo who would look my way and give me the stink eye. It caused me to sink lower into the uncomfortable plastic chair that made my butt go numb after only being on the bus for thirty minutes.

I was almost relieved when I realized I had reached my stop, till I remembered the reason why I was even coming here in the first place.

Nonetheless, I jumped out of the bus in a hurry and walked a few minutes or so when I finally saw a lit up building with the word's 'Portland Hosipital' glowing in bright red.

Hurriedly, I made my way to the entrance, passing people in wheel chairs and another lady who I was positively sure was about to give birth. After that, I didn't pay much attention to the atmosphere around me, nor the fact that I despised hospitals. I was too caught up in finally getting to see Anna that I didn't care.

I made my way to the front desk where a elderly woman sat, typing away and staring at the computer screen. I had to clear my throat just to get her attention.

"May I help you?" She asks rudely and normally I would have taken offense to the tone of voice she was using with me, but then I thought about how I would feel working at a hospital in the dead of night. So I decided to let it slide.

"Yes," I answer slowly, "I'm, uh, looking for Annabelle Steel. Could you tell me what room she's in?"

She raises a brow at me, "Are you family?"

I nod jerkily. "Yeah. I'm her sister."

The lady purses her lips at me, obviously knowing I'm lying but nonetheless she turns away from me and I watch as she types Anna's full name into the computer. She turns the computer away from my sight right when she clicks enter. And immediately, I watch as her mouth twists into a frown as she anazlyes the screen.

"What? What is it?" I ask, leaning over the counter to somehow get a glimpse at the computer screen, but she exits out of the tab quickly.

"It seems there's a little error with the computer. I'll call the doctor down, no worries. Just take a seat and he'll come get you."

"What do you mean an error with the computer? Look-" I begin to say, but the woman cuts me off.

"Please, miss, just take a seat. I assure you the doctor will come to get you and take you to see your... sister." She says and then gestures to the waiting room chairs.

I open my mouth to object, but quickly decide against it. I am not going to start a fight with this chick just to get kicked out.

So I take a seat and tap my foot against the marble white floors while I fiddle with my hands and keep an eye out for this doctor dude or whatever.

It isn't long after that I see a familiar face appear before my sight.

It's Mrs. S and Mr. S, walking along side a man with shaggy blonde hair and pale blue eyes who I automatically assume is the doctor by the white lab coat he's sporting.

And by the look on Mrs. S' face, I can tell something is terribly wrong. Her once neatly combed blonde locks are a mess and her eyes are blood shot with dried tears staining her cheeks. Mr. S is no better.

Instead of running to them like I want to, I stay in my seat and watch as they slowly approach me. I wait till they stop in front of me before standing up and drawing in a shaky breath.

I stare into Mrs. S' blurry green eyes. I search her face for some sign that Anna is okay. That she's still alive and that she's going to make it through this. That Anna's gonna be okay. That Anna will return to school in only a matter of months and that we can be friends again. That we can somehow make up and go back to the way we used to be. But I find nothing but sorrow etched on her features. And it causes my heart to sink into my stomach.

"Is she dead?" I question softly. I know the answer to my question, but I can't help it. I can't help but ask and still grasp onto the ounce of hope I still have left.

A lump forms in my throat as I watch a rogue tear fall from her eyes. And that's it. That's all I need to know.

I turn away, feeling the tears sting my eyes. I hear Mr. S call my name, but I don't look back. I can't. How can I possibly look them in the eye? How can I face them when I know I'm the cause of this? How can I lie to them and tell them it was just some unfortunate accident? Because that's thing. It wasn't some accident. It was Alpha Beckett.

As I sit on the bus, I cry silently. I bite onto the sleeve of my knit sweater to contain the sobs that claw their way up my throat.

I dig my nails into my thigh and I'm pretty sure I've drawn blood, but I don't care. I remain still and let the warm tear trail down my face. I don't bother to wipe them away. I'm too shocked.

Because how can this be possible? How can my best friend be dead?

Just months ago we were fine. Everything was normal and Anna was still breathing. It wasn't until Adam declared that I was going to be his mate that thing's drastically changed for me.

I feel like an idiot. I feel stupid and angry at myself for even being mad at Anna in the first place. Because she honestly didn't deserve it. She was right when she said I was a liar. Or well, when she implied I was a liar. Because I was. Because I am.

I lied to her about everything. About me, about my family, about my past. And I feel like a major bitch for doing that. Maybe if I would have told her about what's going on with Adam, I coulda possibly saved her. And I know that sounds stupid. And it's because I am stupid.

I'm a stupid and weak little girl for letting Alpha Beckett walk all over me. I'm stupid for letting him kill my best friend and ultimately tearing me apart.

And then, along with the tears and evident sadness, my blood boils. And all I can imagine in my head is pounding Alpha Beckett's face in. I can feel my body shake with anger and it gets so bad that once the bus door opens, I leap out.

Once I reach the woods, I shift and run. I run all the way back to my pack territory, where I'm not surprised to find all the houses lights flickered on and my dad standing outside, along with every other pack member. Of course, including Alpha Beckett and Adam.

I shift back to human form once I near and draw their attention. My dad calls my name and demands to know where I have been for the last fours hours. But I don't reply. I simply stare at Alpha Beckett. And he does the same, examining me with a cold and calculating gaze. I can tell he thinks he's so superior. So strong. Well, I'm about to prove him wrong.

"Ronnie, we thought something happened to you. Where were you?" A familiar and concerned voice asks. I let my eyes trail off in the direction of the voice to find Adam looking at me with worry filled eyes. I clench my fist, feeling my nails dig into the palm of my hands. I ignore the pinch of pain and curl my lip up in disgust at Adam. At the monster his father is slowly creating.

He tries to act innocent and good, just like Alpha Beckett does, but it's all a lie. He knows what's wrong. He's knows where I've been. He know's what's happened. He know's that Anna's dead and that his father caused it and still, he has the guts to stand before me and act like he cares about what happens to me.

"Don't give me that whole innocent act, Adam," I spit. "I'm done with playing your games and especially your father's games. I'm done with everything!"

My father steps forward, grasping my arm. "Ron, stop. Let's just go inside and-"

I cut him off when I wrench my arm from his grip. "No! I'm done pretending I'm fine when I'm not! You may not want to stand up to Alpha Beckett, but I am!" I turn to Alpha Beckett, meeting his eyes and before I can help myself, the tears fall and I screech. "Why me? Why did you pick to torture me? What did I ever do to you to cause you to make my life a living hell?"

Alpha Beckett keeps a calm facade, unfazed by my screeching. "I don't know what you're talking about, dear."

I laugh dryly, "Oh please. You know what I'm talking about, you basterd."

"Ronnie!" My father hisses sharply, reaching to grab me but I step back.

"Don't you realize what they've done? Are you blind? Or are you just really that stupid?" I hiss at my father. And for a minute, I feel guilty when a look of hurt flashes across his face, but that feeling quickly disappears, only to be replaced with rage. "He killed Anna. He killed Anna probably just like how he killed mom!" I see my father's face drain of color at the mere mention of mom, and I feel even more completely evil when I utter. "You remember who she is, don't you? Or has your little girlfriend made you forget about her? Have you completely forgotten about the night she was killed? The way she screamed your name but you weren't there to save her. I bet you feel awful."

My father's fact twists into pain and he soon steps back. He doesn't argue back at all. What a coward.

"You're a fool, Ronnie," Alpha Beckett comments, drawing my attention back to him. "Just like your mother. She didn't listen either and look at that, she got herself killed."

"More like you got her killed." I hiss, "What's the real reason you want me so badly to mate with Adam? Huh?"

Alpha Beckett remains silent for a minute or two. Then he says, "if you know what's best for you, you'll turn and walk to your house and I'll be nice enough to pretend like this never happened."

"No way. I'm done with that. I'm done with going along with what you say. I'm no longer your puppet. I reject Adam's offer to become his mate and I officially state that I'm leaving the pack, once and for all."

"Ronnie, dear, you are not thinking clearly." He steps forward, close enough that I can see the ominous flicker in his eyes. "You wouldn't want Liam to get hurt, would you?"

"Of course not," I answer lowly. "And that's why I'm leaving. Because I'm going to take you down."

"Ron, stop, don't do this." Adam pleads from afar. "I never wanted this to happen. I swear. I never wanted Anna to die."

"If you didn't want her to die, then you would have stopped this along time ago." My voice cracks at the end and my vision blurs due to the tear that cloud my eyes. My eyes flicker to Alpha Beckett. "I'm gonna enjoy killing you in the future."

"I hope you know that you're declaring war against me and my pack." He replies. I nod slowly.

"I know," I scan my eyes over the faces of familiar people I've grown up with. The people I use to talk to everyday. But weirdly, they all feel like strangers to me. And I guess it's because I truly don't who they are anymore. And for some reason, it kills me to know that I might possibly have to kill these people who I formerly use to call my pack mates. Then again, they disowned me after my mother's death. If they cared, they would have stickin' up for me when I needed them most. Now there's no going back. This is war. "I hope you're ready when I come for you."

And with that, I turn on my heel. This time, I'm walking away for good. No looking back. No second chances. No nothing.

They let me go and I know it's because Beckett doesn't see me as a threat. But he should. Because when I come back, I won't be alone.

I'm leaving behind everything I've ever known. My home. My friends. Adam. Everyone and everything.

And for some odd reason, there is no ounce of sadness left in me. Only determination.

CHAPTER 25

The news of Anna's death spreads like wildfire throughout the whole town.

No matter where I turn or went, someone is always talking about it. They don't seem to really care if I'm listening or not.

I mean, it's no secret that Anna and I were good friends. They weren't oblivious to that fact, but for whatever reason, they didn't seem to care if them talking about Anna would cause me pain.

Which it did.

But I didn't run away from those feelings like I thought I would. I guess I just realized that by running away from my emotions, I was doing more bad then I was doing good. I had to face the fact that Anna was gone in order to move on.

So, that's why when the funeral happened, I went. I went and I offered whatever words of comfort I could up with to Mr & Mrs. S. They seemed grateful and surprised when I showed up. Almost as if they expected me to ditch out on Anna's funeral.

I guess a lot of people suspected I would. Everyone was pretty shocked that I had decided to go rather then running away, like I did when my mother died.

I had opened up at the funeral. I said a few words before they buried her, though my speech was nothing significant, Mr & Mrs. S still smiled and said thank you. It made me feel good in a sense. Because for once in my life, I felt like I was finally doing something right. And I wasn't doing to make others happy, I was doing it because I wanted to be happy.

At the end of the day, after the funeral was done, I felt better. And as I went to sleep that night, no nightmares of sort plagued me.

Though as the days passed, I had my moments of weakness and perhaps vulnerability, and I let those moments happen, no matter how much I loathed it. Because I knew if I didn't, the thought of Anna's death being my fault would ultimately loom in my mind. I was sure I would drive myself crazy if I held those emotions in, so I let them out.

Just when I was alone, of course. I hadn't taken that big of a step and actully turned to someone in my moments of desperation.

I dealt with them solely alone and it was good enough for me, honestly. No matter how much my mind screamed at me to really just turn to Liam.

Liam.

I still hadn't seen him. And I was beginning to worry more then ever. I had tried going to his cabin and seeing if he was there, but he wasn't. He never was.

And in result, only concern filled me. Because normally by now Liam would have popped up randomly like he always does, but he hasn't. Though I think I've made that point clear by now.

Nonetheless, I carry on as if it's nothing. Attending school and painting like crazy. The week flew by and it wasn't as bad as I thought it would be. Especially when Ms. J delivered some news that Friday.

"Guess what, Ronnie, guess what!" She came skipping into the art room, clapping her hands together and grinning like a mad man. Or well, mad woman.

"Why not skip the guessing part and just tell me what's up?" I suggest as I glance back at my painting, just slightly distracted by her sudden enthusiasm.

"There's no fun in that," She states with a small laugh. "Come on, guess."

"Okay," I nod and turn to face her, giving her my full attention. "Well, first off, does it have to do with me?"

"Of course, why else would I be here?"

"Because you work here?" I shrug and drop my paintbrush onto the desk next to me while shimming off my apron that is covered with paint.

"Yes, but it's four o'clock in the afternoon," She says, "I could be at home right now. Watching TV. But I'm not. I'm here. Isn't that weird?"

"I don't know. Maybe you wanted-" I begin to say, but she cuts me off, clearly because she's becoming rather impatient.

"You know what, forget it! I'll just tell what happened!" She declares, that same creepy grin slithering back onto her lips. "So there I was, just sitting at home, watching Desperate Housewives and then, I got a call."

I raise an eyebrow at the dramatic tone of her voice, but nonetheless, I nod for her to continue. "And?"

"The man who runs the Young Artist exhibit called," She says slowly. And immediately so, she sparks my curiosity. "A visitor at the museum was asking about your painting," She pauses, probably for dramatic effect. "Turns out, he works at some big art college in New York. He wants to talk to you about attending the school, Ronnie."

My eyes widen in shock as she begins to squeal in excitment and embraces me suddenly. "Isn't that amazing, Ronnie?"

I nod, speechless as I grip her back tightly. Finally, I manage to comment, "Yeah. It is. Amazing, I mean," I utter out. "Absolutely amazing."

It all happens really quick. That Sunday, I get to meet the dude that was at the museum and took interest in my painting and me. It turns out his name is Bill Carter, AKA, Mr. Carter. He works at the Academy of Arts in New York, as Dean of admission.

We had met at the small coffee shop in town and immediatly, he begin to dive into what the whole school was about. He explained about the courses and the teachers themselves. He even went as far as to show me paintings from other students attending the school. They were all beyond amazing and the whole time he spoke to me, I couldn't help but wonder what some big time Dean who ran an art school in New York was doing talking to me.

Me.

A not-so-simple girl who lived in a really small town - as cliche as it sounded - and how my painting had caught his eye while there were so many other amazing paintings at the Young Artist Exhibit. Of course, while he was speaking, I couldn't help but blurt that out.

"Why me?" I ask suddenly, rudely cutting him off. Immediatly, Mr. Carter's features twist into one of confusion.

"Excuse me? I don't quite understand what you're asking."

"I mean, why me? Why did you pick to speak to me about the college when there were so many other amazing paintings at the exhibit? Honestly, I don't even think I would be able to pay for the school. It's amazing, don't get me wrong, but I wouldn't be able to afford it." I explain awkwardly.

A grim smile slips onto Mr. Carter's lips. "Because your painting stuck out to me, Ronnie. Your painting was raw and emotional and just down right incredible. You're so young and bright, and I would hate to think that you do not realize that." He says strongly, "As for the money situation, I've reviewed your grades for your other courses. You have relatively good grades and could potentially graduate a year earlier if you wanted," He comments. "The only class I notice problem with is math. But if you are willing to raise that grade and work hard for the rest of the year, we are willing to offer you a scholarship."

I nearly choke at the word scholorship. Scholarship? Is he serious?

"Are you serious? A scholarship? Oh my god, am I dreaming?" I mutter stupidly. He chuckles and shakes his head.

"No, you aren't, Ms. Mars. We will offer you a dorm, of course, at the expense of a having to deal with a room mate and all the tuition paid. Though you would have to deal with your own living expenses. Such as food and so soon and so forth."

"That's awesome," I breath with a giddy smile on my face. "Seriosuly, Mr. Carter, I could kiss you! I won't, but I could. Basically, I'm saying thanks."

He smiles, collecting the papers he has scattered all around the table and shuffling them before slipping them into his briefcase. "You're welcome. But don't rush to answer, you have until the end of the school year to reply to my offer. Hopefully, next year, I will be seeing you at the Academy of Arts, Ms. Mars."

"You will, Mr. Carter." I say, "Again, thanks."

He smiles and places a generous tip on the table for the waitress. He sends me one last fleeting glance as he exits the coffee shop and then he's gone. I begin squealing immediately after, earning a few looks from other customers, but I don't care.

Just like Mr. Carter, I leave a tip on the table and bounce out of the coffee shop, laughing softly to myself in amazment while tucking my hands into my hoodie.

I walk without realizing where I'm going. The whole time I do, a huge smile is plastered on my face. It's because I can't believe what's just happened. A scholarship. To an actual art school in New York.

I let out another soft laugh as I cross the street, fixing my grey beanie and focusing my eyes on the ground.

Once I lap around another block, I finally draw my eyes away from the ground and to the people around me. It isn't long after that I discover a familiar face among the sea of people that surround me.

Though the girl is turned away from me, I still notice something off about her. And how it feels like I've seen her before.

She isn't facing me, so I can't really examine her. But from what I can make out, she's small and has pin straight long brown hair. Nearly black hair.

She stands stiff, staring up at a boy with curly red hair and big blue eyes, who grins goofy down at the small girl.

Though that smile is wiped off his face once he glances up and realizes I'm staring.

Immediately following, he nudges the small girl and she turns slowly and comes to face me. And that's when I recognize her.

It's that girl from the woods! The one I bumped into!

And just like that night, she still sports that angry scowl as she narrows her dark brown eyes at me. Quickly, she whips around, her hair spinning around her as she whispers something to the boy and then she's off.

Something comes over me and before I can help it, I begin to walk after her, fighting my way through the crowd and trying to keep my eyes trained on the small girl.

I lose her several times as I follow her down the road. She's agile, ducking into shops momentarily before reappearing back into my line of sight.

I trail after her for a good five minutes. Then, suddenly, she turns again, heading into an alley.

And that's when I stop. Mainly because I question if it's really a good idea to follow a mysterious girl into a dark alley.

Yeah, definitely not a good idea. But, I'm too stupid to listen to the common sense that is screaming at me to turn away.

Because this girl, whoever she is, has to know something about Liam. She had been running from his direction that night. And even if she didn't know who he was, I was still curious about who she was and what she doing in Portland. And why she reeked of the Purgatory.

I mean, last time I checked, the Purgatory didn't even accept girl members. Maybe only to abuse them or such, but the thing is, this girl didn't look like she had been abused. She had no bruises and overall no evidence of being tortured by them in anyway.

Besides, I was just too curious to turn away from finding out who this chick is.

So I turn into the alley.

At first, I don't see anything. Nothing but the ladder that leads to the top of the building and the stray garabage cans pressed up against the brick wall.

I peer around, my eyebrows furrowing as I glance behind me and forward, but the small girl is nowhere in sight. Nor is that boy with the red hair and blue eyes.

Where did she go? I think, puzzled.

There was no way she could have escaped. At the end of the alley, there was only a brick wall. But perhaps she had clambered over that when she noticed I was following her. What a waste of time.

With a huff, I spin around, ready to walk off when suddenly a fist comes swinging at me.

Just like in the movies, it all happens in slow motion. And for a minute or two, I'm frozen in shock as I watch the fist slowly coming towards my face. Then my reflexes finally kick in and I'm ducking, though the fist skims the top of my head.

And before I can really comprehend what just happened, another fist is flying at me. Again, I quickly dodge, thanking God for my quick werewolf reflexes.

I jump back and manage to get a glimpse of the maniac with flying fists. Turns out, it's the girl with the pin straight hair and nearly black eyes.

For once, she doesn't have a scowl on her face, but a determined look as she swings at me again. I block again, quicker then the other times and I can tell she's surprised that she hasn't landed a hit on me.

Where I lack in strength, I obviously prevail in speed.

But it isn't long that she's got me backed up against the brick wall, still going all mad Rocky on me.

And I have no where to duck but down. So when she swings at me for what feels like the millionth time, she ends up hitting the brick wall and with wide eyes, I watch as a crack forms in the wall.

And though there is no evident damage done to her hand, she still grips it tightly, hissing under her breath. "Son of a bitch. Jeremy, just grab her already!"

Before I can comprehend what's happening, I'm grabbed and thrusted up against the same wall the girl had just punched. An arm is pressed to my throat as well as a knife being pointed at me.

I look up, immediatly recognizing that this was the boy the Rocky chick was talking to just minutes ago.

Instead of wearing a scowl or a glare like his partner in crime is, he simply grins down at me. "Well, that was easy," He drawls tauntingly to the small girl that stands beside him. "I think you're losing your touch, Stella."

"Oh shut up," She snarls at him, still clutching her fist. "If you would have given me back my knife, I could have had her pinned much easier."

"Excuses, excuses," The redhead teases. 'Stella' rolls her eyes at him and then her eyes flicker to me.

I want to shrink away from her heated gaze. Mainly because something about this girl gives me the creeps, and the ominous glint in her eyes do no better to calm me down.

She cocks her head to the side, her dark eyes scanning my face before a look of realizition flashes across her face. "You're that girl," She states simply and quite blandly.

The boy's face immediately contorts into confusion. "You know her?"

Her cold eyes slither away from me to meet his gaze. "Something like that," She answers. "Why were you following me?"

I know that this question is directed at me, but I can't seem to spit out the answer, so I just dumbly keep staring at her.

After a minute or two of uncomfortable silence, I feel the point of the knife dig into the skin of my throat. Helplessly, my eyes flicker to the boy who watches me expectantly. "Well?"

I swallow roughly, "I'm not answering any questions until you get that knife away from me."

"Why? Does it make you nervous?" Stella taunts, a glimmer of sadism in her eyes. "You know, we could just get this over with quickly. Kill you and dump your body somewhere."

"I won't be much use to you if I'm dead, don't you think?" I remark smartly. The redhead scuffs, though.

"You're not much use to us right now and you're alive," He says. To emphasis Stella's previous point, the knife digs into my skin further more, this time, drawing blood. And that's when my heartbeat picks up.

I knew this was a bad idea! My conscious screams at me, you never follow some creepy girl down an alley way unless you want to get killed!

I squirm under the boys grip, now eagerly desperate to escape. But he won't budge and the knife continues to be dug deeper into my throat. And before I can stop myself, I blurt, "Liam won't be happy with you if you kill me!"

That immediately stops the boys action.

He retracts the knife away from me, his blue eyes widening, along with the girl who now stares at me in confusion. "You know Liam?"

So she does know Liam, I think, but how does Liam know her?

"Yes," I utter out. "Are you guys hunting him or something?"

"Are you?" The boy counters.

I shake my head, "No. I know him. He's a... good friend of mine."

The girl - AKA Stella - let's out a dry laugh. "Bullshit," She says, "Liam doesn't have any 'good' friends. He'll only keep you around if you're any convenience to him. So, tell me, how do you really know him?"

I press my lips together, my eyes focusing on the ground as I contemplate lying or telling the truth. Then a thought strikes me. How do the both of them know Liam, anyway?

"First, I want to know how you know him." I state. They both exchange a look at one another. Stella is the one to speak first.

"As long as you tell us who you are. And don't even think about lying, because telling the truth could potentially let us spare your life."

I roll my eyes, "Oh, what are you gonna do to me? Punch a wall again?" I mock, "You couldn't even land a hit on me, last time I checked. What makes you think you'll be able to the second time around?"

The girl snarls and attempts to throw herself at me, but the boy quickly pushes her back. "Ladies, ladies," The boy drawls slowly, "As much as I love a good cat fight," He pauses to add, "Seriously cat fights are hot," Then continues on seriously."But I cannot let you kill each other. Mainly because we both need answers from one another."

Stella growls at him, obviously annoyed, but nonetheless she stops reaching to get me and instead crosses her arms over her chest. She chooses not to say anything after that. And that leaves the redhead to deal with me.

"I'll start off with introductions," He announces. "I'm Jeremy Caverly. And this is Stella Prescott." He motions towards the small girl beside him. "And we know Liam because we have history with him, I guess," He explains, "We keeps tabs on him as well as on each other. We noticed he went missing a few days ago and we have no clue on where he went. Ever since, we've been trying to locate him. It isn't like him to be away for this long."

I study his expression and search for any indication that he might be lying, but he isn't. He's telling the truth and I can tell by the glint in his big blue eyes. And even though this boy - Jeremy - has given me limited information, it's still enough to please my curiosity. For now, at least. So I nod hesitantly, deciding not to press on about how he mentioned they have 'history'.

Last time I checked, Liam had never mentioned anything about these two nut cases. I didn't even think Liam had friends. They obviosuly had to be friends if Stella and Jeremy were willing to go looking for him. I just wondered how they all connected to one another. And why Stella still reeked of the Purgatory.

I want to ask, but I figure now is not the best time. And they obviously want answers from me. And now that they've given me the truth, I am willing to answer their previous question.

"Ronnie," I blurt suddenly. A look of confusion crosses Jeremy's expression, while Stella's only morphs into horror.

Jeremy opens his mouth to say something, but Stella beats him to it. "Wait, don't tell me-" She cuts herself off, pausing for a minute as she examines the ground intensely. Then her dark eyes flicker back up at me. "Are you her?"

It's only now that I've realized Jeremy has released me. I push myself away from the wall with a stiff nod. "If you mean Ronnie Mars, then yes, that's me."

Her eyebrows nearly shot up into her hairline. "Oh my god, no way, no way," She whispers breathlessly, "You're real!"

"I like to think so, yeah," I mutter. "Why is this a shock?"

"Because we thought all that gibberish about Liam finding his mate was bull," Jeremy answers, "But it's real. And let me just say, he is one lucky basterd. Because you are one fine ass b-"

Stella cuts him off by shoving him, "Jeremy, shut up!" She commands, "You're Ronnie! That means you know where he is, don't you?"

"Not really," I reply timidly. It immediately brings a frown to Stella's features. "I mean, he didn't mention anything to me before he left. I kinda figured you would know where he is, that's why I followed you into this alley."

I montion to the dump around me with a meek shrug. Stella groans, running a hand through her hair. "Don't you guys have mate-telepathy or something like that?"

"Yeah, but it isn't really working right now. Probably because he's too far away and he hasn't marked me yet, so the connection isn't as strong as it should be, I suppose." I say. And it's true. I had tried connecting Liam through our weird mind-link thingy for the past few days, but nothing had happened. And I figured it was because Liam just wasn't listening to me or that the connection was too weak to reach him if he was far away.

"Well this is great," Stella mutters.

"Yeah," Jeremy nods. "If only Liam would have left behind his map, then-" He begins, but I quickly cut him off at the mere mention of the word 'map'.

"His map?"

"Yeah, his map." Jeremy repeats. "It's one he keeps of all the Purgatory locations and such. He usually circles off where he's going next or whatever. He's like an animal. Migrating from one place to another."

I ignore his weird analogy and instead focus on the fact that he brought up the mention of a map. A map.

What did a map have to do with any of this? Was Liam freaking Dora The Explorer or something? Why did he have a freaking map? This is-

Oh my god. The map!

It suddenly dawns on me that I know what Jeremy is talking about. Liam's map. The same one I saw him working on when I was healing from the Purgatory gang bang or whatever. I had even asked him about it and why he had it.

I remembered seeing all the red X's on it and everything. And the only circle that really stood out to me was... Riverwood.

No way. Could Liam have actually went to Riverwood? I mean, he had asked me about it and everything. And I knew Liam was crazily hell bent on killing Purgatory members off, but was he that insane to actually travel to Riverwood?

Riverwood was/is commonly known as a popular hang out for the Purgatory pack members. And the place only screamed trouble. And honestly, the more that I thought about, the more I realized that Liam, no doubt, had went to Riverwood.

He is that crazy and stupid. I knew Liam would stop at nothing to take down the Purgatory and even if it meant putting himself in danger, he didn't care. That idiot.

"I know where he is," I declare after a long string of silence. Their attention immediately shoots right back to me.

"What? You do?" Jeremy questions in astonishment, "Where is he?"

"I'll tell you on two conditions," I state. Stella groans, again.

"Of course you wouldn't just tell us," She says. "What do you want?"

"Two things only," I say simply. "Number one; I'm kind of going to need you break into a house for me. But don't worry, it's my old house. Just collect the clothes from the closet and dresser and that's it."

"And tell me why we are going to break into your old house? Why not get it yourself?" Stella asks, quirking a brow at me.

"I got into a... fight, with my pack." I say, "I can't go back unless I want to get killed. And I don't want to get killed. So I need you to get in and get out as quickly as you can without getting caught."

"Wait, are you from Alpha Beckett's pack?" Jeremy inquires.

"I was from his pack, yeah."

"How can you not tell, Jeremy?" Stella rolls her eyes at him. "She reeks of them."

I scuff, "I take offense to that, you know."

"Good," She sneers. "Fine. We'll break into your house or whatever as long as you tell us where Liam is."

"Good," I mock, "Now for my second condition-" I begin to say, but Jeremy cuts me off. I guess it's payback for cutting him off before.

"I think I know where this is going," He concludes.

I raise a brow at him, "Oh, do you?"

"Yeah," He nods and then gives Stella a push. "Go, Stella. I don't want you to see me do this. I'm doing this for Liam." He turns away from the confused girl, sucking in a sharp breath. He faces me slowly, then he purses his lips. "Okay, let's do this."

He begins to lean closer to me and my eyes widen at his actions. "Uh, what do you think you're doing?" I press my finger to his cheek, pushing his face away from me. Jeremy appears dumbfounded.

"Oh, so it isn't going in that direction? I don't have to offer my body to you for information?"

"What? No." I shake my head at with furrowed brows. "I was just gonna say that you guys have to take me with you to go find Liam."

"Oh," Jeremy mumbles dumbly. He starts to rock on heels shortly after, "Well, this is awkward now."

Stella let's out a dry laugh, "I swear, Caverly, you get dumber and dumber each day." She shakes her head at him, her hair swaying from side to side with that one simple motion.

"It's just what happens normally in books or movies, so I just assumed-" Once again, I cut Jeremy off.

"Look, do you agree to my conditions or not?" I say, folding my arms over my chest.

Stella looks to Jeremy momentarily. He stares back at her and then nods, obviously giving Stella his approval.

She twists her body towards me, nodding stiffly. "We agree."

It isn't long after that I find myself cramped in the back seat of a white van - presumably Jeremy's - with a duffel bag of my clothes squashed up against my side along with Jeremy who has fallen asleep after an hour of driving.

Stella is the one driving, though she should probably be focusing on the road, she seems lost in her thoughts. It's obvious when she begins to swerve and if it weren't for my constant screeching, I'm sure we would have crashed by now.

How do I get myself into these kind of predicaments? I question silently as I peer down at the sleeping ginger next to me. He snores, really loudly, along with grunting and mumbling and the occasional kick or two that is, of course, directed at me.

And I can't get away from him, because there is no where else to go. I can't get in the trunk since it's full with all their suitcases and Stella won't let me sit in the passenger seat without hissing at me. So I'm forced to remain in the back.

To pass the time, I go through my clothes in my duffel bag. While I'm doing this, I come to realize why Anna was always bickering at me. It's because all that my wardrobe consists of is: Tang tops, hoodies, plaid shirts, beanies, jeans, and combat boots.

God, I feel like such a hipster.

I sigh and toss the bag aside when I can no longer take shuffling through my clothes. Instead, I focus my attention on annoying Stella with my loud huffs of annoyance and occasionally kicking the back of her chair. But can you blame me? Being stuck in a van with two people you barely know drives you insane.

"Can you stop that?" Stella asks irritably, her eyes meeting mine in the rear view mirror. I flash a sweet smile at her.

"I can," I drawl. "But I won't." I kick the back of her chair again, humming along with the song on the radio.

Stella rolls her dark eyes at me, but doesn't reply. We sit in silence for another thirty minutes, with the occasional grunt or moan from Jeremy. Stella let's out a dry laugh when Jeremy kicks me again.

"I swear, I will strangle you if you kick me again," I mutter as I glare down at Jeremy. He seems to hear me, since his eyes flicker open and a tired smile appears on his lips.

"My bad," He mumbles and pushes himself up into a sitting position with a yawn. "What time is it?"

"Quarter till five," Stella replies with a smirk. "Did you have a nice nap?"

"I slept like a baby," He says with a nod.

"Yeah, really." I mumble sarcastically and I rub at my throbbing thigh. "Thanks for kicking me, too. I think I have a few bruises."

"Not my fault you're so fragile," He comments, giving my thigh a rough pat. "You have to get some meat on you. I swear, it felt like I was kicking a rock. Then I realized I was just hitting your bone."

I roll my eyes at him, did that even make sense?

He hops into the passenger seat, causing Stella to hiss at him. Jeremy merely laughs. "Are you a snake or something?"

"Or maybe she's just Volderment's daughter and she's cursing you off in snake language." I chim. It causes Jeremy to laugh harder.

"Now that you've mentioned that, Ronnie, I do see some resemblances between Voldy and Stella." Jeremy replies teasingly. "They're both grumpy and evil. Stella's nose is relatively flat and I have noticed she's been losing hair lately. Baldness does run in the Dark Lord's family, you know?"

Stella sneers at him. "If I'm Voldermort, then you're that annoying ginger kid."

"Ron Weasly?" I offer and Stella nods. Jeremy fakes a look of hurt.

"You're just jealous of my amazing ginger way," He says.

"Liam can be Harry Potter," I say suddenly. "You know, with the scar he has on his forehead and stuff."

"Very true," Jeremy nods. "And who are you going to be?" He asks, twisting in his seat to face me.

"I'll be Hermione, duh."

"Oh," Jeremy waggles his brows at me. "That means you and me end up together in the end."

"Never mind, I'll be Hagrid." I correct quickly.

"I think that's a perfect choice for you, Ronnie," Stella admires with a smirk on her face. "Both of you are freakishly tall and you did live in a shack."

I scoff, "A midget is freakishly tall compared to you."

Jeremy let's out a snort as he laughs. "Oh, burn!"

"Shut up, both of you!" Stella snaps. And that's the end of our conversation. Or, well, argument.

Night falls as we continue on driving. And it's evident that we're nearing Riverwood when we see bright flashes of lights in the distance and loud music. Once we get closer, we get a glimpse of a warehouse with raging Purgatory members as well as humans who are getting drunk out of their mind. Stella turns to glance at me, raising a brow. "Riverwood is a warehouse?"

"Guess so," I answer. And we all silently slither out of the van, Stella carrying three hoodies with her. Immediately so, I get a whiff of the foul odor that only belongs to the Purgatory. "Man, this place reeks of Purgatory." I comment with a hint of disgust in my tone. Stella nods.

She tosses me a hoodie, as well as one to Jeremy. She shrugs on her own hoodie and hides away her hair. "You might want to put that on," She says, gesturing to the black hoodie in my hands. "I'm not on good terms with the Purgatory right now and I want to avoid being spotted."

"Well it looks like you and I have something in common, then," I tug the jacket over my head and pull up the hood, though I don't tuck my braid away. "I'm not on best terms with them either."

Stella smirks at me, but doesn't question what I mean. Jeremy simply smiles. "Well, aren't you two rebels."

"Stay together. Especially you, Ronnie. Don't stray away from me, okay?" Stella ignores Jeremy's previous comment and gives me a pointed look, obviously trying to get her point across. I meekly agree with a nod.

We begin our short two minute walk until we near the warehouse entrance, where a tall and quite buff man stands. Though he doesn't stink of the Purgatory, nor is he a werewolf from what I can tell.

We stop in front of him as he analyzes all three of us, then he asks, "You're not from a gang or something, are you?"

Jeremy shakes his head, "No, lad. I can promise you that we aren't in some gang."

"Alright then," He nods and opens the door of the warehouse, "Head on in and enjoy your night."

Jeremy beams at us, "Thanks, macho man. Enjoy your night too."

I roll my eyes at Jeremy but follow behind him nonetheless as we enter the building. I feel quite claustrophobic once the man shuts the door, leaving us in a pitch black hallway that booms with music and a few stray couples that lean against the wall, attacking each other faces with frantic kisses.

Stella makes a sound of disgust while Jeremy let's out a whoop and grabs mine and Stella's hand, draging us down the hall and into where the main partying is happening.

I find that the hallway leads to the heart of the warehouse. The room is huge, filled with people and lights and an open bar with an assortment of drink I've never seen.

People are grinding on each other like animals in heat and sweating bullets from the intense heat of the strobe lights that flash all different types of colors. Red, blue, purple, pink. You name it.

I watch with wide eyes as one girl chugs down a whole bottle of vodka before ripping her shirt off, leaving her clad in a bright pink bra. Immediately following, all the guys around her cheer and shout degrading remarks, though the girl doesn't seem to mind. She only giggles and then throws herself onto the first guy she sees. They disappear into the sea of people after that.

I shake my head and look to Jeremy and Stella, who are also shocked about what's occuring before our eyes. Or well, Stella's shocked. Jeremy's just grinning like a mad man and staring after any girl that walks by.

"Where do you think Liam is?" I shout the question as loudly as I can over the roar of music. Stella's eyes dart away from the crowd to me.

"I guess we'll just have to spread out and look around. There's no way we can stick together with this huge crowd," She calls back over the music. And just after she says this, Jeremy shoots off into the crowd. Stella shakes her head, but doesn't comment on it. She only says, "Meet me back here in fifteen minutes. Stay safe."

I nod and wish her luck. And just like that, Stella disappears into the cluster of people and I'm alone.

I remain calm and scan the area for a golden brown haired and green eyed boy, but of course, I don't spot him and I know just like Stella and Jeremy, I'm going to have to journey into the crowd.

I dive into the cluster of sweaty and drunk teenagers, pushing my way through and shoving away at the hands that reach out to grab me and perhaps coax me to dance with them.

Once I get through what appeared to be a never ending crowd, I discover another stray hallway. Though, somehow, this hallway is presumably darker then the other and to my surprise, once I begin to travel down the hall, there are no couples making out over here.

As I get deeper and deeper into the hallway, I begin to notice how the music behind me becomes duller and all I can hear is the sound of my footsteps and soft murmurs that come from down the hall.

I cock my head to the side once I catch sight of a sheer pink curtain and beads that dangle from the ceiling. Through the thin fabric, I see a group of men a few stray woman that cater to them. They chatter softly with the occasional chuckle, but that's it.

I frown and look to my side, realizing that there is more to this hall then just this one room. I take one last glance at the room before me and then decide to keep on traveling down the hall, since it's obvious Liam wasn't in that room.

I continue on for a good minute till I finally reach the end of the hall. But the only thing at the end of the hall is a mere grey door. Without much though, I push the door open, being greeted with fresh air.

So this must lead to back of the warehouse, I think matter-of-factly as I take in the sight of a few girls and boys sitting around a bonfire. They all hold some alcoholic drink in their hand and they occasionally pour some into the fire, watching as the fire grows and licks the sky. They laugh each time and I wonder momentarily of why this is so entertaining to them.

Nonetheless, I walk away from them and soon spot another large cluster of people. Only this time, their circling around what appears to be a... cage?

A fighting cage, I guess. I try to recall where I've seen this before but I end up blank. Till I remember my dad talking to me about UFC. What's that thing the UFC fighters fight in?

The Octagon! That's what my dad called the cage they'd fight in. And well, it seems I listen to my dad without even realizing it.

I walk closer to the Octagon and the people surrounding it, who hoot and holler and throw insults at the people who are fighting in the cage. Or, well, the animals who are fighting in the cage.

I get a look closer of who's in the Octagon once I fight my way through the crowd, catching a glimpse of a grey and black wolf who circle around each other, snarling and swatting their paws at one another.

It isn't long after that the grey wolf takes charge and hops onto the black one, sinking it's large canine's into the others throat.

The people around me go insane, yelling with excitement and pushing to get closer to watch the fight. Ultimately, I'm thrusted up against the cage and in order to steady myself, I loop my fingers through the metal fence part of the Octagon.

I soon realize that this isn't a simple fight or anything, this is a fight to the death.

That's made obvious when the grey wolf behead's the black wolf.

Everyone around me screams and starts chanting for the grey wolf, who takes a lap around the cage, obviously drinking in it's victory.

Man, the Purgatory are sick mofo's, I think as I watch the cage door fling open and not a second later does a man emerge with a microphone and a sadistic smile plastered on his features.

"Again, the winner is Rex!" The man yells, giving the grey wolf a rough pat on the back. "Are you read y for the next contestant, Rex?"

'Rex' howls, an obvious yes, I guess.

"Good!" The man chimes back and his grin widens as his eyes scan over the crowd. "Cause now we'll be picking one of you from the crowd to battle Rex!"

Instead of the crowd becoming scared or sickened at the idea, they merely begin to scream possibly louder while trying to convince the man to pick them. The sadistic man laughs and begins to walk around the cage, just like 'Rex' had been doing a few minutes ago.

He peers into the crowd, pursing his lips. He pretends to pick someone but then quickly kills their hopes once he shakes his head and decides he doesn't want them.

It's only when he gets to my section of the crowd that my heartbeat picks up and my eyes grow wide beneath the hood that covers my face.

I release my grip on the cage and turn, ready to escape the crowd when I feel a tug on my jacket, dragging me back to the cage.

My back slams into the cage and I twist my head around to get a look at the person who grabbed me, only to come face to face with the sadistic announcer.

"You!" He says excitedly. "You'll battle Rex!"

Of course he'd pick me, I think, I have the worst luck in the world!

"What? No, I'll pass, really," I begin to protest, but the man isn't having it. And neither is the crowd.

Hands grab me and push me towards the cage door, despite my struggling and objections.

And once I stand before the cage door, the man grabs a hold of my wrist and throws me into the cage along with the grey wolf.

He yanks down my hood and instead of being surprised that I'm a girl, he simply laughs. "This is going to interesting!" He declares into the microphone and then says directly to me, "You should probably shift once that cage door closes, just letting ya know."

And then he's off and slamming the cage door, along with locking it. I watch him in horror and throw myself against the cage door, desperatly trying to peel it open. "I don't want to fight!" I yell in fear, "Let me out!"

The man shakes his head and winks, "No can do, sweat heart," he turns to the crowd and thrusts his arm outwards. "Let the fight begin!"

The crowd, just like before, begins to hoot and holler and throw insults. Just this time, this is all directed at me.

I turn away slowly from the cage door, seeing that the grey wolf is already in front of me, his lip pulled over his teeth in an angry growl.

I put my hands up, signaling surrender. "Look, Rex, I don't want to fight. Let's be f-" I'm cut off when he suddenly charges forward me.

Now running solely on fear, I jump out of the way and onto the cage as I begin to scale up to the top. Though I realize that at the top of the cage, there's barbed wire.

I guess I'm not the only one that's thought about escaping, I think dreadfully as I peer down at the grey wolf that begins to throw itself against the cage side, snapping it's teeth at me.

Oh god, oh god, I begin to think frantically, I don't want to die. Why does this have to be the second time I am almost die today? I don't want to die! I don't want to die!

"Stella!" I yell over the loud roar of people, "Jeremy!"

"Your little friends can't help you!" One person calls from the crowd tauntingly. And just as he says this, the grey wolf snags my ankle and I can feel it's teeth sink into my flesh.

I let out a scream and with my free foot, I slam my boot into's it's face as hard as I can, though it only causes the wolf to release me momentarily, it's enough time for me to scale across the cage to the other side.

I grip onto the cage with one of my hands, while I wrap my other hand around my bleeding ankle.

The grey wolf is below me again, though this time he begins to leap up to get me and I can feel how much force he's putting into his jumps, since the cage begins to shake.

"Holy shit!" I cuss, kicking out my leg again to hit the wolf down. I land a hit to it's eye, which only causes the wolf to get even angrier. "Leave me alone, you crazy dog!"

Rex growls, swatting his paw at me. This time, he gets my thigh. I cry out once his sharp talons meet my thigh. He leaves three diagnol cuts in my leg, shredding not only my skin but somewhat of my jeans, leaving my upper thigh bare and exposing the deep cuts to the cold air.

"Fuck my life," I hiss under my breath as the warm blood begins to roll down my leg and the pain sinks in.

And somehow, over the roar of the crowd and the growls of the wolf below me, I hear something. Something that sounds like a scream of my name.

"Ronnie!"

I look in the direction of the voice, though I'm met with only the stares of the crowd that are still screaming for the grey wolf to kill me.

"Ronnie!" The voice screams again. "Ronnie!"

And now that's I've heard the voice clearer, I recognize who it is immediately. Because no other person could make shivers ripple down my spine just by saying my name. It's Liam. And there's no doubt in my mind about it.

"Liam!" I call back, my eyes searching the crowd and that's when I catch sight of him. Along with Stella and Jeremy.

They stand by the cage door, Liam prying the lock open while Jeremy shouts at the announcer dude who is shoving them back and trying to prevent them from opening the cage door.

To shut him up, Stella throws a punch. Immediately following, the man is down for the count.

The microphone clatters with the floor, causing a ear-deafening echo. The people in the crowd cover theirs eyes, letting out a cry at the sound.

All I do is stare at my three hero's as they barge open the cage door, catching the attention of the grey wolf who whips around and snarls at Liam, Jeremy, and Stella.

"I'll take this fucker on," Stella declares, a grin slipping onto her lips. "I haven't had a good fight in a while."

"I'll take him, too," Jeremy says, "Go get Ronnie, Liam."

Liam doesn't protest. Though he does help Stella and Jeremy by throwing the grey wolf across the freaking cage.

Jeremey and Stella shift, gallaping after the grey wolf. It isn't long that I hear the disgusting sound of flesh being ripped from the grey wolf's body.

I shut my eyes in order to not see Stella and Jeremy killing the damn wolf.

I only peek my eyes open when I feel the cage shake and I see that Liam is clambering up to me. He stops beside me, holding out his hand to me. I take it and Liam drags me towards him, softly commanding, "Wrap your legs around me."

I do what he says and ignore the pain as I wrap my legs around Liam's waist, as well as circling my arms around his neck.

He climbs down slowly until we reach the ground and once we do, he wraps his arms around my back and shouts to Stella and Jeremy. "Come on guys, we have to go!"

Jeremey and Stella whine, but quickly shift back. Again, I close my eyes in order to avoid seeing the remains of the grey wolf.

I keep my eyes closed the whole entire time Liam runs. I simply press my nose into his neck and inhale his addicting scent. I ignore the pain shooting up my leg and grip as tightly onto Liam as I can, as if I'm afraid he'll disappear. And I guess I am pretty scared he will disappear.

We reach the van shortly and immediatly so, Liam flings open the door and lays me down in the back seat, while Stella and Jeremy hop in the front. "Drive, bitch, drive!" Jeremy commands and I soon feel the car lurch forward. If it weren't for Liam holding me, I'm sure I would have went flying towards the windshield.

Liam detaches himself from me momentairly, ripping a piece of his shirt and then typing it around my leg. "What are you doing?" I ask sluggishly, suddenly feeling lightheaded.

"Trying to stop the bleeding," Liam answers in a raspy voice. Which is incredibly sexy, I might say.

Why are you thinking his voice is sexy at a time like this? A part of me screams, but I ignore it, keeping my eyes trained on Liam's concentrated face. "He cut you really deep, but you'll live." Liam declares as he ties the piece of his shirt around below my wound. "Do you have water bottle or something in here, Jeremy?"

"Maybe," I hear Jeremy faint reply and then I hear him shuffling around the car before he says, "Yes! Found a water bottle!"

He tosses it to Liam, who catches it effortlessly. He tears off the cap and then pours the water on my found.

I whimper, despite the previous urge to choke down the cry. "Liam, that hurts."

"I know, princess, I know." He murmurs, leaning up and pressing a kiss to my sweaty forehead. "Just close your eyes. We'll be back in Portland shortly, don't worry."

I listen to him. Well, for the most part anyway. I listen to him about the part of closing my eyes. But I still worry. Not for me, but for what awaits us back at home.

Chapter 26

The drive back to Portland had been crazy.

Crazy from the start, really. And it had only gotten worse as we continued the long drive back home. It started with Stella and Jeremy screaming at one another, and then me screaming at Liam when he decided he would have to stitch up the deep cuts in my leg.

When we pulled up to a gas station so Liam could retrieve the supplies that he needed to patch me up with, I had meekly tried to escape out of the van. Only resulting in Jeremy having to yank me back into the car and Stella snickering in my face the whole, claiming I was being childish and that it was only a few stitches. Immediately, I commanded her to shut up and continued on trying to escape my fate.

Eventually, once Liam came out with a bag full of supplies, they managed to get situated back into the van. Though it was obviously against my free will.

Jeremy had to hold me down as Liam threaded a freaking needle through my skin. And so I was forced to lay back and merely squirm in pain.

And once Liam was done stitching me up, I discovered the torture I was enduring wasn't over. He had fetched a bottle of Peroxide from the gas station for my ankle. And I had squealed in pain once he poured it over my wound.

Seriously, I was making some sounds that weren't even human. Then again, I'm not exactly human. But still, it hurt.

After putting me through hell, Liam finally let me get some sleep. Though my nap only lasted so long before Jeremy and Stella started screaming again. This time they weren't even legibly fighting over a specific reason or whatever. They were simply bickering and picking out one another's flaws. And it gave me the worst headache ever.

If I didn't have a bad leg, I would have leaped over my seat and pounded their faces in until they decided to shut up.

But I couldn't, as I've said before. So I laid back and endured it. Just how I had endured Liam torturing me.

We didn't reach Portland until it was 6 AM. And by then, everyone was grumpy and tired and pissed off at each other for no reason.

When he reached Liam's cabin, Stella had stormed to the guest room - the room I had been confined to after my unfortunate run in with the Purgatory - and locked the door, even after Jeremy had called dibs.

Jeremy was pissed at her. He had stood outside her door, yelling insults and comebacks I had never heard before. And since Stella had screwed him over, he decided to screw Liam and I over by taking the only room left for himself.

And before Liam and I could even react, he had slammed the door shut and locked the door just like Stella had.

So Liam and I got stuck with the lumpy couch.

It sucked, pretty much. I just ended up sleeping on Liam once we he laid down on the couch. Though Liam didn't seem to mind much. He simply draped a blanket over us and he was out like a light.

I had stayed up a little longer, unlike Liam, Jeremy, and Stella. It was because I was too engrossed in my thoughts and how exactly I was going to explain to Liam that I had left my pack and how I had declared war on them. Or the fact that Anna had died.

Once the thought of Anna filled my mind, I couldn't shake it off. Not even once I managed to fall asleep.

I dreamed about her. Though it was nothing horrifying or repulsive or whatever. It was more taunting then anything. Because in my dreams, Anna looked happy and alive and it pained me to think how I might have caused her death.

I suddenly felt like the biggest hyprocite in the world. I had always been one of those people who preached for people not to blame their selves for every bad thing that happened in their life, but here I am, blaming myself for every little bad thing that happened over the last several months.

But when you really thought about it, I kinda did cause these bad events to happen. All the problems that occurred in the previous months had revolved around me refusing to mate with Adam. And the consciousness I faced from it.

There was only one problem that I hadn't caused. And that was Tara.

Okay, maybe it was a little rude of me to refer to her as a problem, but I couldn't help it. Even though Tara was evidently harmless and kind and overall freaking perfect, that didn't necessarily mean I was fond of her.

I admit, she had changed my father for the better, but it hurt to know some random woman who had walked into his life one day had changed his ways. She made him better, while I couldn't. Then again, I never really tried to help him. If anything, I brought him down. Tara is better and way more supportive then I ever was. And it sucked to really accept that fact.

And there I went, being a hyprocite again. Getting mad over the fact some chick had walked into my dad's life and made him a better person. Because, in reality, that's what happened with Liam.

He had walked into my life one day. Quite literally, actually. Just like the way Tara did. And he had made me somewhat of a better person. He had helped me when it came to me dealing with my trust issues and ultimately teaching me to stop running away from my problems. As corny and cliche as it sounded, he showed me that it was okay to let someone in.

And Tara was just showing that to my father as well. She was showing him it was okay to love again. And it was working, clearly. Because my dad was happier then ever and I didn't want to bring him down from that. Not again.

Sure, Tara wasn't and surely would never be my mom, but he deserved to be happy. If he wanted to go run off with her, then I guess now was the best time to do it. In my mind, as much as

I hated to think about it, I could image them getting married. Perhaps see my dad having another child. One that wouldn't come out as messed up as me.

And that would mean I would have a half-brother or half-sister. I don't cringe or push the thought away, though. I simply reflect on the fact that if they did get married and have a kid, that I wouldn't be apart of their life. Then again, after my mother's death, I had never really been involved in my dad's life. Nor had he been involved in mine.

I had kicked him to the curb just like he had done to me. I couldn't be mad at him. I couldn't blame him or anything. He didn't deserve me screaming at him or just overall silently loathing him. He didn't deserve my feeble anger. And neither did Anna.

At that moment, I made a mental note to speak to my father about it. That is, if I ever managed to catch him straying out of pack territory. Most likely, I would. And I'd grasp that opportunity and tell him I'm sorry. It might be the last time I see him before the whole fight between Beckett's pack and me went down. It was time I faced another fear of mine. And that was finally being able to talk to my father honestly.

And it isn't long after that my dreams slowly morph from Anna to my dad and to my mom. But just like with Anna, the dream isn't neccassirly bad. Nor is it good. Mainly because just seeing her smiling face in my dreams are painful. A painful memory that I've tried to suppress for so long. But it's just another fear I have to face.

That's when my body finally decides to wake up. And I'm slightly relieved when the image of her disappears and I'm left to stare up at the ceiling of Liam's cabin.

I remain like that for a while, until I finally decide I've had enough of laying around and slide off from the couch and Liam. Somehow, with my amazing ninja skills, I manage to get up without waking Liam.

Even though my leg is throbbing and I can't really apply pressure down onto my ankle, I still limp to my duffel bag that I somehow reminded Liam to bring in. I fetch myself a pair of jean shorts and an over sized sweater, along with my other essentials.

I take a bath, simply enjoying resting in the warm and washing away all the impurties of yesterday. Such as dried blood and dirt that has somehow caked itself into my hair.

Once I'm done, I dry off and throw on my clothes as well as my combat boots. I re-braid my hair and then slither into the kitchen, where I work with what Liam has in his fridge.

Which is relatively nothing, really. All he has is eggs and bacon and tea. And then some other old musty jar of pickles I thought Liam threw out. But hey, at least he has breakfast food stocked away.

I make as little noise as I can, but eventually, I hear footsteps behind me and I turn around, expecting to find Liam but inside I find myself staring right back at Jeremy, who flashes me a sleepy grin.

"I smelt food," He says simply. It's enough to make me crack a smile right back at him.

"I should have figured," I reply and with a sigh, I shove the plate of food that was intended to be for me to him. But luckily, I made another plate for Liam, so-

"Who's making food?" Stella's voice rings out and before I know what's happening, the other plate of food is jacked from me and I can't really object to it, since by the time I realize what has just happened, she's already scarfing down the breakfast I made for Liam and myself.

"That wasn't for you," I grit out, glaring at the small girl as she smugly smiles at me.

"Oh, so this was for you and pretty boy over there, eh?" She casts a glance over at a still sleeping Liam, "I would say sorry, but I'm really not."

Instead of starting a fight with her, I merely huff and begin to crack a few more eggs. It's way too early to start screaming at one another, anyway.

Though Jeremy and Stella obviously disagree with me on that. Since they immediately begin to bicker and it isn't long that Liam wakes up from it.

"Do you two ever shut up?" Liam groans and I watch as he slowly pushes himself up from the couch, stretching as he does so.

It's like my eyes have a mind of their own because immediately, I'm following his every action. Just watching the muscles in his back ripple as well as his chest. And man, how hadn't I realized that he had taken off his chest during the night?

"No," Stella replies with a scoff and then her eyes flicker over to me. "And you might want to put on a shirt, pretty boy. You might give Ronnie a heart attack over here."

For some reason, at this mere comment, the blood rushes to my cheeks and I force my eyes to stop inspecting the deep V that disappears into his jeans.

I hear Jeremy laugh at my embarrassment and so does Liam. It isn't long that I feel his presence behind him.

He wraps his arms about my waist, pressing my back to his chest as he bends down to my height and nestles his head into my neck. He presses a gentle kiss to the base of my throat, making me shiver.

"You guys me sick," Stella shudders in disgust at our act of affection, while Jeremy rolls his eyes.

"Jealous, Stella?" He taunts, causing Stella to glower at him.

"No, why would I be jealous?"

"Because you have no one to be mushy and romantic with," Jeremy says. He beams at her. "But don't worry, you'll always have me."

Stella scowls at him, "That doesn't make me feel better at all."

"At least you'll have your hundreds of cats to keep you company once you get older, Stella." I comment with a smirk.

Stella hisses at me. "Now I really wish you turned out to be fake."

"Turned out to be fake? What?" Liam questions from behind him. Stella opens her mouth to answer him, but I quickly intervene.

"Eat now. Questions later." I shove the plate of food towards him along with his mug. He raises a brow at me.

"Are you sure it's safe to eat?"

I furrow my brows at him, "Why wouldn't it be?"

"Because those eggs and bacon have been sitting in that fridge long before I even got here." He says. Immediately, I hear Stella and Jeremy choking on their food.

"Gross!" Stella shrieks, running off to the bathroom to spit out the food. As well as Jeremy that runs after her, fighting his way into the bathroom along with Stella. She screams at him and attempts to shove him, but Jeremy prevails and pushes her to the ground. Only resulting in Stella to grip onto his ankle and scream possibly louder.

Despite the urge to laugh, I detach myself from Liam and turn to face him. "Oh my god! Why didn't you tell me? That could have been ages old and I-"

I'm cut off when Liam suddenly begins to laugh over Jeremy and Stella's screaming and gagging. He laughs so hard that he can barely choke out his next sentence, "What idiots!" He gasps between breathes, "They fell for it!"

"Wait, so it was a joke?" I ask, confusion clearly plastered across my features. Liam nods, still laughing.

I shake my head at him, but laugh along softly, all the while watching as Jeremy and Stella fight over the bathroom.

Can't say they didn't have it coming, I think and with that, I turn and walk off.

It isn't long after that night falls and we can no longer avoid the inevitable conversation that is bound to come.

We get as comfortable as possible, settling around the fire that Liam lit in the fireplace. Shortly after doing so, Stella pulls up another chair from one of the room's and takes a seat beside the couch. Jeremy, Liam, and I sit on the couch.

"So, does anyone want to tell me what Stella meant earlier?" Liam breaks the silence, his vivid green eyes flickering between Stella, Jeremy, and me.

Stella's the one who decides to do the talking, thankfully. "Jeremy and I ran into Ronnie in town," Stella begins slowly, her dark eyes meeting mine. "She was stupid enough to follow me into an alley-"

I cut her off, "I wasn't stupid, I was curious."

She sneers at me, "You didn't let me finish."

"That's because you-" I start to say, but Jeremy annoyingly cuts me off, just like I did to Stella a minute ago.

"Basically, the point is, we ran into Ronnie and kinda had a little fight with her at first-" This time, it's Liam's turn to interrupt. Oh joy.

"A little fight with her? What?" Liam hisses. Jeremy shrugs innocently.

"It was a simple little disagreement, but then we got to talking and we figured out who she was, so we backed off."

I scoff, "Yeah, after I warned you that Liam would be angry if you killed me."

Liam's eyes widen and so does Jeremy's. "Ronnie!" He shrieks, his voice taking on a higher octave. "Shush!"

"What the fuck did you guys do to her?" Liam snarls.

"Nothing!" Jeremy replies quickly.

"You're lying," I say in a sing-song voice. "After Stella was done trying to punch me, Jeremy pinned me to a wall with a knife pointed at me. I felt threatened and frankly, very scared. I mean, I did nothing to them."

"Now you're the liar!" Stella snaps. "You're the one who forced us to bring you with us to find Liam!"

Liam turns to me, his eyes narrowing. "You forced them to take you to Riverwood? Are you crazy?"

"Don't turn this on me," I say, glaring right back at him. "I did it because I was concerned about you. And you didn't exactly warn me about these two nut cases, anyway."

Jeremy gasps, obviously offended. "I am not a nut case! If anyone of us is really crazy, It's Stella! She tried to murder me in my sleep!"

"Lies! You all tell lies!" Stella hisses, pointing an accusing finger at all of us.

"Shut up, Voldermort!" Jeremy snaps back. Stella looks ready to attack.

"As I've said before, at least I'm not that annoying ginger kid!" Stella shouts, "I swear, if you don't shut up with that stupid little insult, I'll murder you!"

"Then stop cussing us off in snake language," I taunt, only making Stella angrier. Of course, this causes her to throw some insults at me and I immediately start screeching them back at her. Calling her evil, and Voldermort, and somehow through our fighting Jeremy begins to point at Stella, yelling random Harry Potter spells. Which makes Stella screech at him to stop.

Basically, the agruement goes like this:

Stella: "Shut up, Ronnie! You don't know anything, you tall freak!"

Me: "I'm not that tall, you're just that freakishly short, you shouldn't be Voldermort, you should be that nasty little creature thing from The Hobbit!"

Jeremy: "Avada Kedavra!"

Stella: "I don't even know who you're talking about! And stop being an idiot, Jeremy!"

Me: "That nasty little creature! What's his name? Gollum! His name's Gollum! And that's you!"

"Crucio!" Jeremy cries, "Die, Voldermort, die!"

And that's when Liam decides to stop the madness. "Guys, stop!" He yells, in somewhat of an alpha tone of voice. But nonetheless, Jeremy, Stella, and I fall silent as we all silently sulk at our argument ending. "You are ridiculous! And frankly, I have no idea what you're talking about. Gollum? Voldermort? What?"

"It's kinda an inside joke," Jeremy mutters sheepishly. "You wouldn't get it."

Liam chooses ignore Jeremy's comment, "Guys, this isn't a joke. With the Purgatory looming closer and Ronnie being forced to mate with Adam-"

"Wait, mate with who?" Stella, genuinely confused now rather then angry.

"Adam Beckett," Liam repeats with annoyance plastered on his features. "He's some annoying little fuck who-"

I cut him off, "Who I'm no longer to be mated to."

Liam turns to me slowly, raising a brow, though he doesn't seem to displeased at my comment. "And why's that?"

"I left the pack," I say bluntly. "But I'll explain it more later. When we're alone."

Liam nods, obviously understanding I don't want to speak about it in front of Jeremy and Stella, but like always, Stella has to comment on whatever I say. "You might as well say whatever you want to say to Liam in front of us. It would help me figure out why exactly the Purgatory are going after you, Liam, and your pack."

My eyes flickers to Stella's, my eyebrows furrowing. "How do you know that they're coming after us?"

She smirks, "I have my sources."

"Like who?" I question, "The Purgatory themselves? I would think so. You reek of them."

Stella let's out a dry laugh, "And here I thought you wouldn't notice. I should've given you more credit."

"Enough with the jokes," I snap. "What are you doing hanging around the Purgatory? And more importantly, why are you hanging around Liam?"

I see Liam smirk out of the corner of my eye. Stella smirks as well. "Possessive, aren't we?" She muses. Her dark eyes slither over to Liam. "Don't worry, Ronnie. Stupid isn't my type," She says. "And it's simple how I get facts out of the Purgatory, I'm apart of them."

"What?" I screech, whipping around to look at Liam. Though he doesn't seem freaked out about what Stella's said or anything. He remains seated, his arms folded behind his head as he remains sitting shirtless. I glare at him, despite the urge to stare at his broad chest. "Did you know about this?"

His cool and collected gaze slides over to me, "Maybe."

"Maybe? Why didn't you tell me?"

"You didn't know about Stella," He replies. "Nor about Jeremy. So I never mentioned anything."

"Yeah, which I'm really hurt about that, Liam." Jeremy pouts. "I thought we shared something special."

Liam rolls his eyes at him, all the while I'm freaking out. "Why the heck is a Purgatory member sitting in our living room? You hate the Purgatory!"

Liam smirks, "Our living room?"

I shake my head at him, letting out a scoff. "This isn't a joke anymore," I say and turn towards Stella. "If you're apart of the Purgatory, what the hell are you doing here?"

"I joined them for a reason," She replies. "It's not that I actually wanted to apart of their little group. Why would I want to be apart of a group that took everyone I ever loved away from me?"

And suddenly, the room is quiet. Quiet and quite awkward. No one even dares to make a smart remark after that. Not even Jeremy. The goofy smile is wiped off his face and he now remains serious. I don't know what to say. And she doesn't give me much time to really think about what she's said.

I glance to Liam and he looks emotionless as he stares at Stella. She glances at him and he shakes his head, as if they're having their own little private conversation.

Her ominous eyes flicker back to me, "Bottom line, just know I am not the enemy. The Purgatory are. And they're planning something big. When? It could happen any day. They haven't told me anything yet," Stella says, breaking the silence. "I think they suspect I'm no longer loyal. Even after I worked months to prove to them I was just as strong as any one of them."

"They're specifically going after Beckett, right?" Liam gruffly asks. Stella nods stiffly.

"Yes," She answers. "They're deciding to break the treaty. They're pissed off and in result, they're going to take more fathers and mothers away from their children. And vice versa. But mainly, they're coming for you and Ronnie."

"Because of Liam killing two of their members?" I say, though I regret it once it comes out of my mouth because suddenly the image of Liam slaughtering that man in the woods appears in my mind.

He did to protect me, I think quickly. Didn't he?

"What? No. Liam has a way longer history with the Purgatory. I mean, all of us do," She gestures between Jeremy, herself, and Liam. "But who wouldn't be after they k-"

"Stella, that's enough." Liam abruptly commands, cutting Stella off. Her eyebrows furrow at his sudden outburst.

"Doesn't she know a-"

"I said that's enough." Liam repeats and I watch as his jaw clenches tightly. "Don't speak about it."

"Why do you always hide things from me?" I ask and twist my body to face Liam. "It's like you don't want me to know anything about you, yet you want to know everything about me."

"Ronnie, we'll discuss this later. That's the end of the conversation for now." Liam declares and when I don't reply, he turns away from me, obviously thinking he's won this little argument.

I stand up and shake my head at him, "No! I'm not just gonna drop it! I'm so sick of you disappearing for days and not having any clue where you are! I'm so sick of you being so angry at the Purgatory and me not knowing why!"

"I'm doing it to protect you!" He shouts back, standing up too.

"That's such bullshit!" I turn away from him, walking into the nearest bedroom and hearing Liam's angry footsteps behind me.

"How is that bullshit? I killed all those Purgatory dickheads for you! I did it to keep you safe!"

"If you're trying to protect me, then why do you leave me alone so many times? You disappear for days and I'm left to be worried sick about you. And I don't need you're protection, I'm fine without you."

"Now that's bullshit," He snarls and grips my arm, forcing me to look at him. Or well, look up at him. "Who was the one who protected you all those times? When the Purgatory tracked you down after the ball? That night in the woods? Me! I was there! Not fucking Adam."

I shake my head at him and attempt to pull my arm out of his tight grip, but it's useless. "What does Adam have to do with any of this? This has nothing to do with him."

"Yes it does," He argues, "I heard about how he wrote that stupid play about you and him. About your childhood. Are you sure you don't love him? I bet you want to be mated to him." He leans down, hissing accusations in my face.

"Are you so blinded by your jealously that you've forgotten how he blackmailed me to be with him?" I shoot back, "I don't want to be with Adam. I left the pack so I could stop being under his and his father's control and most importantly, I did it so I could be with you, idiot. I'm crazy about you and you obviously can't see that. Maybe you would if you were around more."

"Again, I'm doing it to protect you," He repeats and then pauses for a minute or two. "And perhaps for my own selfish reasons, but that doesn't matter."

"Yes it does," I say. "It does matter. And it matters to Stella and Jeremy as well, obviously. What happened with the Purgatory? And how do you know those two people out there?"

"Leave me out of this! Jeremy is not to be involved in this!" I hear Jeremy faintly yell from the living room. Liam growls and peaks his head out the door, telling Jeremy to shut up and mind his own business before slamming the door shut and locking it.

"Liam? Answer me," I demand angrily once he faces me again. His eyes have now taken on a darker tint at the seriousness of this conversation.

He doesn't reply. All he does is stare at the wall in silent rage.

I step forward and refuse to be ignored as I grip his arm, "Liam, listen to-"

"I don't like to talk about the death of my pack, just how you don't like to talk about your mom." He answers sullenly.

I let my grip on him slip. The death of his pack?

And then it hits me. Is this why Liam is so hell bent on killing the Purgatory? Because just like Stella, the Purgatory took his loved one's away from him? Had the Purgatory also killed his sister? His mom? His friends? His old life? Had they ripped away everything from him?

And without even having to ask, I know the answer is yes. I can tell just by the expression on his face. And the hurt in his eyes that he is so desperately trying to conceal.

I suddenly question why we are even screaming at one another. Liam's just returned from being at Riverwood, he's perfectly unharmed, and we should just be celebrating the fact I'm free from Beckett's grasp. But instead, we're screaming at one another like an old married couple. And on top of that, my ankle and leg are hurting like a bitch from running off so angrily.

Luckily, the stitches haven't come out or anything, but the pain is immense. Especially in my ankle. I take a seat on the bed, kicking off my boot and staring at the grossly swollen limb. I hear Liam exhale a cuss.

"You overworked yourself and now you're in pain," He says with a shake of my head. I roll my eyes.

"I'm fine. It doesn't hurt that much."

"Liar," He accuses and before I can say something back, he drags me up to the center of the bed. He leaves the room for a second, only to return with an ice pack. He locks the door, despite Stella and Jeremy questioning him on what he's doing.

He plops the ice bag on my swollen ankle, showing no remorse even when I hiss in pain at both the coldness and the impact of the bag.

"You never listen to me when I tell you to take it easy," He mutters. "Do you just like disobeying me?"

"I'm not a dog," I reply with a scoff. "I'm not just going to follow your every word."

"Technically, you are a dog." He retorts smartly, obviously referring to my werewolf-ness or whatever. I glower at him.

"Are you looking for another fight?"

He sighs and shakes his head. He meekly crawls over me, resting his forehead against mine. "No. No more fighting. I just got back and I don't want to scream at each other anymore."

I'm silent for a minute, staring up into his green eyes till I finally nod, silently agreeing with him.

He places one hand on my neck, while the other rests softly on my cheek. It's only when I don't reply to his show of affection that he removes his hands from me before grabbing my arms and wrapping them around his neck. Once he's assured that I'm not going to remove my hands from him, he places his hands back where they were before.

He leans in slowly, his hot breath fanning over my parted lips as he lowers himself down onto me, though he makes sure to not apply all his weight on me.

Soon enough, every crevice of his body is pressed up against mine to a point where I can feel the warmth radiating off of him. And though I hate to admit, it's a pleasant feeling. And it makes my previous emotions of anger disappear, only to be replaced with affection.

I run one hand from the back of his neck to his bare chest while my other hand finds his hair. I tangle my fingers in his golden brown locks and pull him possibly closer to me, all the while I press myself up against him as well, wishing for no more space to be between us. It's been too long to where we can just enjoy being by ourselves. We haven't had a moment like this in a while.

He leans down, brushing his lips to mine teasingly. I don't move. I'm too scared if I do he'll decide it'll be funny to pull away. So I sit still like a state as I silently yearn for him to kiss me.

He starts by pressing a kiss to the corner of my mouth, to my cheek, to my nose, to my forehead, and then he finally captures his lips with mine. It's starts off slow and gentle, but that quickly changes once I tug on his hair, making a growl rumble in his chest.

He applies more pressure, turning the soft and gentle kiss into a rough one that sends shivers down my spine and makes my toes curls.

I kiss him with just as much intensity, my hands traveling to the front of his chest and traveling down, feeling the muscle ripple under my hands.

He pull's away and allows me to catch my breath, but he robs me of that oppurtunity as his lips trail from mine down to my neck.

He tugs my braid loose and then sweeps my hair behind my shoulder as he leans down to press a kiss at the hollow of my throat. Then his lips travel to where my neck meets my shoulder. He presses kisses to that stop for a reasonable amount of time and it isn't long after that I feel his teeth scrape against that same spot. He bites gently, but hard enough to a point that it'll leave a mark. Not a permit one like it will when he officially marks me, but one that will surely last a while. And I can't help but gasp at the sensation.

His lips travel back up to mine, though this time, the kiss has returned to being softer. He pulls away, his face hovering over mine as he stares me dead in the eye. And all I see in his expression is... love. As corny as it sounds.

"I missed you so much, princess." He whispers, his warm fingertips brushing across my cheekbone.

"I missed you too," I respond honestly and I lean up, pressing my lips to his softly, hoping that I can convey the emotions that

I feel towards him in that one, simple kiss. "You have no idea how worried I was."

"And you have no idea how much I thought about you while I was in Riverwood," He mumbles. "Seriously. All I could think about was how hot you looked in that batman underwear."

I laugh, shaking my head at him. "You nearly gave me a heart attack that night," I reply, reminiscing with the memory of Liam making me think he was a burglar. "I remember I kicked you... ahem, there."

"Yeah," He chuckles. "You almost killed the opportunity of getting to ride this ride." He gestures to his body while waggling his eyebrows. Again, I laugh and semi-playfully smack him in the arm.

"You're a pervert."

"You love it." He whispers and then asks, "What are we going to do, Ron? About Beckett?"

I sigh, tightening my grip in his hair. "I don't know," I state softly. "But we have time to figure it out, don't we?"

He nods, "Yeah. Right now, I just want to enjoy the fact that you're here. And that we're together."

"Well, aren't you romantic, Farley," I tease with a grin. Liam shakes his head at me, though a smile plays on his lips.

"Don't act like you don't throw cheesy lines at me either," He says and he begins to mock me, "'Oh, Liam, you're so strong and tough and manly. Oh, Liam, kiss me. Oh Liam, let me feel up on your'-"

I cut him off, "I've never said any of that! And I do not sound like that," I protest. "And if you even dare to complete that sentence, this time, I will make sure you will never get to ride-" I gesture to my body, "-this ride."

Liam laughs, "Fine, I'm sorry." And then he glances to the digital clock on the night stand and a frown takes over his features. "It's late. You should get some sleep."

"Fine, but get me something to sleep in."

Without moving from me, he leans over and grabs a shirt that was tucked away in the nightstand and then passes it to me.

"I can't exactly change with you on top of me, you know."

"You can try," He teases with a smile. I roll my eyes but give him a shove, though he doesn't even budge. It's only till I glare at him till he moves and takes a seat on the edge of the bed, his back facing me.

"Don't peek," I command swiftly.

"It's not like I haven't seen your body before. Don't be so dramatic."

"Still, have manners and don't peek." I repeat. Liam throws me a grumpy look over his shoulder and then nods.

I throw off my sweater and slide out of my jeans short as slow as possible, just to make sure I don't hit the stitches or my ankle. Once I've got both articles of my clothing off, I toss them to the flower and slide the T-shirt over my head and tug it down, not surprised when I find it fits me like a freaking dress.

"I'm done," I announce. "You can look."

He shifts in his seat, his eyes analyzing my body in his shirt. "Have I ever told you how good you look in my clothes?"

"Have I ever told you to shut up before I smack you?" I drawl and quickly slip under the comforters, tugging them up until they rest on my stomach.

"Yes, you have actually," He replies, appearing to be lost deep in thought. "Many times, really."

I roll my eyes at him and squirm down further into the sheets, resting my head on the plush pillow. Immediately, I begin to grow tired.

I sigh contently, closing my eyes and re-opening them to find Liam staring at me. I smile at him gently. "What?"

"Nothing," He says and then leans closer to where his lips are inches from mine. "You're beautiful."

Instead of objecting, I simply press my lips to his and pull back, remarking softy. "You know I'd pick you any day over Adam, right?"

Hesitantly, he nods. A sarcastic smile breaks across his face. "Who wouldn't? I mean, have you seen this body?"

I roll my eyes, "I'm serious."

"I know you are," He retorts. "And I honestly believe you would pick me over Adam. Sometimes, my stupid jealousy clouds my judgement. It's because I can't bare the image of someone touching what's mine."

My breath halts in my throat at his last sentence. And as sick as it sounds, the sentence isn't repulsive to me, as it really should be. I mean, I wasn't a piece of property or whatever and maybe I should voice this to him, but I don't. For some crazy reason I don't want to object with him. Mainly because I know it's true. Even though he's a possessive ass, I am his. And that's all that mattered.

"Possessive, eh?" I taunt with a smile. "You know, I find it extremely sexy when you're possessive."

"I love it when you talk dirty to me, princess." He growls and playfully nips at my neck, making me laugh.

"Shut up, you idiot. It wasn't dirty talk."

"You're right, it wasn't," He says with a nod. "It was simply the bluntly honest truth and to be bluntly honest as well, I think you look really sexy when you're mad and I kinda like it when you fight with me. Maybe we should fight more just to have crazy make out sessions afterwards?"

"Okay, now that's dirty talk, Mr. Farley."

"No, true dirty talk is me commenting that when you call me Mr. Farley, I think it's kinky."

I roll my eyes, "You ruined the moment."

"We were having a moment?" Liam feigns innocence and again, I smack him. Though harder this time.

"Feisty," He teases. "I like it."

"Okay, that's it, you're getting a kick to your baby maker."

"No! I'm sorry!" He says quickly, protectively covering himself. "It never did anything to you. Seriously, it hasn't. Yet."

I glower at him, "I will seriously kick you."

"I said I was sorry."

"Then made a pervy comment afterwards!"

"Okay. I'm sorry. Again."

I groan and roll away from him, mumbling, "Go to sleep, moron."

"Fine," He whispers and I hear him get to his feet, immediately causing me to whip around.

"Where are you going?" I question with a frown. He looks over his shoulder and gestures to the door.

"To sleep, like you just said to. Or did you forget that?"

"No," I shake my head and bite down my lip, watching as he goes to reach out for the door knob, but my next words stop him. "Stay with me?"

He analyzes my face for a minute, as if he suspects I'm bluffing or messing around with him or something. But I'm not. I'm actually serious. After everything that's happened today, all I want is for him to say with me. To wake up and know that he's there and that everything's okay. "Please?" I whisper, almost desperatly.

He nods and slides in next to me. He motions for me to scoot closer and I comply to his silent command, nestling my face into his neck as I throw my one good leg over his. I fit my body against his perfectly and sigh contently when he wraps his arms around me and presses a sweet kiss to the top of my head.

I contemplate perhaps telling him about Anna, but I figure he already knows. About her death, I guess. Even though he hadn't brought it up, it was obvious. Liam practically knew everything that goes around in our little town. Or, at least he knew everything that went on with me. Nonetheless, I know that this is silent way of comforting me over the death of my friend when he squeezes me tightly and kisses my head again.

I let the idea of springing up the conversation slip from my mind and instead, I wrap my arms tighter around him and pray that I won't lose him. Not like I lost Anna, and certainly not like how I lost my mom.

"Goodnight Liam," I whisper. "Thank you."

He doesn't need to ask what I'm thankful for. He simply replies, "Goodnight, princess."

And that's when I know, without a doubt, that nothing is going to tear me and Liam apart. Not the Purgatory, not Alpha Beckett, and not the fact that he's a rogue.

We're in this together. For good.

Chapter 27

Just walk up to him, Ronnie! My mind screams at me, talk to him! Do it before it's too late!

I shift nervously in my seat and try desperately to swat away my pestering thoughts as I stare out the window of the small and warm and safe cafe.

From beside me, Liam shifts in his seat as well. It seems my nervousness is contagious, but hey, at least I'm not alone.

I force my eyes away from the man that grips the tall blonde to him and instead turn to face Liam. He frowns at him.

"You should go talk to him," He says, voicing my thoughts. His vivid green eyes follow my movement as I lift my hand from my lap and begin to stir my spoon around in my cup. When it's evident I'm not about to reply to his comment, he huffs. "You can't avoid him forever."

"No, but I can try." I mutter defiantly. My eyes flicker away from my cup long enough to notice Liam is scowling me.

"Ron, this might be the last time you're able to see your dad for weeks, or months, or however long it takes before we can get this whole Purgatory and Beckett situation worked out."

"I don't know what to say to him." I answer honestly. I twist in my seat to face him. "I mean, you should have heard the things I said to him before I.. left."

"Exactly. You said some things you regret. This is your last chance to fix them, princess."

Regret? Did I really regret what I said to him? I question silently. Immediately, I know the answer is yes. Because I do regret what I said. I was angry and hurt and so I directed all my bitter emotions at him, when he clearly didn't deserve it. I had done the unspeakable. I had taunted my father about the death of my mom - his mate - the one woman he loved the most in this world. And I had painfully reminded him that she was gone and he could do nothing about that.

In result, I felt horrible. And also even more horrified when I realize Liam is right. I need to speak with him. To put somewhat of a mend on our strained relationship, because just like Liam said, it could be the last time I got to see him for a long time. Or, well, maybe it would the last time I saw him ever.

He deserved an apology, answers, and most of all, a warning of what was to come in the future. Therefor, he would have the chance to run off with Tara and create a new life with her. At least then I could sleep peacefully knowing I had least done something to help him.

My eyes slither back over to window and I watch silently as Tara and my dad fall into step, side by side, merely talking and laughing occasionally.

I suck in a sharp breath, it's now or never.

I stand abruptly, manging to catch the attention of Liam. He gazes at me out from the corner of his eyes, not even phased when I begin to make my way for the door. I stop once I reach the door. I place my hands on the handle and throw a look over my shoulder at a smirking Liam. "You coming or not, Farley?"

He stands and tosses a couple bills on the table before joining me at the door. We exit the cafe wordlessly and begin to make our way towards Tara and my dad.

I'm a bundle of nerves as we near them and Liam seems to sense that. He holds out his hand for me to take and without another thought, I place my smaller hand in his. Liam doesn't hesitate to intertwine our fingers together. He draws me near to him as well, pressing his side up against mine. And I'm glad when he does this, because immediately I feel some ounce of comfort.

I peer up at him, sending him a grateful smile. He returns it with one of his own, his eyes flickering back over to Tare and my dad.

And when I turn to look in their direction, it seems we've already caught their attention. I suck in a sharp breath as my eyes meet my dad's grey one's.

He stands stiff and ridgid and I notice he's incredibly wary of Liam's presence when he draws Tara near to him, wrapping an around her shoulders. Tara doesn't seem to notice his sudden change in mood, all she does is stare at Liam and I, a bright smile on her face as she waves to me.

"Ronnie! It's so nice to see you again!" She squeals once were only a few feet apart from one another. "How are you, sweetheart?"

I ignore the use of the nickname and instead, flash her a bittersweet smile. "I'm good, thanks. Yourself?"

"Oh, I'm doing well. I was actually just talking to your father about you and how we should have dinner again some time."

"Yeah, that sounds great." I nod and my eyes flicker over to my dad, who warily gazes at Liam. "Hi dad."

This seems to catch his attention. He looks towards me, a weak attempt of a smile sliding onto his lips. "Hey Ron."

"Is this Liam?" Tara questions. Liam's quirks an eyebrow at the tall blonde.

"You know who I am?" He asks gruffly. Tara let's out a melodic laugh and nods.

"Of course! Ronnie mentioned you at dinner."

Oh god, I will never hear the end of this, I think begrudgingly as I peer up at a smirking Liam. He waggles his eyebrows at me and then says, "Oh really? What else did she happen to mention?"

"I mentioned that you were incredibly full of yourself. Though that's really no secret." I intervene quickly before Tara get's the chance to respond. She merely laughs while Liam pouts.

"Nice to know you speak so highly of your own boyfriend."

I roll my eyes at him and glance back to my dad. His eyes are once again trained on Liam, his features scrunched in confusion. "I actually came here to talk to you, dad." I state, "If you don't mind, Tara." I add in quickly. Immediately, she shakes her head and nudges my father.

"Of course not! Go ahead and talk." She flashes me a warm and smile and I return it as best as I can.

"Thanks. What do you say about taking a walk?" I ask. Dad's eyes finally drag away from Liam to me.

"I'm not sure, Ron. I don't want to leave Tara all by her-"

"Don't worry, Mr. Mars. I'll look after your girl while you and Ronnie talk." Liam interrupts, sending him a bright smile. I resist the urge to smack him, mainly because him saying that, does not make my father any less wary. I'm pretty sure my dad doesn't trust Liam one bit and honestly, I don't blame him. I mean, Liam is known as one of the most infamous rogues ever.

"I want to have a small chat with you. It'll be quick." I add quickly, feeling his hesitation. "Besides, Liam will take perfectly good care of Tara. I promise."

"You worry too much, honey," Tara says with a small laugh. "I'll be fine! Go, talk with your daughter. I'll be here when you get back."

Finally, dad stiffly nods. He squeezes her to him, "I won't be far away and I have my cell on me. Phone me if anything... happens."

I roll my eyes and detach myself from Liam, grabbing my father's arm and rudely tugging him along with me. "I'll meet you back here, Liam! Don't stray too far away." I send him a playful glare and point a stern finger at him. He chuckles.

"Whatever you say, sweetheart." He flashes a breathing taking smile at me and at that moment, I am oh-so tempted to turn right back around and run to him. Resist, I tell myself, resist his hotness!

I shake my head as if to rid my thoughts and release my grasp on my dad's arm. I stuff my hands in the pockets of my jacket. Unsure of what to say, I wait for him to break the silence. Though I realize he's not going to when I glance over at him to see him mimicking my same posture. Hands dug in his pockets, head bowed, and eyes trained on the ground. He looks so lost. And for some reason, my heart constricts at that mere thought.

I dully wonder if he's acting this way because of what I said.

Obviously, my conscious whispers, you taunted him with your mother's death. Who does that?

Me. Idiot me. That's who does that.

The year's following my mother's death, I had never really called him out on it or whatever. But I had nagged at him. Because I was angry. It seems I say the most stupidest and irrational things when I'm angry.

What the hell do I say now? 'Sorry I waved mom's death in your face'? 'Sorry I'm a douche'? 'Have I told you how nice you look today? Oh, by the way, I totally didn't mean what I said the other day'?

Yeah, that's not a really good way to start this conservation. Instead of just blurting out a sorry, I decide to just bring it up in the middle of the conservation.

"So," I drawl, "How are you and Tara?"

He looks up and lifts a brow at me, "Did you really pull me away from Tara to talk about Tara?"

There goes casually sliding an 'I'm sorry' into our conversation.

"Well, no," I state bluntly. "But I figured I-"

He cuts me off, "Do you really even care about what's happening between Tara and I, Ronnie?"

I bite down on my lip, weighing the objection of telling the truth or lying. Though my silence is already enough of an answer for him, apparently.

"You don't need to pretend to care, Ronnie. I don't expect you to."

My eyebrows furrow, "What's that supposed to mean?"

"I mean I don't expect you to like the women that is 'supposedly' replacing your mother."

"I don't think she's replacing mom," I mutter. It's a lie. And he sees right through my words, since he scoffs and shakes his head, his stringy black hair following his movements.

"Of course you-"

This time, I decide to cut him off. "Okay, I didn't come here to talk about Tara, I admit that. I came here to talk to you about what... happened, the other night. With the pack."

He stiffens, stopping abruptly and in result, I stop as well and face him. "Alpha Beckett isn't happy about it, you know."

"Yeah, I figured," I say with a nod. "But I don't regret it. Well, at least I don't regret leaving the pack. It was the right thing to do."

Dad's eyes widen and he stares at me as if I've just sprouted a second head. "The right thing to do? Ronnie, making Alpha Beckett target you was not the right thing to do."

I scoff and cross my arms over my chest, "So, what was I supposed to do? Remain being his puppet? I don't think so. And besides, he was already targeting me. All for the purpose of mating with Adam. Or did you forget about that?"

Immediately, once I say this, a look of pain flashes across his face. I silently curse myself for having added that last tidbit to the sentence. I'm such an idiot.

"I'm sorry, I didn't-" I start to say, but he cuts me off.

"It's fine. I deserve it, anyway." He let's out a dry laugh, though there is obviously no humour to this situation. "I threw you to the dogs, Ron. Quite literally."

"You don't deserve it." I object, "You didn't deserve for me to scream at you that night and even before you didn't deserve me putting you down. I should have realized that you were just... trying to cope."

"I wasn't trying to cope. I was trying to forget. And I did it in the wrong way," He murmurs. "I left you to fend for yourself. And I should be the one apologizing. I missed out on so much of your life. But I promise you, Ronnie, I will not miss out on your life any longer. I promise."

My chest tightens and I swallow roughly, slowly I begin to shake my head as I stare at him. I don't know how to exactly phase my next sentence. Perhaps I should just be blunt and say it, but for some reason, the word's are stuck in my throat. My mind screams at me to spit the truth out but, again, all I do is stare.

It seems luck is never on my side. Figures that when I suddenly begin to put back the pieces to my father and I's broken relationship that something is just bound to go wrong. It could be weeks, or months, or even years before I ever saw him again. Or maybe this would be the last time I saw him.

And I know it's suddenly weird about now wanting to fix our relationship, but maybe it's because I realized that you could lose people close to you at any time. Any second. Any day.

Anna had died so abruptly so that I never got the chance to tell her I was sorry. That I am sorry. And I don't want that to be the same case for me and my father. If I'm going to die or suddenly go disappearing or whatever, I at least want to know I went without having the weight of never speaking to my father on my shoulder's.

I suppose now is the best time to man up. Or well, woman up, I suppose.

"Dad, I might not be around for a long time." My reply is blunt and simple and straight to the point, but the feeling in my chest only tightens as his features draw into one of confusion.

"What?"

"The Purgatory... they're planning to attack Beckett's pack. Your pack. They're angry and mostly targeting them because of Liam and I. We might have to go missing for a while, perhaps to gather more people to help us, but either way, you need to leave pack territory as quickly as possible. You need to leave the pack."

"What?" He echoes, a look of disbelief now crossing his expression. His eyebrows knit together in confusion and he shakes his head at me. "The Purgatory?"

"Yes," I nod slowly. "They're highly dangerous, but I'm sure you know that. You need to flee, not only because of the attack that's coming, but because of Alpha Beckett as well. He'll use you against me. He'll probably blackmail me with your life, just like he did to Anna. And I know he's not bluffing when he says he won't hesitate to kill those closest to me. Anna dying is the proved point."

He's atonished. Shock. Bewildered. And whatever other emotion that describes shock and confusion, but through it all, he still manages to shake his head and mutter, "Oh my god." He repeats this numerous times.

"You can leave with Tara. Make a new life or something. Whatever you do, just get as far away from Portland as you can. Maybe you could go on vacation or something. I hear Hawaii is nice this time of year, so-"

"Ronnie," He cuts me off from my erratic stumbling with a simple call of my name. "You do realize how crazy this sounds, don't you?"

"Yes," I swallow roughly. "But it's the truth."

"How could I even go off and start a new life when you're fighting with not only the Purgatory, but Alpha Beckett and his pack?"

"I'm not going in this alone, dad. I have Liam, you know."

"He's a rogue, Ron!" He screeches suddenly, "A dangerous rogue at that! He's killed so many people. How can you trust him?"

"It's simple," I mutter. "He's my mate."

"Maybe he's tricking you into believing that!" He huffs, "Maybe he's working with Purgatory or something."

I shake my head, "He's not. He... cares for me. And I know you might not get that and I don't expect you to, but you have to trust me when I say he would never hurt me. He saved me that night, you know. When I was attacked by the Purgatory. That's what I had those bruises."

Dad runs a hand threw his hair, tugging at it with a grunt. "Attacked by the Purgatory? Why don't you tell me these things?"

"Because I thought I could deal with them on my own," I say, "If you haven't realized, I'm not fond of sharing my problems with others. Even those that are closest to me."

He sighs and shakes his head for the millionth time. "So what, you're just going to disappear? Never to be seen again? With some guy who has killed innocent people?"

"It's in his past," I argue. "He's not... he's not like that anymore."

Technically, it's not a lie. He has killed people in the previous months, but they certainly weren't innocence. But I suppose to other's that it doesn't excuse the fact that he took someone's life. As sick as it sounds, I've learned to simply forget about that part of our relationship. That Liam has killed and perhaps will continue to kill. This time around, I know he won't take innocent people's lives. He'll be fighting for me and maybe for revenge on the Purgatory. And I guess I have to accept that.

I guess I'm just going to have to get use to the fact that I might see more lives be taken. And I might have to take a few lives myself.

Suddenly, I wish I hadn't thinkin' that at all. The thought of... killing someone makes my stomach churn.

"So you're telling me that he doesn't kill people anymore?" Dad says, catching my attention.

"He only does it to protect me-"

"Protect you? Is that what he calls it?" Dad sneers. He scowls me as if I'm some foolish child. "He's malicious, cold hearted, evil, ma-"

"And the one person in the world that gets me!" I shout, though I realize how corny my words sound once they leave my mouth. I pause for a minute, looking to rephrase my words into a way that so I don't sound like some stupid irrational teenager that is blinded by love. "As stupid as it sounds, and I know it sounds stupid, he get me. He comforts me in my time's of need and he shows me a side of him that is unknown to other's. I trust him with my secrets and I.. I care for him. More than anything. We may be complete opposites of each other and he may drive me crazy sometimes but that doesn't matter. What we have isn't a fling. It's forever."

Once I finish my rant, I meet my father's eyes. His wide and awed grey eyes. And I'm sure I've just made myself out to sound like that annoying chick from Twilight or something, but the word's I speak are true. And incredibly corny. But I'm not going to go back on them.

"I don't know what to say, Ronnie." He breathes and immediately, I shake my head with a small smile.

"You don't need to say anything. Just know that when I'm gone, Liam will be there with me. He won't let anything happen to me. I promise. Just like how you need to promise that you'll get as far away form Portland as you can, okay?"

He seems uneasy at my words and I'm sure desperation has filled my eyes because not a second later does his eyes soften and he nods. Though it's stiff and forced, I'm still grateful.

For the first time in years, I lean forward and grip him in a tight hug. He seems surprised by my actions, but he wraps his arms around me as well, resting his head on top of mine.

I bury my head into the cool leather of his jacket while I fist the material in my fists. Though, yes, the feeling of giving and receiving a hug from my own father is weird, I still savor it. Not because I'm scared I'm going to die or disappear or whatever, but because even though I've said I don't care about him, I do. There's still a chunk of my heart that holds love for him and both my mother. I don't want to be angry with him anymore. I want to forgive and forget and remember our last moments together.

I pull away from him, not enough to be out of his arms, but far enough that I can look up at him. He gazes down at me with a sad smile and he reaches up, tucking a wisp of my brown hair away from my face. I return the smile as best as I can.

"You and Tara will have a great life together, I just know it." I whisper.

"It'll never replace the life I had with your mother, Ronnie. Tara will never be her, you know that, don't you?"

I let out a soft laugh and nod. "I do now."

"Good," He embraces me again and I don't resist, not like I would have before. "Stay safe, okay?"

"Always." I mumble. And with that, we pull away from each other and walk back to Tara and Liam, who are chatting away happily. Or well, Tara is chatting away happily while Liam seems to be dazed. Once I reach back into his range of sight, a look of relief crosses his facial expression.

I don't comment on it nor do I make it obvious that I noticed he was worried. I simply go to his side and immediately, once I reach him, he pulls me into his side and presses a kiss to my head. He exchanges gazes with my father and when dad gives him a stiff nod, Liam returns it. It's not a sign of acceptance or appreciated or whatever. It's one of respect.

"Two weeks," Stella says for the fifth time.

And for the millionth time, Jeremy replies, "Two weeks until we die."

I scuff at his remark, but decide not to comment on it. Though Liam does. He argues that we're not going to die but Jeremy fires back. He objects that we're doomed and that the Purgatory and Beckett are going to kill us. And though I hate to admit, Jeremy might be right.

Two weeks until the Purgatory goes for the Beckett and most likely, Liam and I. Two weeks until they plan to kill us and bathe in sweet revenge.

And I'm positively scared, but again, I don't voice this. I merely snuggle myself into Liam's side, needing some of his confidence to perhaps float to me.

Of course, at this action, Stella rolls her eyes and makes a snarky remark on how weak I look. I don't have enough fight in me to object, so I take her insults and shove them aside.

"We should leave," Stella suggests. "Bail out until we gather more people to help us fight back. Besides, it wouldn't be smart to stick around anyway. After the Purgatory attack, if Beckett is still standing - which I'm sure he will be - he'll send people after us. And perhaps the Purgatory will do the same once they realize you and Ronnie aren't present. We have the upper hand and we should take advantage of it. We're in no position to fight with only the four of us. You do know that, don't you?"

"I hate admitting Stella is right, but it's the truth. We should leave a week before the attack. Get a head start and everything." Jeremy says.

"And where will our primary destination be?"

"Some place where safety and help is assured."

"Yeah, well, last time I checked, a place like that doesn't exist." Liam snorts, "I don't know if you forget or something, but I'm a wanted man. Since you guys are with me, whatever pack we stumble upon along the way, will make an attempt to fight and kill you as well."

"I'm aware of this, Liam," Stella replies. "That's why we'll do our best to stick to the main roads and never stay in one place for too long. We'll run as long as we have to before we get the help needed."

"So we run like cowards for God-knows-how long?" Liam shakes his head. "That could take years."

"Well, if you have a better plan, then go ahead and let us know, genius." Stella sneers.

"Simple; we fight." He inquires nonchantly.

"Simple; we die." Jeremy mocks with a roll of his big blue eyes. "That is the most stupidest plan ever. Unlike Ronnie, Stella, and I, we are not as trained as you are to fight those Purgatory fuckers off."

"Speak for yourself," Stella hisses. "I have enough experience to take them down. The only reason I suggested running is because I know you and Ronnie would get yourself's killed. Face it, you're weaker then us."

"Hey! I'm not weak!" Jeremy whines like a child. Liam waves off her remark.

"Ronnie may not be as strong, but she's fast. Faster then all of us and she's got quick reflexes."

"You can only block a hit for so long, Liam," Stella says. "Speed might help for a while, but she needs to learn to fight as well to properly defend herself."

"Shouldn't I determined what I need to learn and what I don't?" I say irritably, finally deciding to speak rather then having Stella talk about me as if I'm not in the room.

"No," Stella chirps. I narrow my eyes at her. "This is why we should pick to run. It gives us more time to prepare as well."

Liam is quiet. He appears deep in contemplation and I know he's weighing his options. And just like Jeremy said, as much as I hate to admit it, Stella has a point. It would be wiser to flee and perhaps train ourselves better to take on the Purgatory and Beckett's pack. Besides, going in and fighting isn't really a plan. It's just a stupid and irrational decision. No offense to Liam, by the way.

"Stella's right," I say, though my voice is strained. The words are painful to even utter. "Her plan is... smarter."

Liam quirks a brow at me, "So you're saying mine was stupid?"

Without hestiation, I nod. "Pretty much."

"Even the most stubborn person in the room agrees. That's how you know I'm right." A sly smirk slips onto Stella's lips.

"Maybe. Still doesn't mean I agree." Liam shoots back. Immediately, the smirk is wiped from her features and she glares at him in silent annoyance.

Though the leadership of the group hasn't been spoken about, we all know who runs our little group or whatever you really want to call it, I suppose. Liam is evidently the leader and Jeremy and Stella will listen to his words. Or well, more like Jeremy will listen and Stella and I will argue before we give in. Nonetheless, Liam has the final say and he knows that because he simply smiles wickedly at Stella. Smug bastard.

I huff and fold my arms over my chest, "Don't be so hard headed, Liam. Swallow your pride and accept Stella's plan. Alright?"

Liam curls his lip up at me, obviously disliking the fact that I'm practically bossing him around. In any werewolf relationship of sort - mate or not - the woman is supposed to comply to the male's wishes and choices. That's just how it works. But that doesn't mean I'm going to follow along with that stupid rule or whatever. I like to believe Liam and I can co-exist in equality and I will strive to make that point across to him.

But as the saying goes, I'll probably just be kicking a dead horse already. Either way, I won't give in as easily as I should.

"Ronnie," He murmurs warningly. Again, I roll my eyes and I silently wonder if one day they will get stuck like that. I shrug off the dumb though as quickly as it came.

"Oh please, don't go all dominate wolf on me." I sneer. I remind myself of Stella when I do this. Speaking of Stella, she obviously agrees with me since she flashes me a bright smile of triumph.

He glares at me. Jeremy laughs. "That's right, guuurlfriend. You stick up for yourself because you are a strong woman. Mhmm."

Stella cackles while Liam directs his heated gaze on Jeremy. It looks like Liam is tempted to strangle him. Well, better him then me.

"Fine," He finally growls. "We go with Stella's plan. In a week from now, we leave. Now Ronnie and I are going to sleep. We have school tomorrow. And don't want to hear a peep from you two."

He stands, grabbing my wrist and pulling me up with him. I snatch my wrist from his grasp and walk to the room with a huff. I decide I'm in no mood to argue with him on this.

"Is that code that you guys are going to fuck? Remember kids; no glove, no love!"

Right when I enter the room, Liam slams the door. And soon after, Stella and Jeremy begin to chirp, "Peeeeep!" just to annoy Liam. Instead of being annoyed like Liam, I simply laugh and fall back onto the bed, feeling a sudden sense of sleepiness overcome me.

"You do realize that my animalistic side still isn't happy about you telling me what to do, right?" Liam peers over me, raising a perfect brow at me. I shake my head with a sigh.

"I wasn't telling you what to do. I was simply suggesting. See? There's a difference." I reply innocently.

"Well aren't you just little miss smart ass?"

"Always am." I say with a laugh.

Liam decides to drop the subject, though not for good, I'm sure.

He crawls into bed beside me, pulling me up against him to where my back is to his chest. Though I flip onto my face and press my side into his chest. I find that he has head propped up on the heel of his hand, peering down at me with pursed lips. "The talk with your dad went well, yeah?"

"Yeah," I nod, though I'm in a daze of amazement as I look up into his vivid green eyes. My favorite features of his. Well, besides his muscles, that is.

Perv.

"I don't want to pry, but did you tell him about the attack that was to come?"

"Yes," I mumble."I told him to get as far away from Portland as he could. I think I suggested he should go to Hawaii or something."

Liam chuckles, "Well, isn't that great advice?" He says and then suddenly decides to ask, "Are you nervous for the whole war?"

"Of course," I whisper, weakness invading my words. "But I brought this upon myself. So I have to deal with it. I just don't know how I'm going to be able to... well, kill someone."

Liam stiffens at the words but draws me impossibly closer, wrapping both of his arms around me and giving me an reassuring squeeze. "I know. And though it's clearly inevitable, I hope you won't ever have to. Whether if they're evil or not." He sighs and rest his head on top of mine. "Maybe I'm just being selfish when I say I want to preserve your innocence."

"Innocence?" I echo. "You actually think I'm innocent?"

"In a sense," He mumbles. "You're far more pure than Stella, Jeremy, and I. You haven't killed, you haven't manipulated other people to bend at your will, and you also haven't done something else that makes you quite innocent." He waggles his eyebrows at me and I gasp in horror. I smack him in the chest and Liam merely laughs.

"Shut up, you idiot! That is not funny. How would you even know that?"

"I was your first kiss, princess. I think that explains it all." He says, "But really, I'm flattered I'll be your first for a lot of things." He smirks and I gaze at him, mortified.

"Do you love pissing me off?"

"Maybe," He teases. And without another word, he sweeps down and steals a kiss before I decide to be mean and turn away from him. I pick to not argue with him when he pulls away and buries his head in my neck, pressing a gentle kiss to the base of my throat. "Get some sleep," He commands softly. "We're going to have a long week."

I hum in agreement and close my eyes, glad that I took a shower and changed once I got back from talking with my dad.

There's a dull ache in my ankle from walking so much today and putting a strain on my injury, but I'm sure it'll be fully healed in a day or two. And Liam seems to sense my obvious discomfort, since he runs his hand down to my ankle and rubs soothingly. It gives me the opportunity to get properly comfortable.

I press my head into his chest and inhale his scent. I lean up one last time and kiss him. It's a lingering and lazy kiss and by the time I pull away, I'm already almost fully pulled into darkness that waves sleep in my face.

Before I fall asleep, I can't help but whisper, "This is just the beginning to our crazy adventure, right?"

He's quiet for a minute before he tightens his grip on me and mumbles, "Definitely just the beginning, princess."

Chapter 28

I'm brain dead.

Completely and utterly brain dead as I stare down at the test before me that contains an endless amount of equations I know I will never be able to solve. Maybe I should have paid attention in class. But then again, I'm not even sure if this test is in English or freaking Chinese.

I bite down on my lip and press my pencil into the paper, debating whether if I should put down random numbers and hope and pray that they're correct. I decide it's not worth it when I glance at the clock and see we only have two more minutes left until the bell rings.

I place my pencil next to my paper and cast a glance over my shoulder at Liam, who appears to be in deep contemplation as he scribbles furiously.

Well, guess he's not as brain dead as me.

I let out a soft sigh when the bell rings and everyone around me gets up, walking towards Mr. Matthews desk and handing in their tests. As my classmates begin to walk out the door, he reminds them of what homework we need to do tonight. All he gets is groans of annoyance.

Hesitantly, I rise from my seat and stride towards his desk, placing my blank test in front of him. He gazes at it thoughtfully for a minute, before he whips out a red pen from his desk drawer and draws a big, fat, red F on my paper. I cringe at the sight and Mr. Matthews beady eyes meet mine when he glances up. He gives me a disapproving look and I decide to make a hasty exit before he decides he wants to talk to me about my grade.

Immediately once I step out of the classroom, Liam appears next to me and grabs my hand, threading our fingers together and leading me down the cramped hall that is filled with loud chatter and laughter.

We fight our way out of the crowd until we reach the glass doors that lead us out of a place called high school that I think of as hell. Even once we're out of the school, I still hearing the annoying ringing of the dismal bell.

Liam and I make our way to his car in silence, a routine I've grown use to for the last four days.

Only three more days, I think meekly. Three more days till we leave Portland.

Indeed, the four past following days had gone by quickly. Probably because there was no more drama stirred up at school or with Adam or with anyone else for the matter. For the four past days, everything has been eerily quiet and - dare I say - peaceful.

Peaceful because no one has bothered me nor Liam for any reason. Even Jeremy and Stella had somewhat knocked off bickering. But maybe it was because they were too absorbed in their thoughts about the plan or something.

Each day, after we got out of school, we'd return back to Liam's cabin and continue packing up everything. We discussed the plan more and specific details that I probably should have paid more attention to when they were talking about it. But for some reason, each time the subject came up of fleeing Portland, I sort of mentally checked out.

And I know that's bad of me to do but at those moments, I couldn't focus. I still can't focus. Most of the time, I find myself lost in my thoughts and contemplating everything that could go wrong. Though the plan sounded evidently simple, it wasn't.

Mainly because we had a lot of tracks to cover up. We weren't only disappearing from the werewolf race or whatever, but society. In order for questions not to be raised, Liam and I would have to unregister from school. Basically, I would have to drop out.

And I certainly didn't want to do that. As bratty as it sounds, I had even contemplated trying to convince Liam, Jeremy and Stella to stay here in Portland so I could finish up my last three months of the school year, but I realized that was selfish and stupid and so I never went threw with talking to them about it.

I knew if we stayed around any longer, we would be killed. We were already risking our lives enough and we certainly didn't need to stick around to risk our lives even more. If that makes sense. Does that make sense?

See, this what I mean by brain dead. I think Jeremy's stupidness is rubbing off on me.

With a sigh, I climb into the passenger seat of Liam's car without even realizing what I'm doing. It seems my body is also on auto-pilot.

All I can think about is dropping out school. And yeah, that honestly shouldn't be the biggest of my concerns, but it is. And it's all because of the scholarship I was offered.

Again, I know I'm being selfish when I say I would honestly give up anything to be able to go to art school next year. I mean, it was my dream to go to art school ever since I was young. Before Adam announced that I would become his mate, I had planned applying to some schools and putting all my efforts into escaping Portland. I dreamed of leaving the pack for good and sticking to the one thing I'm good at; art.

But now those dreams that were starting to bloom into reality were suddenly crushed.

I guess I shouldn't be so bitter about the whole situation, mainly because I kinda started this war in the first place.

I should look on the brighter side of things, right? Like how I have Liam. And Stella and Jeremy, even if they do annoy me and I haven't really known them that long. But I know enough to at least put my trust into them and that's all that really matter's currently.

I should be grateful for the fact that I'm not going into this war alone, but still, that little voice in the back of my head is screaming at me for being so stupid. Stupid enough to really ruin my own dreams of going to art school.

I knew that once Liam and I left Portland, people would make assumptions that we ran off to get married or that I got knocked up or something else relatively stupid. They'd probably think of me as another Bella Swan. A girl who threw away her whole youth and life just for a boy.

Even if that boy was incredibly cute and just so happened to be her mate. Then again, people would never really know that. Well, they'd know Liam was cute but not that we were mates, obviously. And there I go again, making no sense.

I subconsciously let out another sigh and I guess this catches Liam's attention since he says, "Are you having trouble breathing or something?"

I gaze over at him, my eyebrows knitting together in confusion at his words. "What?"

"I mean that you've been sighing for the past hour. Are you okay?"

My eyes flicker over to the digital clock on the dashboard. "Liam, we've in the car for five minutes. How could I be sighing for the past hour?"

"You were sighing in math class," He points out. "Seriously. It was distracting."

I roll my eyes and mutter, "You didn't seem distracted. You were writing like a mad man."

"Oh, you saw that?" Liam laughs, "It wasn't even legit answers. I think I wrote down the number of pie or whatever," He waves it off like it's nothing but a speck of dust.

"Well, at least I'm not the only one that majorly failed that test."

"Is that what you're so stressed about? Because you failed Mr. Matthews test?" Liam asks, disbelief clear in his voice. When I don't reply, it's enough of an answer for him. "Ron, it was just a test. Besides, we'll be out of here by the end of the week and grades won't matter anymore."

I pinch my lips together and decide not to object to his words. He's right, anyway. Once I leave the school, grades won't matter anymore. Neither will art school.

Oh, shut up, Ronnie, my mind hisses at me, what would you rather have; art school or Liam?

I know the answer to that question immediately. Liam, of course. And it seems I'm going back on my previous statement, when I said I'd give up anything to go to New York. That doesn't seem to be the case when it comes to Liam. Obviously, right now, I'm giving up art school for Liam.

But maybe once the whole war was over, I could come back and complete my final year of high school and apply to a different school, seeing as I doubt The Academy of Arts would accept me after dropping out of school then re-enrolling. Though, definitely, the new school wouldn't be as great as the one up in New York, I'd still have the opportunity to at least experience college.

Then again, there was always a chance I might not come back.

And I really need to stop over thinking so much.

In order to get my mind off from current dilemma with school, I decide to distract myself by focusing on other things. Though when my thoughts suddenly shift, they land on a rather uncomfortable subject. And can you guess what subject that is? That's right, Adam.

It was no surprise when I arrived at school on Monday to find Adam was missing. Nor was it surprising when he missed Tuesday, Wednesday, and now Thursday. Not that I was complaining or anything, I was just slightly suspicious.

I mean, Adam had to be absent for a certain reason. Whether if it was just to avoid me or Liam or whatever. Or maybe he was just too busy plotting my death with his father. I wouldn't doubt it. Despite my current ugly facts about Adam, I still wanted to see him. Not to say goodbye or whatever, but for answers. Answers on what happened to my mom and what Alpha Beckett did to cause her death.

It was so obvious that Alpha Beckett had something to do with my mom's death. I mean, she had died so suddenly. Without a real reason. I mean, the explanation I had gotten from my father was that the Purgatory had attacked her while she was prowling around. But that didn't really make sense.

Because according to my father, mom hadn't even crossed over the boundary to Purgatory land. So why would the Purgatory cross over our boundary to solely attack my mom? At that time, we had a treaty with them as well. They wouldn't have messed with us unless we did something to them. Or if Alpha Beckett had given them a tip, just like he had given a tip to the Purgatory about me when I ran off from the ball.

Most likely, that was what happened. Alpha Beckett was pissed off, so he gave the Purgatory a tip or whatever and in result, they killed my mother. The only thing that left me guessing was why Beckett wanted my mom dead.

So, that's why, I had to get answers from Adam. I had to somehow squeeze the truth out of him before we went missing. I would get the answers I wanted, one way or another.

"Did you put my suitcase in the truck, Jeremy?"

"No."

"I thought I told you to!"

"What do I look like? A maid?"

"No, you look you're useless," Stella hisses before diving towards him and attempting to smack him. Jeremy squeals in return and begins to try to escape, dramatically screaming for me to help him.

I merely rolls my eyes at him and plop back onto the couch, flipping through channels and trying to find something to watch.

Eventually, when I realize that nothing is on, I toss the remote aside and peer over at Liam, only to find him lacing up one of his boots. I furrow my brows at him and ask, "What are you doing?"

"I'm gonna head over to the auto shop, get the oil changed from the truck before we head out on Monday." He replies nonchalantly, standing and shrugging on his jacket. "You can come if you want."

I open my mouth to agree, but quickly shut it when a certain thought leaks into my mind. This may be the only chance that you get to go see Adam.

"No," I answer casually. "I'll stay. I'm not feeling too good, anyway."

Liam shoots me a wary look and I struggle to keep a straight face as he leans over and presses the back of his hand to his forehead. "You don't feel hot."

"My stomach's just a little upset. Must have been something I ate," I lie. And though Liam doesn't seem to buy it, he still nods.

"Okay," He replies slowly. "Are you sure you'll be okay?"

"Yeah," I nod and shoot him a small smile. "Go. Before it gets too late."

He leans closer towards me and presses a lingering kiss to my lips. It's lasts for a second or two, but it's long enough for that moment to burn itself into my memory.

He pulls back and gazes at me, opening his mouth to say something but quickly decides against it, since the next thing I know, he's saying goodbye to Jeremy and Stella and then he's out the door.

I stare after him for a minute, dazed and confusion and overall, just curious. What was he gonna say?

I decide not to drive myself mad with curiosity and instead, I stand, looking to find Jeremy and Stella still fighting. Nonetheless, I tell them I'm going to bed and the only acknowledgement they give me is a glare.

I head towards Liam's room, shutting the door behind me softly and walking towards the window. I push the curtain back and I'm relieved to see that Liam's car is missing from the driveway.

I pop open the window and climb out. And then I start going to the one place where I know Adam will be; the lake.

Maybe he isn't coming, I think silently as I tug at the bottom of my plaid shirt. For the millionth time, I glance over my shoulder, staring into the plush green forest and silently hoping that he'll appear.

It was cold and dark and honestly, all I wanted was to back to the cabin before I got caught by Liam. Surely he be mad if he found out I had sneaked out of the cabin to go see the one person he hated most in the world besides the Purgatory.

Not to mention he would probably start throwing some accusations that I loved Adam or all along I wanted to be with him, or something relatively stupid and untrue. That's why I had to work extra hard not to get caught, though Adam was kinda making that hard for me to do, since he hasn't showed up.

Then again, I shouldn't have expected him to. He didn't even know I was here. And if he did, I would doubt he would want to face me.

I cross my arms over my chest with a sigh. Once again, I cast another behind me. And again, I find nothing.

This isn't worth it, I think dully, he's not going to show up. I should just go back to the cabin. This was a stupid idea. Stupid, stupid, st-

"Ronnie?" I shoot off the ground abruptly, spinning around to find myself staring back at a confused Adam. "What are you doing here?"

I blink and regain my composure, that is until Adam begins to walk closer and I quickly lose my nonchalant appearance. Instead, I'm rigid and quite stiff when he stops in front of me. Despite this fact, I try to swallow my nerves. "I was looking for you," I say, "I was starting to think you wouldn't show up."

"How'd you know I'd be here?" He asks warily. He gains this panicked look in his eyes as he spins around, appearing to look for something. Or well, someone. "Is he here?"

I don't need to question him on who he's exactly talking about, I already know. "No," I reply. "He's not. I came alone. And I didn't know you'd be here, I just took a guess."

"Why were you looking for me?"

"You ask a lot of questions," I say.

"Well, you don't give much answers."

"Now you know how I feel whenever I speak to you." I reply. I curse myself silently when Adam begins to shake his head.

"Answers? Ron, if this is about my dad, you know I can't-"

I cut him off, "It's not about your dad. Well, your dad has something to do with it, but it - my questions - have to do with something else. Well, someone else."

"And that person is...?" He trails off, gazing at me expectantly.

"My mom," I spit out before I lose my nerve. "I wanted to ask you questions. About her death. You must know something. I mean, you're the Alpha's kid. You probably know everything that goes on with the pack."

"That doesn't mean I'm entitled to say anything," He argues. "I shouldn't even be talking to you. If my dad found out, he'd..." He trails off as he pinches his lips together "Look, you should go."

"I'll go if you give me answers," I say. But despite my words, he begins to turn away, probably to flee, but I'm tired of all this. I'm tired of the lies, I'm tired of running, I'm tired of everything.

"Adam, please, this might be the last time you ever see me. Just give me a few answers!" At the sound of desperation in my voice, he faces me. His jaw is clenched tightly and he's obviously having some kind of mental debate with himself. His eyes dart to the forest, then back to me. "Please?" I whisper.

He's silent. Completely silent.

All I can hear is the soft lapping of the lake's waves and Adam's deep breaths. I'm about to say something, but Adam's bitter laugh fills my ears right when I'm about to.

"I should have figured this was the only reason you'd come to see," He mutters. "Just like everyone else, you want something from me."

My brows furrow in confusion. "I just want the truth."

"Fine. You want the truth? Okay, I'll give you the truth," He spits angrily, "My dad knew your mom, Ronnie. He wanted her from the beginning. Not because of her beauty, or her personality, or whatever. But because of the fact she was the Purgatory Alpha's daughter. Did you ever really think of why they hate us so much? It's because my grandfather, just like my dad, wanted to take her away from them. So my dad could mate with her and they could create a stronger line of Alpha children. My grandfather tried to force her to comply to the mating. And at first, she agreed, for the sake of her own father's life.

But she rebelled once she met Lucas, or well, your dad. My grandfather tried to speed up the mating, but it was already too late. She was marked by your father and of course, you can't break a bond like that. They killed her mother and father and in result, another pack member took over the Purgatory with a vengeance. It wasn't until twelve years after she gave birth to you and my father took over the pack that he killed her. The Purgatory didn't kill her. He did. And he made me watch. He made me watch as he killed her and I just couldn't face you after that. So I stopped being your friend."

Shock. Shock is my only emotion as I stare at him and it isn't long after that I feel the tears begin to well up in my eyes, but Adam doesn't care. He continues on, spewing the truth. More of the truth I asked for. "I knew if I didn't, he'd... he'd be angry. He'd think I was weak and he'd take his rage out on me. So I did what he said. And when it was time for me to mate, he chose you. Because you were the only girl with Alpha blood in you. Even if it was Purgatory blood, it didn't matter. When it was obvious you didn't want to agree with it, he did the same thing his own father did. He blackmailed you and he hurt you like he hurt me and then he killed Anna. This whole time I know I should have done something, but I was scared, Ronnie. I am scared.

I'm scared and stupid and I'm sorry, Ron. History is repeating itself and I should have done something to stop it. I'm sorry, I'm s-"

"I can't believe this," I choke out. I pinch the bridge of my nose, shaking my head. He reaches out for me and places his hands on my shoulders, trying to get me to meet his eyes but I refuse. Especially not when I'm starting to become a sobbing mess.

"I'm sorry, Ron, I'm sorry." He pulls me into a hug and I'm too weak to push him off, I merely try to contain my broken sobs. Pull yourself together, Ronnie. Pull yourself-

"Ronnie!"

Great. This is great.

I peek out from Adam's arms, catching a glimpse of a furious looking Liam as he storms over to us. Immediately once, he reaches us, he shoves Adam and I apart, glaring furiously at Adam.

"What the fuck do you think you're doing?" He hisses, grabbing a fistful of Adam's shirt and picking him off of the freaking ground. "Who the fuck do you think you are for touching my mate? I should have gutted you like the fucking pig you are that night of the party. No worries, I have all the time of the world to do that now. Maybe that'll teach you a lesson to stay the fuck away from Ronnie!"

It's all a blur. A crazy blur and all I hear is grunts of pain from Adam and more spiteful words from Liam.

I step forward, grasping Liam's bicep and trying to pry him off Adam before he beats him to death. "Liam! Stop! You're going to kill him!"

Liam drops him and I get a glimpse at him, only to find his nose is crooked and blood is dripping from his mouth. I cover my mouth in horror and look up at Liam, only to find him panting and seething with rage.

"And you! How could you lie and sneak out to me Adam? How long has this been going? Have you been lying to me this whole time?"

"No!" I screech, "No! I haven't even been seeing Adam!"

"Then why were you hugging him?" He sneers and he turns once Adam begins to try to stand, "Move and you'll get more then a fucked up face, Beckett!"

"I came here for answers, Liam. Answers about my mom and her death." I explain, my voice cracking weakly on my last word. It only reminds of what Adam's just told me. "He told me. He told me everything and I.. I broke down and that's why he hugged me."

"You could have pushed him off!" Liam shouts.

"I just found out Alpha Beckett killed my mother, Liam! I just found out that I've been lied to all my life! I just found out that I'm related to the Purga-"

I'm cut off. Not from Liam or Adam.

But by the sound of a scream. A mortified scream, one that sounds somewhat familiar, because the scream is of my name. And immediately, without a doubt, I know the scream has come from the direction of where my old home resides.

And again, without a doubt, I know that Alpha Beckett is preparing to take the life of another person I care about. My dad.

Epilogue

The scream rings in my ears, making the blood in my veins run cold.

I stare in the direction of where the scream came from. I'm frozen. Completely frozen and stiff and I certainly don't need a mirror to know my face is turning blue just from holding my breath.

My legs itch for me to run while my mind screams at me to stay. It could be a trap, after all. I bet Alpha Beckett was doing this to lure me. To get me to come to him and then make me watch as he slaughtered my father.

I bet he would enjoy watching me as I pleaded for my father's life. And as much as I hate to give him that pleasure, I can't just stand back and let my father die. I have to go to him. I have to, I have to, I have to.

"Ronnie," Liam calls to me, anticipating my motives. "Don't."

The sound of desperation in his voice pulls at the strings of my heart. I'm tempted to comply to his command or well, plead. But I can't. I can't when my father's life is being waved in my face. I don't want him to die. I don't want to be the blame of another person's death.

Anna nor my dad didn't ask to be mixed up in my problems. It was time I took responsibility. Even if it meant putting my life in Alpha Beckett's greedy hands. I'd do it not to play hero, but to avoid letting Alpha Beckett take another person I loved away from me. He had already taken my mother and Anna. My dad wouldn't be the next.

So without another thought, I shake my head at him, turn, and begin to run.

I run and run, hearing my dad's battered screams in my ears.

My legs burn and my hair whips around me as I swat away at branches and leap over fallen trees and roots. In the distance, over the horrified screams of my father, I hear Liam yelling. Telling me to come back.

But the sound of him calling me is soon over powered by the blood pounding in my ears. And all I can do is hope he has enough common sense to stop chasing after me and go retrieve Stella and Jeremy.

Because, obviously, our plan of escaping has ultimately been canceled. There is no doubt in my mind that tells me I will be drawn into a fight with Alpha Beckett and perhaps the Purgatory. I was stupid. Stupid for believing that we could run away from them. This whole fight was inevitable. I just wish I would have realized it sooner.

Now I'm running into this fight completely blind sided. Not to mention, Beckett has the upper hand. He has my father and he knows I will submit to merely preserve my dad's life. He has me right where he wants me. But I'm too panicked and overwhelmed to stop and perhaps debate a plan of any sort.

So I keep going, keep striving forward to get to him.

"Dad!" I shout, nearly tripping as I stumble over a tree root, "Dad!"

My heart slams against my chest as I near the scene, swatting away at the last branches that hide my father and Alpha Beckett from my sight. But before I can break into the clearing, something - someone - rams into my side. And in result, I'm sent flying to the ground.

I impact the ground hard. Face first. And not even a second later do I feel the throbbing in my side from where I took the hit.

Despite the pain, my mind screams at me to get up. To keep going.

I roll onto my back, looking up and meeting the angry eyes of an unfamiliar wolf. Though he seems to recognize me, since he snaps his teeth at me and lunges forward.

My reflexes quickly kick in and I dodge the attack, rolling away from the wolf and hopping to my feet.

But the unfamiliar wolf isn't quite keen on giving up, so once again, it lunges at me. I avoid the attack once again, but I skid back, desperate to avoid it's sharp teeth from sinking into my skin and in result, I find myself standing right in the middle of the clearing.

Where there isn't only one wolf, but more. Much more.

They surround me like a swarm of bees and I'm trapped. Evidently trapped and I know who's behind this all once I turn and find myself staring right into Alpha Beckett's eyes.

I hold his cold and calculating gaze for a minute or two, that is, till I hear a strangled gasp and my eyes instead flicker to where the sound came from.

And there I see him. My father at his knees and numerous gashes decorating his chest.

I flinch when the smell of coppery blood reaches my nose and I stare as more blood oozes from the many gashes.

As I glance beside him, I look to see several black duffel bags, all ripped open with my father's clothes scattered around him and Alpha Beckett and the other two men that are currently restraining my father from moving.

Weakness and desperation leaks into my system and unable to resist, I take a step forward and reach my hand out to him. "Dad," I breathe.

But my action is halted when the wolf in front of me growls and snaps at me, forcing me to take a step back although my legs itch to run to him.

"I wouldn't come any closer, Ronnie," Alpha Beckett warns, a twisted smile spreading across his lips. "Unless, that is, you want one of your former pack mates to take a chunk out of you."

Former pack mates, huh? I do a complete 360, slowly making a circle and staring at each and everyone one of the wolves. Most of them I don't recognize, probably because I never really saw them in wolf form, but some I do.

Like one wolf, with honey brown eyes and golden brown hair. Mandy.

And then the wolf next to Mandy. Green eyes and blonde coat. Jessica.

And then the next one is all too familiar. Black hair and cold hazel eyes. Cliff.

My fist clench at my side at just the sight of him. At the sight of Anna's supposed boyfriend and the one who set her up from the start.

Vaguely, I wonder if he ever really liked her. If he ever cared for her like Anna cared for him. I wonder if he knew Anna was going to die. I wonder if he simply let it happen or if he wanted to stop it.

Who am I kidding? Cliff was just following orders from Alpha Beckett. He never cared for her. He never liked her. He didn't care if she died or not.

I grind my teeth together, my fist clenched tightly at my sides as I stare down at him. I hate him, I determine. I hate him and he wil lbe the second life I will take beside Alpha Beckett's.

That is, if I can even manage to somehow worm myself out of this predicament.

"I would think it's hurts, you know, to have your whole pack turn on you," Alpha Beckett says abruptly, catching my attention. I glance over my shoulder at him, once again meeting his twinkling eyes filled with amusement. "But then again, you turned on them as well."

For some reason, I can't find my voice to speak back. To object to his words, but I guess it's because I realize his words are true. I have turned on them, just as they've turned on me.

But I don't feel guilty about it.

Because then again, we were never truly a united pack. They never had my back, just as I never had their's. They would have never risked their life for me, just as I wouldn't have risked mine for their's. We were selfish people, I suppose. Only caring about ourselves and never about one another. And that's where Alpha Beckett doesn't realize the flaw in his pack.

I bet they'd turn on him twice as quick if they weren't so blinded by the monster that leads their pack.

And I want that chance. I want the chance to expose Alpha Beckett for what he truly is. A monster. A murderer. A liar.

But I fear I might not possibly get that chance. And can you blame me? My odds of getting out of this situation is zero to none.

And as I look out towards the forest, into the thick brush, I detect no movement. Which means Stella, Jeremy, And Liam aren't close by. Which means I might be in this alone.

Don't be stupid, Ronnie, my mind whispers, they wouldn't leave you to fend for yourself. Especially Liam.

That's true. Liam would never leave me to fend for myself. Perhaps Stella and Jeremy wouldn't either. They're probably just thinking out a plan.

And all I can do is hope they think out a plan oh-so-quickly.

"Looking for them, are you?" Alpha Beckett muses, "He's not coming, Ronnie. He's a rogue. He doesn't care for anyone but himself."

Something in me snaps and I whip around to face him. "You don't even know what you're talking about."

Alpha Beckett merely laughs, despite my harsh tone of voice. He takes a step forward, raising his hand off from my father's shoulder and joining me inside the circle of wolves. "Farley made you believe he cared for you. That he liked you. Perhaps even loved you. And you were that foolish to fall into his little trap. And now where is he?" He gestures to our surroundings. "Nowhere! Nowhere to help you!"

"Liam's my mate. He couldn't leave me behind, not even if he wanted to." I spat in defense. Alpha Beckett waves me off.

"From what I've heard, Liam has left you behind in the past. Numerous times. And for what? For revenge on the people who killed his beloved pack."

I swallow roughly. I can feel the angry scowl slipping from my features, only to be replaced with wariness. "You don't know what you're talking about," I echo. It's the only thing I can think of to say.

"I do," He replies calmly. "Liam's going to leave you behind. Just like your mother."

My angry edge is back just at the mere mention of my mother. "My mom didn't leave me behind! You took her away from me!"

Alpha Beckett eyebrows shoot up. Yeah, who's what they're talking about now? "Took her from you?"

"I know everything, Beckett," I hiss lowly, edging closer to him and pointing an accusing finger in his face. "You killed her. I know. You killed her just because she didn't want to be with you. Because she didn't want to have a monster's child."

I know I've hit a nerve when Alpha Beckett's clenches his jaw tightly. "That's all a stupid lie. The Purgatory killed your-"

I cut him off, "Why would her own pack kill her? That's the thing, they wouldn't. That's why the Purgartory hate you. That's why they hated our pack and targeted us! Because you killed the Alpha's daughter!" I pause, sucking in a shaky breath and exhaling just as shakily. "You're the reason the Purgatory hate us. You're the reason many of us have died due to fighting the Purgatory. You're a monster. A murderer. And my mother realized that."

"And she got killed for that reason! She got killed because she refused! And you're going to end up just like her. Dumb and dead." He hisses back just as cruelly.

And before I can stop myself, I suddenly fling myself at him with an angry cry, swinging my fist at his face.

My fist doesn't even make impact with his face. He quickly catches my hand and twists my arm behind my back.

I manage to break free by elbowing in the ribcage, but as I spin around, I'm too late to realize his hand is flying at me.

He backhands me straight across the face. And hard.

I stumble and reach up, pressing my hand across my cheek and desperately trying to swallow down the wail of pain that climbs up my throat.

"Stop!" My father cries. "Stop, please, Alpha Beckett. Please."

Alpha Beckett turns and I have a feeling that the cold and calculating attitude he once had has vanished. For good.

"Stop? You want me to stop?" Beckett hisses, inching closer to the bleeding man known as my father. "You're partly at fault for this, Lucas. At the beginning, you promised she would comply to my wishes and mate with Adam. I told you to make sure she didn't get out of hand. You failed. And then you tried to run like the wimp you are." Beckett took a step closer, kicking a stray black duffel bag aside. "Maybe you should have listened."

He begins to walk closer to my dad and that's when the panic builds up in me. I start after Beckett, but of course, the wolf in front of me stops me from moving any closer and possibly helping my dad.

Even after these people have heard the truth, they still decide to stick with Alpha Beckett, I duly glance down at the wolves around me and shake my head. Maybe it's because they're monsters too. Or they're scared. Scared just like Adam.

As Adam's name repeats in my head, I look around, wondering where he is and if he too had decided to run off and avoid the fight.

And even if he did decide to run off, I wasn't mad. Because at least he had told me the truth. He told me the truth when no one else would. And for that, I was grateful.

Grateful to know that this whole time, Adam was afraid. Afraid of his father and I could only wonder what Alpha Beckett did to put so much fear into him. It must have been traumatic, because when we were little, before my mother died, he wasn't afraid. Not of his father and not of the world. He was brave and daring and so was I. Maybe that's why I was so reluctant to let go of Adam and our friendship. Because he made me stronger. Braver. More confident.

I cared for him beyond belief. And I couldn't help but feel slightly guilty for making myself stop caring about him once we got older. I should have seen the signs. I should have realized that Adam was only trying to please his father and avoid getting hurt. I should have realized. Yet I was blind and just as foolish as Alpha Beckett claims I am.

I am dumb. I am foolish. I am weak. And I'm going to be dead soon enough.

The tears build in my eyes as I watch the two men release their grip on my father and let him fall. I flinch when he makes impact with the ground and let's out an agonized groan.

Before I can comprehend what's happening, the two unfamiliar men - probably new recruits- are marching their way over to me. They grab both of my arms, holding me back and I don't realize why until Alpha Beckett sends a hard kick to dad's side.

I let out a strangled gasp, shaking my head and just beginning to fight against the men's grip once Alpha Beckett kicks my dad again. Harder this time. So hard that I can hear his ribs crack under the force.

"No," I breathe, the tears becoming more persistent in my eyes. "No. Stop!"

My pleas are useless. They fall deaf to Alpha Beckett's ears and all I can do is watch as he slowly lures my father closer to his death.

I let out useless cries, the tears running down my cheeks as I flail in the men's arms, trying desperately to get to my dad. To somehow stop Alpha Beckett. But I quickly become limp in the men's arms when I realize there is nothing I can do. I can't help my dad because I'm weak. All too weak and out numbered.

So all I do is cry. It's the only thing I can do, then again.

Liam? Where are you? I scream in my mind. No reply. I get no reply and I stupidly begin to believe Beckett's words. I believe that Liam has ran and taken Stella and Jeremy with him. Maybe he realized I wasn't worth fighting for. Maybe he realized I wasn't worth all the trouble I brought with me.

It isn't till my father is coughing up blood and beaten battered that Alpha Beckett steps back with a low laugh.

He roughly digs his bloody fingers into dad's hair, pulling his head up and snarling in my father's face. "You brought this on yourself, Kevin. You should have listened. You should have listened!"

Beckett bangs his head against the ground, nearly giggling when my father cries out in pain. He releases him, stepping back and whipping his bloody hands on his shirt. And then he glances at me, taking in my tear stained cheeks and horror filled eyes with a smile. A sick smile that makes my stomach churn.

He stops to where he's at eye level with me and hesitantly, he reaches out, tracing a finger down my cheekbone. And with this simple action, it reminds me of Liam. Because Liam has a habit of doing that. Especially when he wants to catch my attention.

Just the thought of Liam makes my chest clench in pain.

I banish Liam from my head, meeting Alpha Beckett's eyes as my stomach churns, my chest hurts, and my cheek stings. Beaten. I am beaten down, not only physically but emotionally.

The tears run down my cheeks more quickly now, making my eyesight blurry. I choke out a sob, causing Alpha Beckett to laugh at my obvious distress.

"You look so much like her, Ronnie," He mumbles tauntingly. "And you are so much like her. Weak. Pathetically weak."

I want to reply, to simply say that he's already mentioned this before, but I can't. So I only resort to letting out more pain-stakin' sobs and cries and falling helplessly to the ground once the men release me.

I begin to crawl towards my father, and when the wolves around me go to stop me, Alpha Beckett stops them, letting me pass and reach him.

Once I do, I let out another loud sob, gripping the back of his shirt and trying to flip over, just to see him. To know that's he breathing, at least.

I manage to flip him onto his back and I'm almost relieved to find familiar grey eyes staring back up at me. Almost.

I take notice of how shallow his breaths are and how much blood he's exactly losing.

I grab his head, placing it onto my lap and brushing the black lock's of hair that are coated in his blood. I cradle his body close to me, peering down at him and watching as the tears fall from my cheeks and onto his face.

"Stay awake," I whisper. "Stay awake. Stay with me. You can't leave me alone. You can't."

"You're not gonna be alone," He gurgles. "Liam... you'll have Liam."

"Liam's gone, dad," I cry. "He's not coming."

"He is," My dad argues, raising his voice and attempting to push himself up. He fails, falling back into my arms. "He's not leaving you. He's not leaving you behind like I did."

I shake my head weakly and bite down on my lip. So hard that I draw blood and soon enough the taste of coppery blood fills my mouth. "It wasn't your fault. You were hurt and-"

"There's no excuse, Ron," He cuts me off gruffly, heaving up more blood. "No excuse for what I did. Liam isn't going to screw up like me. That day... with Tara... he looked at you with an emotion I couldn't understand at first. That is, till I went home that night and thought about it.." He trails off momentarily, his murky grey eyes drifting off towards the forest. "He cares about you a lot, Ronnie. I didn't believe it at first, but you are mates. True mates. He's not going to leave you behind because.. because he lo-"

He's cut off. Not by someone or something, but by a sound. A sound in the distance. I raise my head up, searching in the direction of where the sound came from, my eyebrows furrowing, along with Alpha Beckett's.

He, too, looks puzzled by the sound. So puzzled that he doesn't even begin to bark orders at the troubled wolves.

I strain my hearing, trying to detect what the sound is. A stampede?

A stampede of what? More wolves?

It's footsteps. Thundering footsteps. And I wonder if Alpha Beckett is just playing dumb or if he is truly behind the whole cause of the sound.

It has to be more wolves. No humans can make that sound. Those thundering footsteps that are nearing closer and closer by the second.

I look down towards my father, surprised to see a grim smile slipping onto his lips. "Told you," is all he says. And I wonder what he means by that. I quickly get my answer when the familiar twinkle of laughter reaches my ears and I suddenly catch movement out of the corner of my eye.

At first, all I see is her long, straight brown hair flying around her. It isn't till she looks away from the direction of where the sound is coming from and looks towards me, a devilish grin on her lips that only promises danger.

It's Stella. Crazy Stella Prescott. Laughing her head off as she looks away from me, to the wolves surrounding us, then to Alpha Beckett.

"Heads up, Beckett," She says in a sing-song voice, "You've got trouble."

And then she's off again. Her hair flying around her and her musical laugh following.

And we're all left completely confused by her statement, but it isn't till the thundering footsteps are only feet away that the awful stench reaches my nose. Purgatory.

Why would Stella lure them here? Was she stupid? Was she crazy? Or both?

Before I can come up with a possible conclusion, the Purgatory emerges. All of them.

The familiar blonde and black-eyed man is the one leading the pack and he seems to be the only one in human form. That is, despite another familiar person in the back, lurking behind one of the big wolves.

It isn't till they shove this person forward that I realize it's Adam. Adam?

The nameless man grabs him roughly by his neck, thrusting him towards Alpha Beckett. "Now, tell me, Beckett, why the fuck did I find your son on my property?"

"On your property? What?" Alpha Beckett asks, astonishment clear on his features. And though I am not the one bit pleased to see that blonde haired, black-eyed monster once again, I am relieved that he's at least distracting Alpha Beckett.

Distracting.

This is the plan! It has to be!

Unable to resist, I look back down at dad, gripping him tighter to me and lowering my head to whisper softly, "We're going to be okay, dad. We're going to get out of this. Hold on."

He gurgles an incoherent response, shutting his eyes for a second or two, before opening them again and offering me a reassuring smile. Though it does nothing to put me at ease, I glance away from him, long enough to see Adam on the ground with the blonde haired man lurking over him.

"Oh, I'm sorry, did I stutter, Alpha shit face?" The blonde haired man mocks angrily, "He was there. On my property. And when the little fucker ran and we finally managed to catch him, he claimed that you sent him. You sent him to scope out on us, when we had an agreement to never step onto each other's lands, that is, unless you wanted to start trouble. Did you?"

"No! Of course not!" Beckett bites back, "I never sent Adam there. I didn't. Adam wouldn't say that, either, would you, Adam?"

Alpha Beckett directs his attention to Adam, who raises his head and meets his father's gaze, unwavering.

Wait, I think, was Adam apart of the plan? Was this all just a set up?

"Your kid begs to differ," The nameless man snarls. "Tell him what you told me, kid." The Purgatory leader roughly nudges Adam, but surprisingly, Adam doesn't falter, nor emotionally or physically.

His features remain in a calm expression and it stays that way as he meet's his fathers eyes. "I told them everything, dad. About how you've been sending me to scope out on them for a while. I can't lie anymore. I can't do it."

Alpha Beckett's features twist into horror, unlike his son's calm expression. "What? Adam! I haven't.. I didn't.." He trials off, unsure of what to say. The Purgatory leaders snarls.

"Even your son is tired of your shit, Beckett," He hisses, "I should have known something was up once you started giving us tips about Farley and his mate. You probably just wanted to distract us and take care of your problems as you planned to start another war with us. This time, I bet, you were planning to take us down for good."

"It's not what you think!" Alpha Beckett objects, shaking his head, "I-"

"Don't worry, Beckett," The man snarls. "You want a fight, we'll give you one."

And that's when all hell breaks loose.

Suddenly, the man shifts and the Purgatory are charging at Beckett's pack. And as they clash together, all I hear is the wails of pains and growling and howling and then the sickening sound of flesh being ripped apart.

I watch as the Purgatory leader clashes on with a newly shifted Beckett, though Beckett quickly manages to squirm his way out of the fight by sending in his pack mates to fight for him.

And then it's a blur. Incredible blur as I realize Alpha Beckett is running towards me. Probably because he's angry. He knows Adam isn't behind this entirely. And I bet he's blaming this all on me.

Before he reaches me, my instincts quick in and I shift as well. You can't run away from this situation, Ronnie, my mind screams and I vaguely agree. It's time to fight.

And that's the reason I meet Alpha Beckett head on. Ramming into him with all the strength I can muster, despite my panicked father screaming my name.

I knock him back due to all the force I put in the hit, but it doesn't take long for Beckett to retaliate and suddenly, he's running at me again, snarling and growling.

I scurry out of the way, jumping around him and watching him come to a skidding stop to realize I've avoided his attack.

He charges at me again and by a stroke of luck, I dodge that hit as well. But it isn't long that Alpha Beckett finally manages to knock into my side, making me impact the ground and Alpha Beckett takes the chance to jump right on top of me.

He snaps his teeth dangerously close to my face and I do the same, snapping my teeth at him while squirming to get away from him. I manage to do so, bucking him off me with an angry snarl.

I jump up, ready to run around him so I can hit him where it hurts, but he anticipates my motives, and I am not as quick as I think I am, because he catches my leg in his jaws and bites down. Hard.

So hard that I feel his teeth sink into my flesh and it isn't long that I can feel the familiar trinkle of blood running down my leg.

I yip in pain, trying to shake him off my leg and for a minute, he releases me, only to knock me right back to the ground and this time, I don't get the chance to fight him off, because the next thing I know, his teeth are scraping up my stomach, following up the path to my throat.

I desperately squirm underneath him, despite the pain that hits me like a ton of bricks.

But I can't break free and I can only watch in horror as his his raises his hand up, then brings it back down, clamping his teeth right around my throat.

I release a loud wail, feeling him press down on my windpipe with his sharp canine's, but before he can crush my air way, the pressure is suddenly gone. And it isn't until I blink and hazily peer around that I notice he's been knocked off of me.

I catch the sight of coppery brown fur and that's when I know it's Liam. Liam.

I shouldn't be surprised, really. Because whenever I'm in a time of need, Liam always seem to appear. But I am surprised. Because my dad's words are true. Liam wouldn't leave me behind. He wouldn't. And perhaps I was foolish to ever think that.

Too weak to hold up in wolf form anymore, I shift back. And as I go to possibly move, I stupidly remember that I can't. I can't because when I glance down at my body, I realize that I'm bleeding. And quite profusely.

A large gash runs from my navel right up underneath my breast. The blood stains my white tank top and when I reach up and touch my neck, I feel hot blood under my fingertips. Though the wound on my neck isn't as bad as my stomach and bleeding leg, it's still worrying. Mainly because I am losing way too much blood.

My head spins and my vision blurs momentarily. Despite the blurry figures swaying around me, I manage to catch sight of a familiar red head boy.

"She's losing a lot of blood, Liam," Jeremy states the obvious, and I hear Liam respond, but I can't make out what he said. His voice sounds far away. So far away.

My limbs feel as if they weigh a thousand pounds and so do my eyelids. But I fight the sleepiness and instead try to push myself up. To fight the numbness that is slowly spreading throughout my body.

My eyes roam the perimeter, hazily, I see fighting figures and Alpha Beckett, who lays unconscious next to Liam, who is now in human form.

I know he's not dead when I look towards his chest. Rising and falling. Rising and falling.

I glance away from his body, to Liam, who crouches down next to my numb body. He strokes his fingers across my cheeks and I watch as his lips move, forming my name, although I can't hear him.

My thoughts are hazy and so the only thing I manage to do is furrow my eyebrows at him. And then suddenly, as if a light switched has been flickered on, the sounds around me come back quite forcefully and I am once again awake and aware of what's going on around me.

"We have to get going, Liam," Jeremy says, "We can't stay around. We have to leave before we catch both the Purgatory and Beckett's pack attention."

"I know," Liam gruffly replies, "Stella is coming around with the van. She ran back to the cabin to pack everything up. She's close."

"Guys!" I hear an familiar voice shout and once that the person that the voice belongs to get's close enough, I realize it's Adam when his voice comes into my sight. "Guys, what are you still doing here? You have to go. Now!"

"We're going, idiot!" Liam hisses spitefully, "We can't exactly move Ronnie without flaring up some kind of pain."

"Well, it's either you let her lay here to die or you pick her up and take her to the van and get her some help. You don't have many objections here, Farley. Get moving!"

Liam cusses at him but quickly comes to recognize that Adam is right. If they leave me here, unattended, I am sure to die.

Jeremy goes to help lift me, but Liam warningly growls at him. Jeremy backs off, very quickly, I might add.

Liam slides his hands under my mid frame, hoisting me up, despite my slight whimper. Once I'm secure in his arms, he raises up slowly and unable to control my body's movements, my head lolls to the side, to where my eyes are directly focused on my dad. My dad's unmoving body.

"Dad," I breathe. And suddenly, Liam is walking away from him. We're walking away from him. "Dad," I repeat louder. Louder that I catch the attention of Liam and Jeremy and Adam as well, who is only a few feet away from me.

"I'll take care of him for you, Ronnie," Adam says, though his voice quivers. "For as long as I can. Take care of yourself and stay safe."

"No," I shake my head. "Please, just take me to him. Please." My words are slurred but somehow Liam understands me.

"Ronnie, you can't see him. We have to go."

"Please! Just quickly! Please!"

"Ronnie, you're bleeding, you can't stay any longer!" Liam argues.

"Just give her to me!" Jeremy suddenly snaps, reaching his arms out to me, though Liam steps back and raises his lip up in a snarl. "This might be the last time she sees her father, Liam.

Give her to me, go find Stella, come back, and we'll go as fast as we can. There's no time to waste. Hand her over!"

Unable to argue any longer, Liam hands me over and as Jeremy carries me over to my dad, I watch Liam sprint off into the huge mass of fighting and then shift.

I look away once's I get close enough to my father's body. As if Jeremy reads my silent pleas, he settles me down next to my father and I do not hestiate to weakly slide my hand underneath his head and bring it right back onto my lap.

I don't care about the pain anymore. I don't care if I'm bleeding to death. All I want is to see him. To know he's still awake and he hasn't slipped away from my grasp.

"Dad?" I whisper. And in response, he opens his eyes, glancing up at me with glossy eyes. "You're still with me."

I'm slightly relieved, that is, till he opens his mouth to say something but can't. He's choked up. Not with tears or words or whatever, but with more blood. The horrifying thought of my father dying leaks into my mind and I can't get it out once it seeps into my thoughts.

"It's okay, you'll get help soon enough," I mumble, my voice cracking and tears pricking at the corner of my eyes. "You'll get through this. Maybe you can come with us. Maybe-"

"I can't." He manages to choke out, "I can't."

I furrow my brows at him, "Of course you can," My hazy mind argues. "You-"

"No. He'll find me. You go. Go find help." His utters out, coughing up more blood. I watch as a trickle of blood runs down his chin.

"I can't leave you behind," I choke out. "I can't just leave you here to die."

The tears run down my face as I weakly clutch him to me. Maybe he won't have to die here alone. Maybe I'll die here with him.

I lower my head, pressing my face into the crook of his neck and letting my tears splatter against his unnaturally cold skin.

"Let go, Ron," He murmurs. "You have to go."

"No," I whisper. "No. I'm not going. I'm staying. Staying here with you."

I hear the pounding of footsteps and then uneven breathing and I don't even have to glance up to know it's Liam. "Stella's here with the truck. We have to go. We're catching Purgatory attention. They're coming for us and Alpha Beckett is gonna wake up soon. His pack members might be down for now, but they aren't down forever. We have to go."

I feel Liam shuffle around my father and I and it isn't long that I feel his hands on my back. "We have to go, Ron. Come on."

And then, before I know it, I'm being pulled away from my dad. And I'm not strong enough to possibly hold onto him.

"No, please, take him with us. We can't leave him!" I screech, but all Liam does is shake his head and so does my dad.

"No time. We have to go, Ronnie. I'm sorry." And then once again, I'm being pulled away from my dad. Towards the van. Towards Stella. Towards, perhaps, my future.

But in result, I'm being pulled away from Adam and dad. Hopeless looking Adam who stands next to my father's body. "Ida Walsh!" He shouts, "Wisconsin. Good luck."

My brows furrow at his words but I vaguely note what he's said. Ida Walsh. Wisconsin.

And then I look back towards my dad, staring at his unmoving body. And then the panic is back and I'm suddenly wailing and screeching and clawing away at Liam. To somehow get back to dad. To somehow save him like I planned to from the start.

"No!" I scream, "No! Dad!"

My screams are inhuman and blood curling and the tears are pounding down my face twice as hard. My eyesight becomes blurry once again and all I can make out is my father's face. My father's grey and glossy eyes as he watches me being carried away. The last time. This is possibly the last time he will see me and I will see him. And it only causes me to scream and cry louder.

"Dad! Dad!"

The van door opens and I'm placed in. Liam tries to soothe me, but I don't listen. I don't listen as the blood leaks from my side. I don't listen when my cheek stings and my head spins and my leg throbs. All I do is bring my bloody hands up to the window, banging my fist on the window and screaming for him, over and over again.

And somehow, in the distance, I see his mouth move and I'm able to form out the words. I love you, sweetheart.

My heart breaks and my hoarse sobs fill the air as Stella fires up the engine and we rocket off. Into the thick brush of the forest. Away from Portland. Away from home. Away from Adam. Away from Beckett. Away from my childhood memories and most importantly, away from my dad.

And all I do is scream. Scream as I bang on the window and watch my father disappear from my sight. Perhaps for forever.

www.ingramcontent.com/pod-product-compliance
Lightning Source LLC
Chambersburg PA
CBHW060754210726
48292CB00013B/110

9781933121765